She was t──oo good to be true...
He was to── o bad to resist...

MEASURE FOR MEASURE

As she stood there, mesmerized, he parted the measuring tape and slid his hands down her sides, slowly, gently, tracing her shape, verifying those numbers experimentally. Trickles of excitement wended their way along the underside of every exposed inch of her skin. Suddenly, all she could see were his full, ripely curved lips.

"Thirty-eight . . . twenty-four . . . thirty-six. You do indeed have curves, Mad Madeline," he said huskily, staring into her eyes. "But now the question is, are those numbers the result of your reformed foundations, or are they just you?" He let the tape drop to the floor and brought one hand up to stroke the curve of her cheek.

"There is only one sure way to settle the matter," he said, brushing his fingertips down the side of her neck and down her shoulder so that they came to rest on the top button of her tunic. With a deft twist of his fingers, it was freed from its velvet loop. . . .

BETINA KRAHN

The Unlikely Angel

BANTAM BOOKS

New York   Toronto   London   Sydney   Auckland

THE UNLIKELY ANGEL
A Bantam Book / May 1996

ISBN 0-553-56524-9

Published simultaneously in the United States and Canada

Bantam Books are published by Bantam Books, a division of Bantam
Doubleday Dell Publishing Group, Inc. Its trademark, consisting of the
words "Bantam Books" and the portrayal of a rooster, is Registered in
U.S. Patent and Trademark Office and in other countries. Marca
Registrada. Bantam Books, 1540 Broadway, New York, New York
10036.

PRINTED IN THE UNITED STATES OF AMERICA

OPM   0 9 8 7 6 5 4 3 2 1

For my own, personal angel,

Donald Robert Krahn
January 3, 1948–November 18, 1995

With all my heart.

The
Unlikely
Angel

1

It wouldn't be a large inheritance. Once the bequests were made and the estate taxes and legal fees were paid, there would be just enough for a modest annual income. But a modest inheritance was perfectly fine with her, Madeline Duncan told herself as she climbed the sweeping marble staircase of the East India Building. The years she had spent tending her aunt Olivia during a prolonged illness had been the old lady's true legacy to her . . . filled with learning and discussion, illuminating thoughts and broadening horizons. Whatever provisions Aunt Olivia had made for Madeline's future would be more than enough.

Hurrying around the domed and columned rotunda, Madeline looked from the letterhead on the paper she gripped to the names emblazoned in gold on polished mahogany doors. Her stomach began to draw into a knot. The gleaming brass, carved marble, oiled leather, and faint redolence of ink and cigar smoke bespoke great expenditure and even greater income. She had heard the names of her aunt's solicitors many times, but she had not known they worked in such splendor. It occurred to her that their fees would undoubtedly be commensurate with the elegance of their surroundings. Pausing in the hall before an ornate set of doors reading Ecklesbery, Townshend, and Dunwoody, Ltd., she squared her shoulders and revised her modest expectations for her future . . . downward.

The door closed with a solid thud behind her, a subtle reminder of the weightiness of the legal establishment housed within. Madeline found herself in a paneled reception room hung with somber portraits and furnished with stuffed chairs and a carved foyer table with an ornate bronze scale sitting on it.

She pulled her long woolen cloak tighter around her and approached the clerk's desk, clearing her throat. The clerk, a wiry young man, shot to his feet at the mention of her name. But before he could speak, the door to one of the inner offices flew back with a bang and a portly, well-dressed man burst through the opening. "She's swooned! Go for a female—that charwoman, downstairs—" He wheeled and charged back into his office without closing the door.

"Yes, Mr. Townshend," the clerk muttered, and bolted for the hall.

Left abruptly alone, Madeline edged across the reception room and peered through the open doorway. In a spacious wood-paneled office, a woman in black was dangling precariously over the side of a chair. Three gentlemen crowded around her, staring at her with a mixture of consternation and annoyance.

"Dashed widows—they're always going off like this," the heavyset Townshend was saying as he snatched up a pillow from the nearby sofa and gave the woman a fanning. "Always seems to happen just before dinner," observed a second fellow with a dapper gray mustache. He glanced at his pocket watch. "Most inconvenient . . ."

"It's the shock. Silly females. Haven't a clue to their circumstances." A rail-thin older gentleman hastily poured a glass of water from the carafe on the desk and turned back to the chair—only to realize that the unconscious woman could not possibly make use of it. Scowling, he bent to peer at her face. "I say, Townshend, should we do something?"

"Looks deuced uncomfortable," the mustached gentleman said, leaning down to scrutinize her as well. "Is she still breathing?"

"Difficult to say, Dunwoody, with her all twisted about and hanging upside down." Townshend glanced over his shoulder with a twitch of irritation. "Where is Tattersall with that female person?"

"Perhaps we should stretch her out somewhere." Dunwoody gestured to the tufted leather sofa.

"Stretch her out? *Carry* her?" Townshend drew a sharp breath.

"Touch her personage? Highly irregular." The older fellow scowled at his colleague. "Not to mention improper."

"But what if she isn't breathing?" Dunwoody looked a bit nervous and tugged at his mustache. "Women do wear contraptions that sometimes interfere—"

"Dunwoody, *really*." The thin fellow raised his nose an indignant inch.

Madeline's eyes widened, then narrowed. *Silly men. There they stood, posturing and pontificating, while the poor woman was all but expiring!* Never one to stand idly by while something needed doing, she sailed through the open door, startling the trio of solicitors. As she advanced, they abruptly retreated.

"Perhaps *I* can be of help." Madeline knelt by the chair and raised the woman's drooping head, brushing a silk mourning veil out of the way. The woman's face was pale and clammy and there was a tinge of blue about her lips. "As I suspected," Madeline said, lifting the woman's upper half back into the chair. "She needs air. We must move her to the sofa."

The men looked at each other, clearly appalled by the prospect of personal contact with a person of the female persuasion. But when Madeline looked up expectantly, Townshend and Dunwoody reluctantly went to help her.

When the woman was safely deposited on the sofa, Madeline asked for smelling salts and a bit of privacy. The gentlemen solicitors fairly stumbled over each other in their haste to quit the room.

Madeline knelt, listened to the woman's shallow, troubled breathing, and ran her fingers over the woman's impossibly narrow waist. "Small wonder she's fainted," she muttered. "Cinched up worse than a Suffolk sausage." She rolled the woman onto her side and worked the fierce little buttons of the black bombazine dress. Then she struggled to loosen the laces of a vicious steel-boned corset. "Infernal inventions . . . distorting women into ridiculous, unnatural shapes . . . cutting off their very life breath. And we call the Chinese barbaric for binding feet. If I had my way—"

Once released to more natural proportions, the woman took a shuddering breath and settled immediately into a more restful state. Shortly, Madeline answered a quiet rap on the door and found the clerk outside with a vial of smelling salts and a wan smile of gratitude.

After a whiff or two from the bottle, the woman roused, averting her nose. Madeline helped her to sit up.

"I loosened your laces so you could breathe properly," Madeline told her, giving her hand a pat and sliding onto the sofa beside her. "You'll be fine now."

The woman looked blankly around the office, then turned to Madeline with anguished recollection. "No, I won't. I will not be fine—ever again!" Sorrow too fresh and too large to be contained by ladylike sufferance spilled forth. "I am ruined—penniless," she choked out. "My dear Theodore was ripped untimely from my arms. And now the lawyers say that he had borrowed on everything he owned. I am left with two little boys to raise and scarcely a penny to my name. Oh, my babies—my poor sweet darlings—whatever shall I do?"

Madeline impulsively put her arms around the weeping woman. Through the ensuing outpouring of tears and troubles, Madeline found herself drawn into the woman's story, imagining the terrors of being left penniless and ill equipped to deal with the world. In so many English minds, a woman was expected to be "the angel of the house," and kept ignorant of the world and its "corrupting" influences: money, commerce, debt, and legal maneuverings.

Now, like so many others, this particular "angel" had been rudely cast out of her nuptial paradise and into the real world. Madeline's mind filled with images of the delicate young woman with two rosy, tousled cherubs in her arms . . . destitute, frightened, bravely trying to keep body and soul together.

She shook her head. If only she could do something to help . . .

Another knock came at the door, followed quickly by an invasion of solicitors. In the interval, the gentlemen of the firm had learned Madeline's identity from their clerk and now insisted on ushering her into another office for the reading of her aunt's will.

The woman held her hands tightly to delay her, looking up with eyes that bore traces of sorrow and fear. "Thank you, miss, for your kindness to me."

"Take heart," Madeline said quietly. "You'll find a way to go on. You have to believe that in order to do it. And you do have to go on, for the sake of your children." Madeline read her doubts and gave her a smile that was a blend of understanding and confidence. "You are stronger than you know, Mrs . . ."

"Farrow. Mrs. Theodore Farrow," the woman said in a

whisper, searching Madeline's face and seeming to take something from her determined reassurance.

As the lawyers ushered her out into the hall, Madeline saw the young widow collect herself and rise with what seemed a heartened attitude. Only then did her mind turn back to her own situation. Her inheritance. Her own uncertain future.

The second office was even grander than the first. A shaft of sunlight from the tall arched window illuminated a pair of chairs situated before a massive mahogany desk. The Oriental carpets were deep, the wood was polished to a high gloss, and the sun-warmed leather upholstery gave off a musky scent that had a distinctively male character. As she was being seated, a smartly dressed man stepped into that stream of daylight. It took a moment for her to recognize him.

"Gilbert." She greeted her boyishly handsome cousin with a polite nod to cover her dismay at seeing him here. She supposed she shouldn't have been surprised. Gilbert Duncan had been largely absent during his elderly relative's last weeks, but naturally he would present himself now, when he had hopes of inheriting a portion of the estate—perhaps even the substantial house that had been Madeline's only home since she was seven years old. Madeline felt a clutch of anxiety.

"We are indebted to you, Miss Duncan, for your assistance with that unfortunate situation in Townshend's office." The dapper Mr. Dunwoody settled into his high-backed leather chair across the desk, and began untying the scarlet ribbons binding the folio of legal papers before him. "Difficult business, the law." He sighed with a martyred air. "At times downright disagreeable."

Madeline shifted uncomfortably in her chair and wondered if he was just making an observation or preparing her for what was to come. From the corner of her eye she saw Gilbert take the chair beside hers and noticed the other solicitors posting themselves at Mr. Dunwoody's right and left. *A gathering of eagles.* She groaned silently.

"Miss Olivia Duncan was a woman of definite ideas," Dunwoody began. "She insisted upon writing out her will in her own hand and in her own words, subject to advice from legal counsel, of course—she was a very *prudent* woman as well. Let us hear now her final will and testament." He lifted a document and resettled his rimless spectacles to read: " 'I, Olivia Marie Duncan, being of sound mind but deteriorating health, do undertake to set my worldly affairs in order, so that I may leave a legacy to the world which will enrich and improve the lives of my fellow human beings. . . .' "

The words caused breath to catch in Madeline's throat. She could almost hear the old lady's once-commanding voice, made papery with age and infirmity, speaking those words. She felt a wave of fresh grief.

Olivia Duncan had been her guardian, teacher, and entire family since her parents' death many years before in the mission fields of West Africa. She had arrived in England a child of seven years who had been raised in the wilds under primitive conditions. Tall, rod-straight Aunt Olivia had seemed quite severe as she worked to establish "sensible" boundaries for her charge. Madeline had been deathly afraid of the old lady, until she began to catch the glimmer of amusement in the woman's eyes.

Sensible, Madeline had come to learn, was the old lady's credo. She lived it, she preached it, and she prescribed it for her ward with unrelenting zeal. However, as Madeline also learned, Aunt Olivia's version of "sensible" was sometimes at odds with the rest of society's notions. Aunt Olivia was one of a kind: an individualist, a bit of a social philosopher, a teacher without peer. She was a *thinker* by nature, with enough insight to realize early on that Madeline's dynamic personal energy would make her a *doer*. In their years together, Olivia Duncan had helped her determined charge learn to channel her impulse for "doing" into "doing good."

Surfacing through a flood of memories and emotions, Madeline had difficulty concentrating on what was being read. She straightened in her chair and shook her head to clear her thoughts, just in time to hear the fateful words: " 'To my consummately resourceful grandnephew, Gilbert, I leave the sum of fifty thousand pounds . . . to be paid out in cash from my accounts in the Bank of England.' "

Solicitor Dunwoody paused and looked up at Gilbert. Gilbert's eyes widened and he gripped the arms of his chair.

"*Fifty th-thousand?*" he choked out. "In coin of the realm? *Currency?*"

"The very same," Dunwoody intoned, adjusting his pince-nez with a prim bit of satisfaction at having delivered an unexpected stroke of fortune. "We shall arrange for a transfer of funds whenever you like. If you will just give us the name of your banker . . ."

"Fifty thousand!" Gilbert forgot gentlemanly pride and decorum for a moment and bounded up, his face reddening with excitement. "I never expected—my dearest, most *beloved* aunt Olivia! Why, I had no idea!"

Nor, as it happened, did Madeline. Where had Aunt Olivia gotten fifty thousand pounds to leave Gilbert? They had always been frugal regarding household expenses. There had always been good food and wine, books had been purchased, and the salaries of the servants were always promptly paid. But it had all been managed through economies employed elsewhere—she knew because she wrote the drafts that paid the bills! She had never suspected that Aunt Olivia had a fortune saved away for a grandnephew who had been such a stranger to her. After Gilbert resumed his chair, Mr. Dunwoody turned to her with an arch little smile and continued reading.

" 'Aside from the above-named bequests to my nephew, to certain charities, and to my faithful servants, the entire remainder of my estate, along with all my love and gratitude, shall go to my beloved grandniece and companion, Madeline Duncan. I am keenly aware of the sacrifices of youth and freedom she has made in caring for me in my declining years.

With this bequest I wish to repay in some small part her generosity.' " Dunwoody paused and frowned at the next phrase as he read it. " 'My very final bequest, and perhaps my most important, is to the world at large. To my fellow humankind I leave . . . my niece, Madeline.' "

Madeline glanced from one solicitor to the other, trying to read in their faces what was meant by her aunt's cryptic wording. Her aunt willed her the rest of the estate . . . and then willed her to the rest of the world? What in heaven did that mean? A thought struck her and her heart began to beat erratically.

"Who does the house belong to?" she asked breathlessly.

Dunwoody chuckled and glanced at his colleagues. "Which house? Scofield Manor in the West Country? The town house in Mayfair? The villa in Florence? Or the plantation mansion in Barbados?"

Madeline stared at him in confusion. "I mean, the house in Bloomsbury, where we—I—live."

"But of course it is yours. Along with all six others," Townshend announced, beaming. "And may we be the first to congratulate you on your good fortune, Miss Duncan. We at Ecklesbery, Townshend, and Dunwoody will be pleased to serve you as diligently as we have your dear, departed aunt Olivia. We, of course, have been appointed trustees of the estate . . . given the charge to oversee your affairs and provide for your needs."

"Without boasting, Miss Duncan, may I say that our firm has taken meticulous care of your aunt's business dealings," the tall fellow, Ecklesbery, said as he tucked his thumbs into his vest pockets. "Under our keeping, her substantial fortune has grown handsomely. You are an extremely wealthy young woman."

"Wealthy?" Cousin Gilbert came crashing back to reality at last, and turned to stare at her in astonishment. *"Extremely?"*

Madeline was shaking her head in disbelief.

"Quite," Dunwoody replied. "The estate has a number of lucrative properties and investments, and a quite substantial cash reserve—all of which needn't trouble your pretty head in the least, Miss Duncan. We shall see to it that you have plenty of money for servants and bonnets and new dresses— all the female luxuries and extravagances you could possibly desi—"

Townshend cleared his throat and leaned toward his partner's ear. "The letter, Sir Edward."

"Letter? Oh, yes. Your aunt gave us an envelope for you, Miss Duncan. To be opened after her passing." Dunwoody retrieved it from the folio and handed it to Townshend, who ferried it to Madeline's hands. "As I was saying, for a woman of such means, your aunt chose to live a curiously frugal existence. We certainly understand—even expect—that you may wish to do things differently." He cast an eye over her simple woolen cloak. "We can recommend the finest silk drapers and dressmakers and milliners in London. We shall be pleased to see that you have introductions into the very first circles . . . invitations from the best of families."

His voice faded from Madeline's awareness as she stared at her name on the envelope, written in her aunt's afflicted but still recognizable script. She tore into it and opened the letter with trembling hands. On the page was just one short sentence.

What would you do, Madeline, my dear, if you had a million pounds?

She stared at the words, feeling a complex jumble of emotions: startlement, recognition, incredulity, and finally amusement born of unexpected understanding. The question was the basis of a game she and Aunt Olivia had played many times over the years. In the midst of spring cleaning, or a bit of needlework, or a story being read, the old lady would pause and fix her with a quixotic look and demand to know: "What would you do, Madeline, my dear, if you had a million pounds?"

As a child of ten, her answers had been predictably impractical: buy a pony, a shop full of sweets, featherbeds stacked to the ceiling, and her own private sailing ship to take her anywhere in the world. But as she grew older, her answers had matured. She would buy a grand house . . . a woodland with a stream so she could give animals a home . . . a beautiful farm with bountiful gardens and orchards to grow lots of food . . . eventually a whole village, where she would make the rules and where everyone would work at what they liked and would have plenty of everything and would be happy.

She came abruptly back to her senses and sat forward urgently, gripping the edge of the desk.

"How much is it all worth? Tell me. If you had to reduce it all to a single sum, how much would there be?"

Dunwoody tucked his chin. "Well, I've never actually—"

"Quite a little," Townshend put in with a scowl.

"Quite a *lot*," Ecklesbery corrected him with a sniff.

"Is it close to a million pounds?" she demanded, her mouth drying and her heart pounding wildly.

Dunwoody resettled his spectacles to give Madeline a much keener look. "It would be in that range, I suppose. We have never thought it necessary to tally all of Miss Duncan's holdings together in such an . . . *indiscriminating* . . . manner."

"A million pounds," Madeline repeated to herself several times, trying to comprehend what was happening. She stared at the letter—at the black ink undulating across the creamy vellum—and felt curiously as if Aunt Olivia were reaching across the boundaries of mortality to play their game one final time.

On afternoon picnics, when they lay on a blanket in the grass, staring up at the clouds, and on dusky evenings, when they sat in the arbor at twilight, the million-pounds gambit had always seemed Aunt Olivia's way of making moral instruction and critical thinking exercises palatable to a willful young girl. For each time she asked the question, it would provoke a challenging discussion, ranging from moral philosophy to social theory, economics to the arts, history to the tenets of the great religions.

Now, staring at that single sentence, it struck Madeline that Aunt Olivia hadn't been playing a game at all. She had been preparing—*preparing Madeline*—for this very moment.

What will you do, Madeline, my dear, with your million pounds?

Color burst in her cheeks and she swayed on her chair. Townshend bolted instantly for a pillow, Ecklesbery frantically poured a glass of water, and the pair fairly trampled Cousin Gilbert in their rush to her side.

It was no longer a matter of hypothetical debate or philosophical dabbling. Aunt Olivia had given her a million pounds and now wanted to know what she intended to *do* with it. Which of her desires, ideas, and heartfelt convictions would she act upon? Which of her dearest longings and most daring dreams would she choose to pursue? What would she do with her newfound wealth?

Her time?

Her life?

She came to her senses to find Messrs. Townshend and Ecklesbery hovering over her, ready to fan or hydrate her at the first hint of the vapors. Her gentlemen trustees clearly expected her to be overcome by her great fortune, then to plunge deliriously into a torrent of luxurious living. They offered to help her acquire a fashionable wardrobe, develop stylish tastes, take up expensive pastimes, and even cultivate an elite circle of acquaintances. Travel, possessions, luxury, acceptance, even renown—her fortune could buy her virtually anything she desired. And for the first time in her adult life, she was responsible for no one but herself.

She was extraordinarily rich and utterly free.

It was overwhelming. Her chest tightened; she could scarcely get her breath. Feeling alone and uncertain, Madeline gazed down at Aunt Olivia's final question, searching the old lady's script for comfort, for direction. As she eyed those familiar strokes, the constriction around her heart loosened and a sense of calm settled over her.

It was still a game of sorts, she realized—*their game.* She was being given a chance to *do* . . . to act on the ideas and realize the dreams she had spun in the cocoon of her life with Aunt Olivia.

Her thoughts raced. A torrent of ideas poured through her mind . . . a thousand things she could do to improve the lot of her fellow humans . . . her fellow women . . . like that poor Mrs. Farrow. It left her tingling with the energy of possibilities, of potential. Slowly, she squared her shoulders and raised her gaze to her aunt's solicitors.

"Those won't be necessary, gentlemen, I assure you." She waved away the pillow and water and shrugged out of her thick woolen cloak. "I have never swooned in my life."

Their expressions were suddenly aghast, and it took a moment for her to realize that their dismay was caused by the sight of her scarlet jacket banded with black velvet. She glanced down.

"I suppose you may wonder about this." She smoothed her fitted bodice, which skimmed her waist and ended just past her hips. It was layered over a tailored black skirt that ended abruptly, shockingly, at her knees. "Scarlet was Aunt Olivia's favorite color, and I promised I would wear it for her in mourning. Suitably banded, of course. It may seem unusual, but I believe it is far more sensible to dress in a way that honors the one who died than some dreary and restrictive social custom."

"O-of course," Dunwoody said, looking at the others with dawning alarm.

"Now, gentlemen . . ." She slid back into her chair and folded her hands in her lap. "I shall need a complete inventory of the estate's assets: the properties, investments, business concerns, and accounts. And I should like to see the most recent accounting of each asset's condition and worth." She smiled encouragingly at them. "From the smallest to the largest . . . please, leave nothing out."

The gentlemen solicitors missed the twinkle of excitement in her eyes. They were busy staring at her ankles, which were plainly visible beneath fine white stockings and below a pair of gathered trousers. Turkish trousers. *Bloomers.*

Townshend fanned himself with the pillow.

Ecklesbery drank the entire glass of water himself.

"Miss Duncan!" The words were forced from Dunwoody as he sat down in his chair with a plop. "Really!" Gentlemanly shock coupled with professional indignation momentarily robbed him of further speech. It fell to Townshend to express their common distress.

"Obviously you do not understand what you are asking, young lady. A list of assets and a full accounting of every bit of property, every enterprise, will take days—weeks!" He gripped his vest and looked disapprovingly down his nose at her. "What could you—a mere wisp of a girl—possibly do with such a bewildering mountain of facts and figures?"

Madeline folded her arms. She hadn't been "a mere wisp of a girl" since she was six. She sighed quietly. It was probably going to take them some time to get used to her.

"I shall do precisely what my aunt Olivia intended—use my fortune to 'improve the lives of my fellow human beings.' " She glanced at her slack-jawed cousin, then back at the trio of disapproving solicitors, and broke into a beaming smile. "And I intend to start by ridding the world of women's corsets."

Dunwoody stared at her in horror.

Ecklesbery made a graceless strangling sound.

Townshend clapped a hand to his head and spoke for them all.

"Dear God."

2

May 1882

The city of London awoke in layers. Each morning, at the break of dawn, scullery maids, printer's devils, boiler tenders, produce peddlers, and milkmen were the first to set about their daily tasks. By seven o'clock, shop stewards, senior clerks, and ladies' maids were bustling. Half past seven was the hour for merchants, mill supervisors, bankers, solicitors, department store managers, and undersecretaries of bureaus to greet the day. The luxury of eight o'clock was reserved for members of Parliament, mill owners, ministers of government, bishops of the church, and women entitled to be called "your ladyship." A select few, indeed, were entitled to the extravagance of half past eight—dukes, archbishops, and the justices of her majesty's royal bench—which explained in large part the fact that the courts of law never commenced session before half past ten.

It was precisely half past ten that gray, moisture-laden morning when Cole Mandeville was admitted through a side door to the Law Courts of Justice in the Strand. He had been standing at the entrance to the honorable justices' chambers for five full minutes, feeling his collar tightening, his hatband constricting, and his severely starched shirt chafing tender elbows—annoying reminders of how he had passed the previous night. He was on the verge of heeling off, when an aged bailiff appeared. The bailiff examined the note he held, and led him down a labyrinthine set of passages which—like the law itself—doubled and redoubled bewilderingly and had to be traversed with great care.

As they passed through the corridor, Cole heard what he could have sworn was monkey chatter coming from one of the justices' chambers. Bizarre counterpoint was provided by parrot screeches from a half-open door across the way. In close succession, they encountered a cloud of camphor vapor, the musty smell of old books, the mingled aroma of day-old sausages and stale cigars, and the stomach-turning sound of someone either gargling or singing a Welsh folk tune. Steeling himself, Cole resisted peering through those open doors. He already knew more than he cared to about the British legal system and the men who ran it. Those peculiar sounds and smells only made him more determined to make this interview with his uncle as short as humanly possible.

The senior justices were housed in the chambers nearest the courtrooms, at the heart of the building, and Sir William Rayburn, Cole's maternal uncle, was as senior as it was possible to be on the queen's Chancery bench. He had been a justice for twenty-five years, the last twenty here in the civil branch dealing with contract and testamentary matters. Through a canny combination of legal acumen, family connections, and raw ambition, he had carved a reputation for himself in the world of British jurisprudence. There was scarcely a barrister in London who didn't know and dread appearing before "William the Conqueror."

A bellow issued from a door ahead, and the old bailiff waved Cole onward. Just then, a man rushed out of the doorway, grabbed a hat from the rack on the wall, and dashed apologetically down the hall around them. It took a moment for Cole to recognize his uncle's beleaguered clerk, Foglethorpe. As the bellow faded, Cole took a deep breath and strode through the closetlike antechamber, where Foglethorpe usually sat in danger of being crushed by toppling stacks of documents and banded legal folios.

Every available inch of Sir William's spacious office was lined with shelves crammed with leather-bound volumes that overflowed into stacks on the worn carpet. In the center of the room a massive oak desk was littered with papers and books. Around it was a motley assortment of chairs. Behind the desk hung the portrait of a veritable bulldog of a man dressed in a periwig and legal robes. And sitting at the desk, thrust back in his chair, was the living—and considerably aged—subject of that portrait. One of his legs, heavily bandaged, was propped up on the desk.

"Damned well about time you arrived!" The old man shot up as straight as his raised foot would allow and fixed Cole with an irritable stare. "Almost gave up on you, boy— I'm overdue for opening session." His regard became razor-edged. "Some of us do still *work,* you know."

Cole's face heated, but the rest of him remained stubbornly cool. "Sorry if I've inconvenienced you, Uncle. I had a rather"—he raised the back of a gloved hand to stifle a forced yawn—"late night of it." His smile grew as pointed as the old man's glare. "But I'm sure you've had a late night or two . . ."

"Not in decades—*centuries.*" Sir William leaned forward, winced, and gingerly lifted his foot down to a pillow atop an ottoman. "I can't remember what it's like to go to bed past ten o'clock, much less wake up in a strange set of sheets. Hell—I can't even remember what a decent glass of port tastes like!" He shook a fist at his bloated and bandaged leg. "Damnable gout. Nibbles away at a man inch by inch, robbing him

of every pleasure in life, making each day a wretched trial to
be wrestled and overcome!"

The old man's dark eyes burned as hot and imperious as
ever, but beneath them were dark crescents of strain and
around them were lines etched by age and physical suffering.
The wrestling had obviously taken a toll. The realization
struck Cole in an unexpectedly vulnerable place. Sir William
had always seemed indestructible, one of those rare creatures,
born under a turbulent moon, who blew through life with
the force of a typhoon run aground. He certainly had cut a
wide swath through Cole's adolescent life some years back.

"Your florid past catching up with you," Cole declared
lightly, standing straighter to compensate for the sinking sensation in his chest. "No doubt there are a number of wretches
in Newgate and country poorhouses who would give a year
off their lives to see you thus."

"No bloody doubt of it." Sir William heaved a disgusted
breath and dismissed the topic of his condition with an impatient wave of a hand. The gaze he turned on Cole pene-
trated his gentlemanly attire and impeccable grooming and
laid naked the man beneath—mind, body, and soul. It caught
Cole off guard. He felt an absurd adolescent impulse to hide,
followed by chagrin at having let the old man's suffering disarm him.

Sir William had a disconcerting talent for cutting through
the usual social and emotional defenses to poke about in the
inner composition of his fellow humans. Cole had learned
long before that one's only hope under one of Sir William's
inquisitions was brutal honesty.

"I had dinner with Van Druesen a few days ago," Sir
William declared, watching Cole's reaction—or lack of one.
Cole drew a slow breath, knowing instantly what this sum-
mons was about.

"My condolences. I daresay, he bored your socks off with
that story about his prize kumquat . . . or whatever the hell it
is he grows on his farm in Lower Dingleberry."

"Lower Darlington." Sir William's mouth quirked up on one side. "An Australian kiwi fruit." The half-smile faded. "As Head of Chambers he is rather worried. Says you haven't taken a case in six months or even set foot in the offices in three."

Cole stuck out his chin. "So, that is it. I've been hauled into your lair for an avuncular dressing-down, have I?"

"Your mother also paid me a call. She is concerned."

"Is she now? About my abandoning what she has always considered a tawdry and distasteful occupation? How very peculiar. If I remember correctly, it was she who spoke so fervently against a career in the law, wept copiously, suffered vapors at the mere mention of 'that horrid, grubby little trade.' "

"Van Druesen says you were on the verge of litigatory brilliance. Had a partnership in the vest pocket, so to speak."

"Van Druesen is a self-absorbed, ineffectual wheeze."

"I myself have heard your name bandied about in connection with a plummy London assize. The judiciary before thirty-five would be quite an achievement."

"Achievement?" Cole strolled to a well-padded chair and sank down in it, propping one long leg casually over the arm. "Sounds more like a life sentence to me. A premature burial in the catacombs of the law." He doffed his hat, tossed it carelessly onto a nearby chair, and began to remove his gloves with exaggerated motions. His actions and appearance were the epitome of the indolent young aristocrat. But he sensed that his pose was not having the desired effect on Sir William, who had been his mentor at law.

Silence settled between them, laden with memories and expectations. After all he had done to encourage Cole in the profession, the old man probably deserved an explanation. Cole lowered his leg and sat up straight, looking in his uncle's direction while avoiding those probing eyes.

"The truth? I left because I was bored witless. Endless details . . . absurd, insipid clients and even stupider colleagues

. . . endless incompetence. . . . I was strangling, drowning in it all. I awoke one morning—after God knows how many sleepless nights—facedown in a pile of papers on my desk." He smiled with purposefully dissolute charm. "Since that day I have made it my sole occupation to wake up each morning facedown in a comfortable bed and—whenever possible— next to an accommodating female."

Sir William studied him carefully for a moment, then pronounced his opinion.

"Horse manure."

Sir William's clerk, Foglethorpe, rushed into the chamber just then, wheezing and red-faced from running. He had a blue apothecary bottle in one hand and a spoon in the other. "Beg pardon, I didn't realize . . . Your medicine, Sir William. And the court has been standing ready for some time now."

Grimacing, Sir William waved the clerk closer and took the bottle. After dosing himself with two spoonfuls of pungent brown liquid, he shuddered. "Damnable stuff—if it weren't for the work, I'd say to hell with it and bite a leather strap instead."

He turned to Cole. "I've not done with you, boy. There's more here than meets the eye, and I mean to have the entire truth and nothing but the truth from you. Just now I have this damnable case—" Glancing at his pocket watch, he frowned, then decided the problem in characteristic fashion. "Wait for me," he ordered, punching a finger at Cole. "Better yet, sit in on the session."

"Sit in on a session? In *Chancery*?" Cole snorted. "I never realized you harbored me such ill will, Uncle."

"Don't be an ass, boy. This is my life's work." Sir William struggled up, leaning heavily upon a gnarled walking stick. Foglethorpe scurried forward to settle his long white wig and help him into his robes. When properly gowned, the old man leaned on the side of the desk with a pained laugh that once again caught Cole in a vulnerable place. "Life's work—hell—this is my *life*." He leveled a look at Cole that was part command, part challenge. "I'll have your opinion on the proceedings afterward. No sense letting your mind go to rot just because your soul has. Interesting case. I vow you'll not see another like it in a lifetime. Female plaintive."

"An inheritance gone awry, no doubt." Cole rose and resettled his vest.

"Suing her lawyers for the release of her trust money."

"How novel," Cole said acidly, reaching for his hat and heading for the door. If he hadn't turned back for his gloves, he might have seen the glint in the old man's eye. When Sir William passed into the hall, he planted himself and his bandaged leg so as to block the exit. The only avenue of egress was down the hall leading to the courtroom and the visitors' gallery.

"If you fall asleep up there, make certain you don't snore." Sir William summoned his infamous courtroom demeanor as he ordered Cole ahead of him with a brusque wave of hand. "I fine snorers."

The courtroom was of recent vintage—the courts of Chancery having moved from Lincoln's Inn a mere eight years earlier—and a prime example of the current fashion for Gothic architecture. Its small windows set high in the walls and dark, massive woodwork lent a suitably gloomy atmosphere to sorting out the tangled obligations and intentions of the dearly departed. Since the courts of Chancery were concerned primarily with contracts and the disposition of wills, there was no prisoner's dock or jury box. The larger part of the main floor was taken up by several long tables, where barristers and junior barristers in solemn black robes were clustered like a flock of fastidious crows. The justice's bench sat at the front of the hall on a raised dais. A small gallery ringed the rear of the hall.

Not surprisingly, the gallery was virtually empty. The only people who attended Chancery hearings were anxious plaintiffs, solicitors, and legatees. Usually, after a few days of enduring the endless nitpicking of procedures and the windy discourses on the nuances of the Latin that peppered many wills, even the most litigious parties staggered from the courtroom dazed and bewildered. Notorious inheritance cases came up only once a decade, and the rest of the time Chancery was so deadly boring that news writers were known to use the galleries to catch a few winks of sleep while following more sensational cases in other courts.

Cole climbed the side stairs and took a seat halfway up, along the side, folded his arms, and settled back with a resentful glower. The smell of the aged wood, the parchment, the ink, and the musty robes brought back a swirl of memories and emotions he had to work to suppress. He squeezed his eyes shut, so determined to control his emotions that he scarcely heard the bailiff announce "the Honorable Sir William Rayburn. The court will be upstanding." When the sound of participants being seated wafted up to him, he opened his eyes and watched the Clerk of Court read the action being brought.

It was then that Cole noticed a curious imbalance in numbers on the two sides of the floor below. On the left side of the courtroom were at least a score of black robes, with senior barristers at the front table and junior members of the defense's representation filling the long table behind them. On the right was a single barrister, a gnarled old fellow with a wisp of white hair poking out from beneath his periwig, a rumpled robe, and a definite stoop to his shoulders. Stacks of documents and books containing precedents and intended evidence were piled on the tables in the midst of the throng on the left. The old man had but a single slim folder on the table before him. Cole frowned.

Turning his attention to the defendant's front table, he was startled by the sight of one of the senior partners of his own legal firm: Sir Harvey Farnsworth, barrister, counselor to the wealthy, and blowhard extraordinaire. He scowled at

Farnsworth, then at his meddlesome uncle. An "interesting" case, the old man had said, knowing all the while that Cole's former firm represented the defendants. He didn't know whether to be intrigued or outraged at the old man's attempt to—what? Goad him back to the bar?

He was surprised again to recognize Farnsworth's clients as Sir Dennis Ecklesbery, Carter Townshend, and Sir Edward Dunwoody, partners in a firm of solicitors with offices in the East India Building, where his own firm of barristers resided. These were men he knew by both reputation and professional association. Reputable, well-heeled, dependable, and scrupulous to a fault, they were part of the bedrock of the London legal establishment. According to the cause being read by the clerk, they had refused to release funds and properties to one Miss Madeline Duncan.

Miss Duncan, whoever she was, didn't have a snowball's chance in hell of getting her money out of Ecklesbery, Townshend, and Dunwoody, he thought grimly. *Or out of Chancery.*

Chancery was a veritable tar pit. General wisdom held that heirs who fell into its unplumbed depths could flail and protest and petition all they wanted, but they were stuck there until either fossilization or the Second Coming, whichever claimed them first.

Sir William hammered down a lengthy recital of "where-ases" and "pursuant untos" and peered down over the bench at the venerable counsel for the plaintiff. "Sir Richard Pendergast. Your opening statement."

When the old fellow struggled to make it to his feet, Sir William watched for a moment, then waved him back down. "Bother it all, Pendergast, save your breath. From the looks of you, you'll need it. Suffice it to say, your client wants her money released from trust." Then he turned to Farnsworth with an impatient glare. "Get on with it, man. State your case."

Sir William's judicial demeanor was frequently characterized as being in the style of a Socrates—bitten by a rabid mastiff. Cole smiled.

"Your Honor." Farnsworth positioned himself before the bench and gripped the folds of his robe in an oratorical pose. "My clients have been given a weighty and most solemn charge. It is their somber and often lamentable duty to act in the guise of a guardian . . . to see to the best interests of their clients, especially when their clients' judgments fail them. It is my clients' sworn duty—as charged by the law, by their profession's noble ethics, and by the terms of the testaments they execute—to protect their clients' good names and good fortunes.

"This action is wholly derived from their solemn and even sacred sense of obligation to their clients, both past and present. For these good gentlemen—Sir Dennis Ecklesbery, Sir Edward Dunwoody, and Mr. Carter Townshend—do not believe that their responsibility to their clients ends even at the very threshold of heaven." He gestured expansively. "They are honor bound to carry out the functions and duties devolved upon them through the final wishes of their clients. It is a rare and precious trust they bear, and they accept it in solemn—"

"Yes, yes, Fartsworth, we all know what a sterling bunch of fellows they are," Sir William declared, waving an impatient hand. "Get on with it. This Miss Duncan wants her money and your clients won't give it to her. Why the hell not?"

Farnsworth opened his mouth, closed it again, and his fleshy face turned red. The others seated at the tables behind him looked at one another, wondering if they had misheard the magistrate. In the gallery Cole had choked on an inhaled breath and began to cough.

Dunwoody came to the barrister's rescue, springing to his feet. "We believe it is in Miss Duncan's best interest, Your Worship. If you will permit me . . . you see, our client—"

"*Unwilling* client."

Sir William scowled at the plaintiff's elderly legal representative. "Wait your turn, Pendergast." As the old fellow sank back into his voluminous robes, Sir William turned back to the defendants. "Proceed"—he waved a hand perfunctorily—"Dimwitty."

Dunwoody started, aghast at Sir William's mispronunciation, not to mention the omission of his title. "It is *Dunwoody,* Your Worship."

Sir William produced a pair of pince-nez spectacles out of his robe and peered through them at the array of documents spread before him on the bench. "So it is. Continue, Dumwoody."

Dunwoody stood for a moment, rigid with indignation, then sat down abruptly. A testy and determined Farnsworth resumed his discourse, proceeding straight to the arguments themselves. "Your Honor, my clients' *unwilling client* is the heir of a deceased lady of considerable worth, Miss Olivia Duncan. Over the years their firm has cared for Miss Olivia's affairs as if they were their own. In their hands her investments and properties flourished so that she died with a very fine fortune, the bulk of which she left to her grandniece, Miss Madeline Duncan." He moved closer to the bench, as if to enlist Sir William's understanding, man to man.

"If it please Your Honor"—his voice lowered—"Miss Olivia was a rare soul who lived a most unworldly life. And Miss Madeline Duncan is of the same constitution and background. They are women of very high ideals but with little experience in the real world. What Miss Madeline Duncan proposes to do with her new fortune shows an ignorance of both society and humankind. As Miss Olivia's executors and as trustees of Miss Madeline's fortune, my clients cannot permit her to squander her resources so frivolously and irresponsibly."

"Oh? And just what does she intend to do with her money that they find so objectionable?" Sir William demanded.

"It is all in the court briefs we've submitted," Dunwoody muttered, still stinging from Sir William's misuse of his good name.

"But, of course, we shall be pleased to review for Your Honor," Farnsworth hurriedly interposed, shooting Dunwoody a narrow look. "It seems Miss Duncan has rather quaint notions of reforming the world . . . beginning with the very *foundations* of womanhood."

"Foundations?" Sir William leveled an impatient look at the barrister. "What the devil do you mean, Fartsworth . . . *female foundations*?"

The barrister reddened and appeared to be sorting his words. "To put it bluntly, Your Honor, female 'improvers.' " At the blank look on Sir William's face, Farnsworth said bluntly, "Miss Duncan wishes to rid women of their *corsets*."

Sir William's eyes widened on the barrister, requiring him to continue.

"In Miss Duncan's opinion, female corsetry ranks as the eighth deadly sin." She proposes to launch a crusade against that particular female unmentionable and the fashions that require it."

"And how, pray, does she mean to do this? Petition Parliament? Revive the clerical courts? Accost women in the streets and rip the lacer-uppers from them?"

"Nothing quite so public, Your Honor . . . yet," Townshend put in, rising. "She intends to convince women to abandon their 'smalls and propers'—along with their good sense—by enticing them to wear 'reformed garments.' "

"Reformed garments? As opposed to what?" Sir William's mouth twitched at the corner. "Incorrigible garments?"

"As opposed to *regular* clothing, Your Honor. Time-honored and traditional garments. Decent and commonly accepted raiment. There is a small but vocal group of malcontents in our society agitating for reform in clothing. Lunatic fringe, mostly. They would have us all dress in peasant shirts and wooden shoes—"

"Pssst!" An audible hiss came from across the way, and when Cole looked up he found a woman in black bending over the railing, trying to get the attention of the plaintiff's counsel. "Sir Richard!" she whispered loudly. "Say something!" When he didn't respond, she tried again. *"Pssst!"*

Sir William heard her and looked toward her and the old man. "Dickie! Dickie Pendergast!" he thundered. The old man started and jerked his head up from his chest. "I believe your client wishes you to wake up and attend the proceedings." He pointed to the gallery, and the old man turned to see the woman making furious hand motions.

The aged barrister turned back and raised a gnarled finger into the air.

"I object!"

"Do you indeed?" Sir William said dryly. "On what grounds?"

Old Sir Richard rose unsteadily and scratched beneath his wig. With a scowl of confusion, he again consulted the woman at the railing.

Miss Duncan, no doubt. Cole shook his head. Whatever the woman's case, with such representation her cause is hopeless.

The unlucky Miss Duncan whispered something the old boy was apparently at a loss to hear. Exasperated, she finally said loudly: "Tell him you wish to call a witness!"

The plaintiff's counsel teetered forward to face the bench and raised that arthritic finger once again. "I wish to call a witness."

"Outrageous, Your Honor!" Farnsworth stalked forward. "We have not yet concluded our opening arguments, much less entered into eviden—"

"Stuff the outrage, Fartsworth. I've heard all I need from you for now." Sir William glowered, then turned pointedly to the other side of the court, leaving Farnsworth with his chin on his chest, gasping like a beached whale.

"Proceed, Dickie."

The old barrister teetered around to face the gallery, where the woman was growing steadily more frustrated by her failure to communicate. She finally demanded aloud: "Call *me* to give testimony!"

Sir Richard's head bobbed. He turned to Sir William and steadied himself on the table. "Your Honor, I wish to call Miss Madeline Duncan to give testimony."

Without waiting for the bailiff to summon her, the woman hurried down the side stairs, her long black cloak billowing around her. Cole watched in bemusement as she took the stand by her barrister and began to speak without being sworn in.

He winced. *Hopeless.*

Sir William halted her with a raised hand and ordered the oath administered. She had old Dickie object on the basis that her solicitors had spoken in court without being sworn in. Sir William glowered, then had the lot of them sworn in by his beleaguered bailiff. As soon as the others were seated she began to speak, but was again stopped by an objection from Farnsworth, who was mightily affronted by her addressing the court from the floor, a privilege afforded only to members of the legal profession. He was instantly overruled.

"Your Honor, I simply cannot allow these charges to go unanswered," Miss Duncan said in a clear, steady voice that had nothing of the withered spinster about it. "The products I propose to make at my Ideal Garment Company are anything but ridiculous. In point of fact, they are the complete opposite of the cruel, absurd, and oppressive garments currently foisted upon my fellow humans in the name of fashion."

"Oh? It's a company now, is it?" Sir William leaned forward, intrigued.

"I am working to establish a business concern that will produce a decent and human alternative to the dangerous devices now in widespread use."

"And just which 'dangerous devices' do you refer to,

Miss Duncan?" Sir William said, studying the clear, slightly flushed face turned up to him.

"Steel-boned corsets, unbending backboards, strangulating collars . . . heavy, unsanitary petticoats and bustle frames that distort the spine and collect every sort of dirt and vermin . . ." She saw the surprise on Sir William's face and smiled apologetically. "Forgive my frankness, Your Honor, but things that are 'not-to-be-spoken-of' can never be changed. At virtually every social function in society there is at least one swoon caused by overlacing, and on warm days untold numbers of women are rendered unconscious by their desperate pursuit of the infamous eighteen-inch waist. Young girls who grow up with such brutal bindings never draw a free or normal breath. They have ribs broken and spines weakened by corseting and they suffer from air starvation and develop weak and unhealthy constitutions as a result. Their children are born small and sickly and their childbed experiences rank as unspeakable terrors, all because of the ridiculous whims of fashionmongers. I believe they should be given another choice, a healthy and gracious alternative. And corsets are but one of the horrors I mean to liberate my fellow humans from . . ."

"Just what do you propose women wear instead, Miss Duncan?"

"Female trousers, Your Honor," Farnsworth blurted out. "*Bloomers!* She wants to dress women in absurd, indecent garments more suited to heathen harems than to decent London streets!"

"There is nothing indecent about such garments," she declared, her voice rising.

"She would have women bare their arms and their . . . chests!"

"Only in summer, during the hottest weather. And somewhat less 'chest' than is revealed by *proper* debutantes in *proper* society."

Open talk of petticoats, corsets, and "chests"—Cole

thought as he leaned forward—small wonder the old man was so keen to hear this case!

Madeline Duncan glared at the opposition and flung her cloak aside, baring her own garments. "I ask you, Your Honor, are these clothes indecent? offensive? apt to cause riots in the streets?"

Sounds of indrawn breaths were audible throughout the courtroom. Miss Duncan was clothed in what appeared to be a long scarlet jacket, superbly tailored, with offset front buttons and black velvet collar and cuffs. The garment skimmed her narrow waist and the contour of her hips and ended at her knees. Below it was what appeared to be a narrow black skirt—until she moved her feet and the garment parted. She wore trousers, cuffed at the bottom like a gentleman's.

There was considerable murmuring as Sir William hoisted himself up and leaned across the bench for a better look. In the gallery Cole was on his feet and moving down to the railing for a better view.

Madeline Duncan's tunic was a vibrant slash of red in that sea of austere robes and weathered oak. Her womanly silhouette seemed to glow in the hazy light coming from the high windows as she turned slowly, lifting her arms, inviting inspection.

Cole found himself accepting that bold invitation. With a connoisseur's eye he examined her broad shoulders, narrow waist, and ripely curved bottom—which were free of frames and pads and weighty layers of petticoats. Her garments were tailored yet far from mannish—quite flattering to her figure. With mild surprise Cole realized that she was younger than he had first supposed. Certainly more curvaceous . . .

"See for yourself, Your Honor. If I hadn't moved my feet, you wouldn't have known I was wearing a bifurcated garment at all. There is nothing the slightest bit indecent about my clothing. In fact, it is the height of sensibility. I have arranged a demonstration for comparison's sake. If you will indulge me for a moment . . ."

Despite objections from the other side, Sir William was of a mood to do just that. At his nod, she hurried to the rear of the courtroom to admit a young woman wearing a long cloak. Miss Duncan led her before the bench and removed the wrap. The young woman was clad in an elegant mauve and black satin ball gown made with beaded straps over the shoulders, a plunging neckline, a torturously narrow waist, and an elaborate bustle—the height of current fashion.

"I purchased this gown two weeks ago from one of the city's leading dressmakers," Miss Duncan declared. "It is precisely the sort of thing worn all over London for evening parties and social gatherings. Notice the depth of the neckline and how much skin is displayed. Notice also how the use of a corset thrusts the young lady's . . . attributes . . . well, more into view." No man in the courtroom could help noticing. Miss Duncan had cannily chosen her model to maximize the "more" that would be "thrust into view." Cole's eyes gleamed with sudden admiration for the intrepid Miss Duncan.

You sly thing. Flash them a bit of flesh for comparison, will you? He propped his chin on his fist, on the railing, and stared at her.

"You may also note the rigid bodice and the elaborate and cumbersome bustle and train," she went on, "that serve no purpose whatsoever except to emphasize and draw attention to the lower parts of a woman's *anatomy*. Along with Mr. G. F. Watts, I loathe fashion's suggestion that the feminine half of humanity is furnished with tails." She nodded at the shocked murmurs her words elicited. "You might well take offense at my blunt words, good sirs, but they should shock you no more than this lady's dress. This is the very sort of crippling garment women are routinely tricked up into, to be sent out among the throngs to display their 'marital wares.' " She folded her hands with genteel determination.

"By contrast, I offer a wholesome aesthetic alternative. Which of us, Your Honor, shows more flesh?" She posed beside her model. "Which of us shows more bodily parts?" When sufficient time had passed for them to draw the inevitable conclusion, she continued. "And from a practical standpoint, which of us is more capable of normal daily functions?" She dropped a handkerchief on the floor and waved the young woman to retrieve it.

When the model was unable to bend or do more than just look helpless, Miss Duncan stooped gracefully, her back straight, and picked it up.

"Come here, young woman. I want a closer look at those clothes," Sir William ordered, using his gavel to wave her around the side of the court and up the steps to his bench. He enthusiastically set his hands to her waist and reported tartly: "For the record, Miss Duncan apparently practices what she preaches. She is not wearing a corset." The mutters of outrage that wafted through the court became gasps when he lifted the bottom of her jacket and peered beneath it. "Can't see an inch of flesh. Not even a glimpse of ankle. A pity, Miss Duncan." He gave a wry chuckle. "Many a gentleman has been started on the path to the altar by a glimpse of a well-turned ankle."

"Your Honor, we object most strenuously to this tawdry theatrical display!" Farnsworth erupted in a voice pitched faintly toward hysteria.

"Overruled!" Sir William snapped, and turned back to have one last peek under the hem of her jacket before dismissing her.

As she recrossed the dais, Madeline Duncan passed through a beam of late morning sun giving off a flash of red serge and burnished hair. For a moment Cole couldn't seem to clear the sight of her from his vision. His hands fairly itched to investigate those unique garments, and he realized, looking around the court, that nearly every man present was suffering the same impulse.

Clever chit. What else do you have up your reformed sleeve?

"Your Honor, my clients' refusal is not based solely on

the garments in question, but on how she means to produce them." Farnsworth tried yet again to state his case, this time with better luck. Sir William's attention shifted pointedly to him.

"What?" William the Conqueror snapped. "She intends to knit them all herself?"

Farnsworth paused to rein in his tongue and collect his composure, then proceeded. "Included in Miss Duncan's inheritance was a small woolen mill in a dying village in East Sussex. A place called St. Crispin on Crewes. The place has long since been abandoned and has fallen into a pathetic state. There is no longer any demand for the coarse fabric it once produced, and the village itself has lost much of its able-bodied population. There is no longer an adequate supply of workers. The rail line passed the place by, leaving it without transportation suitable for manufactured goods. The village is dying."

"Miss Duncan, however"—Dunwoody popped up again—"proposes to prolong its misery by pouring a great deal of her capital into the place. She wishes to reopen the mill and transport a throng of London rabble out to occupy the cottages and work in her factory. And that is only the start. She plans to fund new trades and services in the village, hire artisans and craftsmen to teach trades to these escapees from the London stews."

"She intends to turn the place into a 'worker's paradise.'" Ecklesbery rose beside his partner with a disdainful air. "Speaks of guaranteeing them a wage, taking care of their dependents, hiring a physician, a schoolmaster."

"In short, Your Honor," Farnsworth declared, taking charge once more and giving his clients a glower, "she wants to build not only a garment factory, but an entire village, an ideal community, a *utopia*."

"Utopia, eh?" Sir William stroked his chin. "Moneyed females gadding about the countryside, turning dying villages into utopias . . ." He scowled. "A disturbing prospect, I'll grant you. But not strictly illegal. What does the firm have against the building of a utopia? Or perhaps it is Sussex they object to. . . ."

Cole was watching the proceedings with an intensity he hadn't felt in several months. It was pure sardonic pleasure to watch Sir William put fat, arrogant Farnsworth on edge and reduce him to saying what he meant in plain words. With age and infirmity, Uncle William had grown less tolerant of strained legal niceties and social restrictions. Cole glowered at his overweening former partner, realizing that he and Sir William shared both a hope of justice and a despair of the law.

Make him sweat, Uncle.

". . . laudable impulses, certainly noble intentions. These are admirable ideals indeed." Farnsworth pulled a handkerchief from his pocket to mop his corpulent face. "But the scheme is doomed to fail and, in the process, to lay waste a goodly part of Miss Duncan's worldly substance."

"Doomed to fail, you say?" Sir William snatched up his gavel, propped his gouty leg onto the bench, and used the handle to scratch beneath its bandages. When he turned back to the proceedings, he was obviously in discomfort. "How so?"

"If it pleases Your Honor . . ." Ecklesbery stepped around the table with an expression of cloying concern. "The entire notion is the epitome of impracticality. The sort of people Miss Duncan intends to employ are unused to work of any kind. They are perennial hangers-on, crude, shiftless, and incapable of bettering themselves. Even if they could be taught, even if she could get them to work, the venture would still fail. Such a business enterprise requires acumen and efficient management. Ask her, Your Honor, who she intends to superintend this 'factory.' "

Sir William did indeed put the question to her. She straightened her spine and stood her ground. "I intend to oversee the work myself, Your Honor. I am well acquainted with financial matters—I ran my aunt's household quite efficiently for a number of years. Since January I have read extensively on the subject of industrial processes and management. And I have already hired an experienced engineer and a number of carpenters and journeymen toolmakers to refit the factory."

"Your Honor, she is a young, unmarried woman." Farnsworth planted himself before the bench with his fists at his waist, demanding the court's undivided attention. "What does she know of the daily workings of factory life or of the sort of people who work in factories? Factories require tending at all hours, in close confines, in close contact with men of the working class. A delicate young woman should be concerning herself with more seemly matters—social events and making suitable connections, possibly even matrimony."

"How dare you?" Miss Duncan's face reddened and her hands fell into fists at her sides as she faced first Farnsworth and then Sir William. "Finally we hear the truth of it, Your Honor. They refuse to release the money because they cannot abide the thought of a young *woman* living her life and running her business affairs without a man's governance. If I were a *man* of twenty-five, would they murmur one word of opposition to my starting a business concern of my own?

"But because I am a woman they tell me not to 'worry my pretty little head' . . . to go plan a party or a holiday in Paris . . . to buy a new hat, a new dress, or a whole shop full of new dresses. My gentlemen solicitors wouldn't bat an eye if I sent them bills for thousands of pounds spent on extravagant jewels and clothing. But let me speak of using that very same money to clothe ragged children and give them food and schoolbooks . . . let me propose creating honest, decent work for those same children's parents and suddenly I'm impractical and ridiculous, a sentimental female, a cockeyed idealist!"

Dunwoody sprang up, ruddy with indignation. "What she proposes, Your Honor, is no less than a doomed social experiment! She even speaks of having her workers run things—take over the place."

"I simply want to give people a chance to work hard and make a better life," she countered. "It has happened before—in the colonies—America, Australia. Poor people can learn to help themselves."

"Help themselves to her money, she means," Farnsworth growled.

Well, it is her money, after all, Cole thought.

"Well, it is my fortune, after all," Madeline Duncan declared as if she had somehow perceived Cole's musings.

Smart girl. Cole focused on her, trying to make out whether her hair was truly red or if its vivid appearance was just the reflection of her audacious coat. *What would I argue next if I were in charge? The will itself, perhaps—could that be of any help?*

"My plans for the money are perfectly in keeping with the wishes my aunt Olivia expressed in her will," she continued. "She knew and approved of my interest in helping others. She would have applauded my intention to rebuild the factory and to use it to produce sensible clothing. In fact, Your Honor, my aunt was a personal friend of those forward-thinking Americans, Dr. Mary Walker and Mrs. Amelia Bloomer. For the last two decades my aunt Olivia wore 'female trousers' herself."

"Did she indeed?" Sir William rubbed his chin thoughtfully and looked down at the documents attached to the briefs submitted by both parties. "I have read the will of Olivia Duncan. It seems straightforward and sensible. Miss Duncan is to have the balance of her estate with no entailments, codicils, or conditions attached. And there is a clear humanitarian bent to the wording."

Cole grinned as his irascible old uncle responded to Miss Duncan's cleverness and heartfelt convictions. *He's on the fence, sweetheart. Give him one last nudge and make it good,* Cole thought. *Something sentimental but smart.* What were the odds that she could come up with something that would qualify on both counts?

"Your Honor—" Just as she started to speak, Farnsworth came forward with a stack of documents nearly two feet high, brandishing them before the bench and then depositing them with a flourish on the desk of the court clerk.

"Your Honor, we have thoroughly studied the matter, including the deceptively simple wording of the will and the relevant applications of testamentary law. We submit these documents for your consideration, along with the correspondence from the agents we asked to investigate this village and those Miss Duncan has contracted with to perform work on the St. Crispin factory."

Madeline Duncan stared in visible shock at the documents. They had used their considerable resources to amass a case against her, and Cole saw her shoulders round as the significance of that mountain of legal paper settled on them. He felt an odd tug of sympathy in his chest.

Hopeless, he thought. They had law and precedent and worldly prudence on their side, and this was a place where such things held sway. Below him, Madeline straightened and approached the bench.

"By all means, Your Honor, do read and study the evidence they have compiled against me," she said in a voice constricted by earnestness. "But as you do, keep in mind that the things that truly matter in this case will never be found in tallies of figures and interpretations of dusty legal codes. What matters is what my aunt Olivia wanted in creating her will. What matters is that she wanted to help her fellow human beings and said so. What matters is that she entrusted me not only with her fortune, but with her desire to help others. She willed to me not just her money, but her hopes, her aspirations . . . her beloved ideals.

"Let me ask you something, Your Honor." She grasped the edge of the judicial bench and looked up at him intently.

"If you suddenly—today—came into a million pounds, what would you do with it?"

The courtroom grew abruptly quiet as all strained to hear both her question and Sir William's reply.

"Would you indulge in brandy and cigars . . . fine meals . . . a new suit of clothes? How many suits could you buy before buying a suit gave you no more pleasure? When you had a surfeit of brandy and cigars and suits . . . what then? At some point there would be more money than you had needs or desires. Would you then be under any moral obligation to help others? To share your good luck? To do something decent and worthwhile with the fortune you were given? I believe I am. Aunt Olivia believed so too. She left me a letter to be opened after her death."

She reached into her pocket and produced a folded piece of paper. Opening it, she introduced it into evidence with the court clerk, as Farnsworth had done, and the clerk immediately handed it to Sir William.

What a quick study you are, Miss Duncan.

"As you can see, she asked me the same question I just asked you. And she did so because she knew my answer would be . . . what I would choose for myself and for my fellow human beings."

Cole found himself nodding. That arresting question, the letter, and Madeline Duncan's heartfelt entreaty should prove damn near irresistible for an aging, gout-riddled man with a penchant for poking around in other people's souls. Miss Duncan had laid out her dreams, her values, and her passions for the old man's judgment.

Sentimental and smart. An inspired gambit, sweetheart. You may have just evened the score.

After a moment's silence Sir William stirred. Glowering at all parties, he announced: "I've heard enough. I shall return presently to deliver my decision."

The court stared in shock and staggered to its feet as the

justice gathered up his papers, rose, and hobbled from the bench.

Ecklesbery, Townshend, and Dunwoody erupted all at once as Sir William cleared the door.

"This is unheard of—unconscionable—unthinkable!"

"He hasn't read a single brief!"

"It's an outrage, it is!"

Cole was as surprised as the defendants by his uncle's abrupt declaration. Watching Farnsworth try to calm his clients, he couldn't help enjoying their outrage. Clearly, they had counted on the legal process not only for a verdict, but also for a substantial delay. Chancery courts were generally known to move at the pace of a snail on hot pavement. Despite recent reform attempts, it was common for an inheritance case to take a year or two to complete. Madeline Duncan's solicitors had obviously been counting on frustration and endless continuances to wear down her enthusiasm for her absurd plan.

As he watched the plaintiff conferring with her barrister, it struck him how surprisingly intriguing her wretched case was. Her petition was a legal lost cause, of that he had no doubt. Trusteeships were established to prevent precisely the sort of ruinous tangent Miss Duncan seemed hell-bent on pursuing. They were held to be nearly inviolate by the courts.

People who inherited fortunes were prone to spend the money on things they would almost certainly later regret. Most went on buying sprees and socialized recklessly, some drank to excess, gambled, and took up with flashy companions who tried to relieve them of the burden of their new-found wealth. An ill-fated few acquired a taste for even deeper vices—games and manipulations, an endless quest for sensation, a descent into the world of the flesh.

Miss Duncan, on the other hand, suffered not from hedonism, but from idealism run amok. From all appearances she was a true believer, convinced of the goodness and redemptive possibilities in humankind.

Cole's jaw tensed as he studied her with that unsettling thought in mind. In the end, he realized, her devotion to her own impossible ideals would likely prove more dangerous to her than a bout of self-indulgence. Like most idealists, she would refuse to see the world as it really was—the rampant disease, decay, and avarice all around her. She would wear herself down to bare bones, doggedly pursuing her vision of mankind's "nobility," until her fellow humans drained every last drop of substance from her and left her as destitute and disillusioned as they were.

Ridiculous female, he thought, staring at her with new eyes. *Why don't you just do as they say?*

Get a corset.

Find a man.

Have a brood of red-haired brats. . . .

3

With each moment that passed, the suspense thickened and the atmosphere in the courtroom became more charged. Ecklesbery, Townshend, and Dunwoody conferred with barrister Farnsworth in jealously guarded whispers, casting glowers Madeline's way while she sat primly by her dozing lawyer, refusing to look at her opponents and seeming confident she would soon receive the court's approbation and her money.

Inwardly, however, she was far from certain that her suit would succeed. From the start she had understood that her fate would depend primarily upon the justice assigned to hear her case. And she'd had either the fortune or the misfortune to come before crotchety old Sir William Rayburn. Protected by judicial privilege, reputation, and seniority, he took liberties with courtroom decorum, the barristers appearing before him, and social propriety. He was gouty and rude and impatient with both man and God. And he might just be the answer to her prayers. Who else but a cantankerous old eccentric would dare deliver a judgment against the cream of London's legal establishment? Who else but an aging man with plenty of regrets, misspent years, and long-dead ambitions would dare give legal sanction to her headlong pursuit of a dream?

Her nervous sigh was in reality a prayer for a favorable verdict. Without one, she might well find herself in the poorhouse before long. In the last three months she had spent herself into something of a financial fix.

Anticipating the release of her money, she had begun work on the factory in St. Crispin, recruiting workers and resettling them in the deserted village. There were a thousand details to attend—endless renovations, hiring, purchase of equipment, transportation, permits, agreements with suppliers—and every one of them seemed to require crossing someone's palm with silver. Soon she had spent both her first year's income and the wardrobe money her solicitors had provided, hoping to pacify her. When they learned she had gone ahead with her plans despite their disapproval, they stopped releasing the funds they held in trust, and she had been forced to use her last personal funds—a small legacy from her deceased parents.

Now her financial resources were depleted. Work on her factory had come to a dismal halt, and things would stay halted and dismal unless she prevailed in this proceeding. She caught a glimpse of scarlet at the door and her heart began to pound; Sir William was thudding back into the courtroom. Rising with the rest of the court, she tried in vain to read some sign of her fate in the old man's countenance as he maneuvered into the great chair behind the bench.

"Beauty," Sir William declared after a lengthy pause, dropping each word as if it were a pearl, "is said to reside in the eye of the beholder. The same might also be said of pomposity, vulgarity, absurdity . . . decency, generosity, and idealism. All are judgments that depend upon the viewer's values and standards. No doubt, at each of the great advancements of mankind there were people present who labeled the proceedings reckless, ridiculous, or even profane. And yet, miraculously, there have always been those courageous few who were willing to risk much to give something beyond the ordinary to their fellow humans. We have them to thank for our continued progress as a species."

He leaned forward on the bench to stare at Madeline, and she tried not to flinch under his piercing examination. "I have no way of knowing whether Madeline Duncan is a great visionary, a garden-variety prodigal with a novel approach to wasting a fortune, or a most peculiar species of lunatic." He turned to glare at the defendants. "But I do know that idealism—however naive or out of fashion—is most assuredly *not* the same as incompetence or irresponsibility."

Ecklesbery, Townshend, and Dunwoody cast looks of alarm at barrister Farnsworth as, before their eyes, Sir William's fleshy face transformed into a mask of judicial hauteur.

"It is the judgment of this court that Miss Olivia Duncan was perfectly clear with regard to her final wishes. There is no need for protracted examination, interpretation, or elaboration of the documents. The funds and properties belong fully and irrevocably to Madeline Duncan. However, mindful of the responsibilities of Ecklesbery, Townshend, and Dunwoody as trustees, it is the ruling of this court that Messrs. Ecklesbery, Townshend, and et ceteras release up to one quarter of the estate for Miss Duncan's use."

Stunned silence greeted his decree. Savoring the drama of the moment, he turned to Madeline with a smile. "I've a mind to see Miss Duncan's 'reformed garments.' God knows, there must be *something* better to garb the human form than torturous lacer-uppers and strangulating collars." He gave his own neckpiece a restive tug. "I am giving her the chance to construct both her clothing and her factory. . . . "

Madeline gasped and reached for Sir Richard's hands, squeezing them. The first flush of jubilation at having won the right to the money was so heady that it took her a moment to realize there was a codicil to Sir William's approval.

". . . under reasonable and prudent constraint," he continued. "The court shall appoint a fair and impartial overseer, an agent of the court whose duty it will be to report to the court on the progress of her factory and production. Said overseer shall have the authority to approve or disapprove capital expenditures and the weighty responsibility to protect Madeline Duncan from her own magnanimous impulses."

The court began to buzz, then to hum, and finally broke into a roar of voices.

"Objection!" Farnsworth was on his feet in a shot, and Ecklesbery, Townshend, and Dunwoody sprang up behind their counsel.

"This is an outrage!"

"Preposterous!"

"Utterly without precedent!"

Madeline rose an instant later, no less appalled than they were by Sir William's decision. An overseer? She was to have a court-appointed interloper to say her yea and nay on every detail? Evaluating her every movement? Reporting on her to the court? "Sir Richard"—she seized the old gentleman by the arm and tried to get him to his feet—"you must object. Tell him that I don't need to be overseen!"

"But, Your Honor, Miss Duncan already *has* trustees— my clients!" Farnsworth was already lodging a vehement protest. "It is *their* task to watch over her expenditures and keep her from reckless—"

"My ruling requires no amendment, Fartsworth," Sir William snapped, snatching up his gavel and holding it threateningly, ready to censure Farnsworth's next word. "Your clients are openly hostile to the entire notion of Miss Duncan's enterprise. They could no more be objective about it than the queen is about Albert's passing. It is the court's intention to give Miss Duncan a reasonable chance while at the same time guarding her interests."

He lifted his bewigged head and scanned the courtroom thoughtfully. "What is needed here is someone familiar with the law and with financial dealings. Someone who is not easily swayed by idealistic emotional pleas . . . a disinterested party . . . one with his feet firmly on the ground and no illusions about the grandeur of the human race. In short, what Miss Duncan needs to oversee her experiment is a bit of a cynic."

An enigmatic smile appeared on his face as he fastened his gaze on someone in the gallery.

"By happenstance, there is just such a man in court today. The court appoints Lord Cole Mandeville as its representative and overseer of the development of Miss Duncan's Ideal Garment Company. It is the court's direction that Lord Mandeville travel to the village of St. Crispin on Crewes, for a period of three months, to observe firsthand the progress toward Miss Duncan's goals, and that he present a report of his findings in writing to the court on Monday of each week. At the end of said three months, we shall reconvene here. The progress of the venture—or lack thereof—will determine the final disposition of Miss Duncan's fortune."

While all in the court were grappling to comprehend Sir William's decision, he banged his gavel, sealing the order, and it was done. Madeline steadied herself on the table, blinking.

She was to have a Lord Somebody-or-other as an overseer . . . regulating her spending . . . scrutinizing her every decision . . . dictating her dreams. She didn't have a father or a husband to control her, so the court had graciously appointed a man of her own to— The rest of Sir William's words stopped spinning in her head long enough for her to understand: It wasn't just any man. It was . . .

A cynic. She was being saddled with a heartless, pinchpenny male for three interminable months!

Through the red haze rising in her vision she was vaguely aware of Sir William quitting the courtroom, of Sir Richard's confusion, and of her erstwhile solicitors' fury in the face of what they considered judicial caprice. From the gallery came a muttered oath, the sound of feet hitting steps, and reverberations from the slamming of the doors at the rear of the gallery.

She stood a moment with her fists clenched and her cheeks on fire, trying to plot a rational course. She would talk to Sir William, convince him that she needed no supervision. Let him give *her* the money and the three months. Then let him take her to task for what she *did,* not for what they were all afraid she *might do!*

Without a thought for courtroom proprieties, she skirted the opposition's barristers and headed straight for the door Sir William had used at the front of the court. She was halted there by a formidable bailiff, who informed her that none but the justice was permitted to come and go through that entrance. Arguing and even pleading were of no avail. She headed for the doors at the rear of the court, determined to be heard.

Finding the way to one of the chief justices' chambers took a bit of doing; the directions seemed to be as closely guarded as the entrance to a pharaoh's tomb. In desperation, she crafted a story that she was Sir William's niece by marriage, late for an appointment with the old fellow, and a knowledgeable clerk took pity on her. She arrived at the door of Sir William's chambers overheated and out of breath and just in time to hear her name being taken in vain.

"The minute I saw Farnsworth, I knew you had called me down here to meddle in my life," a deep male voice was declaring. "But you've exceeded even my most jaded expectations—saddling me with some damned-fool female out to save the world. This Duncan woman is nothing short of a lunatic—a full-bore, bleeding-heart, go-down-with-the-ship martyr. Did you plan this all along, Uncle, or was my being pressed into your service just an impromptu bit of manipulation?"

Madeline halted just inside the door, her face as scarlet as her tunic. Sir William, still in his robes and wig, was ensconced behind a large desk with his bound leg propped on an ottoman, being read the riot act by a tall, dark figure looming over the desk.

"A *lunatic*?" she said. Sir William looked up, his accuser started and wheeled, and both men looked at her as if she had two heads.

"Good Lord. There she is now," the man said, tugging both his ire and his vest down and into place. "Madwoman Duncan."

"That is *Madeline* Duncan, thank you," she said sharply. "You, I take it, are my proposed keeper."

"Not if I can bloody well help it," he declared. "I have better things to do with my time than prevent some idiot female from spending herself into oblivion." He glanced at Sir William, then turned a glare on her that would have sent a lesser woman into vapors. "If I could tolerate such duty, Uncle, I'd have taken a wife by now."

Madeline drew up her chin, studying him with the same fierce regard he aimed at her. He was an intimidating figure— tall, dark in coloring, and dressed in a charcoal-gray suit that bespoke both money and the leisure to submit to a tailor's ministrations. Out of pure habit she took in the details of his garments—the broad padded shoulders of his coat, the close-cut waist, the tight standing collar, and the tuck-front shirt that was so overstarched, it looked like paint on clapboard siding. He wore a black silk cravat with a diamond stickpin instead of a tie, his shoes were covered by dove-gray spats, and precisely one inch of Chinese silk showed above the breast pocket of his coat.

She groaned mentally. If Sir William had combed the city, he couldn't have found her an overseer less sympathetic to her cause—*a fashion-conscious cynic*. Pulling her gaze from him, she advanced on the desk, determined to hold her own.

"As you can see for yourself, Your Honor, this 'arrangement' you have proposed—"

"Ordered," Sir William corrected her.

"—*ordered*—is unworkable. Can you in any way call this

man objective? or reasonable? He's already named me a lunatic, an incompetent, a wastrel, a bleeding heart, and a martyr."

"Ahhh"—Sir William raised an excepting finger—"but those are merely *personal* opinions. I have every confidence that his *professional* assessments will be considerably more objective."

"The hell they will," her overseer declared, folding his arms.

"The hell they *won't*," Sir William said with sudden furious calm. "You are a member of the bar, Lord Mandeville, and in court you are subject to my authority." His volume rose with each precisely chosen word. "You will indeed serve the court as overseer in this case . . . unless you would prefer to continue in your contempt and find yourself sitting in a cell in Scotland Yard."

"A cell does have a certain appeal, considering . . ." Lord Mandeville looked Madeline over with an expression men usually reserve for something they've stepped in while crossing a street. Then he turned to Sir William, meeting him eye to eye, glaring, testing the old justice's resolve and finding it as firm as Gibraltar. After a long, tense moment he struck his colors and surrendered. "Damned if you wouldn't do it."

"I most certainly would. And so, Lord Mandeville, shall you, since you seem to have nothing better to do with yourself." That settled, Sir William's mood brightened as he looked up at Madeline. "I am certain, Miss Duncan, that Lord Mandeville will exercise every bit of objectivity and restraint he possesses in overseeing your enterprise."

"What he will exercise, Your Honor, is his prejudice. To put him over my Ideal Garment Company is to condemn me to failure!"

"And to condemn me to three long, suffocating months of having to nursemaid a pigheaded female who insists on stirring up the social order and meddling in other people's lives," Mandeville said testily. "All because she has nothing worthwhile to do with herself."

"Nothing worthwhile?" She turned to face him and realized that stretching to her full height and rocking up onto her toes could not compensate for the difference in their sizes. She struck back with the only weapons at her command: words. "You don't see the value of freeing women's bodies from the tyranny of cruel fashions? You find nothing worthwhile in helping the working poor make a better life? You cannot appreciate the benefit of a workplace that enhances human dignity and fosters creativity?"

He paused a moment, staring down into her face, examining the stubborn set of her jaw and the determination blazing in her eyes.

"None whatsoever," he declared tautly. "Leave the poor alone, Miss Duncan. They suffer enough misery without having to put up with reformers and idealists. If females want to squeeze themselves in two with corsets and flaunt their bosoms in public, I can't see that it's any business of yours. In fact, the world could do with a bit *more* bosom and a good bit *less* high-minded moralizing. It's the idealists of this world who get mankind into trouble. Leading people to believe they are entitled to a better lot . . . promising impossible solutions—"

"Impossible solutions?" she demanded, swallowing hard. "There is no help for humankind? Just gloom and despair and hopelessness all around?"

"I'd say that rather sums it up."

They had come virtually nose to nose, each refusing to give an inch in this ideological battle of wills. Her heart was pounding and blood was roaring in her head. But through that inner tempest she could feel heat radiating from him, engulfing her senses. Her head filled with the scents of starch, soap, and sandalwood carried on a distinctive current of musk that was foreign to her but that she sensed had to do with "male." His face was suddenly all she could see—an intriguing blend of planes and angles too sharp and bold to be merely handsome. His eyes were a striking hazel-green, a snatch of autumn forest—jade and amber—changeable. Her gaze fled down the curve of his cheek to his mouth. She'd never seen lips like his—broadly curved . . . sensuality inscribed in every contour. . . .

Startling new sensations washed through her, heat as palpable as physical contact. She'd never imagined it was possible to feel a person without touching. But then, she'd never been this close to a man befo—

That thought booted her sharply back to reality. Color flooded her face as she scrambled to retrieve her self-possession. Wretched man, intimidating her with his size and upper-crust disdain. She couldn't let him get away with it.

"Spoken like a overindulged upper-class male who has never had to strive for anything," she declared, answering his condescension with a bit of her own. "How sad to have been handed everything from the moment you were born. Nothing to dream. Nothing to hope for. No ideals to struggle toward." She shook her head with suddenly genuine sympathy. "No wonder you see everything in shades of gloom."

Her words sank unexpectedly into the dark centers of those jaded autumn eyes, but she turned to Sir William before she could discern their full impact. "It would appear that Lord Mandeville, like my noble-spirited trustees, has a thing or two to learn about ideals. Well, where better to learn such lessons than at the Ideal Garment Company?" She leaned over the desk and lowered her voice. "I will open my factory and produce my garments and sell them at a profit, no matter what obstacles my trustees and my court-appointed 'nanny' erect in my path."

She caught a glimpse of Lord Mandeville's face as she turned to go. It was red and set, filled with patrician outrage. Her first impulse was a shameful surge of triumph. But by the time she reached the door, it struck her that she had just goaded the very man who held her fate in his hands.

Perhaps Lord Mandeville was right, she thought as she charged down one hallway after another, searching for the blessed exit. Perhaps she was Madwoman Duncan after all.

As Cole Mandeville stormed out of the gallery, slamming the doors back against the walls, a shabby, unshaven man in a brown checkered coat popped up out of the last row of benches. "Wha-at the—" The fellow blinked, rubbed his reddened eyes with ink-stained fingers, and glared at the figures making noise below on the courtroom floor.

"How dare you inconsiderate clods raise such a ruckus when a bloke is tryin' to catch a few winks up here in the pews?" he grumbled. "This is Chancery, after all."

A moment later that fact brought him fully awake. A ruckus in *Chancery*? He shot to his feet and intercepted a dapper young gentleman on his way out the doors.

"Say, guv, what's got the wigs all in a dither down there?"

"Out of my way." The fellow tried to shove him aside, but Rupert Fitch, one of London's most tenacious penny-press news writers, was not easily dissuaded when he was hot on the trail of a bit of news.

"See here, guv, I'm a journalist with *Gaflinger's Gazette*." He grabbed the man's sleeve, sensing in the fellow's agitation a tale just waiting to be told. "It's my job to report on the dread workin's of Her Majesty's Law Courts, especially if there's a foul miscarriage of justice afoot." The young gentleman winced as he peeled Fitch's stubby fingers from his sleeve, but then seemed to have second thoughts. Pausing, he glanced over his shoulder at the chaotic scene below.

"There has been a miscarriage of justice, right enough." The fashionable gent scanned the courtroom, his mind working visibly behind his boyish features.

"Good-fer-nothin' lawyers." Fitch snorted sympathetically.

"Oh, no, my friend, not the solicitors and barristers." The young gentleman smiled. "They are the most earnest of fellows. It was the lord justice who perpetrated the outrage here, a buffoon and an incompetent if ever there was one. He's just handed over a small fortune to an ignorant slip of a girl who intends to throw it away." In anger, his face lost much of its charm. "She has vowed to invest a quarter of a million pounds in developing an enterprise aimed at ridding women of the bondage of corsetry and petticoats. It's positively"—he caught the gleam in Fitch's eye and reined in his tongue—"heartbreaking. If it is allowed to go forward, I fear for the poor girl's reputation, if not her sanity."

Fitch instantly discerned the salacious potential. Prospective headlines—*Heiress Wages War on Corsets!* and *Heiress Strips Off Her Petticoats!*—flitted through his mind. He was just as quick to perceive the hint of self-interest in the fellow's tone.

"And this misguided young thing . . . she is a relative of yours?" he inquired.

"My cousin." On those handsome lips the words had a strangely unpleasant ring. "She got the lion's share, you see. While worthier relations were—well—" The young gentleman's smile suggested that he was too much a gentleman to elaborate.

"Say no more, Mr. . . . ."

"Duncan. Gilbert Duncan. My lady-cousin is Miss Madeline Duncan."

"A millionairess with a loathing for boning," Fitch said, measuring each word as if readying it for lead type. A tobacco-yellow smile bloomed on his stubbled face. "Well, Mr. Duncan, I can see ye've got a terrible burden to bear. And old Rupert Fitch here has a willin' shoulder to lend . . . and a willin' ear."

Cole Mandeville stormed out of the Law Courts like a man possessed. And indeed he was possessed—by two stunning blue orbs, an oval of luminous ivory, and a cloud of burnished silk, all wrapped around the steely core of a genuine do-or-die social reformer. Moments ago he had found himself standing flatfooted and speechless, staring down into Madeline Duncan's remarkable blue eyes and seeing into her blasted soul.

Her inner landscape seemed as pristine and unsullied as a newborn babe's. No avarice. No guilt. No sinkholes of self-interest. No gaping wounds to compensate for. It just wasn't possible. No human being could survive to her age without a few ravages to the soul, not even the most sheltered or privileged.

Not that she was particularly ancient, he thought furiously, hailing a hansom cab and feeling his vest riding up again as he raised his arm. Nor particularly hard on the eyes. It ought to be a law of nature that strange females had to *look* strange.

Giving his vest a savage jerk, he settled back into the worn leather seat of the two-seater cab and squinted at her memory, searching it for the flaws he knew must be there— a hint of orange in that perfect chestnut, a taint of muddiness in that penetrating blue. Under such heated examination her image evaporated and he was left glowering at the horse's rump through the carriage glass and feeling very much like one himself.

He should have known his uncle was up to something, should have headed for the door the minute he spotted his former colleague at the counsel table. He had presumed the old boy intended to treat him to the spectacle of "Fartsworth" at work, expecting it would somehow lure him back into the profession. He never imagined the old goat had more direct designs on him—involving him in the case itself!

And such a case. A damned infernal female with delusions of messiahship out to save the world from the twin evils of corsets and poverty in one fell swoop!

Corsets and poverty. The absurdity of it struck, and he began to laugh.

When laughter had purged much of his tension and he sobered, the smile that lingered on his lips slowly acquired a bitter edge. The chit wasn't just idealistic, she was downright ignorant. If life in the law had taught him anything, it was that people didn't want to better their own lot; they wanted somebody else's lot to better them. People didn't want to be delivered from their vices; they wanted to learn how to pursue them without getting caught. Given a choice, human beings would always choose their own comfort and self-interest above grandiose abstractions like devotion and loyalty and justice. The unlucky few who somehow became yoked to such ideals were doomed to disillusionment and despair.

Unbidden, her face invaded his mind once more—earnest, determined, and so insufferably righteous. So the brazen chit intended to give him a lesson in ideals, did she? Well, not before life gave her a lesson or two in the grim reality of the human condition. A vengeful pulse of satisfaction went through his veins at the thought that he was going to be there—front and center—to see it happen.

What was it Uncle William said? Part of his charge was to save "Mad Madeline" from her own magnanimous impulses?

He smiled.

Like hell.

4

When the sun came up over the village of St. Crispin a fortnight later, Madeline watched it as she had every morning for the past two weeks—from her second floor bedroom in the superintendent's house that nestled beside her factory. She cradled a cup of tea between her hands and savored occasional sips as she stood by the window, surveying the wakening village.

This was her favorite time of day and her favorite way to spend it: overlooking the modest stone houses lining the cobbled lane and the rectangular patch of green at the heart of the village. In that first golden light of morning the limestone of the buildings glowed as if gilded and the grass and trees appeared like a deep teal velvet. Each morning she absorbed the sight and stored it in her heart, feeling like the richest woman alive. Each morning it renewed her determination to make a success of her factory and of the garments that would free women to live fuller, more productive lives.

"Another drop of tea, Madeline?" a voice

asked from behind her. She started out of her thoughts and turned to find her stout, round-faced housekeeper standing by the writing table where her breakfast tray sat.

"No, thank you, Davvy. I need to get to the office early this morning. The first shipment from Manchester is due anytime, and I have two more families arriving today."

"And *him*." Mrs. Davenport folded her hands at her waist and leveled a narrow look at Madeline. "You do seem to keep forgetting that *he* is arriving today."

"How could I possibly forget?" Madeline set her cup back in its saucer on the table. "You haven't ceased mentioning it since his wretched letter arrived."

"Only because you have refused to mention it since the letter arrived." Davenport studied her as she paused to peer at herself in the mirror of the dressing table. "We should have made arrangements."

"I have made arrangements . . . of a sort," she said, tucking an unruly lock of hair back into the ribboned net around her simple chignon.

"What do you mean 'of a sort'?" Davenport frowned and folded her arms over her ample bosom. "This is no time for any of your stubbornness, Maddy Duncan. We should be gracious and hospitable—prepare a welcoming dinner at the very least." When Madeline didn't agree straightaway, a glint appeared in the housekeeper's eye. "Your aunt Livvy, bless her, always said the route to a man's goodwill was through his stomach."

Madeline halted in the midst of reaching for the long blue smock that hung on the open wardrobe door. She knew full well what Davenport was up to in invoking Aunt Olivia's name, but was somehow unable to dismiss it. "No, Aunt Olivia always said the route to a man's goodwill was generally through his prejudices. *You're* the one who always insisted that men think with their stomachs."

Davenport gave a harumph of annoyance. "Well, at least think about it."

Out the door and hurrying down the narrow footpath leading from the house to the factory, Madeline took a deep breath of country air and did think about it . . . or, more accurately, about *him*.

Her last glimpse of Lord Mandeville was as he stood in the justice's chambers, livid with outrage at the affront she had just dealt him. If she hadn't forgotten, it wasn't likely he had either. And it was even less likely that his opinion of her and her venture had improved in the intervening two weeks.

Strangely, his ire wasn't the only thing she remembered. She had never been one to recall faces well, but for some reason she could recall every line, every curve, every shading and texture of his. In the quiet of her room at night, in the privacy of her inner thoughts, she also remembered the curious and somewhat worrisome tingling she had experienced as he loomed over her. It wasn't merely the excitement of verbal combat or of the passionate defense of her strongly held beliefs. It was something else, something she had never experienced before. Something alarmingly personal. And feminine.

All the more reason for her to see that his lordship's stay in St. Crispin was unexpectedly brief. She had to get rid of him. It was the only sensible thing to do. And in order to get rid of him, she had decided, she would have to convince him that both his oversight of the Ideal Garment Company and his presence in St. Crispin were unnecessary.

To that end, she had plotted a strategy along two separate but complementary fronts. She planned to convince him of her sound management and the ability of her employees by demonstrating the progress they had made in clothing designs, the manufacturing process, and the factory itself. Only the most narrow-minded and vindictive of men would refuse to see the good that was happening here. Despite the animosity between them at their first meeting, she hoped that Lord Mandeville's professional objectivity was worthy of Sir William's high opinion of it.

Her secondary strategy addressed his presence in the village. A man of his elegance would no doubt find St. Crispin's meager accommodations difficult. With a little help they might become altogether intolerable.

Looking up, she found herself a short distance from the front doors of the factory. She paused. As always, her worries and cares began to fall away at the sight of the tall brick-and-limestone building and the freshly lettered sign over the main entrance identifying it as THE IDEAL GARMENT COMPANY.

The factory was simply the most beautiful thing she'd ever seen, a dream in the making. The large windows on the first and second floors still awaited a coat of paint, and the roof, which had suffered moisture damage during the years of neglect, still had holes here and there. The entry yard needed a great deal of stone to make it passable in wet weather, and there was a good bit of cleaning and painting to do all around. But such exterior flaws were easily remedied, minor compared to what had been accomplished inside the building.

Rolling up the sleeves of her blue smock, she headed inside and up to the offices, stepping carefully around the defective boards in the stairs, which were due to be repaired any day now. As she strolled through half-finished cutting tables, envisioning them piled with layers of cloth and surrounded by cutters and apprentices, she was startled by a snarling sound from a nearby stack of lumber. Investigating, she discovered a man sprawled on his back on top of a pile of boards, snoring furiously.

It was Fritz Gonnering, her German-born engineer. Her first impulse was to awaken him, but then she spotted the dark circles under his eyes and the pallor beneath the stubble on his face. *Exhaustion.* He had probably been working into the wee hours again. He had designed a system of pulleys and shafts to run an entire factory of cutting and sewing machines from a single coal-fired engine and now was laboring night and day to install and perfect it. Madeline shook her head, suffering a pang of conscience at how hard he was working.

Then she hurried on through the cutting rooms and up the back stairs to the offices.

Proceeding past the clerks' desks and the door to the superintendent's office, she headed straight for the sample room. It was here, in this spacious area flooded with light from newly installed windows, that the designs and patterns for her new garments were being painstakingly assembled.

The litter of creativity was everywhere. Bolts of fabric were propped against table legs and cabinets; sketches, drafting squares, and curve templates hung on pegs near the door; and pattern books and drawing pads were stacked on shelves and spilling over onto the worktables that lined the walls. Half-cut pattern pieces, palettes of fabric swatches, bolts of trims, and huge spindles of thread and rubberized elastic were piled higgledy-piggledy on every horizontal inch. In the center of the room stood a pair of wire dressmaking forms wearing a collage of paper patterns and pieces of fabric.

She felt a surge of warmth in her chest. The room was a mess, but in some ways it was her favorite place in the entire village. It was here that she started every morning, thinking, imagining, helping Jessup Endicott, her pattern maker, translate the ideas in her head into manufacturable pieces.

A commotion outside drew her back down the hall, where she discovered Emmaline Farrow, standing in the middle of the main office with her shawl hanging from one shoulder, looking distraught and clutching a wriggling eight-year-old in one hand and a six-year-old in the other.

"I'm so sorry that I am late . . ."

"I only just arrived myself," Madeline responded.

"It was just . . ." Tears were working their way up Emily's throat into her eyes. "I tried making porridge again and it scorched and stuck to the horrid pan and I had no time to do it all over again. . . ." The boys set up a wail as they buried their heads in their mother's skirts, and she looked as if she might swoon.

This was the third time this week that widowed Emily

Farrow had ruined her children's breakfast and arrived in the offices looking frazzled and overwhelmed. She was having a difficult time adjusting to a life of reduced means—cooking her own meals, laying her own fires, doing her own laundry, and looking after her own children.

Madeline peeled the children from her secretary's skirts and took their damp faces in her hands. "Theodore, Jonathan . . . Mrs. Davenport has some scrumptious buttered toast and jam left from our breakfast. I believe she may have some kippers tucked away somewhere too." She looked up at Emily. "Why don't you take them over to our house for a bit of breakfast? Beaumont will be here at any moment, and we'll manage for a while without you."

Poor woman, Madeline thought, leaning against the door frame and watching as Emily's darlings pulled her toward the stairs, then abandoned her to race down the rotted steps. She didn't realize she had also spoken it aloud, until a voice answered her.

"She's in a bit of a fix, all right." She turned to find Beaumont Tattersall standing behind her, watching Emily too. "Trying to keep up with those two . . . keep up her house . . . keep up her work . . . all while keeping up the old standards. It's a lot."

Madeline nodded ruefully. "But she'll learn. She just needs a bit of help now, at the start." She headed for the sample room to do a bit of sketching. "When Endicott arrives, tell him I want to see him straightaway."

"Miss Duncan, before you begin . . ." Tattersall called her back with an apologetic tone. "I've a stack of drafts for you to sign and, while you're at it, I'd like you to go over the accounts with me. I fear a number of bills have come in over the initial estimates."

She glanced wistfully at the sample room, then retraced her steps. Where would she be without Beaumont? The wiry, self-effacing little man was the epitome of organization. Small wonder Ecklesbery, Townshend, and Dunwoody had gone into near apoplexy the moment he announced he was leaving their office to join Madeline's Ideal Garment Company. His defection to her cause had proved the last straw where her gentlemen trustees were concerned. Knowing now just how much of a loss they had sustained, she could scarcely blame them.

Together she and her head clerk went over each invoice, bill, and entry in the account ledgers, scarcely noticing Emily Farrow's return. But they couldn't help noticing when a hollow-eyed Fritz Gonnering barged into the office, dragging two terrified boys by their Lord Fauntleroy curls, growling that if Emily wanted them to survive to grow up, she should keep them on a leash. They watched in sympathy as she dragged her weeping children up onto her lap, dried their tears, and then sent them outside with the admonition to keep their white lisle stockings and velvet knickerbockers clean. Madeline made a mental note to speak with Fritz Gonnering about being a bit more understanding with Emily's children. Poor, fatherless things. Of late they had subsisted almost exclusively on a diet of tears and burned porridge.

Shortly after things settled down again, a burly workman clomped into the office with his woolen cap in his hand, asking to speak with the proprietor. He scowled and shuffled his feet when Madeline presented herself and demanded to know his business. He explained that he was the foreman of the crew laying water pipes through the village and they were nearly finished with the job. He was there to collect his workmen's money.

"You've finished?" Madeline brightened. It was the best news she'd had in weeks. "You're ready to turn the wheel and fill the pipes—set it in motion?"

"Well . . ." He scratched his head and looked a bit uncomfortable. "That ain't my job. That 'ere en-gineer—that'd be his say. Turnin' wheels an' such, that ain't my place." He drew a sweat-stained piece of paper from his belt and peeled it open. "Now, about this here bill—"

"But if the pipes are all laid and the pumps are in place, it should be ready to use, should it not?"

"Well, I ain't responsible for—" The fellow shoved the bill into her hands. "If'n ye'll just give us our money, me and my blokes'll be on our way."

This was a momentous day indeed for Madeline and the resurrected St. Crispin. A safe and plentiful water supply piped into each cottage was her first major step in revitalizing the village itself. Now, after months of planning, that goal was finally being realized. She was seized by a fever of excitement.

"I want to see it work. I want to see water running in each and every cottage!"

Beaumont, Emily, and the sputtering foreman were hard put to keep up with her as she hurried through the cutting rooms, down the steps, and out into the yard. Getting her bearings, she headed for a clutch of men standing by the open ditch that snaked along the lane running through the center of the village. The workmen doffed their caps and stepped back to give her access. She stood admiring the thick iron pipe at the bottom of the ditch, then, the light of discovery in her face, located a junction with a smaller pipe that led into a nearby cottage.

The pipe ran beneath the side wall of the cottage's front room and ended in a pump attached to a dry sink. Emily, Beaumont, Fritz Gonnering, and a number of the village's old and new residents crowded into the doorway or peered through the broken window, watching her inspect it. Feathering a touch over the pump handle, she savored the accomplishment for a moment, then turned to them with her face glowing.

"Let's fire up the pump!"

The sun was high in the sky when Cole Mandeville crested the last rise on his big bay gelding and paused to scowl at the village below. After four miserable days and three interminable nights on the road—thrashing through half a dozen ditchwater places with names like Stonecrouch, Flimwell, and Three Leg Cross, following the locals' vague and erroneous recollections of the way to St. Crispin on Crewes—he was hot and sweaty and cross as a cat stuffed down a rain barrel. It seemed Madeline Duncan's village had not only died, it had also been forgotten.

Now that he had finally located the accursed place, he was greatly annoyed to discover that from the top of that rise it appeared perfectly idyllic. A score of stone cottages dotted the rolling hills and clustered along a winding lane that descended gently through a little valley. Mature trees formed picturesque clusters along a stream—presumably the less than noteworthy Crewes—and there was the odd sheep grazing here and there on verdant slopes. The spire of a quaint church nestled at the near end of a greensward and a large brick and limestone building were visible at the far end of the resurrected hamlet.

It looked like Eden reopened. A little slice of heaven newly reissued to earth.

And he was there to give its guardian angel a sound thrashing.

With a glance back at his carriage lumbering up a rise on the road behind him, he started down the sloping lane leading toward the center of the village. Surprisingly, the closer he came to the cottages, the worse they began to look. Many of the roofs were swayed or buckled; most of the windows had been removed, leaving raw holes in the stone walls; and from what he glimpsed through the gaping doors inside, many had only dirt floors. When he turned his attention to the surrounding countryside, he discovered that what had appeared to be lush pasture from a distance was actually coarse grass infested with burdock and thistles. And the road itself was degenerating into a rutted, scarcely navigable track.

He brightened. With each hovel he passed, the grim set

of his jaw eased and he relaxed a bit in the saddle. This, he told himself, was more like it.

At the edge of the main part of the village he noticed a freshly dug ditch running the length of the lane. He steered his mount closer to have a look. The iron pipe at the bottom of the trench and occasional offshoots of smaller pipe toward the cottages suggested some sort of public works in progress. It seemed rather small for a sewer. He edged his mount closer, frowning. A water supply pipe, perhaps.

His horse danced skittishly as he urged it still closer, studying the layout, trying to see the full extent of the project. The big bay tensed and laid its ears back, listening, alarmed by something. It took a moment for Cole to perceive the low rumble that worried his horse. It seemed to be coming from the ditch . . . that pipe . . . He increased the pressure of his knees and leaned far to one side, listening, focusing his attention on the middle of that trench.

Water suddenly came shooting out of the pipe in all directions, startling Cole's horse and setting it rearing. Jolted out of the saddle, he flailed and grabbed handfuls of saddle pad and mane, trying to avoid tumbling headlong into the open ditch. Struggling back into his seat, he fought to regain control of his plunging mount. It was only when he realized that they were being pelted with water that he urged the frantic animal out of range. Panting, his heart pounding wildly, he reined up and turned to discover circular flumes of water rising above the trench at regular intervals.

Further commotion followed as a dozen people rushed from a break in the line of cottages and came to a halt, staring in dismay at the spewing water. A figure in pale blue pushed through to the front of the crowd and quickly dispatched some of the others back the way they had come.

Before long the impromptu fountains lowered, sputtered, and then died with a gurgle. In the shocked silence Cole shivered and looked down at his clothes. He was half soaked.

His gaze raking over the onlookers down the lane, he fastened on the one he deemed responsible and made straight for her.

". . . simply won't do," Madeline Duncan was saying to a surly, platter-faced fellow as Cole rode up. "We'll lose half the water before it reaches the cottages—not to mention the possibility of contamination. I'm afraid, Mr. Gibbons, that you and your men shall simply have to—"

"Miss Duncan!" Cole called out in a booming voice. "What in infernal blazes is going on here?" He reined up at the edge of the crowd and sat glowering at her. She seemed startled by the sight of him—or perhaps by the water dripping from his hat.

"Your lordship." She held her ground, though her face suffused with color. "It seems you arrived just in time for the first test of our new municipal water system."

"A test?" He clamped his jaw together while he waited for the impulse to climb down from the saddle and give her a good throttling to pass. "Well, I'd say it failed the test. So much for wasting money on absurdities."

"It's not an absurdity. The village needs a safe, plentiful water supply," she pointed out. "We'll have it running properly in a few days."

"No, you won't," he declared, straightening in the saddle. "Water systems qualify as capital expenditures, and as such they come under my authority. I refuse to allow good money to be thrown after bad"—he glared at the now-muddy trench—"into an accursed hole in the ground."

"You can't do that!"

"Oh, but I can." He located the fellow Madeline Duncan had been laying down orders to and spoke directly to him. "Gibbons, is it? Pack up your men and leave. Your boondoggle here is over."

Shocked mutters wafted through the onlookers.

"For your information, Lord Mandeville, these workmen have already been paid for much of the work." She planted herself before his horse, which reversed its ears and eyed her nervously. "Now it is up to him and his men to make it right—to rejoin the pipes and stop the leaks. It makes no sense at all to send them packing and leave the village without water, when a few more days would see the system finished and functional . . . as well as paid for."

Undercut by her logic, he retreated into aristocratic disdain. "We shall discuss this further"—he raked a glance over their gawking audience—"in private. Now, if you will be so good as to point me toward my accommodations, so that I may change these wet garments . . ."

"Six miles." She flung a finger at the horizon. "Back the way you came."

"Six *miles?*"

"The nearest inn."

Was it possible the chit would refuse him—the court's designated agent in her affairs—the basic courtesy of accommodations? She expected him to travel six bloody miles to—"You mean to say there isn't an inn or boarding establishment in this wretched hole?"

"Not a one. The closest thing to a room to let is in Netter's Tavern, and I fear it wouldn't be up to your usual standards." She seemed inordinately pleased to conclude: "The only *suitable* accommodations for you are six miles away."

He glanced around for evidence to the contrary, but found none. When he looked at her upturned face again, he caught a glint of challenge in her eyes. She was serving notice that she intended to keep him at a distance, to diminish his involvement and authority here. The thought rankled. "I shall be the judge of what is suitable and what isn't."

"Suit yourself," she said, and headed off down the lane toward the factory, drawing several members of the crowd along with her.

He watched her go, feeling the same burning frustration he had experienced in his uncle's chambers—from the same cause. How was it that both of their meetings had turned into confrontations, and both times it felt as if he had come out on bottom?

"Beggin' yer pardon, sarr." A toothy fellow in a soiled, haphazard apron stepped out of the dwindling crowd and gave an awkward bob of respect. "I be Hiram Netter. If'n ye plan to stay . . . I got th' only room to let, o'er my tavern."

Cole looked back down the road, thinking of the miserable miles he had just traversed. What choice did he have?

"Lead the way."

Netter's Tavern proved to be nothing more than one of the larger cottages converted to public use. It was filled with sundry crude tables and benches, and a makeshift bar of barrels topped with a plank. The single guest room was actually the cottage loft, recently closed off by a few hastily nailed boards and accessed by a set of steps that looked like a ladder with a case of the bloat. Once upstairs, Cole discovered he couldn't straighten without banging his head. When the carriage arrived with his manservant minutes later, Cravits took one look at the place and went into a decline.

With determination fueled by discomfort, Cole climbed down the steps and sought out tavernkeeper Netter to demand water and clean linen. The fellow behaved as if he hadn't heard of the latter and the former was well beyond his technical capabilities.

"Have to haul water from the commons well," he said, scratching his chin and then his chest. "Ain't got no help fer that."

Cole climbed back up the steps, ripped off his coat, shirt, and breeches, and managed to replace them with dry alternatives. Cravits roused from wilt in time to help Cole with his collar and to clean and buff his riding boots.

Shortly, Cole was stalking along the lane, headed for the Ideal Garment Company and the pigheaded female who was responsible for it, and the reason he was there. But as he crossed the village green and neared the factory, he was revisited by the memory of Madeline Duncan's impossibly blue eyes and the look on her face minutes earlier. He slowed. It occurred to him that each time he had seen her, she had managed what London's wiliest prosecutors, magistrates, and high-court judges had failed to do; she had made him lose his temper. He'd have to watch that.

Across from him stood the Ideal Garment Company factory, a rambling architectural nightmare, brick and stone used seemingly at random, pretentious Georgian parapets, oversized windows with unpainted wooden frames, precariously tilted chimneys, and a roof that looked as if it had been struck by lightning—several times. Trenching for the water main had torn up a good portion of the yard, and in the rest, mud had dried in ruts the size of Venetian canals. The place was every bit the disaster he had expected.

At a cry of protest from on high he looked up and spotted a shirtless, muscular young man on the roof, lurching up to a sitting position. Over him stood another brawny, half-naked fellow with a dripping bucket in his hand, laughing. The pair began a raucous game of tag across the rooftop, scrambling over and around gables, dodging holes, and slipping on loose shingles. The chase ended when the prankster disappeared down one of the holes in the roof and pulled the ladder in after him, leaving the other fellow stranded. The victim poured a few choice threats down the hole, then thudded back across the roof to his overturned toolbox and stretched out adamantly beside it to finish his nap.

Part of Madeline Duncan's "Ideal" workforce, no doubt.

Cole straightened his coat and headed for the front doors of the factory. Inside, he was immediately required to choose between going up or down stairs. Darkness was below. He chose to go up toward the light. Halfway up the stairs he felt a step giving way beneath him, flailed, and just managed to catch himself on the board tacked as a makeshift railing against the wall.

Hanging on for all he was worth, he slid his free foot to

more solid wood, then extricated his trapped foot from the spongy mass that had once been a substantial stair tread. As he hauled himself hand over hand up the edge of the steps, his knee began to burn, and the sensation spread up his thigh. At the top of the steps he assessed the damage and discovered a nasty scrape up the front of his boot and a tear in his good riding breeches. He glared back at the stairs.

The bloody place is falling down!

Looking around, he discovered he was at the edge of a hall the size of a small cricket field. The light that had attracted him came through a row of huge windows newly set in the thick masonry walls. Above, there were rafterlike trusses supporting cylindrical iron shafts with sundry mechanisms attached. Underfoot were floors of aged oak. Lumber was stacked here and there, and the tools and residue of carpentry work—augers, chisels, and hammers; dust, plane curls, and chips of wood—littered the floor.

He strolled around the space, testing both his aching leg and the sturdiness of the floorboards with each step. A number of partially constructed tables sat at one end of the hall. While giving them a cursory inspection, he noticed a man at the far end sitting on a stack of lumber.

"Can you tell me what is going on here?" Cole called. "What are you building?"

The only response, as he approached, was a soft snore.

Another wretch asleep on the job.

He cleared his throat as he rounded the stack of lumber, but the fellow was apparently dead to the world. As he bent over him to investigate, he was struck by the sickly-sweet odor of anise on a strong undercurrent of alcohol, and jerked back. He caught the glint of metal in the fellow's hand—a battered hip flask.

Not merely asleep—dead drunk!

He headed irritably for a nearby door, intent on finding Mad Madeline, but instead found himself in a storage room stacked with forty or fifty identical crates, several barrels, and what appeared to be schoolroom desks. Poking around in an open crate, he uncovered a sewing machine—spanking new from the looks of it. He mentally tallied up the expenditure this represented if all the crates held the same thing.

Two thousand pounds sterling . . . sitting idle . . . like the rest of the cursed factory.

As he rounded the stacks of crates to investigate another door, he came across a burly, graying man engrossed in a book, sitting by a dusty window. The fellow didn't seem to notice that he was no longer alone as Cole leaned down to read the title on the front of the book . . . John Wesley's *Methods of Piety.*

He straightened in disgust. Too bad it wasn't John Wesley's *Admonition to Get Off Your Fat Arse and Earn Your Wages*!

He strode back through the hall, now more determined than ever to find and confront Madeline Duncan. He was just deciding whether to brave the stairs again, when he spotted a pair of high-buttoned shoes descending them. A pair of black-cuffed trousers appeared next, then a border of red below an expanse of powder blue. A moment later he was staring into Madeline Duncan's flushed face.

"Lord Mandeville. I was just about to send Beaumont to find you," she said, picking her way carefully down the steps and, with a gesture, reminding those coming behind her to do the same. "Did you find 'suitable' lodging?"

Her ill-suppressed smile told him that she knew precisely what he had found.

"I have made arrangements. I have a few words for you, Miss Duncan."

"I'm certain you do. But first perhaps I could show you the progress we've made. I was just familiarizing our new head seamstress with our factory. You may come along." Joining Madeline was a pleasant-faced middle-aged woman in traveling clothes and a dark-eyed young girl with a nubile shape and a flirtatious smile. "Permit me to introduce Mrs. Maple

Thoroughgood and her daughter, Charlotte. They will be teaching our seamstresses to use the sewing machines."

"About those machines," he said, fixing his gaze on the slight dent in the tip of Madeline's nose in an effort to avoid looking into her eyes. "They represent a monstrous expenditure to have sitting about idle."

"You've seen them?" She frowned at the realization that he had been prowling about on his own. "The sewing tables have just been finished, and we still have a few seamstresses to hire. First things first, your lordship." Without waiting for a response, she gestured to the hall around them.

"I take it, you've already seen the cutting floor as well. This is where the fabric will be readied and the pieces cut according to pattern. There are actually three levels in the factory. Storage and shipping are on the ground level; the cutting floor and classrooms are here on the first; and the sewing floor and offices are on the second. We're in the process of making a number of renovations."

She led them toward the tall windows overlooking the rear of the factory and into a bath of sunlight. "We've replaced all the windows with much larger ones that can be opened for healthful ventilation. I'm especially proud of them—they represent our heartfelt commitment to the well-being of our workers. The carpenters will be painting them any day now. On the far end, as you can see, there are fans in the wall to draw out stale or dusty air. They're not hooked up yet." She led them along the edge of the hall and halted to point out the long shafts sticking up from the floor and the mechanized racks and arms overhead. "These are part of a system designed by our engineer, Fritz Gonnering." Something at the far end caught her eye, and she brightened. "There he is now—Fritz! Fritz Gonnering!"

The fellow snoozing on the stack of lumber at the far end started, snapped upright, and lurched to his feet. As they hurried toward him, he straightened his clothes and wiped his mouth on his sleeve.

"Fritz is a pure genius with mechanicals. He has had to invent tools and pieces of equipment for us." She lowered her voice as they approached him. "He has been working so hard, I fear it may be affecting his health."

As the fellow stumbled over a greeting, Cole was thinking that one look at those bloodshot eyes, one whiff of that anise-and-alcohol aroma, should have been enough to alert any normal, reasonable person as to what was truly affecting the wretch's health. Not Mad Madeline, of course.

Despite a dry mouth and intermittent cough, Gonnering managed to explain: "Racks overhead . . . for moving boltz of cloth. Und die grosser metal shaften in das middle *ist* power supply for cutting tools. Interchangeable parts. Gud idea, ja? Die zewing machines upstairs musst haf power also, und . . ." After thanking Fritz, she led Cole and the others over to the burly fellow Cole had seen reading in the back room. He was now making a racket with a chisel and hammer.

Madeline ran her hand along the newly planed surface of a table under construction. "These are the cutting tables. When they are finished, two long rows of them will sit above the power shafts. Up to eighteen cutters will work here at a time."

Cole studied the planks and leg pieces scattered around the floor. "And when will that be?" He just managed to keep from suggesting: *the next century*?

"Soon enough," she answered tautly, as if she had heard his thoughts. Catching the eye of the graying, barrel-chested fellow who was creating joints for the table legs, she waved him over and introduced him. "This is Harley Ketchum, the Ideal carpenter. He and his sons are doing the repair work and renovation. When the factory work is done, they will begin renovating the cottages, to make them more habitable."

Harley's broad smile and extended hand caught Cole off guard, but no more than the stupendous bellow he aimed at the rafters. "Ketchums!" he shouted at the top of his lungs. "Get down 'ere!" Then he stalked to the nearest window and roared the same thing outside.

At the commotion overhead, Cole looked up and was startled to see two young men scurrying deftly through the wooden rafters and dropping to the floor. Another swung in through the window and still another came sliding down a set of ropes inside a metal cage in the far corner. In a wink, four muscular young hulks with sun-burnished faces and tousled hair, varying shades of blond, were lined up before Cole, staring with fascination, not at him, but at the fetching, dark-eyed Charlotte Thoroughgood. Cole recognized two of them as the ones he had seen playing "tag" on the rooftop.

"These here be my boys, yer lordship," Harley declared with a broad, toothy grin. "Matthew, Mark, Luke, and Calvin. The wife—bless her sainted heart—named 'em. She were a Methodist. Say yer respects, boys." He gave the nearest a jab in the ribs.

Their spines straightened, their chests swelled, and they hurriedly swished hands back through their shaggy hair. Appreciative grins appeared as their eyes continued to drift toward Charlotte's curves and coquettish smile. They each mumbled something on the order of "it be an honor, yer lordship." Their father scowled, sensing the waywardness of their thoughts.

"That'll be enough o' that. Get back to work, the lot of ye!" He had to give the nearest one a shove to get them moving. One by one they disappeared the same way they had come, with a display of brute strength and agility. Cole stared after them in disbelief. He could only hope Mad Madeline wasn't paying them by the pound.

They toured the classroom, the room just off the cutting floor, where the sewing machines were being stored. Here, Madeline explained, training and worker meetings would be held. As she explained to Maple Thoroughgood her ideas of "worker participation," Cole made a noise of disgust and strolled over to one of the newly installed windows. He rubbed a clear spot on a dusty pane and peered out over the rear of the factory. There, under a tree, two men were lying . . . to all appearances napping . . . with shovel handles clasped in their hands.

More "Ideal" workers, he thought. *Was everyone in the bloody place asleep at the tiller?* When he turned back, he caught Madeline's eye and gave her his most sardonic smile.

They toured the lower level, which contained dryers and pressing machines, shipping crates, Fritz Gonnering's workshop, and an old dyeing room filled with ancient stone vats. Then Madeline led them up a short flight of steps to the yard at the rear of the factory: "Here is where we will have the gardens," she announced.

"Gardens?" He scowled.

"The area closest to the factory will be primarily flowers and herbs"—her expressive hands conjured a lush vista—"with a background of flowering trees and shrubs. I've had plans drawn by a master landscape architect in France."

"A pleasure garden?" He was a bit annoyed by his own surprise. "In a factory?"

"Creative people need stimulating surroundings to enhance their productivity. William Morris fervently believes that improving the aesthetics of the work experience will ultimately improve the products. And I agree."

She led them down a narrow, weedy path toward the center of the yard. "Farther out we will have kitchen gardens, which the families will each donate time to tend. In return, each will receive a share of the produce."

As Cole followed her, he found himself scrutinizing the movement of her bottom half beneath that voluminous blue smock. Appalled by the direction of his thoughts, he focused instead on wondering how she would react at discovering two of her precious workers asleep under a tree.

But Madeline called ahead: "Algernon! Roscoe!" and by the time they arrived, the two were not only on their feet, but had managed to work up the appearance of exertion. The pair stood by a modest hole, leaning on their shovel handles and mopping their faces. All around the weedy yard were strings tied to stakes, crisscrossing each other, creating a maze that Cole and the others had to mind their feet to navigate.

"How is the work coming, Roscoe?" Madeline asked with a smile.

Before they could answer she turned to Cole. "Let me introduce Roscoe Turner and Algernon Bates, your lordship. We were fortunate to catch them between jobs. They were with Lord Aisencot's gardens at Quincy before moving to London to work in Kensington Garden. It was a pure stroke of luck that their previous project ended just as I was looking for someone to put in the gardens here."

"Roarin' fine to make yer acquaintance, yer lordship," Roscoe declared as the pair snatched off their headgear for a moment, then replaced it. One looked for all the world like a beanpole that had sprouted ears and the other like a shifty-eyed radish in a silk-lined bowler. Their ferret-quick gazes were sizing up him and the Thoroughgood women with a shrewdness that owed nothing to planting periwinkles or trimming topiaries.

If this pair had worked Kensington Garden at all, it was more likely as a file and his stall than as gardeners.

"I'm glad ye come, miss, on account of we run into a bit of a hitch here," Roscoe declared, motioning to the hole at their feet. "We got us a *rock*. Show Miss Duncan, Algy." Algy dutifully plunged his shovel into the dirt beside the rock visible at the bottom, and it resounded with a minerallike "chunk." He tried it a second time, on the other side, with the same result.

Roscoe rocked back on his heels and tucked his chin, looking grave indeed. "What we got here is a two- or a three-man rock smack in the middle o' what should be yer cursantheemums. Can't grow no cursantheemums on bare rock."

He looked at his partner. "There's but one thing fer it, right, Algy?"

Algy nodded, his eyes wide and earnest. "Right."

"Dig it out," Roscoe said in tones somber enough to be a declaration of war.

Madeline Duncan frowned at that innocuous bit of stone. "What did you call it—a 'three-man rock'?"

"'At's the way rocks is measured, miss," Roscoe said with an indulgent smile. "By th' number o' blokes it takes to heft 'em. A two-man rock takes two blokes to heft. A three-man rock takes three, an' so on. Algy an' me, we'll have 'er shifted out o' here soon enough. But added diggin' will slow us down a mite."

Madeline sighed, contemplating that information. "Well, do what you must. I'll check in with you tomorrow and see how it is coming along." As she led them inside, Cole looked back over his shoulder and caught sight of the pair stealthily slipping back toward the base of that tree.

A bespectacled middle-aged fellow in a vest and sleeve garters met them on the rear stairs of the factory. Madeline Duncan introduced him as her head clerk, Beaumont Tattersall, and asked him to conduct the Thoroughgoods to their new residence and see them settled. Cole did not miss the way the fellow looked at her, as if he'd walk through fire for her if she asked it.

Madeline then led Cole up the rear stairs to the top floor, describing the expected schedule of repairs and renovations and emphasizing how much had already been done. But Cole's attention drifted once more to what would have been the swing of her skirts—if she had been wearing skirts. Then his gaze slid to her combination of mannish trousers and high-buttoned shoes. A novel pairing. A rather intriguing one. What, he found himself wondering, did she wear beneath those imitation male garments? He became intensely aware of his own trousers and how they rode against his most sensitive skin. Did her trousers rasp and rub the same way?

By the time they reached the top of the stairs, he was lightly winded, faintly aroused, and ripely annoyed at himself. He could scarcely listen to her prattle about the offices and the general organization, or her introduction of a petite woman with a harried look. Emily somebody, a secretary. They were rudely interrupted by two young boys in velvet Fauntleroys who raced into the office, caked with mud and wailing at the top of their lungs that they had been bullied and beaten by big, mean boys.

Madeline dismissed her overwrought secretary to take the crying children home. Continuing the tour, she led him into a large, airy room lined with shelves and worktables laden with every sort of textile and tailoring tool.

"Endicott?" she called, peering around a corner at an abandoned drawing table and an empty hat rack. "Where could he—"

"There you are, dear Madeline!" a high, nasal voice called from the doorway behind them. Cole turned to see a slender, long-haired fellow in velvet knee breeches and a flamboyant red and purple velvet vest poised in the doorway. "I've had a brainstorm, a stroke of absolute brilliance! You're going to simply love it! Here it is: *Leaves*. Wonderful graceful designs taken from genuine leaves. We'll wrap women in pure, unsullied *nature*—women everywhere will share Mother Nature's beguiling glory! Wait—don't tell me what you think—not until you see my designs!" He rushed past them and grabbed a sketch pad and pencils from the desk. On the way out the door he paused to shimmy with delight. "It will be spectacular! I'm going out upon the sun-drenched hills and into the cool, shaded vales to absorb the shapes and colors—to find inspiration in communion with nature!"

Deep silence followed Endicott's dramatic entrance and precipitous exit. Madeline blinked and scrambled for an explanation.

"That was Jessup Endicott, my designer and pattern maker," she said, her voice cracking slightly. "He's a pure genius with textiles and patterns. He was one of William Morris's protégés at The Firm. In fact, he was one of Mr. Morris's favorites. He has the finest design credentials and a very . . . *creative* . . . mind.''

"Ummm" was all Cole said.

Ignoring his blatant skepticism, she turned to the bright sunlit space, arms out, as if to embrace it.

"This is what we call the sample room. Here our designs are developed into pattern pieces, and sample garments are constructed. It's a most dynamic and creative undertaking." She noticed that he was eyeing the cluttered tables and littered floor. "Creativity is sometimes a rather messy process."

"Ummm." His attention began to settle once more on that billowy blue smock. Forcing his gaze away, he strolled around the workshop. "Where are they, then, these 'sample garments'? I don't see any."

"That's because we're still working on the ideas for them."

"Am I to understand that you will soon have an entire factory retooled, refitted, and refurbished, and you don't even have an *idea* for a product?"

"Oh, we know what we'll produce, all right: reformed clothing." She crossed her arms and tucked her chin. "And where better to start than with the very foundations of women's clothing?"

"Corsets again." He strolled closer, glancing at her eyes, trying to see what was in her head without having to deal with what was in her heart. "Tell me, *Mad Madeline*"—his voice softened and deepened in spite of himself—"what do you have against corsets anyway? Did someone stuff you into one once and refuse to let you out?"

"Don't be absurd. This has nothing to do with me personally." Her chin rose a notch. "Liberating women from their corsets is a perfectly reasonable and humane course of action."

He laughed softly. "A sentiment that would be heartily seconded in the gentlemen's clubs of St. James's."

He headed for one of the worktables, where sketches sat in piles, pinned to swatches of fabrics. "Let's see some of these 'reformed' garments of yours."

He picked up, perused, and discarded several sketches of tunics and smocks, with a long-suffering expression. Then he came upon a drawing of a pair of ladies' knickers. His interest was piqued by the swatch of filmy silk that was attached.

Madeline watched the smirk spread across his face and felt strangely that her very person was somehow being invaded. She snatched the sketch from his hands and cradled it against her. But he simply picked up another one showing the silhouette of a woman's unclothed body with a bandeau bodice drawn over the bosom. Holding it up, well out of her reach, he gave it a thorough inspection.

"Tell me, Mad Madeline, just what is this bit of stuff"— he twanged the rubberized elastic attached to the sketch— "meant to do?"

Mayhem, she told herself, was out of the question. Throttling was probably out as well. Imagine having to face Sir William. *I'm sorry, Your Honor, but he indecently fondled my swatches and I had to shake him until his teeth rattled in their sockets.*

"It provides support and shaping," she said with more heat than was prudent.

"Support and shaping for what?" His gaze flickered speculatively over her.

"For a woman's . . . *shape.*" When he raised a skeptical brow, she carefully elaborated: "Women wear boning because they think they need support and shaping beneath their garments. We will give them an alternative. Something soft and flexible. Something that permits freedom of movement but still provides support."

He raised the sketch to eye level and pointedly looked between it and her upper half. Then with a shake of his head he tossed the drawing onto the table.

"Women wear corsets because they want *curves,* Mad Madeline. What woman in her right mind would give up an eye-catching hourglass figure to look like a twig?" He smiled vengefully. "Or a mossy tree trunk . . . with plenty of *leaves?*"

He was making fun of Endicott's ideas and her plans. *I'm sorry, Your Honor, I have no idea how those scissors got into Lord Mandeville's heart. I wasn't even aware he had a heart.*

"My clothing will not make women look like twigs, logs, or tree trunks. My designs will use rubberized elastic to support and enhance a woman's natural shape . . . curves and all."

"How do you know what they will do?" he said, moving closer to her and intruding on her senses with his size and personal intensity. "You haven't even made a sample garment yet."

There it was again, she thought. That worrisome tingling she had experienced when her head filled with his bedeviling scents. Sandalwood. With a hint of spice and vanilla. *I'm sorry, Your Honor, but Lord Mandeville smelled so good that I simply forgot he wasn't cake and bit him.* Jerking back, she put several paces between them.

"I don't need to make samples to know that the garments function properly."

"Oh?"

"I wear them myself. I have for years."

He scowled, regarding her baggy smock, then gave her a superior smirk. "You really are in trouble. No woman I know would trade in her lacing for a frumpy blue barrel, no matter how comfortable it is."

"I am not wearing a *barrel.*" Her fingers flew to her buttons and in a moment she had shed her smock and was smoothing the midriff of a scarlet tunic identical to the one she had worn that day in court.

"Barrel . . . barberpole . . ." he said with a taunting smile. "Where's the difference? Neither has curves."

"That's not true, I have—" She bit it off, realizing the

folly of proclaiming she did have plenty of curves. What would she have to do when he took exception to that? She had to think of another way to put it. "There is considerable variation in my circumference, even in reformed garments."

"How much variation?" he demanded.

"Really, your lordship!" The man had crossed the line, demanding the facts and figures of her figure!

"Well, there is one sure way to settle the matter." He turned to rummage through the equipment on the table and came up with a linen measuring tape. "You're wearing the samples. We'll just measure you."

"Don't be absurd." She backed up a step for each step he took toward her, eyeing the dangling tape measure as if it were the Serpent in the Garden.

"If you truly have curves, as you claim, then there's nothing for you to worry about, is there? It requires only a simple empirical investigation. Unless, of course, you're afraid to put your garments to the test." His autumn-forest eyes grew flinty with challenge. "You can be sure other women will before they buy." He had her right where he wanted her, and he knew it.

"Very well. I'll measure myself." With her face aflame, she snatched the tape from his hands, wrapped it around her waist, and noted the measurement. Then she lowered it to her hips, whereupon he objected.

"For the sake of accuracy, I should at least have the right to verify the numbers." The wretch. For a minute she just stared at him, telling herself to ignore the angular strength of his jaw and the well-tended sheen of his dark hair.

He sank down on one knee before her and scrutinized both the linen tape and the part of her it encompassed. A low whistle expressed his opinion.

"Thirty-six." He glanced up with a insolent male grin. "Even in country terms I believe that would qualify as 'bountiful.'" When she bit her tongue and jerked the tape to her waist, he had the cheek to readjust it, sending a curious shiver up her side. "Ummm." He stared judiciously at the measurement. "It's plain to see that you're not a slave to the eighteen-inch rule."

"It's twenty-four," she snapped. *I'm sorry, Your Honor, if a tape measure seems undignified for a member of the bar, but it was all I had to strangle him with at the time.* "Which makes a twelve-inch variation from the other measurement. That should be proof enough."

"Ohhh, no." He wrested the tape from her fingers and slid it up to her bosom, catching her gaze in his as she attempted to pull away. "I would almost think you were embarrassed, Miss Duncan, if I didn't know that you are far too sensible and forward-thinking for such maidenly folderol. And much too old."

In any other situation she might have used those very words to describe herself. But coming from him, as he stood there with his knuckles pressed intimately against her breast, they sounded positively insulting. Worse yet, his smile let her know he was enjoying the way she was toasting on her own flaming pride. Shamed by her own missish impulses, she lifted her chin and endured his final measurement.

"Thirty-eight here, I'm afraid. Not very consistent of you." His voice acquired a thick quality that poured through her like honey—sweet and clinging.

She looked at him and was caught in his hazel-green eyes. The nape of her neck prickled, and her breasts, near his hands, began to tingle. The sensations released a subtle physical awareness that she hadn't realized had been locked away.

As she stood there, mesmerized, he parted the linen tape and slid his hands down her sides slowly, gently, tracing her shape, verifying those numbers experimentally. Trickles of excitement wended their way along the underside of every exposed inch of her skin. Suddenly all she could see were his full, ripely curved lips.

"Thirty-eight . . . twenty-four . . . thirty-six. You do indeed have curves, Mad Madeline," he said huskily, staring into her eyes. "But now the question is, are those numbers the result of your reformed foundations, or are they just you?" He let the tape drop to the floor and brought one hand up to stroke the curve of her cheek.

"There is only one sure way to settle the matter," he said, brushing his fingertips down the side of her neck and down her shoulder so that they came to rest on the top button of her tunic. With a deft twist of his fingers, it was freed from its velvet loop.

5

"Miss Duncan?"

Beaumont Tattersall's voice broke over them from the doorway and they jolted apart.

She stammered, "I was merely acquainting his lordship with the . . . design process." Lord Mandeville became suddenly engrossed in a giant spool of cotton thread.

"Daniel Steadman and his family have arrived. I thought you would want to know," Beaumont said. Madeline seized the opportunity to escape what she was certain would be Lord Mandeville's mocking smile. Declaring that she needed to greet her new cutting-floor foreman, she excused herself and hurried from the factory.

It was only as she strode along the village lane that the insinuation in Cole's last remark registered fully with her. She glanced down at her unfastened button and was instantly livid. The crust! How dare he barge into her factory, scoff and sneer at everything in sight, and then take liberties with her person? She hurriedly refastened that dangling button. Obviously he had mistaken her progressive social views for moral laxity and felt free to use the personal nature of her products as an excuse for inappropriate and offensive intimacies.

But as she walked, the breeze drew some of the heat from her burning cheeks and pride, and she realized her charge against him wasn't entirely correct. His actions had been inappropriate, but they had not been entirely offensive to her.

She stumbled and had to catch herself. All the more reason for her to see him gone.

Cole Mandeville had also fled the factory in a temper, disconcerted by his sensual impulses toward Madeline Duncan. She was so much the opposite of the sleek, subtle, mysterious women of the world he had always found desirable. She was appallingly wholesome, forthright, and transparent, an unabashed innocent. His hard-won experience and sophistication counted for nothing with her. She hadn't the faintest notion of what the world was about, or even of how close she had come to being backed up against one of those tables and kissed within an inch of her virtue.

He knew, however. Just like he knew that her precious workers were a pack of weak sisters, idle good-for-nothings, drunks, peacocks, and sharp charlies who were collectively taking advantage of both her ignorance and her largesse. They lolled and snored and drank and chased butterflies and each other—until she hove into view and they became all earnestness and diligence and industry. The wretches.

But, in all honesty, it probably didn't take much to convince her they were geniuses, artisans, or just decent-but-downtrodden folk. Those wide eyes saw only what they wanted to see. And when he looked into them, he could see only the pain in store for her when she finally faced the truth about her "noble" workers.

He ground his teeth and tried to banish that pristine blue and her inevitable disillusionment from his mind. Never mind the satisfaction of being proven right, suddenly he just wanted to put miles between them and forget he had ever seen her.

He made straight for the tavern, for paper and ink, and penned his first report to his uncle. It was short and to the point:

> *The Honorable Sir William Rayburn*
> *The Royal Law Courts of Justice*
> *The Strand, London*
> *Your Honor,*
> *I was right—she is a madwoman. Get me the hell out of here!*
>
> > *Your suffering servant,*
> > *Lord Cole Mandeville*

By nightfall that report was tucked safely in a leather pouch on a mail coach speeding toward London . . . right next to a letter from Madeline Duncan:

> *The Honorable Sir William Rayburn*
> *The Royal Law Courts of Justice*
> *The Strand, London*
> *Your Honor,*
> *I am writing to beg deliverance from the difficulties brought upon me by your appointment of Lord Mandeville as my "overseer." He arrived only today and, straightaway, set about jumping to conclusions and issuing absurd edicts regarding my enterprise. He has derided every aspect of "ideal garments," including the very notion of reformed clothing, and has extended his offensive assumptions into the personal sphere.*
> *The beast is incapable of objectivity in his dealings with me. I respectfully request that he be withdrawn from St. Crispin immediately and that I be permitted to proceed without further interference. I appeal to your sense of fair-*

*ness and your avowed intention to support my development
of the Ideal Garment Company.*

> *Awaiting your mercy,*
> *Madeline Duncan*

The next morning Cole stumbled down the ladder from
his lodgings, having slept poorly and having performed his
morning shave from a bucket of stale, rusty water. The smell
of the main room of the tavern—soured ale, stale tobacco,
sweat, and greasy ash—washed over him like stagnant water.
He held his breath and headed straight for the door. As he
stood in the entrance, gulping in fresh air and vowing never
again to take for granted the simple act of breathing, a flash
of scarlet across the way caught his eye. It was Madeline Duncan, tripping down the steps of a substantial brick house
tucked away next to the factory.

He hadn't noticed that house before, set back as it was
from the common path. He hadn't thought about the fact
that *she* had to live somewhere, and that *her* dwelling probably
didn't smell like the bottom of a bait bucket. His eyes narrowed. She was unmarried and had no dependents. That
meant she had that sizable house all to hersel—

"Somethin' to break yer fast, yer lordship? I reckon ye'll
be hungry, what with ye havin' no supper an' all."

Hiram Netter's voice startled him, and he turned to find
the tavernkeeper holding an iron kettle filled with suspicious-
looking sausages wreathed in slimy onions and bobbing in
grease. He closed his eyes, but not before he noticed the grime
caked on the fellow's apron and fingernails.

"I'm not much for morning food, I'm afraid."

Tugging his vest down into place, he struck out across
the green in the direction Madeline Duncan had taken.
Somehow he would wangle an offer of better accommodations from her. After passing several newly occupied cottages,
he came across one with a pony cart in front of it. The cart

was filled with shabby household goods as well as a squalling baby. A racket loud enough to drown out the growling of his stomach was coming from the open door. As he approached, he caught a glimpse of red inside.

"A right peach of a place, miss," a soss-bellied fellow was declaring above the roar of a woman scolding and snatching at a number of rambunctious children racing about the cottage. "Afore long Bess'll have 'er right as pie, won't ye, Bessie?"

"What?" A tall, lanky woman with a face like a hatchet turned on him, scowling, then seemed belatedly to understand. "Oh . . . aye, Miz Duncan. Right as rain."

"I've brought you a few things to help set up your kitchen." Madeline gestured to three willow baskets filled with bags of flour and sugar, jars, crocks, tins, and a huge shank of a ham sitting on a wooden pushcart parked by the door. "If you need more to tide you over while you're settling in, just see Beaumont or myself at the factory. Thomas, we'll need your help setting up the machines and worktables tomorrow."

"I'll be there, miz, never fear." Thomas was scratching his chest and eyeing the ham with undisguised delight.

Cole stepped back as Madeline exited the cottage. For the brief moment that they came face-to-face, all he could see was the pleasure shimmering like sunlit water in her eyes. He backed two more steps.

"Hard at it already, I see," he observed. It was annoying that she was granting shiftless ne'er-do-wells the hospitality that she had so emphatically denied him. His gaze caught on the red-gold threads the morning sun painted in her hair, and that annoyed him too. "Just how much did all this cost, Miss Duncan?"

The pleasure in her face dimmed noticeably. "A bit of flour, salt, and tinned fruit scarcely qualify as capital expenditures, Lord Mandeville. Not that it is any concern of yours, but I like to greet each family as they arrive, bring them a few supplies, and see them settled into their new homes."

"And into the lining of your purse," he added.

"Well,"—her eyes narrowed—"it is *my* purse, after all. You lawyers do seem to have difficulty remembering that." With that, she turned her back and began to remove the enormous basket of food from the cart.

She tugged and lifted and finally succeeded in wrestling it to the edge, where it teetered dangerously until she secured a grip on the handles. With a heroic heave she lowered it to the ground, while burly Thomas and strapping Bessie stood in the doorway behind her, watching her struggle single-handedly with the hamper that would feed them and their brood of children for the next week.

Furious with the feckless pair for not helping her, with her for not demanding that they do so, and with himself for caring one way or another, he carried the hamper to the door for her, then stalked off down the lane toward the factory.

"Who be that swell?" Thomas asked, scowling after Cole Mandeville's retreating form.

Madeline followed his gaze as she dusted her tunic.

"That? I'm afraid that's Lord Mandeville. My court-appointed nanny."

Thomas Clark shook his head. "Testy sort, ain't he?"

Her smile bore a defiant hint of mischief.

"He probably didn't sleep well."

Madeline greeted two more families that morning before returning to the factory. On the way back she prepared herself for her next encounter with Lord Mandeville, determined not to be caught at a disadvantage again. It was the surprise of walking out of the cottage and straight into him that had rendered her so witless, she told herself. That, and his breeze-ruffled hair and the newly wakened look of his eyes, the impossible breadth of his shoulders and the insolent cant of his mouth—the wretch was a walking heap of distractions. And for some reason, around him she was appallingly distractable.

It wasn't at all like her to respond so physically to another person. She was comfortable with herself as a thinker, a human soul, and an agent of social change. But now she realized there was a part of her she had never acknowledged before: the elemental female part. How unsettling that it was arrogant, overindulged Lord Mandeville who seemed to bring it out in her.

By the time she set foot in the offices, she had fortified her defenses and felt reasonably well prepared to deal with his cynical snarling. She was not at all prepared, however, to have Endicott come charging out of the sample room and down the hall with his velvet frock coat flapping and his eyes wild.

"He's a beast, I tell you!" he declared, pressing his fingertips to his temples. "An insensitive lout—a pure philistine! His aesthetic sense is so stunted that he could not recognize Mother Nature herself—much less a principle of natural design. I simply cannot work under such conditions, Madeline—look at me, I'm a shambles!" He held out a pale, artistic hand to show her how it trembled. "I must flee to nature's bosom—to let her beauty and symmetry restore my creative balance!" With a toss of his long, romantic locks, he sailed out the door.

Madeline hurried into the sample room and found Cole Mandeville poised before a fabric-draped dressmaking form with silk pins in his mouth, tilting his head from side to side.

"What on earth do you think you are doing?" she demanded, halting several paces away with her arms stiff at her sides.

"Trying my hand at this 'design' business," he answered, taking the pins from his mouth and stabbing them into a pincushion. He adjusted something on the front of the form, then stepped back and eyed it approvingly. "I don't see what's got your Endicott's drawers in such a bunch. This is not so all-fired difficult. In fact, I believe I may have something here. What do you think?"

His expression angelic, he turned the dress form toward

her. She was startled by the sight of leaves pinned over the female form's breasts and private area. Real leaves. From trees.

"Of course they're not genuine fig," he said, stepping to the side to view it from a new angle. "To get the full effect, one really should have fig leaves."

She looked up at the gleam in his eye and had to struggle with the violent impulses that seized her. *Of course I regret stabbing Lord Mandeville with a whole box of silk pins, Your Honor. Silk pins are very expensive these days.*

"You truly are despicable," she said, sounding a bit hoarse in her own ears.

"Well, you did say you believed garments should be as natural and comfortable as possible." He smiled. "What could be more natural than this? Though, I must confess, the idea is not entirely original."

Aunt Olivia had always admonished her to make her tongue follow her brain rather than the reverse. Just now that advice, though difficult to follow, served her well.

"Why don't you go home, Lord Mandeville? You don't want to be here, and heaven knows, I don't want you here. You have no sympathy for our goals and purposes, and"— she cast a furious glance at his "design"—"you certainly have nothing to contribute creatively."

She felt some satisfaction in seeing the curve of his mouth straighten.

"I would be more than willing to send you all the reports and descriptions and sketches you could possibly need," she continued. "I could even have Beaumont copy our ledgers for you to peruse at leisure . . . in the comfort of your own home. Sir William need never know you didn't stay the entire three months." The look she leveled on him and his design was hot enough to boil water. "I've come this far without your helpful *advice*. I believe I can manage the rest of the way on my own."

For a moment she thought she saw signs of his turgid

male pride wilting. But in a wink he was in complete control again and tossed aside the pincushion.

"I'm not going anywhere, Miss Duncan. Like you, I have a task here, and it's high time I got on with it." His expression sharpened as his eyes took in the chaos of the sample room. "I want to see some actual reformed garments—not just fanciful sketches. I want to know precisely which items you intend to manufacture first, and I want a timetable for the completion of the first shippable product. And while you're at it, I believe you need to explain just how and where you intend to sell your garments—what sort of customers you will try to attract and how you will go about letting those unfortunates know that your clothes are available."

She studied the flecks of fire in his eyes and realized that her steeled manner had struck a bit of flint in his core. He had obviously expected a different reaction to his "design," and since he hadn't gotten it, was reverting to his officious legal persona.

"I've told you what garments we intend to make first: the bandeau bodice and knickers. You've already seen the sketches—"

"Which were most unsatisfactory," he said, settling back on one leg and looking speculatively at what she was wearing. "I want to see the finished articles."

"Well, we don't have them read—"

"Oh, but you do. According to you, you're wearing them even now."

She felt her cheeks grow hot in spite of her determination to remain cool. "Lord Mandeville, I do not intend to throw open my tunic and haul up my skirts simply to satisfy your curiosity." She halted and made herself take a calming breath. "However, if you would be so good as to accompany me to my office, I can easily meet your other requirements."

She was out the door before he had a chance to respond.

The superintendent's office from which she planned and conducted her business was a modest room containing a desk, a long, paper-laden worktable, a cabinet for filing documents, and three worn but comfortable-looking wooden chairs. She directed him to a seat and turned to the neatly labeled stacks of documents on the worktable, selecting papers from first one, then another.

"You asked for details . . . ." She turned to him, scanning the document on top of the stack in her arms. "We have hired most of the workers we need, and the factory itself will be fully functional by the end of next week. Tomorrow we will set up the sewing machines, and on the day after, Fritz will connect them to the power shafts by means of his belts and pulleys. We will begin with twelve machines, and once our production level is established, within a month or so, we will add a second tier of seamstresses, bringing the total to twenty-four. Depending upon orders for the garments, we could add a third tier before the year is out.

"As soon as the machines are installed, Maple and Charlotte will begin instructing the seamstresses in the use of them and give the women a chance to practice . . . by week's end if everything goes according to schedule."

"And if it doesn't?" He propped an arm on the back of the chair, looking roundly annoyed by what he was hearing.

"We have built into the schedule some 'oops time,' at least, that is what Fritz calls it. Unexpected things will come up in a first-of-its-kind venture such as this, and we are prepared to handle them too." She glanced back at her papers. "Then, while the seamstresses are being instructed, Daniel Steadman will set up the cutting floor and train-in several new cutters. Since cutters can cut so much faster than seamstresses can sew, we'll begin with a half dozen of them, and add another half dozen by year's end." She sorted through the stack in her arms, selected a number of documents, and thrust the lot into his hands. "These will explain the budgetary specifics of each stage of development." He gave them a perfunctory scowl, then irritably plopped them on the desk beside him.

"About these exemplary workers of yours, how many of them have ever worked in a garment mill?" he asked.

She paused, assessing the question and the possible motives behind it. "Only Daniel Steadman has actually worked in a clothing factory before. But every one of our employees has skill relating to the task they were hired to do. A number of the women have worked in dress shops and all of the men have worked with machinery of various sorts, except for Harley Ketchum and his sons, who are adept at carpentry."

"And just how do you intend to sell these wonders of sartorial ingenuity?" He was studying her out of the corner of his eye. Something in that appraisal sent a tremor through her.

"I've made plans for the marketing as well." She shuffled through the documents in her arms and pulled out a sheaf of papers. "I intend to send letters describing our philosophy and our garments—perhaps even a few samples—to a carefully selected list of women. I shall ask for opinions and endorsements, and then, using those testimonials, I shall personally call upon a number of reputable and forward-thinking department stores to suggest that they offer our garments to their customers on a trial basis. Once the outlets are in place, I will place advertisements in various ladies' publications and journals and—"

His hand had gone up to halt her.

"Who is on your select list of women?"

She referred to her list, not because she didn't know the names by heart, but to escape his glowering countenance. "Viscountess Harberton of the Reform Dress Society, Mrs. Oscar Wilde, Mrs. Annie Besant, renowned suffragist Miss Ada Ballin, social reformer Mrs. Josephine Butler, Dr. Elizabeth Blackwell and Dr. Elizabeth Garret Anderson, the first women admitted to the British medical profession, the trade unionist Mrs. Emma Patterson, journalist and lecturer Mrs. Florence Fenwick Millar, Lady Goldsmidt, Mrs. Millicent Fawcett, Mrs. Emmeline Pankhurst."

"Good God." He snorted. "It's a damned gallery of viragos."

She bristled. "Hardly. All these women are at the forefront of their fields. I also mean to approach a number of society patrons—Lady Maria Ashton, Mrs. Tyler-Benninghoff, Lady Hargraves, Mrs. Edith Evanston, Beatrice St. James, the Countess Sandbourne . . ."

"The dragons of the 'Upper Ten.'" He rolled his eyes. "You haven't a prayer."

"You think not? Lady Ashton and my aunt Olivia were girls together in Brighton and kept up a lifelong correspondence. I have had several notes from her since Aunt Olivia's death. And Lady Beatrice is a distant cousin of my deceased mother's. She has always consulted Aunt Olivia in matters regarding fund-raising for her charities. Each of these ladies has some personal connection to me or to my aunt. I believe they will at least do me the courtesy of listening."

Cole's jaw clenched as he looked over the stacks of paper on the table. Each was labeled with what looked like a place card identifying some function vital to the Ideal Garment Company: hiring, equipment, transportation, materials, records, garment design, advertising, sales, finances, facilities.

The size of those stacks of paperwork finally registered in his mind, evidence of the planning she had invested in her "mad" venture. In terms of sheer quantity, the output would be worthy of an entire government bureau. And as for quality, she had clearly thought through every possibility. He looked up at her with grudging respect.

Red crept up his ears as he realized just how much he had let his prejudices interfere with his judgment. Even having glimpsed something of her true nature on that very first day, in the courtroom, he had still completely underestimated her. According to his worldly frame of reference, idealism such as hers could come only from a thorough ignorance of reality. Now, faced with her logic, her energy, and her sensible strategy, he felt his condescending assumptions being knocked end over end.

And if there was anything Lord Cole Mandeville, Barrister at Law, could not abide, it was being blindsided by the facts.

"Very well, you have made plans, I'll give you that," he declared, rising to his full height in an unwitting effort to regain his sense of superiority. "But plans on paper are a far cry from a functioning factory turning out a salable product." His gaze slid over her hair, trying to avoid those dangerous pools of blue that seemed to hold such an unholy fascination for him. "Putting your plans into action may prove more difficult than you realize. There are other factors to consider. The motivation of your workers, for instance."

"My workers are very dedicated."

He smiled tightly. "To their own comfort and well-being, perhaps. But what about your crusade to rid the world of corsets and reform the way people dress? How do they feel about that?"

Madeline stared at him, hoping her surprise didn't show in her face. In truth, she had never really given thought to how her workers might feel about her reformed garments. She had simply assumed that they would support the rightness of her endeavor.

"They are eager for the chance to improve their lot and in the process to do something constructive for the world," she said determinedly. "They know an opportunity to better their lives when they see it."

He chuckled. "On that, Mad Madeline, we most certainly agree." His gaze settled on the top button of her tunic, then veered away. He cleared his throat. "But I cannot help wondering how they will feel when they learn you mean to garb the women of Britain like *beefeaters* on parade."

"B-beefeaters?" She looked down at her scarlet tunic with its velvet trim and her trousers, and her face flamed.

Snapping her head up, she glared at him. "My garments don't look the slightest bit like a royal guardsman's uniform!"

"Other than the red frock coat, the trim, and the trousers, you mean?" His amusement at her rising outrage was insufferable. "If that is your idea of salable clothing, I shall have to report to the court that you're going to be bankrupt very soon."

"How dare you!" She took a step toward him, the blood roaring in her head drowning out more prudent voices. "Our designs have graceful, supple lines and construction that allow for freedom of movement. In Ideal garments women finally will be able to breathe healthfully, to bend and stoop and reach while working or engaging in exercise. My garments will free women to be and to do whatever they want!" What *she* wanted to do right now was to smack the amusement from his face. "You want to see garments?" she demanded. "Come with me!"

Sailing out the door, down the rear steps, and into the garden, she led him quickly along a narrow foot trail leading toward the rear of her nearby house. As they reached the edge of the proposed gardens, Roscoe suddenly appeared and planted himself in her path.

"Beggin' a minute o' yer time, miss," he said, dragging his incongruously elegant bowler from his head. "But me an' Algy, we run into another hitch."

"What?" She glowered at this intrusion into her righteous indignation.

He led her toward the center clearing and there she spotted Algy leaning on his shovel beside a hole that was wider but no deeper than when she'd seen it last. At the bottom of their shallow excavation was a broad, rounded stone at least four feet across.

"It be that rock, miss." Roscoe stuck his thumbs under his suspenders and contemplated the obstinate mineral. "What ye got here be a six- or seven-man rock." Algy vigorously nodded his agreement. "It'll take a site more diggin'."

She glared at that widening impediment, sorely tempted to name it "Lord Mandeville" and take a pickax to it. "Can't you plant around it?"

"It's smack in th' middle o' yer cursantheemums, miss," Roscoe pointed out. "Ye move 'em and ye got to move somethin' else . . . then somethin' else. Afore ye know it, yer garden's sprawled from here to Dover!"

She made a noise of disgust. "Then get help and dig up the wretched thing!"

Brushing past Cole, she headed for the path once more and Cole followed. Not, however, before he saw the broad smiles Roscoe and Algy exchanged.

He trailed her to the rear yard of the sizable brick house he had noticed earlier that morning. Once inside the rear door, he found himself in a roomy, open-beamed kitchen furnished with surprisingly modern conveniences; a porcelain-clad stove with double ovens, a water pump in a copper-lined sink, and racks of shiny copper pots and utensils hanging above the long table. Smells of fresh-baked bread, roasting chicken, and something richly seasoned and being baked au gratin seized his senses and interfered with his motor skills. He suddenly had difficulty putting one foot before another. His mouth began to water. His vision began to narrow.

"Your lordship?"

At Madeline's prompting, he cudgeled his senses back under control and forced his feet to move in her direction. She led him through a pleasantly furnished dining room and into the front hall, where she instructed him to wait in the parlor while she fetched the garments. His head still swimming with the intoxicating effects of those aromas, he ambled through the indicated doorway and found himself in a handsomely appointed sitting room.

The clean, restrained lines of Hepplewhite furnishings, the soft drape of ivory brocade over interior shutters at the windows, the muted tapestries, the cream watered-silk up-holstery, and the thick ruby-colored Persian rugs underfoot surprised him. The room registered in his mind not as grand or fashionable, but as wholly refreshing in its texture-rich simplicity. More important, it had an air of ageless, timeless comfort about it, just the sort of place a man could take his friends for a drink and a quiet bit of conversation. His shoulders rounded and he began to relax all over at the prospect of—

Enjoying that comfort. He surfaced abruptly from that fantasy. This was *her* house. These were *her* delicious aromas. This was *her* comfort, not his. While he was bumping his head on rafters in a musty old loft, acquiring God knows what infestations from sleeping on moldy straw ticking and going delusional from lack of food, she was ensconced in this cozy little house, sleeping like a princess, eating like a queen, just waiting for him to give up and—

Like hell he was going home!

He charged out the door. For a moment, standing in the hall, he was unsure where to go. Then with sudden resolve he began to climb the stairs.

6

Determined to call her on her little game, he invaded bedroom after bedroom—four to be exact—before he found her. When he threw open the door of the fifth, there she was, standing before an open wardrobe with her arms full of garments.

"Your lordship! I was just about to bring the samples downstairs," she said indignantly. She hurried toward him with an arm outstretched, intending to sweep him back out the door.

"No need to empty your wardrobe when I can see them here." He deftly sidestepped her and began to stroll about the warm, sweetly scented bedchamber, peering into boxes on her dressing table and fingering the counterpane and curtains on her bed. Then he caught sight of garments tossed across a chair and strewn over the bed and swung around one thick bedpost for a closer look.

"What is this?" He picked up a long-sleeved cotton garment and turned it this way and that.

"A blouse," she snapped. She suddenly realized that what she was holding in her arms was a stack of intimate garments. Reddening, she pulled them protectively against her. "Really, your lordship—"

"I claim no expertise in female fashion, but this looks like a fairly ordinary blouse to me."

"It *is* an ordinary blouse. And it is worn with an ordinary overskirt and trousers. Now, if you will just—"

He discarded the blouse in favor of a bit of muslin printed with soft geometric designs and trimmed with delicate tatted lace. Dangling the garment by a short puffed sleeve, he looked at her in bewilderment. "And what is this?"

"A dress," she said through her teeth.

"Are you quite certain?"

"I designed it myself. It conforms most specifically to the Reform Dress Society's guidelines for aesthetic and appropriate garments: classical lines, an unconstructed bodice, a high waistline, a simple neckline, a softly shirred skirt . . ."

"Looks more like a handkerchief to—"

She snatched it from him before he did something vile, like blow his nose in it. But a moment later he invaded her wardrobe, pulling out one garment after another until he came to a bit of brown wool serge.

"A divided skirt?" He held the garment up by its bifurcated bottom, staring at the place where the parts that covered her limbs were joined. He looked askance at her. "Good Lord, don't tell me you're one of those frenzied female bicyclists as well as a rampaging idealist. It's got so a fellow can't go for a stroll in the park on Sunday afternoon without putting himself at risk of being run down by Amazons on wheels." He dropped it as if afraid of contamination and continued to pillage her closet, dragging out a long gored skirt, another high-waisted dress, and one of her Chinese-style tunics.

"And this—what in blazes is *this* thing?" He hauled out a combination garment made of fine pintucked cambric and held up one of the abbreviated legs. "Ye gods—it looks like one of those hideous Jaeger suits. Not his 'sanitized woolen'

model, however. Where is the rest of the legs? the sleeves?"
Suspending it in midair, he examined the garment visually,
then transferred his scrutiny to her. "I confess, Miss Duncan,
I am shocked by the thought of you gadding about in public
in such scandalously flimsy foundations."

"My 'foundations' are neither scandalous nor flimsy."
Madeline tilted her nose to ward off his stare. The bounder.
She had dragged him there to prove her point, and he was
turning the tables on her yet again, taking advantage of her
professional attitude to indulge his juvenile curiosity about
her undergarments.

But before she could elaborate, he was on to the next
outrage.

"Ahhh, here they are! The infamous female trousers."
He turned back from the wardrobe with a pair of black serge
pantaloons pressed to his waist, then held them up to the light
for a better look. "Not much to them, I daresay." When he
looked at her, his face was bronzing and his eyes were beginning to glow. "Hold on, they aren't red. I thought you always
wore red."

"Only in public. And only in mourning." She refolded
her arms defensively around the garments she held. "It is not
my color."

"Oh? I would say it suits you perfectly. Red hair. Red
clothes. You're the proverbial red flag . . . waving yourself
before society's horns." He took a step toward her, and she
jerked back, smacking into the bedpost. He struck a pose,
holding the trousers out to his side toreador-style, and jan-
gling them at her. A moment later he swung them out of the
way with a flourish and an indecently handsome smile.

"Olé!"

"I am not waving myself or my garments before society's
horns," she insisted frigidly.

"Of course you are." He dropped the trousers and looked
pointedly at the garments in her arms. "You're challenging
long-established standards of propriety . . . tweaking society's

upturned nose." One corner of his mouth quirked lazily. "Interesting of you, actually. It makes one wonder just what set you so at odds with all that's considered proper and decent for a woman."

"Clearly you haven't understood the first thing about what I've been telling you." She struggled not to react to that oddly unsettling smile of his.

"Just what have you been telling me, Miss Duncan?"

"I am trying to make the world a better place, Lord Mandeville." *Trying desperately to think of a way to get you out of my wardrobe, my bedroom . . . my life!*

"Come now, Miss Duncan, this is hardly Hyde Park." He edged closer. "Climb down off that soapbox and talk to me human to human instead of saint to nonbeliever. Just what do you intend to get out of all this charity and humanity?"

There it was, she realized, the thorn that had been stuck in his paw since he first set eyes upon her. According to his cynical philosophy, no one did anything for nothing.

"I'll not deny I want something from all this," she said, feeling her heart racing as her gaze drifted toward his. "Contrary to your peculiar delusion, I am *not* campaigning for canonization." She drew a deep breath and met his gaze full on.

"I make no secret of what I expect in return. . . . it's the same thing I am providing for my workers. I want a reason to get up each morning, a chance to make my days count for something—in short, a purpose in life." She searched his eyes for some glint of understanding. "Is that so terribly difficult to comprehend?"

Cole had allowed his gaze to meet hers, and from the instant he slid into that seductive blue, he knew he had made a fatal error. The truth was all there, written on her soul in large, indelible script. Earnestness. Honesty. Integrity. She truly wanted to use her fortune in a way that would give her life structure and depth and meaning. He did understand. He understood so well that an ache bloomed in his chest.

For a moment he felt drawn to her, drawn to the clarity

and certainty in her, the sense that here was something to fill the emptiness within. But then he banished that sentimental notion, deciding that what he really felt within was hunger. Only this time it wasn't merely his stomach that was demanding satisfaction.

He reached for one of the garments in her arms and gave a slow, irresistible tug. The piece slid and finally popped free, and he found himself holding a sleek strip of ivory silk awash in lace. With eyes glittering, he looped fingers through two straps and held up the garment.

"What is *this*?" he demanded.

"Our first product. A bandeau bodice."

"This little thing?" It was made of a fine silk foulard, a fabric considered by society's arbiters as too indecent for undergarments. He held the garment up to the light coming from the nearby window and wriggled his fingers behind its translucent fabric. His voice lowered a full fifth. "What does it do?"

Madeline watched him fingering her favorite bodice, and a spurt of confusing heat shot through her veins. She snatched it away from him and shoved it behind her back.

"It covers and supports a woman's—" She swallowed and tried again. "It's very like a corset cover or a camisole, only foreshortened and with cleverly placed darts that make it conform to a woman's . . ." She couldn't have uttered the word "bosoms" if her life depended on it.

One of his eyebrows rose in comprehension.

"It has buttons down the front so that a woman can fasten it herself," she said, pressing her spine harder against the bed-post and trying not to breathe too deeply of the dangerous scent of elemental male swirling around her. "All of our Ideal designs are predicated upon the notion that grown women in British society should be perfectly capable of dressing themselves."

"And *un*dressing themselves?" His voice was suddenly

like Barbados molasses and his eyes were darkening in the centers.

"That goes without saying," she whispered, feeling another garment sliding from the stack in her arms.

He raised a pair of short, flounced knickers between them and rubbed the light fabric slowly between his fingers. "Rolled silk. Very nice."

"The Ideal ones will be made of a specially knitted cotton that will provide a healthful give against a woman's . . . a woman's . . ."

"Shape," he supplied.

"Shape," she echoed, feeling some of her tension slide. Or was it her defenses?

He was so close that the heat radiating from him seemed to be melting her knees. As he drew the clothing piece by piece from her arms, she was grateful for the support of the bedpost at her back. With each garment he examined and discarded, he edged closer, until both their hands were empty and the front of his coat rested against her tunic.

"So, it might be said that with an Ideal bodice and Ideal knickers, a woman might have an Ideal shape?" A deliciously wicked grin drew her gaze to his mouth. Bold, sensual lips . . . nubile and expressive . . . the texture of dusky sateen. "Like yours."

"M-mine?"

"Half the women in London would give a year off their lives to have your thirty-eight, twenty-four, thirty-six. After seeing what you wear beneath your 'reformed' exterior"— he dragged his knuckles down the side of her cheek—"I am forced to conclude that those noteworthy curves have little to do with Ideal garments. Those curves, my mad little Madeline, are very simply you."

She couldn't respond on any level to his words; she was too busy responding on every possible level to his silky dark hair, his glowing eyes, and his rough-soft voice. When he lowered his head, she lifted hers to protest, and their mouths met.

His lips poured over hers, softly at first, experimentally, and her surprised thought was that his touch seemed to somehow assuage the heated, tingling sensations that she had come to associate with him. That sweet burn of anticipation now muted into a ripple of warmth that spread slowly through her.

She had never been this starkly intimate with another human being in her life—pressed body to body, mouth on mouth. His arms slid around her waist and her senses filled with enthralling new perceptions. How could she have known that the feel of a man's lips would change from moment to moment—soft, hard, flexing, slanting, parting, coaxing, commanding? How could she ever have imagined that a mouth—his mouth—actually had a taste of its own? It was salty-sweet, like buttered toast with jam. And how could she have guessed that he would smell like warm wool and sandalwood, spiced with a tang of male heat that resembled the aroma of Ceylonese tea. The man was a pure feast for the senses.

How long his lips explored, teased, and caressed hers she had no way of knowing, for it seemed as if the world gradually slowed on its axis and the normal motion of the cosmos came to a grinding halt. The moment stretched around her—extraordinary, brilliantly vivid, exquisitely infinite. And when the cogs of reality began to turn again, the universe had assumed a slightly different rotation.

Cole opened his eyes first, and the sight of her feathery lashes and flushed skin took a moment to register through the steam in his head. When they did penetrate, it took another moment to comprehend the ramifications of the jasmine and heliotrope filling his head and her mouth soft and pliant beneath his.

He broke off the kiss and lurched back a step. He had just been kissing Madeline Duncan for all he was worth. And—sweet heaven—he'd been enjoying it.

Madeline was somewhat slower to react. She lowered her eyes in confusion and discovered she was standing in a circle of discarded undergarments. The sight cleared away the haze of pleasure from the fact that there she stood, in a heap of her own unmentionables, being kissed to abandonment and back by the very man who was supposed to be objectively supervising her business.

How in infernal blazes had she gotten into such a mess?

She stumbled aside, smoothing her tunic and her shattered composure; he wheeled away and jerked his vest and his self-possession back into place. When they turned to face each other across the corner of the bed, they were both uncharacteristically at a loss for words. Finally Cole snatched up a bodice from the floor and dangled it from one finger.

"So this is your Ideal product." The curl of a nostril made his opinion of it plain. "Have your workers seen this?"

She stooped to rescue the rest of her fallen foundations. "I do not make a practice of showing my undergarments to my workers, Lord Mandeville." The fact that she was showing her most intimate apparel to *him* suddenly struck her full force. She suffered a brief and nasty vision of his report to Sir William: *"Miss Duncan showed me her undergarments, and I found them sorely lacking. Especially in fabric."*

"So, then, none of them have actually seen these contraptions," he concluded. "And what will they think when they learn they are here to produce female bosom binders and fast drawers?"

Bosom binders and fast drawers. One minute he was kissing her, the next baiting her, she thought, and she honestly didn't know which she found more contemptible.

"They will think the garments are . . . refreshingly sensible," she declared.

"Refreshingly sensible?" He hooted a laugh and eyed the bodice hanging from his finger. "Harley Ketchum and his herd of young stallions will find these lacy bits . . . *sensible*?"

"They won't be lacy. . . . And naturally they will appreciate the freedom in my designs," she insisted, welcoming the renewed anger she felt.

"Are you certain?" He inched forward. "Certain enough to put it to the test?"

"Of course."

"All right, then, call a meeting of your 'exemplary' work-force. Show them the garments you intend to produce and let's see their reaction."

Stretching to her tallest, she defiantly held his gaze.

"Very well," she conceded. "Seeing a bit of democratic management in action might do you a world of good. I shall call a meeting as soon as they are settled in, and let *them* prove how wrong you are."

With a sardonic smile, he gave her a nod and strode from the room.

Collecting the rest of her undergarments, she vented her annoyance by throwing them onto the bed. Impossible man. In the midst of tossing her divided skirt onto a nearby chair, she suddenly recalled the guarded depths of his eyes and halted, staring fiercely into that memory.

She had glimpsed something there within him, some-thing fleeting and light-shy, something he hadn't wanted her to see. Something behind the walls he had erected. Behind the intellectual pride, the cultivated condescension. The ram-pant skepticism. Hunger. Conflict. Pain.

She straightened.

For the first time since their meeting, she wondered why he had such antipathy for her project, sight unseen. Why was he so determined to believe the worst of her and her workers? Why was he so eager for her to fail?

And why was she having these wretched weak-in-the-knees and ache-in-the-chest feelings at the idea that Cole Mandeville might have some hurt buried inside him?

The last thing she needed just then was a soft spot for the hardheaded cynic bent on bringing her to her knees.

• • •

That evening Cole retired early to his cramped loft and tried by the light of a smoky tallow lamp to read one of the journals he had brought with him from London. But as the noise from the tavern increased, his concentration grew steadily worse. Finally he gave up reading and doused the lamp.

Strident male voices battered the planks of the floor and the meager door as the patrons below indulged in ale, cards, and dice. Three times Cole sprang up off his pallet, meaning to storm downstairs and demand some peace. The first time he bumped his head, the next stepped barefooted in the middle of the empty dishes on the tray by the door, and the third time, the noise abated abruptly as he reached the door. Giving Cravits an envious look, wishing now that he had accepted the valet's offer of a sleeping draft, he crawled back onto his lumpy straw mattress. As he lay tossing and turning, the name "Charlotte" wafted up to him and he realized that some of the voices—the younger ones—belonged to the four Ketchum offspring.

Growing desperate, he rolled off the pallet and rummaged about in his trunk for a bottle of Scotch whisky. But the liquor served only to stoke the heat already smoldering in his belly. Somewhere in the midst of that slurry of voices and tavern noise he heard a reference to "Miz Duncan." Immediately he stilled and strained to hear, now thwarted by the very drop in noise level that he had longed for moments earlier.

He scowled at a burst of laughter from below, conjuring up a dozen possible contexts for Madeline's name being bandied about in such a setting; Miss Duncan's deep pockets and crazy notions . . . Miss Duncan's generous nature and extreme gullibility . . . Miss Duncan's scandalous trousers and penchant for talking openly about ladies' corsets and drawers. Perhaps they knew more than it seemed, and her titillating undergarments were indeed the topic of the hour.

Even worse possibilities struck. They could be discussing

her admirably displayed thirty-eight, twenty-four, thirty-six . . . her fire-kissed hair and enormous blue eyes . . . her wet-satin lips . . . her tempting skin . . . her empty and beckoning bed.

Lips? Bed? Such salacious possibilities would occur only to someone who had direct experience with her measurements, had touched her hair, had tasted her lips and felt the welcome in her.

Cursing softly, he lurched up and headed for the door. But as he stomped down the ladder into the smoky, beer-laden atmosphere of the tap room, the main door flew open and in charged Harley Ketchum, his jaw set like stone and his eyes blazing.

"Jus' like I thought!" Harley bellowed. "Helpin' old Fritz tonight, are ye?" he demanded, glaring at the table where his offspring sat with their hands full of cards and tankards of watered rum.

"Now, Pa—" One of Ketchum's strapping sons dropped the pasteboards and sprang to his feet, wiping his hands nervously on his thighs.

"We can explain," one of the others began as the remaining brothers scrambled to their feet as their father approached.

"There be naught to explain—I got eyes!" Harley roared. "Here in this den of iniquity, swillin' rum and sportin' and gamblin' like the devil's own spawn!" He overturned the bench they had been sitting on and it smacked the floor with a bang, setting loose a flurry of motion as the other patrons scurried out of the way.

"But, Pa, there ain't nothin' wrong with a jot o' ale now an' again," the one who looked to be the eldest protested. "Till Ma died, you took a nip right regular yourself."

The wrong thing to say, apparently. Harley flew into a rage, quoting both Scripture and his staunchly Methodist wife as he declared judgment, decreed punishment, and proceeded to carry it out. Overturning tables and breaking crockery, he stalked, seized, and duly thrashed each of his hulking, way-ward sons.

Cole retreated back up the ladder and sat on his sour, lumpy bed in the darkness, enduring the howls and grunts and the miscellaneous sounds of breakage that seemed to go on forever.

By morning he was hollow-eyed, ravenous as a regiment of regulars, and desperate enough to try anything for a decent bit of sleep and a palatable meal. By half past seven he had roused poor Cravits and innkeeper Netter, had dressed and packed, and was marching across the green to Madeline's comfortable brick house. He would see whether he could bully some hospitality out of her.

He pounded on the door with the heel of his fist until the panels vibrated. When the door was opened by a stout woman in somber garments, his righteous anger propelled him straight past her into the entry hall. There he braced, announced that he had come to stay, and demanded to see Madeline straightaway.

"So sorry, your lordship," the woman said with a beatific smile. "Madeline—Miss Duncan—has already gone to the factory this morning." She looked at the baggage in Cravits's and Netter's hands. "She is an incorrigibly early riser, always up with the sun."

"How typically unladylike of her" was all he could think to say.

"I have your rooms all ready, your lordship."

"You—you have?"

"I've been expecting you." She smiled and nodded. "And I imagine you'll be wanting a bit of breakfast. We have plenty of kippers, eggs, and scones with marmalade and pear honey. Oh, and coffee. Unless you'd prefer tea of a morning." She raised her brows in question.

Cole wondered whether he was hallucinating. He said faintly, "Coffee will be fine, Mrs. . . . Mrs. . . ." His mouth was watering prodigiously.

"Davenport. I am Madeline's housekeeper and longtime friend. Now, if you and your gentlemen will just follow me."

Beaumont Tattersall came rushing into the sample room at half past nine with his face flushed from running up three flights. "It's here, Miss Duncan. The cloth—"

Madeline looked up from the design she had been working on with Endicott. Dropping the pencil she held in her hand, she headed for the steps, Tattersall and Endicott at her heels. As they passed through the offices and sewing room with Tattersall relating what was happening, Emily, Maple, and Charlotte Thoroughgood, Daniel Steadman and engineer Fritz Gonnering fell in behind and followed them down the three flights of steps to the shipping area.

There, several heavy trucks were being unloaded, their cargo rolled bolt by bolt down a specially prepared ramp into the receiving room. The dust, the scent of newly dyed cloth, and the musty smell of the room filled Madeline's senses as she waited, clasping her hands to keep from rushing over to help Harley's sons roll the massive bolts aside as they came thundering down the wooden incline.

When she could bear the suspense no longer, she chose a bolt well out of the way of the unloading and began to tear away the heavy brown wrapping. To her confusion, what met her eyes was the sight of dark blue woolen cloth where there should have been pristine knitted cotton. She tore through the rest of the paper, then stooped to examine the end of the bolt. Poking and prodding, she managed to insinuate her finger between the tightly wound layers just enough to feel the soft wool.

Beaumont, too, was staring at the fabric in bewilderment. "It's woolen. How can that be?" he said.

Fritz was peeling back the paper covering on another nearby bolt, and she hurried over to see what he discovered.

It was the same blue woolen. Her eyes were wide with alarm as they attacked a third bolt, then a fourth.

It was all the same, every last roll. Dark blue woolen. Fine-quality cloth to be sure, but entirely the wrong stuff for ladies' unmentionables.

"We ordered *cotton*—Lawrence and Haviland's finest, softest cotton knit!" she exclaimed, suspended somewhere between despair and outrage. "And they sent us—Lord, I didn't think they even produced woolens in Manchester!"

"Here is the answer," Beaumont said, approaching with the bill of lading in his hands. "The shipment came from Lawrence and Haviland—of *Leeds*." He scowled. "Apparently there's been some sort of mix-up . . . and the order was sent to Leeds instead of Manchester. They've sent us forty master bolts of their best woolen jersey."

Knitted woolens. Those massive bolts that only moments before had made Madeline's heart race with anticipation now made it sink with distress. Forty bolts of wool that would make women's tender parts—

"Well, well, what have we here?"

It was Cole Mandeville's voice, of course, cutting through the dusty air and through her assembled staff, who stepped aside at his approach. He made a deliberate detour to give the fabric in one of the opened bolts a considering stroke before reaching her. "This is your textile? A bit chafing for intimate lady-wear, isn't it?"

It was times like this that she regretted not acquiring a huge, insanely protective dog. One with a taste for noble shins.

"It appears we have just experienced our first 'oops.'" Madeline conceded coolly. "They've sent us the wrong fabric. The mistake will be set right, but it will involve an adjustment in our schedule." She paused, looking over that growing sea of unwanted woolen. "We will simply find a way to minimize that delay."

Madeline was suddenly conscious of her employees looking on anxiously. This was their first crisis, the first real test of her leadership. It had to be solved by combining their strengths and ideas—a true community effort—if her idea of worker participation in the company was to have any meaning.

"Well, this appears to be a perfect opportunity to demonstrate to Lord Mandeville the advantages of participatory management. Several heads are always better than one." She hoisted herself to a seat on one of the bolts and declared: "We need ideas! What can we do to get proper fabric here within the week?"

For a moment they stared mutely at one another, accustomed to following orders, not to being asked to think for themselves. Then Daniel Steadman spoke up.

"Sending this lot back and ordering again could take weeks. Which do you have more of, Miz Duncan, time or money?"

With a look at Cole's adamantly crossed arms and disdainful expression, Madeline replied: "Neither, unfortunately, is in great supply."

"Well, with enough money you could buy fabric from a closer supplier, enough to get us started and keep work going for a bit."

"A closer supplier. Good idea." She refused to look at Cole. "If we have sufficient capital. What else?"

"Use vat we haff," Fritz said, waving with Prussian pragmatism to the room full of woolens. "Make . . . zomet'ing else."

That possibility had already occurred fleetingly to her and been dismissed. "We have the design and the patterns ready— we're committed to women's foundations."

Daniel Steadman spoke again. "Well, then. You'll have to find another supplier, someone who has good cottons at a fair price."

There was a moment of silence, then Beaumont Tattersall brightened. "While at my former employer I made the acquaintance of the head clerk at Liberty. They are often approached by wholesale linen drapers and manufacturers. Perhaps he could put us on to a source of good cotton."

"Excellent." Madeline smiled brightly. "Would you be willing to contact him, travel to London yourself, and pay him a call? I could give you authorization, as our Ideal agent, to strike a bargain within the cost limits we've set. You know how we arrived at our estimates and you're familiar with our production constraints."

Tattersall seemed a bit startled at being offered such an important charge, but quickly straightened his shoulders and nodded.

Relieved that the catastrophe could be averted, Madeline turned to Cole Mandeville, only to see that he was heading for the stairs. She suddenly remembered the fresh capital she was going to need—the purse strings of which were held in the tight, unsympathetic grip of Lord Mandeville. Clearly, they weren't out of difficulty yet. Grimly she went after him.

Before she could catch up with him, Roscoe Turner and Algy Bates came tromping in from the rear yard with another fellow in tow.

"There ye are, miz," Roscoe began, wagging his head. "I'm afraid we got us a bit o' bad news." His voice lowered and filled with dire portent. "That rock, miz . . . it's a mite bigger than we reckoned. Ten- or twelve-man, at least."

"A right heavy bugger," Algy put in with a nod, over his partner's shoulder.

"But I thought you were taking care of it," she said, her frayed patience obvious in her voice.

Cole Mandeville had paused and was standing in the doorway with his arms crossed. She felt his gaze on her.

"Oh, we will, miz. Found us someone to help wi' the diggin.' A feller willin' to work for the same wage as us." He gestured to the short, wiry fellow in a fancy bowler standing a few feet away. "Miz Duncan, this here be Rupert Fitzwater.

Come from London to visit his sister over by Flimwell. Says he's dug up a bit o' dirt in his time."

"Miss Duncan." The fellow dragged his hat from his head and smiled, baring yellowed teeth in a grizzled face. He was dressed in a frayed woolen coat, trousers in dire need of a good pressing, and shoes that had seen better days. "I'd appreciate the opportunity, miss. When I got a job to do, nothin' stands in my way."

"Well, Mr. Fitzwater, that being the case, I suppose you're hired. You shall have to find accommodations among—"

"Oh, he can put in wi' me an' Alg, Miz Duncan," Roscoe assured her. That seemed to suit Mr. Fitzwater, who nodded, and the matter was settled. The threesome exited into the garden to begin work anew.

Her attention returned to Cole Mandeville, leaning against the door frame, wearing an irksome smile.

"More problems, Miss Duncan?" he asked as she approached. "*Tsk, tsk.* I'm afraid you're going to need a good bit more of that 'oops' time before you're through."

"What I need, Lord Mandeville, is a good bit less of your condescending attitude." She halted a pace away, matching his crossed arms with hers.

His eyes narrowed. "What you need, St. Madeline of the Bleeding Hearts, is a walloping great wad of cash to pay for your unfortunate little 'oops.' And to get it, you have to have my approval."

"Your approval," she said with a genuine spurt of anger. "To spend *my* money."

"That's the long and the short of it," he declared. "My solemn and binding legal duty, you know, protecting you from your own magnanimous impulses."

"A task made ever so much more difficult by the fact that you wouldn't know a magnanimous impulse if you saw one."

A muscle in his jaw flexed as he straightened abruptly and

headed for the stairs. She followed, determined to have her say—and her money.

"What do I have to do?" she demanded of his back as he mounted the steps. He stopped several steps up, and after a moment turned. "What will it take to convince you that the Ideal Garment Company is a viable business concern? That I am both serious about this work and capable of carrying it out? What is the price of your prejudice, Cold Mandeville?"

Anger flickered across his bronze features.

"What did you call me?"

It had been a slip of the tongue; wholly unintentional. But it was so fitting that she realized some part of her had meant it.

"Cold Mandeville," she replied, squaring her shoulders.

"That's what you think I am? Cold?"

"If the shoe fits . . ." she said. "You have yet to demonstrate the slightest bit of human warmth or compassion or generosity of spirit. Since you arrived, you have done nothing but stalk about snarling and passing judgment on everything you see—even though you know nothing of working-class people—their lives, their problems, or their dreams. And you know even less about having dreams of your own."

His eyes hardened.

"Cold?" he said with a hard-edged laugh. "You haven't seen *cold,* Saint Madeline. Cold would be looking the other way while this collection of dolts, whiners, and tuppenny dodgers take advantage of a naive young do-gooder who never learned to say no." He stepped down heavily onto the lone stair tread between them. "Cold would be letting you spend yourself into oblivion trying to provide for people who sleep on the job in every available nook and cranny, drink themselves into a stupor by noon, and refuse to lift a finger to carry food into their house—when it's been delivered to their bloody doorstep." He bent close to her. "Cold would be prizing my comfort more than my sworn duty and stalking off back to a life of pleasant, idle debauchery in London."

He took her chin in his hand and tilted her head. She could feel his breath on her face. Her heart skipped erratically as his voice became like rough velvet.

"*Cold* would be taking you into my arms right now and kissing you until you melted."

The touch of his lips would most certainly make her melt—she was perilously close to liquefying at just the touch of his hand. Anger warred with desire, and for a moment, all she could do was stare at his mouth. . . .

When he turned and continued up the stairs, she abruptly came to her senses. There she stood in the ruins of her righteous indignation, unkissed, unmelted, her pride and lofty ideals still intact, still St. Madeline of the Bleeding Hearts. With a hot rush of confusion, she couldn't decide if he had decided to let her stew in her own longings or had declined to humiliate her with her own responses. Was he torturing or protecting her? The worst of it was: She hadn't the foggiest idea whether she should be furious or grateful!

Still struggling with her emotions, she climbed the stairs and stood in the middle of the sewing floor, trying to recall just what it was she had intended to do that day. Stacks of sewing tables, crates full of sewing machines, a series of power shafts—she began to remember as she surveyed that idle lot, including Thomas Clark, who was lounging across the way on a stack of spare lumber. The sight of Thomas's well-fed face and propped feet sent an unfamiliar trickle of annoyance through her. And where were the others she had asked to be here?

"Thomas Clark!" she called out. With a start, he rolled off his seat and stood, shifting his considerable weight from foot to foot. "I need you to go and find the others—Ben Murtry, William Huggins, Bernard Rush." When he looked confused, she explained: "Your new neighbors. We need them here to help unpack and install the sewing machines."

He nodded and ambled toward the stairs. There, he spoke to a ragged, barefoot boy of about twelve years, who was hanging on the banister. A moment later the boy slid down the railing and Thomas sauntered back to his former seat. In response to her scowl, he smiled with earnest indolence.

"That be my eldest. He'll fetch them others for ye."

Fritz and Daniel Steadman arrived up the back stairs just then. Immediately they spread out a set of drawings on one of the tables and set to work laying out and marking the work stations for the seamstresses. Before long, more male workers arrived and stood bunched near the stairs, looking around the hall and seeming somewhat reluctant to venture farther.

With some relief, Madeline welcomed them and set them to work in teams of two, carrying and positioning tables, loading and unloading sewing machines on the lift at the far end, and helping Fritz unpack machinery. Shortly, some of the women arrived, bringing with them a number of their children. They perched on the chairs stacked at the end of the hall and, in the way of women everywhere, soon began to visit, leaving their children to race, crawl, climb, hang, squeal, poke about, and generally interfere with the business of creating a clothing factory.

More than once Madeline had to peel children away from half-installed sewing machines, warning them of the dangers of getting too close. Setting Emily to ask the women to watch them, she returned to the task of doling out assignments and helping Fritz and Daniel make final decisions. But before long she was having to remove children from stacks of crates and shoo them from underfoot again. It finally occurred to her to send for Maple Thoroughgood and Charlotte, to have them lead the women to the downstairs classroom and begin teaching them to use the machines. Since the younger ones went with their mothers, that alleviated part of the children problem.

Increasingly, Madeline found herself having to be in four places at once, responding to questions, corralling children,

directing the placement of the equipment, and constantly repeating directions. The men had a disconcerting tendency to
do one task, then to stand and wait to be directed to another—even if it was the same one—over and over. Patiently,
Madeline explained and re-explained what needed to be
done, hoping they would soon take the initiative and continue the work on their own.

Clearly, they were unused to being in charge of their own
work. Such a momentous change was bound to take some
getting used to. Immersed in a constant flow of demands,
decisions, and activity, she was far too busy to worry about
Cole Mandeville and his judgmental attitude—for the moment.

7

But Madeline continued to occupy Cole's thoughts as well as his vision. He stood just inside the office doorway with his arms crossed and his feet spread, watching every nuance of Madeline's expressions and movements. He didn't understand the dangerous fascination she held for him.

Why didn't he just give her all the financial rope she wanted and then step back and watch her hang her saintly self with it? More to the point, why *hadn't* he grabbed and kissed her until she was a helpless puddle at his feet? What in hell was he doing, protecting her from his desires and her own stubborn idealism?

A disturbing possibility occurred to him. Was he, in fact, doing what he knew in his bones to be the right thing . . . no matter how it annoyed or inconvenienced him? The ramifications of that rattled him to the core. Some unexpunged blot of idealism must still lurk deep inside him.

Damn and double damn, he thought, retreating from the all-too-absorbing sight of her, into the superintendent's office. It had taken a lifetime of hard lessons, disappointments, and familiarity with the gritty realities of the world for him to achieve the cynicism he was so comfortable with. Now St. Madeline of the Infernally Helpful had reminded him that he, too, once harbored pathetic dreams of making a difference in the world.

The ache beginning in his chest was proof of just how painful those old ideals had been. He knew from experience that the only cure for a virulent case of ideals was a near-lethal dose of reality, having your dreams kicked in by someone in whom you have misplaced your faith. And the more he watched Madeline with her chosen lot of slackers, sots, and cloak twitchers, the more certain he was that they would be administering that bitter draft of reality someday soon. And the plain truth of it was that he didn't want any part of it, not even a glimpse.

He sat down in the one padded chair in her spartan office, propped his feet on the desk, and stared at the stacks of paper that were the outward manifestation of the astonishing orderliness inside her. She was an interesting woman despite all that unfortunate optimism. Also intelligent, energetic, logical, opinionated, and utterly unaffected. In point of fact, it had been a long time since he encountered someone as individual, independent, or inventive as she was. Thoughts of frothy silk knickers popped into his mind, and he couldn't help wondering what it would be like to have her employ those creative instincts in more pleasurable endeavors.

Pushing away those dangerous musings, he rose and went back to watching her from the doorway as she supervised the unpacking of the sewing machines. It was chaos around her, yet she dealt with obstreperous children, dubious workers, and frustrated engineers with extreme patience. Every time she turned so that he caught a glimpse of her flushed cheeks or the flash of her quick smile, he felt a worrisome sliding sensation in his middle and prayed it wasn't the feel of his hard-won common sense deserting him.

• • •

Later in the afternoon, as Madeline was cleaning a newly un-packed machine, she realized that things had become strangely quiet. She looked up to find the sewing floor empty except for a clutch of men standing near the stairs, surveying the sight of ladders, half-assembled machinery, empty crates, and the litter of packing wool and wood shavings all about. She set her hands to the small of her back, stretching, feeling for the first time the deep, throbbing ache of exhausted muscles.

Where was everyone? The women, the children, her newly employed cutters—even Daniel and Fritz were no-where to be seen. Only Thomas Clark, Ben Murtry, and Will Huggins were left. She looked at the dwindling stack of crates against the wall—only five more. How good it would feel to be done.

The top crate was well over her head, but she managed to find a grip on its wooden framing and give it a tug. It didn't move, so she braced and pulled again. This time the entire stack swayed. Her workers should not have left such a precarious vertical stack, yet another example of their poor judgment. With another heave and tug, the top crate began to slide. Steadying the crate below it with her other hand, she looked around for help from the men.

Surely they could see her predicament. "Thomas, I need some help," she called as she turned back to give the crate another pull. It slid more easily than expected, and she sud-denly found herself bearing more weight than she'd bargained for. "Aghhh! Thomas!" She looked frantically over her shoul-der, only to see the last of three heads disappearing down the stairs.

The crates tipped and wobbled. Just as she shut her eyes in panic, her burden abruptly eased. Male hands were lifting that box above her head and lowering it safely from the stack. The hands were attached to dark-clad arms finished with pristine cuffs. When she turned, Cole Mandeville was standing behind her, holding the heavy box and glaring.

"Biting off more than you can chew again, St. Madeline?" He delivered the machine to one of the unoccupied tables and deposited it with a thud.

"I—I didn't realize they were leaving," she said, reddening. "I thought . . ."

The disgust in his expression made his opinion of her workers quite clear. Muttering something she didn't catch, he strode past her to the stack of machines and transferred the remaining crates to unoccupied tables.

"There," he said, straightening his clothing. "I've done more work in three minutes than most of your precious employees did all day."

If Cole had looked back as he exited the room, he would have been treated to the extraordinary sight of Madeline Duncan kicking a hunk of packing felt and sending it flying. Fortunately for Madeline's dignity, he did not look back. If there was anything she hated more than a cynical, unfeeling overseer, it was a cynical, unfeeling overseer *who was right*. She couldn't deny the disappointing performance her workers had turned in on their first day on the job.

Wholeheartedly confused, she picked up a pry bar, shoved a chair over, and climbed up to open one of the crates. She savagely jabbed the metal bar between the boards and pushed and levered the slats apart. With a crash the lid fell to the floor, followed by a bushel of packing wool and wood shaving.

Thomas Clark had left her there, in trouble, with a costly piece of equipment teetering overhead. He and the others had walked away as if they hadn't heard anything. She paused in the midst of removing the front part of the crate and leaned on the wood. Well, of course she couldn't blame them for what they hadn't heard, could she?

Grimly, she opened more crates, cleaning off the packing materials and removing the leather shipping straps, then clearing away the debris and situating the machines in the slots on the tabletops.

It wasn't until Emily came out of the offices, whirling a shawl around her shoulders and bidding her a good evening, that Madeline realized the sun was setting. Looking around, she wondered briefly where Fritz had gone. It wasn't like him to quit work so early.

For some reason, Cole Mandeville's voice stole into her mind, saying that some of her workers "drink themselves into a stupor by noon." Scowling, she thought of the times she had smelled spirits on Fritz's breath and of the scent of the overpowering anise drops he seemed to favor. Was he . . .

"That's what I loathe about you, Cold Mandeville," she snarled, lighting a lamp and setting it on a nearby table. With angry vigor she attacked that last wooden crate. "You spread your little seeds of cynicism and stalk off, leaving them to sprout and take root in the first available doubt."

It was sometime later that Madeline closed and locked the office door, paused to let her eyes adjust to the darkness, then made her way from the factory. Her muscles ached, her nose and eyes burned from the lint and dust, and her head throbbed. Just putting one foot before the other took nearly all her concentration, leaving only enough to fasten on the promise of a warm, soothing tub and a glass of wine.

She let herself into her house knowing that Davenport would be in the kitchen at this hour. She thought of asking for a tray in her room, but the long flight of stairs convinced her that the dining room was a good idea.

She made her way to the dining room, poking her head into the kitchen to let Davenport know she was home. As she sank wearily into the chair at the head of the dining table, closing her eyes gratefully, it occurred to her that it was brighter than usual in the room—Davenport seemed to have lighted two sets of candles. Moments later she was roused by the housekeeper's voice saying cheerily, "It's about time, Maddy Duncan. We were beginning to think we might have to send out a rescue party. If the soup is cold, your lordship, you can blame Miss Diligence Duncan."

That peeled Madeline's eyes open and brought her bolt upright in her chair. There at the side of the fireplace, his arm propped on the mantel, stood Cole Mandeville, fully rigged out. A tailcoat and trousers, black as a raven's wing, with a silk brocade vest, tucked shirt, and high collar, he was in full evening dress. Madeline could not suppress the groan that escaped her.

"What on earth are you doing here?"

"Anticipating dinner, I believe," he responded, raising his glass to her and then to his lips. "A very smooth bit of grape, I daresay."

"Dinner?" She turned a fierce look on Davenport, who merely smiled and waved to Mercy, the housemaid, to bring the platter and tureen for serving.

It must be a bad dream, Madeline thought. Before she could put words to her outrage, Cole Mandeville was taking the chair at the opposite end of the table, and Davvy was ladling some deliciously aromatic concoction into Madeline's soup bowl.

Davvy explained. "His lordship found Hiram Netter's accommodations a bit—"

"Primitive," he supplied.

"Primitive," Davvy echoed, clasping her hands at her waist. "From now on he'll be staying with us."

"He most assuredly will not," she said, glaring between the pair of them.

"Oh, but he will." Davvy didn't bat an eye. "I've already invited him and settled him and his man into the front bed-rooms."

"*You* invited him?" Madeline was stunned. She never really thought of Davvy as a servant or employee, more as one of the family. Still, it floored her to have the staunch housekeeper flagrantly contradict her expressed wishes.

"Of course I invited him." Davvy's smile bore a familiar hint of stubbornness. "I decided to take that decision off your shoulders, Maddy dear. Worker participation, don't you know. You're always ballyhooing it—"

"I-in *the factory*," she stammered.

"Well, I am part owner, after all," Davvy reminded her with steely pleasantness. "It was my money that bought those fancy new windows, was it not? Gave to the cause without a murmur, if you'll recall. I'm only looking after my investment, Maddy dear."

"Ah, yes, your quaint notions of worker participation." Cole addressed her with a taunting smile. "It has always seemed to me that such policies must have drawbacks for an owner. *Loss of control,* for one." Beaming infuriating good humor, he sniffed the soup Davvy was ladling into his bowl and picked up a spoon. "Damned if this isn't the best thing I've smelled in weeks."

Silenced by the treachery of having her own ideas wielded against her, Madeline tapped her wineglass sharply and Davvy filled it with the white wine Cole had just complimented. Madeline downed it quickly, seeking its heat in her parched throat, hollow middle, and aching limbs. The soup was one of Cook Hannah's specialties and one of Madeline's favorites: a rich mixed-poultry broth with rice and sage. She consumed the entire bowl before looking up again to behold Cole Mandeville leaning back in his chair, savoring another glass of wine and looking outrageously content.

Even knowing he wasn't welcome, he insisted on staying in her house. And short of hiring a pack of thugs to come and evict him bodily, there seemed precious little she could do about his presence. For tonight, anyway. *I'm sorry, Your Honor, I haven't the faintest idea how that arsenic got into Lord Mandeville's coffee. I was rather counting on smothering him with a feather ticking myself.*

Jabbing her fork into her orange and endive salad, she signaled Davvy for another glass of wine. As she lowered her gaze, it caught unexpectedly on his smile. Of course he was smiling, he'd gotten exactly what he wanted. She scowled and stuffed her mouth full of salad. She might have to suffer his presence, but she didn't have to extend him more than bare civility.

They ate in strained silence, the only sounds in the room the tick of the mantel clock and the occasional scrape of silver or clink of crystal on china. The chicken en croustade was magnificent—she managed two bites. The braised trout with spring vegetables was positively succulent—she propped one cheek on her hand and filled the other with trout before realizing she scarcely had the energy to chew. Fearing that she would be stuck looking like a squirrel for the rest of the night, she managed to down the fish with the help of some wine.

Every time Davenport appeared with another course, Madeline gave her a dark look and she returned a spitefully cheery smile. She had apparently been planning this little feast for some days: She was serving all of Hannah's best dishes. By the time the braised beef in Bordeaux and mushrooms, the steamed asparagus with hollandaise, the brandied pears à la Hélène, and then the cheeses and cordials arrived, Madeline was sagging in her chair and listing to one side. Fortunately, the chairs were provided with old-fashioned wings that for generations had served to keep overstuffed gentry's heads from drooping.

Cole watched her closely through the meal, partly to show how little her hostility daunted him and partly to satisfy his bewildering craving for the sight of her. And she was indeed a sight. Her hair was coming undone, her blue smock was covered with dust and lint, wood shavings were stuck in the net around her chignon, and there was a healthy streak of dirt across her cheek. Her skin seemed pale despite her tippling, and beneath her closed eyes were dark smudges that spoke of fatigue.

If he had any lingering doubts about her commitment to her Ideal Garment Company, watching her today and seeing her tonight would have dispelled them. She was devoted to her cause body and soul, so determined to help others that she willingly sacrificed her own time, energy, and resources. She had worked herself to near oblivion today, moving, cleaning, organizing, delegating, encouraging, teaching, arranging, supervising, approving. And she did so without the cloying air of martyrdom that characterized so much of the "charity" in society of late.

Simply put, she was a giving sort of woman. Warm and giving. Delectably warm and giving. Lushly delectable, warm, and giving—and if he didn't cease this line of thinking at that very moment, he would be forced to sit in this chair with a table napkin over his trousers for the rest of the evening.

Just how long he sat there, watching her slide deeper into unconsciousness, he had no idea. But when her shoulders rounded and she surrendered utterly to gravity, he sensed it had been quite some time. It was clear that neither the housemaid nor the intrepid Mrs. Davenport would reappear anytime soon, so he gave in to the impulse to rise from the table and move closer to her.

Ripe-as-peaches lips. Long, curly lashes. Threads of gold in her auburn hair. Sweet, silky skin visible on the nape of her neck, beneath her small, sensible collar. She had an air of innocence about her, an angelic quality that would have made her perfect for a Rossetti painting—except that Rossetti's women always seemed so aloof and untouchable. And Madeline Duncan was supremely touchable.

He swirled a fingertip around one of the silky wisps of hair that had escaped her chignon, watching with pleasure as it wrapped around his finger. His hand strayed to her temple, where he brushed stray hair back, then ran a knuckle across her cheek. She stirred lightly, and he feathered a soft stroke down her nose and across her lips. Roused by that touch, she ran her tongue over her lips.

Soft little tongue. Just then it would taste like a strawberry cordial. . . .

Perhaps it was the wine that led him to bend and gather her into his arms, lifting her against his chest. It was as if an electrical circuit had been completed in him; his blood began to hum at the contact. By the time they reached the bottom of the stairs, she was awake.

"What's hap-pen-ing?" She rubbed her face, squinted up at him in the hall light, then began shoving. "Put me down— what on earth are you doing?"

"You're exhausted and I am taking you to bed," he said, setting her on her feet with genuine reluctance. He was quickly rewarded by the feel of her body swaying and finding support against his.

"I can take myself . . . th-thank you," she said, pulling away. Then she stumbled and went down on one knee when she attempted the next step up.

He caught her and hauled her to her feet with an arm around her waist. Over her objections he helped her climb the steps and led her down the hall to her bedroom. A single oil lamp had been left burning for her, casting a golden glow over the room. He led her to the bed, stood her against the foot post, and braced her there with his lower body as he unfastened the buttons of her voluminous blue smock.

"I . . . I can do that," she said, trying to bring up her arms to take over.

"Let me," he said dryly as he watched her arms flop back down her sides. "It will be my thrill for the evening." As he peeled the dusty smock from her and tossed it aside, she started to sink, and he caught her against him with both arms. Looking down into her unfocused eyes, he felt something within his chest tighten. "A pity you don't wear laces, St. Madeline." He caught her face in his hand and tilted it to his. "I could offer to loosen them for you."

"I c-can undo my own . . . boddie," she said, doing her best to relieve him of the burden of her weight.

"I'm certain you can. But think of how interesting it would be to have someone else undo your 'body' for once." He knew she meant bodice, but somehow the words registered in him just as they were spoken. *Body*. He wanted nothing more at that moment than to "undo" her entire body, bit by responsive bit, inch by voluptuous virgin inch. His arousal as he stood pressed against her was instant and urgent. Every sinew in his body was suddenly hot and primed.

He sat her down on the bed, wrapped her arms around the foot post—and quickly left the room.

At the sound of the door closing, she roused enough to know that she was on her own bed, safe, with delicious impressions of hard male warmth lingering all along her body. With a wistful smile no one could see and she wouldn't remember, she climbed up into the middle of the bed and abandoned herself to a soft, enveloping cloud of sleep.

She awakened some hours later, her mouth dry, her eyes grainy, and her senses disoriented. When she sat up, she was relieved to recognize her own bed and the clothes she had worn the previous day. She felt thick and leaden as she crawled from the bed, shed her clothes down to the skin, and pulled a nightdress over her head. It caught on her chignon, and she freed it, then plopped down at her dressing table to loosen her hair and give it a few hasty strokes with the hairbrush.

Her head was pounding and her stomach was growling. What she needed was a megrim powder and something to eat. She glanced longingly at the bed, but knew she would only toss and turn if she went back to bed hungry and hurting. She pulled a dressing gown over her shoulders, then padded barefoot down the stairs.

In the kitchen she turned up the lamp that was left burning at night.

She rummaged about in Cook's medicinals, assembled a

dose of headache remedy, and downed it. Minutes later she was perched on Cook's tall stool with a slice of cold cottage pie in one hand and a glass of milk in the other. It took her back to the days when she used to sneak downstairs at night to the kitchen of their house in Bloomsbury. Aunt Olivia always seemed to know she was up and would come floating downstairs in an exotic Persian robe and night turban to supervise . . . or to join her.

A noise startled her, and she whirled on her stool, half expecting to see the old lady come sailing through the door with that memorable light in her eyes. Instead, coming out of the hallway darkness was Cole Mandeville, in shirt-sleeves, no collar, and rumpled evening trousers. A lock of tousled hair hung over his forehead, and he looked as if he hadn't slept a wink.

There was just no getting rid of the man.

He paused inside the kitchen door to stare at her, and it was a measure of her surprise and confusion that she didn't think to close her gaping robe or cover her bare legs, which were propped on the stool rungs and visible from the knees down.

"What are you doing up at this hour?" she demanded. She was beginning to recall how she had come to be sleeping in her clothes, on top of her bedcovers. A pink tinge crept into her cheeks.

"Much the same as you, I expect." He studied her a moment longer, then headed for the pie safe. "Couldn't sleep. Must be all this peace and quiet. A few nights at Netter's establishment make a lasting impression on a body's nocturnal routine." He turned back with a slice of gooey mulberry pie in his hand. "I came downstairs to see if you had any reading material and found a rather cozy little library with an astonishing array of books. Yours?"

She nodded and swallowed a mouthful of her own pie. "Mine and my aunt Olivia's. She loved books and taught me to love them too. Half of those volumes were gifts from her to me or from me to her. There is another whole collection at our house in Bloomsbury."

He had located a glass, poured some milk, and now came to sit at the worktable beside her. She watched him, strangely mesmerized. Odd that she hadn't noticed his extraordinary grace of motion before. Just now he seemed so long and lean . . . every swing of his legs seemed to inscribe a flawless arc. His shoulders moved with a relaxed confidence, and, seeing him in shirt-sleeves, she made the discovery that the breadth of his coat shoulders owed nothing to padding after all. As he slid to a seat at the table, she watched his upper arms flex beneath the snug linen of his sleeves, and it took a moment for her to realize that he had said something.

"You changed clothes, I see." He gave her thin night-dress an inquisitive look. "Your reform garments must live up to your expectations if they allowed you to undress yourself in the state you were in." He took a bite of pie and washed it down with milk. "But, I must say, I am a bit surprised to find your choice of nightwear so conventional."

She looked down at her robe, snatched the sides together, and reddened.

"No bloomers?" His eyes roamed over her. "No woolly combinations or leather leggings or health suits? Not even a hair shirt?"

She scowled. "There is nothing unhealthy or uncomfortable about a regular nightdress. If a garment is already well designed, I will happily wear it."

"More's the pity," he said with insouciance. "I was rather looking forward to an entertaining episode with your nightwear."

She paused with her nose in her glass, then lowered it without drinking. "You really are the limit. How would you feel if someone made free with your most intimate garments?"

He chuckled. "I think I could bear up." He leaned toward her. "I might even come to like it—especially if I were wearing them at the time."

She felt her skin heating under his amusement, but, never one to shrink from a challenge, she returned his scrutiny. "You are without a doubt the most outrageously self-possessed human I have ever encountered."

"Don't get around much, do you?" His eyes twinkled; he was obviously enjoying himself.

"I'll wager you got by with murder as a child," she said. "Mama's favorite and Nanny's darling . . . born with a silver spoon in your mouth, never denied a thing. Spoiled rotten. Now you think you have only to wish a thing and you make it happen."

He stilled, and the light of amusement in his eyes became a focused gleam. Then he looked away with a wry twist of a smile. "Yes, that's me . . . spoiled forever by too much attention from the women in my early life. My lady mother and dear old nanny loved me so slavishly that I now expect every woman I meet to feel the same." He flashed her a look that was positively coquettish. "It's quite a burden actually, being this adorable."

She couldn't prevent the smile that tugged up the corners of her mouth. But even as she gave in to a laugh, it struck her that everything he said seemed to carry with it another, quite opposite meaning. It made her feel a twinge of sadness. She couldn't help recalling the pain she had glimpsed in him the other day. . . .

"But as to getting whatever I want just by wishing— you're wrong there, St. Madeline," he continued. "I'm afraid that getting what you want in life requires more than wishing, even for arrogant, overindulged aristo-brats."

"Oh?" She thought that over for a moment. "And what does 'getting what you want in life' require?"

"A providential birth, a handsome face, an extroverted nature, and an exceedingly thick skin." He assumed the pompous, faintly bored manner of an Oxford don. "One can survive a burden of intelligence if it is held closely in check. But scruples, ideals, sentiment"—he wagged his head—"those are generally insurmountable obstacles. Many a promising young life has been ruined by them."

"Including yours?" she asked, suddenly knowing the answer.

"Mine?" He hesitated, clearly trying to decide how much to say to her. "Very well. I make no secret of it. Shocking as it may seem, I was once a victim of idealism run amok myself. Against my family's wishes I studied for the bar and joined a firm of barristers. Interesting business, the law. For every yea there's a nay, for every absolute, an exception. One's opinion need never ever be wrong. And there is always plenty of quid pro quo to go around."

"Something for something," she translated.

"Ahhh, an educated woman. Assets. Transactions. Compensation. *Gain.*" He took a deep breath, and when he exhaled, some of the tension in his shoulders eased. "I wasn't especially quick to catch on to the way of things. Had those damned-fool ideals in my eyes. All I could think about was justice, equality, human dignity, making a difference in the world—that sort of nonsense." He fixed her with a gaze that reminded her of her scalding remarks on the stairs. "So you see, you aren't the first person ever to suffer delusions of a 'greater good.' "

She resisted an impulse to squirm. A cynic, she had heard long ago, was an idealist disappointed. Before her sat living proof of that old saw. His behavior suddenly made a strange kind of sense. She felt foolish for not seeing it earlier, for having made the wrong assumptions about him.

"I had no idea," she said gently.

"I'll take that as a compliment." He flashed a defiant grin.

She gave him a dark look. "What happened to dispel your 'delusions'?"

He finished his milk and sat searching the white puddle at the bottom of his glass. "Nothing. Everything. Things I wanted to do. Things I couldn't bear to do. The weight of a thousand little victories and a thousand little failures." He set his glass down and rubbed his hands down his thighs. "I simply woke up one day and realized that it wasn't going to change. That nothing I did would make that much difference. I began to see the world the way it is instead of the way I wanted it to be." Looking at her, he said quietly, "I strongly suggest you do the same."

His opinion of her had not changed, but understanding something of where it had come from softened its grating effect.

"I see the world realistically enough," she responded. "I know you think my workers are a shiftless lot looking for a soft bed and an easy meal. It's true that so far they haven't shown much initiative, but that is a quality that can be encouraged by example and opportunity. They have willing hearts and trainable hands and heads. That's all I ask. And if they nip a bit too much or nap occasionally, well, they will outgrow old habits when production gets under way."

He studied her. "I suppose you really believe that."

"I do."

"Then I'm afraid you're headed for heartache, St. Madeline."

She smiled. "Well, it is my heart after all. You do seem to keep forgetting that."

"No, I don't," he responded, his voice lower. "It's not possible to forget your heart for a moment."

"It's not?" She felt the organ under discussion beating erratically.

"It is always in plain sight." His mouth crooked up ruefully on one side. "On your sleeve."

The warmth in his voice sent a shiver along her shoulders. "If you are half as cynical as you'd like me to believe, why would you care what happens to my heart?"

His wry look smoothed into a sensual, teasing smile. "It is my duty, remember? I am required on penalty of imprisonment to report to the court regularly on the state of your heart. And on the success or failure of its magnanimous impulses."

"And what will you report this week?" She couldn't seem to break the spell of his gaze.

"That you're stubborn as hell, you work like a fiend, and you're in more trouble than you know."

No truer words were ever spoken, she realized, for she felt a delicious tingling in her lips even as he warned her to guard her heart.

"That is all? You won't tell Sir William about the progress we've made in renovating the factory, that the sewing room is nearly ready, or that we'll begin sample production next week?" She folded her arms and raised her chin. "That's hardly fair."

"If you insist upon thoroughness, I could also report on a costly water system that has yet to work, a garden in which the only thing growing seems to be a certain rock, and a fairly catastrophic mix-up regarding the materials you need for production. I would also be compelled to include an in-depth description of my examination of your 'sample' garments." He paused and gave her a heated look that set her pulse fluttering. "And a detailed account of our midnight meeting . . . in a darkened kitchen . . . in our nightclothes."

"Not true." She shrank back on her stool, glowering at his evening trousers and rumpled dress shirt. "*I* am in nightclothes, but you aren't."

"Oh, but I am. Beneath these clothes I wear precisely what I sleep in." He chuckled. "I can see you require proof." He stood and began to unbutton his shirt.

"No, no—" She stood up as well, feeling both excited and appalled, unable to tear her eyes from the slice of bare skin appearing between the parting edges of his shirt. Smooth, hard flesh, dusted with dark hair, glowing with male heat. What on earth was he—good Lord—did he mean to imply he slept in nothing but his skin? When she jerked her head up, his eyes were gleaming in a way that made her knees weak and her throat constrict. Her voice sounded hoarse and distant.

"Really, your lordship—"

"Don't you think it's time you called me Cole?" He reached for her hands. "Such formalities seem rather pointless when you've seen me in my . . . nightwear."

She would have pulled away, but he pressed a soft kiss into one of her palms and brought the other to his chest, spreading it against his open shirt so that her fingertips rested on his bare chest. That contact, restrained as it was, sent a volley of shock waves through her.

And through him. The touch of a woman's hand on his naked skin was more than familiar to him. But it hadn't prepared him for the effects of her tentative, whisper-light touch. Heat and chill raced through his skin, and a sweet ache began around his heart and slid slowly down toward his loins.

From the moment he had stepped out of the dark hallway into the circle of her lamp, he'd felt desire for her, drawing him. After dinner, when he'd "escorted" her to bed, it had been by the narrowest of margins that he hadn't taken advantage of her sweet vulnerability. He was spending altogether too much time thinking about her, watching her, arguing with her—and enjoying every bit of it.

Then he strolled into the kitchen and saw her curled up on that stool with her nightclothes swirled around her, her tousled hair gilded by lamplight, and her slender feet and ankles bare. The resolve he had been bolstering these last few hours in the library withered like a morning glory at midnight. He wanted nothing more than to take her into his arms.

Now she was there, in his embrace, soft and yielding, reminding him of things he knew spelled trouble. She was beguiling hope . . . sweet, deceptive dreams . . . a forbidden joy he had long since refused to seek. He ought to have known better—he *did* know better. She was a sure passage to despair. Pain just waiting to happen. And he was lowering his lips to hers, sinking into the lush comfort of her kiss, reclaiming the temptations of a sensual passion that led to feeling, then to caring, then to living . . . perhaps loving.

From the moment his lips touched hers, all rational thought dissolved. She could recall nothing in all her life that resembled the power of feeling him against her, the raw pleasure of skin against skin, the mysterious sweetness of warmth seeking warmth in another's being. His touch sent jolts of pleasure skittering along her muscles and racing through her nerves. Each motion, each nuance of texture and pressure, became a template for the one to follow. And each that followed added a wealth of new sensation to the storehouse of pleasures she was discovering inside her.

When the kiss ended, she staggered back. She could scarcely focus her eyes, but some inner compass turned her toward the door.

His grip on her hand halted her, and when she turned to him, he reeled her back and pulled her into his arms.

"Ah, St. Madeline, you're a pure temptation, you are."

Their second embrace was somehow softer, sweeter than the first. His lips raked hers ever so lightly, preparing her, provoking her response, holding the sweet completion of a full kiss just out of reach. He held her lightly, teasing and toying with her lips until she slid her arms around his ribs and rocked up onto her toes to meet him as an equal, responding as she had just been taught. They explored the feel of each other, kissing again and again—short, playful nips and soft, resonant strokes and slow, deep joining.

When he released her, she turned once again for the door, floating, unable to feel the floor beneath her feet. The boundaries of her body seemed to have dissolved. She was air and element, free, unencumbered—until she felt his hand on her wrist and realized he was going through the door ahead of her, pulling her into the darkness of the hallway with him.

This time, when his arms closed around her they bore her back against the wall and clasped her fiercely. His mouth came down on hers with full hunger, taking the sweetness of

her tongue, claiming the moist recesses of her, burning his
need into her lips, her mind, her heart. This time, as his body
pressed hers his hands moved feverishly over her shape, exploring her, learning her through her thin garments. He cir-
cled her waist, ran his hands up her ribs to cup her breasts,
then slid them down her back to clasp her buttocks, murmuring approval of all he encountered.

She was suddenly on fire, trembling, learning the sleek
skin and crisp hair of his chest, the strong column of his throat,
the coarse rasp of beard on his jaw. He tasted the same salty-
sweet as before, only now with mulberries and milk. She was
suddenly ravenous with unrecognized need. Arching, thrust-
ing toward his hands, she moaned softly when his fingers
found the burning tips of her breasts. Pleasure washed through
her in lush, drenching waves that drained slowly through her
body, leaving a delicious heaviness, a longing in its wake.
More. She wanted more. . . .

When he raised his head to search their surroundings for
a more accommodating situation, he was surprised to realize
they were in the hallway, coupled fiercely while pressed hard
against the side of the stairs. It took only a moment for the
surprise to mature into a recognition that things could go no
further there. He stepped back enough to allow her to regain
her balance, and she swayed against him.

Steadying her, he took a deep breath and struggled for
control. With his eyes now adjusted to the darkness, he could
see her plainly—glowing skin, a torrent of dark hair, a pale
nightdress hanging askew on her shoulders. She was nothing
short of adorable, especially now, looking love-warmed and
rumpled, her eyes glistening with new passion. Passion.

Merciful God. What had he done?

A moment later she tried once again to withdraw gracefully. With her head up and her robe hanging precariously
from only one shoulder, she glided down the hall, turned too
early, and smacked straight into the thick, carved banister.

"Ohhh!" She recoiled, rubbing her head, and he lurched to her side to see if she was all right.

"Lord—let me see," he demanded, prying her fingers from her head.

"It's fine . . . it's nothing . . . really." Her voice was breathy and distracted, but he couldn't feel a knot forming on her forehead. He tilted her chin to look into her eyes and she gave him a glowing, somewhat unfocused look that warmed into a dazed smile.

"Bloody hell," he groaned, taking her hand and pulling her around the banister to the bottom of the stairs. "Come on, I'll see you up the steps."

But, in fact, he saw her to her door, into her room itself, and even pulled back the covers of her bed for her. Then he performed the alarmingly gallant act of turning on his heel and leaving her there, on her bed, alone.

She sat for a while with a radiant countenance, her eyes half closed, holding on to the sensations of his kisses. As they faded, she began to feel the cold floor and the soft bed beneath her. Reality gradually returned, and, shivering, she slid her legs between the bedclothes and lay back on the pillows. These were wonderfully contradictory feelings—cold and hot, aching and soothed, uncomfortable and yet oddly pleasant. Combined, they created a breathtaking sensual arousal. Desire.

Long ago she had read and thought about pleasure, and had sensibly consigned it to that region in her being where she kept unsolvable quandaries and irrelevancies. Sexual passion was a curious and confusing part of human life, a basic animal instinct that she had been grateful not to have to deal with. The destiny she had inherited and the path she had chosen both seemed to call her beyond such an expression of humanity's most rudimentary nature. Her life was to be about service and giving and helping.

Just now, however, passion seemed anything but basic or animal or irrelevant. It was overwhelming and complex and enthralling. And so very personal. Why, there must be millions of variations on just a kiss. And imagine the delight of discovering, of exploring every single one of them with—

Oh, dear.

In London, Sir William sat in his chambers that same night, his gouty foot propped up on a stack of pillows on the ottoman and two oil lamps blazing on his desk. In the midst of a veritable deluge of legal papers, he held a pair of letters in one hand and wiped his eyes with the other.

"She's a raving madwoman and he's a bloody beast," he said to his clerk Foglethorpe, then went off in another booming peal of laughter. When he sobered, he stared at the writing once more and sighed wistfully. "I would give my good foot to be a fly on the wall when those two go at it."

8

The sun had been up for more than an hour when Rupert Fitch-cum-Fitzwater sauntered down the lane toward the tavern anticipating a breakfast of that juicy sausage and onion gallimaufry that was Hiram Netter's morning specialty. He paused by the muddy trench that divided the village and stared at the lengths of pipe strewn about the bottom. A glint appeared in his eyes. He fished a small pad from one pocket, produced a pencil from another, and began to scribble a few notes. It wasn't enough to base a newspaper exposé upon, but in his business every little bit helped.

He was still scribbling when the morning air brought him the sound of a door closing across the way. He looked up to witness Miss Madeline Duncan exiting her house in something of a hurry, her head down and her shawl pulled tightly about her. Since it wasn't a particularly cool morning, her appearance and behavior struck him as odd. And "odd" always brought Rupert Fitch to attention and set his nose to the air for a whiff of scandal.

As he watched, the front door of her fine brick house opened and out stalked none other than his high-and-mightyship, Lord Mandeville, clad in riding breeches, boots, and a shirt that was scarcely half buttoned. Rupert Fitch had made a career out of creative arithmetic; in his tallying, one and one always made at least four. From Cole Mandeville's tousled appearance, Fitch deduced that he was recently risen. And from the fact that he appeared half clothed in Madeline Duncan's doorway, Fitch deduced just where the young lord had been abed. Those two conclusions, in the fetid slurry of Fitch's mind, brought forth a vile third—about the source of the lord's annoyance.

"So," he muttered, his eyes lighting with prurient glee as he added some hasty scratching to his open and receptive pad, "she's found a way to make his lordship come to heel, has she? Smart girl. A pity she ain't learned to use the *back* door for such capers."

After a few more strokes he looked at what he had written and smiled broadly, showing his yellowed teeth. "She'll learn." Folding the pad and tucking it securely away, he shoved his hands into his trouser pockets and strolled on toward Netter's Tavern, whistling. "She'll learn."

By midmorning the sewing floor was again chaotic, filled with sounds of talk and movement and sawing and hammering mingled with the scent of oiled metal and the acrid smell of turpentine. While the place was being cleared of debris from the frenzy of unpacking on the day before, bleary-eyed Fritz and his newly arrived mechanic tried to concentrate on attaching sewing machines to the power takeoff, and the Ketchums worked to repair the steps and paint the windows. Adding to the confusion were Maple Thoroughgood and Charlotte, who were trying to outtalk the noise to instruct their seamstresses in the cleaning and preparation of the new sewing machines. Their job was made harder by the fact that the sewing floor was overrun with new cutters and pressers, who hoisted a crate here and moved a table or a bit of packing material there but generally spent most of their time visiting with their new neighbors and distracting the seamstresses with their comments and laughter. Meanwhile, a harassed Daniel Steadman was steering cutter candidates, recently come down from London, in and out of the offices to be enrolled as new employees.

In the midst of it all Madeline was trying to keep both things and people moving in the right direction. Early that morning, before anyone else arrived, she had stood surveying the littered sewing floor and assessing the previous day's work. In her mind she identified several key mistakes she had made in structuring the tasks and atmosphere, and she was determined not to repeat them.

Straightaway she had taken Maple and Daniel and Fritz aside and delegated tasks for the day, emphasizing how much she counted on them to see things through. Then she positioned herself in the main entry, directing everyone reporting for work to the appropriate floor and supervisor. It should have functioned like a clockwork. And it did . . . for nearly an hour.

What she hadn't counted on was the free migration between floors and work areas. No one seemed to stay at their post for very long. Then there was the disconcerting influx of children, who in addition to the noise and injury hazards they created posed a considerable distraction to mothers and their fellow workers. She peeled little ones from walls, windows, and machinery; wiped wet paint from sticky hands; and sent group after group outside to play, where they were promptly evicted from the rear garden or extricated from the muddy trench in front and sent back inside to their mothers.

Cole had to wade hip-deep through children playing on the stairs as he made his way to the offices. They stared at him, pulled on his coat, and asked bold as brass, "Where'd ye nick them boots?" He managed to extricate himself and made it most of the way up the stairs before a toddler, still un-breeched, took a fancy to his glossy footgear and attached himself bodily to Cole's leg.

Unable to detach the child without provoking a pitched fit, Cole was forced to carry the child along to the office, where he demanded: "Will someone please get this creature *off my leg?*"

Madeline, who had seen him limping across the sewing floor and into the office, groaned quietly and handed Maple Thoroughgood the sewing machine instruction sheet she had been reading aloud. After their intimate encounter the previous night, facing Cole under any circumstance was going to be uncomfortable. But in the middle of a situation she herself found nearly intolerable . . . she would rather have had a few molars extracted.

After locating the child's mother and peeling the toddler's grubby little fingers from his boot, she stood and faced him, expecting the worst. He did not disappoint her.

"What in infernal blazes are all those br—children doing here? It's a madhouse out there!" he roared.

"A slight miscalculation," she said, picking up some papers from Tattersall's vacant desk and pretending to be more interested in them than in his developing tirade. "The workers I hired in London turned out to be a bit more . . . *productive* . . . than I realized."

"The hell they are!" He flung a finger toward the sewing floor. "Faces are the only thing that scurvy lot know how to produce. And hungry mouths. You cannot seriously expect to get anything done with herds of wild offspring rampaging through the factory at will. Something must be done."

"They are hardly rampaging at will," she declared. She forced herself to look directly at him, hoping her all-too-vivid recollections of the night before did not show in her face. "Something will be done. I have already set in motion a plan for dealing with our Ideal children. Unfortunately, the schoolmaster and schoolmistress I have engaged will not arrive for another month." She glanced toward the gaggle of children hanging on the coat hooks and climbing about on chairs stacked against the far wall of the sewing room. "I hadn't counted on quite so many children, or on providing a school for them quite so soon."

"A schoolmaster?" He eyed the ragged and quarrelsome bunch tussling for a place on the top chair of the stack. "You must be joking. You're going to try to teach *that* lot the three Rs?"

"Education is the very foundation of civilization, Lord Mandeville."

"Of all the cockeyed, harebrained ideas of yours, this has to be the most idiotic. It's not enough that you give them houses and food and jobs, you have to keep their blessed brats occupied too!" He reddened and fished about in the inner breast pocket of his coat for an envelope. "Very well—here it is." He slapped the envelope into her hand. At her frown of confusion, he told her, "It's all the rope you'll need. Try not to hang yourself with it."

She watched him stride across the sewing floor and battle his way down the steps before opening the envelope. In it was a letter to the officers of the Bank of England authorizing carte blanche whatever drafts she would make against the encumbered funds of her trust. He was giving her the money she needed for the replacement cloth and anything else she might want. Why?

Why now? She scowled, realizing he must have written the letter sometime that morning. After last night. After he had tempted and tantalized her, enjoyed and explored her. Was it payment for services rendered or something to oil the way for future liberties? She should probably hand it right back to him, let him know she wasn't for sale, not even for a "greater good." But if she did refuse it, how would she fund her factory, her dream? Was she going to let a bit of pride ruin everything?

Blast his dark heart! When did everything get to be so

complicated? He had just managed to make her first major victory too fraught with worries to enjoy.

It was just past noon, and many of the workers were heading home for a bit of dinner, when Emily Farrow's boys came racing up the main stairs, wailing and sobbing as if their hearts were breaking. They were so loud that every woman on the sewing floor turned to see what was going on.

Jonathan's and Theodore's velvet jackets were ripped, their lace collars hung in tatters, and their mud-caked lisle stockings flapped on their legs, trailing from their ruined black slippers. Worse yet, their shoulder-length curls were smeared with mud and a hank of Jonathan's hair, near his face, was missing altogether.

Emily heard their cries and ran from the office to meet them. They threw themselves into her arms and wailed that they had been attacked by bigger boys.

The women left their stations to investigate. Most were mothers themselves, and there was a wide range of emotions in their faces as they watched Emily's reaction to her children's story.

"Th-they called us sissies and nancy boys," Jonathan gasped out.

"Th-threw mud . . . an' knocked us down an' tore our clothes." The tears from Theodore's big blue eyes left clear tracks on his mud-streaked cheeks.

Emily raised an anguished face to Madeline. "This isn't the first time this has happened, Miss Duncan. My poor, sweet babies—something must be done this time!"

Madeline groaned privately. This was all she needed—to have to mediate childhood squabbles on top of everything else. Trying to think what to do, she knelt by Jonathan and Theodore and lifted their faces. "Who did it? Do you know their names?"

Both boys shook their heads and burrowed into their

mother's shoulders with fresh wails and sobs. Madeline rose and looked in appeal at the other women. They regarded her with blank looks and skeptical frowns.

"Well, I'm afraid we can't do much unless we know who the culprits are. But I think this is a good opportunity for all of you to speak to your children about—"

"Oh, but we do know who the culprits are," came a booming male voice from across the sewing room. The women parted to reveal Cole striding toward them, dragging a mud-caked urchin in each hand. He hauled them up before Madeline and released them with a glare that warned them to stay put. "They're right here," he declared, then pointed to Emily's boys. "And right there."

"Wh-what?" Emily pushed to her feet, paling, and pulled her children tighter against her. "That's absurd. One look at my poor babies proves they are the victims!"

"And one look at these two will reveal the damage your two inflicted," Cole countered.

Before Madeline stood two shoeless young boys, eight or nine years old, wearing cast-off adult breeches cinched with frayed cord, oversized shirts hanging half off their shoulders, and a generous smattering of drying mud. Their clothes were ripped in places. Beneath their defiant eyes they had nasty scratches on their cheeks.

"Jack? Willie? Why, them's my—" Bess Clark hurried from the far side of the worktables, bringing several others with her. She stopped just before she reached her offspring and folded her arms. "Whad've ye been up to?"

"Nothin', Ma, honest," one said, cowering behind his older brother.

"It weren't us. Them's what started it!" The older one pointed at Emily's boys. "Called us gutter wipes an' whop-straws, poked fun at our clothes." He hitched up his oversized pants with a defensive glower and pressed his arms to his waist as if trying to hide his rope belt. "They said we wus ragpickers, thick wi' fleas."

"An' lousy," the smaller one put in. "I ain't got no lice—look, see!" He offered his head for inspection, but all attention was turning to the spectacle of his mother's reddening face and blazing eyes.

"Snooty little tits." She glared at Emily's boys, causing them to shrink against their mother. "Call my boys names, will ye? Deserved a right good thrashin' if'n ye ask me." She pulled her offspring to her sides by their ears. "Fancy little nibs in their velvet 'n lace—think they're better'n the rest, do they? I could show 'em *better*—"

Madeline was suddenly caught between two furious mothers: Emily Farrow and Bess Clark, scowling at each other, each threatening to take the other's children in hand if they weren't rightly punished. The rest of the women murmured to one another, frowning and beginning to take sides.

"Look at Jonathan's and Theodore's clothes!" Emily insisted, outraged.

"Look at Jack's an' Willie's faces!" Bess countered. "Them two went for blood!"

"It seems to me"—Cole's booming voice halted every word mid-utterance—"that both pairs got in a few good licks."

"They cut my Jonnie's hair!" Emily held up the truncated lock.

"Them two blacked little Willie's eye!" Bess grabbed the boy's face and thrust it out in evidence.

"While I was out walking the grounds, I happened to see what occurred," Cole announced, his expression daring anyone to contest it. "There was an inadvertent trip . . . a bit of laughter, a few taunts . . . a shove, then a shove back. Before long all four were on the ground, thrashing and scratching and flailing, until they rolled down into the mud of the watermain trench. From what I saw, they bear equal blame. Of course, it's not up to me to decide what should be done."

When he looked to Madeline, laying the problem squarely at her feet, the others did too. She stood for a mo-

ment, trying to look composed and thoughtful while frantically trying to think of where to go from there. A moment
later she came to life and addressed first Emily, then Bess
Clark.

"Take your boys home and get them cleaned up, both
of you. I'll see the lot of you in my office tomorrow morning,
first thing." She broadened her orders to include the others.
"Until then, I suggest that all of you give your children a
sound bit of parental guidance on the virtues of tolerance and
charity."

Emily seemed shaken by Madeline's stern look, her hands
trembling as she ushered her darlings to the stairs. Bess gave
the closest of her boys a flip on the ear to get him moving
and could be heard railing at the pair as they tromped down
the rear steps. Afterward, Madeline bid the others return to
work, then headed to her office for a minute's peace.

"You see what's happening, don't you?" Cole said. She
turned to find him leaning a shoulder against the door frame,
wearing a knowing look.

"You were a fat lot of help," she said irritably.

"You're welcome. It's jealousy pure and simple, you
know. With helpings of envy and distrust and prejudice
thrown in for good measure." When she scowled, he clari-
fied: "It's a quintessential clash of classes, St. Madeline. Probably inevitable in this unlikely stew of workers and
management you're brewing up. Little Fauntleroy Farrows
don't bide well alongside the guttersnipe Clarks of this
world—and vice versa."

Was he taunting her or offering her insight? "They're
just boys. They don't have a class," she insisted.

"What cave have you been living in? Some boys are born
with a burden of wealth, some with a burden of poverty, but
all bear the weight of their father's class on their shoulders
from the minute they are born. I should know . . ." He
looked as if he might say more, his eyes suddenly darkening
with something remembered. Then he gave her a taunting

smile and turned to go. "You have a problem on your hands, St. Madeline."

So she did. She sat down in her padded chair and closed her eyes. She had anticipated a vast array of pitfalls and problems, but this was certainly not one of them. She hadn't bargained on quite so many children, or on a children's squabble rousing such resentment and division between adults. Much as she hated to admit it, Cole was right; this had to be quashed before it affected morale. She had to do something. But what?

Who would have thought that something as ridiculous as children's clothes could possibly pose a thr—

Clothes, ridiculous?

That brought her up short. Why would children's clothes be any less important than men's and women's? Clothing certainly played a huge part in limiting the lives of women. That was what her venture was all about—freeing women from the tyranny of their garments. But what about freeing children from the tyranny of their garments?

Now that she thought about it, there were a number of people in the dress reform movement who had taken up the issue of restrictive children's clothing. In the middle and upper classes, many children were corseted and bound to backboards from an early age. And one look at Emily's boys—with their tight velvet coats and delicate lace collars, their long curls and prissy black slippers—illustrated how absurd children's fashions could be.

Madeline headed for the sample room, where she did her best thinking.

"You want what?" chief designer Endicott said, blinking in disbelief. "When?"

"Final sketches and pattern pieces. By tomorrow morning." She gave him a look of unadulterated faith and expectation. "I know it's a lot to ask, but I really need something to show them. You have such a genius for analyzing a garment and knowing just what pieces would be needed where. I did some calculations and I think we'll need only three sizes of each. The rest can be altered up or down from them."

He gave her a narrow look, then glanced at the fading light coming through the windows. "But it would mean working half the night! And you know how I need my sleep," he moaned. "I'm just no good at all without eight blissful hours in the arms of Morpheus." Looking back at her and at the drawings she clutched against her, he winced. After a moment his shoulders rounded, and he held out a hand for the sketchbook. "All right, then, give them to me. I probably wouldn't sleep a wink tonight anyway, for seeing that woebegone look on your face every time I closed my eyes."

The next morning the seamstresses reported promptly at eight for work, but their minds were not on learning to use the machines with which they would earn their living. Their true attention was on the office door, where both Emily Farrow and Bessie Clark disappeared at Madeline's bidding.

When they reappeared sometime later, they looked solemn and subdued. Before questions could be asked, Madeline Duncan directed everyone down the stairs and into the classroom. There she laid out for them a proposal that took them all by surprise.

"I've had a wonderful idea that may solve many of our problems. You need something to work on as you become familiar with the machines, and we need to do something about the children's clothing problem. With that in mind, it struck me that children are just as much in need of sensible clothing as women are. So with the benefit of Endicott's creative genius, we have come up with an Ideal design for children! As it happens, we have a generous supply of the very fabric most recommended for active and growing children: woollen jersey."

Her face alight with excitement she opened her sketch-book to the first design, a middy blouse and trousers for boys.

It was greeted by silence and blank looks.

After a few moments one woman declared: "Why . . . it looks like a sailor's shirt 'cept for th' color."

"Because that's exactly what it is," Madeline responded, refusing to be dismayed by their lack of enthusiasm. "It's made of sturdy woolen jersey with a healthful give, to allow for boys to climb and run and move easily. And it has doubled knees to cut down on repairs."

Still the women hesitated, some trying to be polite, others blatantly skeptical and shaking their heads.

"The first to wear these garments will be your very own children. The children of St. Crispin will all be wearing *equally* new and *equally* attractive clothing. Never again will any child look down on another because of what he is wearing."

"Yer sayin' ye want to dress our young 'uns like swag-gerin' tars?" Bessie asked.

"Hardly like swaggering tars . . ." she replied, taken aback by the question and the attitude behind it. Before she could continue, Cole Mandeville strolled into the room and she had the distinct impression that he had been eavesdrop-ping for some time.

"Well. I was passing and heard what you said about your little project," he declared, sauntering over to take the sketch from her. A look of indignation dawned on his face as he studied it. "You propose to make *these* for the local children?"

"I do," she said irritably. Oh, why couldn't he leave well enough alone!

"Surely this is a jest. You know perfectly well you cannot make clothes like this for . . . ragamuffins." He tossed a haughty glance at her seamstresses. "Why, the queen herself designed these suits for the princes royal some years back. Since then they've been stitched by only the finest tailors and reserved for only the noblest of families. It would be unthink-able to dress *these* children like princes of the realm."

His words and his arrogant attitude, displayed so callously before the children's mothers' eyes, were the last straw.

"I based my design on those sailor suits, but there are important differences—improvements, in fact. And just who do you think you are to come waltzing in and tell me what I can and cannot produce? If I want to dress our Ideal children like princes of the realm, it's no blessed business of yours. You're here to oversee and advise—not to establish yourself as the Ideal arbiter of class distinctions!"

She pointed to the door. "If you don't mind, your lordship, we are trying to do something useful and productive here, and we don't need interference."

His smile did not seem at all abashed. He bowed with a degree of irony and obligingly made his exit.

Madeline took a moment to collect herself after he had gone, then turned back to her seamstresses. It seemed to her that their expressions had changed. They were now looking at her as if to their savior or champion.

"And what about the girls?" asked a woman from the back. "What would they wear, Miss Duncan?"

Madeline released the breath she had been holding and hurried to pull out another sketch, a clever dropped-waist dress with a pleated skirt and a sailor's collar.

"I had this in mind for the girls."

The collective oohs and nods and smiles were gratifying. Madeline began to relax.

"There are several variations on this basic design that would allow for individual tastes. Would you care to see?"

That night Beaumont Tattersall returned from London in a wagon laden with bolts of bleached muslin and fine-gauge cotton knit. He had managed to strike a deal with a cloth jobber, even convincing the fellow to accept a postdated bank draft.

When the wagon load of fabric pulled up before Madeline's house, it was a welcome excuse to avoid having dinner with Cole. She spent the better part of the evening inspecting the new cloth and supervising Maple Thoroughgood as she tried out one of the sewing machines to make sample garments. Things went fairly well and the hours slipped by. It was late indeed when she returned to the house. Catching sight of a lamp burning in the library window, she hurried straight up to bed without a stop in the kitchen.

The next morning she rose a bit before her customary hour of seven and grabbed a mug of coffee and a leftover scone on the way out the rear kitchen door, thus avoiding an encounter with Cole over breakfast. She had a great deal to do and the thought of starting her day with a fiery confrontation was less than appealing. His behavior the previous day in the classroom was unforgivable. And coming so soon after he had given her the financial freedom she so desperately wanted and needed, it was also incomprehensible. Unless— the ugly thought arose in her—he did think that if she had plenty of financial rope, she truly would hang herself.

More troubling, however, was the question of what had happened to him between that night in the kitchen and the very next morning. That night he had been the very essence of roguish warmth and reckless tenderness. He had teased and talked with her, dazzled her with the pleasures he summoned from within her, and then gallantly refused to take advantage of her vulnerable state. The next morning he was a changed man; scowling, contemptuous, and eager to challenge her and find fault with everything he laid eyes upon—even children, for heaven's sake!

It was as if in the mere act of rising, shaving, and dressing he had recalled who and what he was and what he— The act of dressing? She thought about that for a moment. Was it possible that in buttoning himself up in his too-tight vest and wrapping himself in a restrictive collar he somehow squeezed and stifled his better nature?

As she stood musing on that fanciful thought, she suddenly realized she was standing in the future garden, staring at the sunken boulder that had grown to massive proportions in the past two days. It seemed the more Roscoe, Algy, and that new fellow dug, the more they had to dig. There was now a crater at least twelve feet in diameter and at least four feet deep at the sides surrounding that accursed hunk of mineral. She frowned, thinking she could just as well have done without her precious "cursantheemums" if she had known they were going to cause this much trouble.

Walking around that massive hole, contemplating it, she decided to take another look at the plans she had commissioned to see if there wasn't something she might do with that huge, annoying rock besides dig it up.

Just as she was turning toward the factory door, Roscoe and Algy came around the corner of the factory, yawning and stretching and having a good morning scratch on their way to work. When Roscoe spotted her, he gave Algy a thump on the shoulder to bring him alert, and together they hurried to intercept her.

"Mornin', miz," Roscoe called. "Out an' about—givin' 'er a look-see?"

"Good morning!" she called, halting and looking back at the garden. "Not much to see except that awful rock." She grew pensive. "At this rate you'll never get it out of there. I was just thinking . . . perhaps I should look at the plans to see if there is something we might be able to do around it—or with it."

Roscoe looked troubled in the extreme. "But what about yer cursantheemums, miz? Ye had yer heart set on cursantheemums—I know ye did."

Her head was beginning to ache; she rubbed her temples. "Yes, yes, well, the reality seems to be that I won't have *cursantheemums,* at least not there." She sighed. "I'll get over it. Right now it's more important to see some progress, and if you can't—"

"Oh, but we can, miz," Roscoe assured her. "We'll soon

have 'er shifted outta here. A sixteen-man rock takes a bit o' time, ye know."

She studied both Roscoe's genial face and Algy's habitually doleful one, then looked back at the rock and the trench growing around it. "All right, a few more days. But I don't want to get past prime planting. I want to see a few flowers here before autumn."

The pair watched her pull her shawl close about her and walk into the factory. Roscoe rubbed his stubbled chin and frowned, while Algy fidgeted beside him.

"What'll we do, Roscoe?" Algy finally broke the silence.

"We be good for a few more days, I reckon," Roscoe answered, walking over to the edge of the crater to study the situation. After a few minutes of deep contemplation, he wagged a finger. "You know, Alg, I bet we *could* move this here rock . . . if'n we wuz to try."

"Move it?" It seemed a rather radical concept to Algy. "How?"

"Hell, them engineer fellers does it all the time. If th' likes o' them can, *we* can." He pulled his coat aside and stuck his thumbs in his braces. His eyes narrowed. "Know what the secret to movin' a big rock is, Alg?"

"What, Roscoe?" Algy listened with widened eyes.

"*Horses,*" Roscoe announced. "An' plenty of 'em."

9

The factory was humming that morning when Cole arrived. There were still children everywhere, but there seemed to be more industry about the place. When he looked into the cutting room on his way upstairs, he was surprised to see the tables fully assembled and being waxed by several men under the direction of Daniel Steadman. In the middle of the tables, down a center alley left to provide access to the mechanical shafts, Fritz Gonnering and his beleaguered new assistant were working feverishly over some machine.

Cole paused to watch the engineer, whose eyes were red but whose hands seemed as steady as a village parson's. He couldn't help noting the expert way the German handled his tools and the intensity with which he became absorbed in his work. Cole had to admit that despite his drinking, the man had managed to accomplish a great deal. His mechanical cutting system, if it worked, was a genuine innovation.

After studying it awhile, he saw Fritz coming out of the center alley and strolled over to ask him a few questions. The engineer was explaining to him that his center shaft and belt system was also being tried on the Continent, when there was a cry of terror from overhead. All eyes turned upward to see little Theodore Farrow hanging from one of the rafters—just above a whirling metal shaft fitted with spinning wheels and belts.

Cole called for him to hang on. Other men broke out in shouts and confusion, some climbing up on tables to try to reach him. Cole gave Fritz a shove, ordered him to disengage the power shaft. But even as Fritz raced off, one of the boy's shoes fell off and into the main mechanism, dislodging belts and sending pieces of shredded shoe flying in all directions. Would-be rescuers went scrambling off the tables, dodging and ducking.

Before the leather had stopped flying, Cole had ripped off his coat and was charging across the tables and up onto the machine frame between spinning wheels and flapping belts. As he climbed steadily higher, there were gasps and mutters from those below. When he was as high as he could go, he stretched taut, grabbed the boy's foot, then secured a hold on his calf, then thigh. "Let go—I have you!"

It took some desperate coaxing, but Theodore finally gave up his grip on the beam. They teetered precariously for a moment as Cole struggled to keep his balance and lower the boy at the same time. Only when the child was safe against him did he glance down at his precarious footing . . . on metal braces no more than three or four inches wide, with a power shaft and wheels grinding along only an inch from the toes of his boots, eight feet off the floor.

There were gasps and shouts of "careful now!" as he began to make his way back down the machinery, finding footholds where there seemed to be none. By the time he was once more on the floor, the pulley wheels were finally slowing and the men were converging on him, laughing in astonishment and exclaiming over what they'd just witnessed. He set the weeping Theodore on a tabletop and barked out:

"What in hell possessed you to climb up there in the first place?"

"I—I j-just wanted to see what it was l-like—"

Cole gave a snort of disgust and thrust the boy into someone's arms, ordering: "Here—take 'Christopher Columbus' here to his mother . . . and tell her to keep him under lock and key." Then he grabbed his coat and strode out.

It wasn't until he was well away from the factory, headed up a slope overlooking the village, that he began to calm down and think about what had happened. As he recalled balancing above the whirling machinery, he suffered a startling upsurge of old memories. Grinding gears and shafts, standing above them on a narrow bar of metal, watching the blades twisting and turning below . . .

Something heavy settled in his chest, squeezing his lungs. Recollections mingled powerfully with present sense—fields of ripened grain, the scent of the dust and the sweet smell of straw as it was cut, the feel of the sun pricking his skin, the chunk of metal gears, groan of wheels, shoosh of blades, and the creak of harness as the reaper turned at the ends of the rows.

He had stood on the top of the mechanical harvester, hanging on, balancing like a tightrope walker, waiting for John Macmillan to stop and order him and Little John down to clear out the rocks and debris that had jammed the machinery. Even on that first day he hadn't been at all afraid of the height or the whir and snap of the blades; he had felt only a sense of mastery, a pride in being truly good at something. At the end of the day John Macmillan had chuckled at his bravado and called him a born daredevil.

He remembered it as if it had all happened yesterday, with recall so vivid that the re-experienced joy and freedom and sense of belonging made him tremble. And hurt.

Rolling his shoulders to shake off those troublesome feelings, he struggled to shove the memories back into the darkest, most remote recesses of his being. He hadn't thought of those days in years—never so vividly. He looked over at the factory building nestled in the valley below, and blamed it and the idealist who ran it for that unnerving remembrance.

Damn and blast, he thought. Her and her precious workers, with their scores of brats climbing all over, running thither and yon without the slightest supervision. The boy might easily have been maimed or killed. Someone had to talk some sense into that woman, and since he appeared to be the only one around with the slightest grounding in reality, it looked like he would have to be that someone. He started back, determined to corner St. Madeline of the Young and Reckless and read her the riot act.

Nearing the factory, he heard a commotion like a scuffling and several raised voices coming from the gardens and quickened his step. Thuds and jangles that sounded like harness noise reached him just before he rounded the bushes and stepped into the main clearing. He was greeted by the sight of four men, two of whom he recognized as Madeline's "gardeners," exhorting two massive horses in heavy harness to pull harder on a set of ropes and log chains that seemed to be attached to nothing at all.

It dawned on him that those ropes were likely attached to the infamous "rock" in the middle of the garden—if it could be called a garden. Just then it resembled more a construction site on the London Metropolitan Railway. Huge piles of dirt were banked up on two sides and the shrubs and greenery already present had been trampled beyond recognition. Digging tools were scattered higgledy-piggledy all around, and in the middle sat the largest single boulder Cole had ever seen.

He watched the horses straining and the men adding their efforts on the ropes, all to no avail. He strolled closer and climbed up a mound of dirt to get a closer look. The amount of rope they had tied around the rock would have rigged a full-sized clipper ship. Calling a halt to rest and assess their progress, they noticed him standing nearby, and Roscoe and

Algy came climbing out of the hole, wiping their brows of something Cole was certain must be a novelty for them: honest sweat.

"Yes sir." Roscoe struck a pose, stuck his thumbs under his braces, and surveyed with great pride the chaos they had created. "A right good bit o' work, haulin' out that there rock. A twenty-manner, we reckon."

"Well," Cole responded dryly, "at least we know it's more than a four-man-two-horse-er." That seemed to make perfect sense to Algy, who nodded earnestly. "Horses are the traditional method, of course. But I am a bit surprised to find you using only two."

"Two was all we could get, sir. Seems there's a right good bit o' plowing goin' on." Roscoe looked perfectly serious as he concluded: " 'Cause it's spring, we reckon."

"Most likely." Cole cleared his throat of the smile he had swallowed. "Still . . . four or six horses would give you more force and better leverage."

He left them there, pondering that jewel of advice, and told himself he had nothing to feel guilty about if they went rampaging about the countryside pilfering horses and got caught and were hanged. He would probably have done St. Madeline a favor.

Madeline stood in the middle of the sample room with her hands pressed to her temples, feeling both taut and frazzled, trying to think what to do next. The cutters were trying out Fritz's new system on the patterns for the children's clothing, and it seemed to be working. As pieces came up from the floor below, the seamstresses were starting to put them together with the new sewing machines, which were proving quite usable. Maple Thoroughgood was working hard to construct the samples of her bust bodices and knickers—they would be finished anytime now. Mr. Gibbons had assured her the water system was coming along and would be ready for another—hopefully final—test by the following day. Looking out the sample room window, she saw activity in the garden below, and even if she couldn't tell quite what it was, it still felt reassuring.

For the moment everyone was actually busy. If Cole Mandeville were to come swaggering in just then, she thought, he wouldn't have a single thing to complain about.

Cole did come through the door a heartbeat later, and from the tone of his voice as it drifted back from the outer office it seemed he had managed to find something to annoy him. The knot that had begun to loosen in her middle now cinched tight again.

"There you are," he announced from the doorway. She turned and found him filling the opening—and only avenue of escape—with his excessively wide shoulders and long legs. His face was ruddy and he was breathing hard, most likely from a quick trip up the stairs. "I have something to discuss with you."

"When don't you?" she muttered.

"Something must be done about the children running hog-wild about this factory," he declared irritably. "They are a pure menace to life and limb. Just a short while ago one of the little wretches slipped off one of the rafters above the cutting room floor and narrowly missed being chewed up and spat out by Gonnering's machinery."

She scowled. "Theodore. Yes, I heard. But they said he was only—"

"They clog the stairs, distract the workers, poke fingers and God knows what else into every available hole, nook, and cranny—even the machinery. They handle and smudge and plunder and mess—even as we speak, half a dozen of the littlest ones are crawling around the sewing room floor, leaving highly suspicious puddles in their wake." He looked with indignation at his besmirched footgear. "A fellow never knows what he'll shove a boot into from one step to the next—"

"Are you quite finished?" She folded her arms to keep them from doing something she might regret later.

"Almost." He stalked into the room, seeming to push all the air out as he advanced. "This impromptu little scheme of yours—to level society and equalize the social classes by giving them all the same thing to wear—won't work."

"You think not?"

"If it were that simple to erase class distinctions—providing that such a thing is even *desirable*—it would have been done long ago."

"Those women out there"—she strode toward the door, pointing to the sewing room—"are delighted with the prospect of making garments for their children . . . of seeing them in sensible, long-wearing, and yet stylish clothing. Come and see, if you don't—"

"Of course they're pleased." He caught her by the arm and pulled her back. "They're getting something for nothing. You're providing the designs, the cloth, and machines—hell, you're even paying them wages to produce the bloody things. And in the end, what will be any different?" He loosened his grip. "Nothing, that's what. The Farrows and the Clarks of this world will still call each other names and push each other into mud puddles, and you will be even deeper out of pocket." He caught her gaze briefly in his and released her. "They won't even thank you for it, St. Madeline."

"I don't expect thanks," she said, pointedly brushing her sleeve. "I expect only cooperation."

"And you'll play hob getting even cooperation out of this lot."

"Miss Duncan?" A woman's voice from the hall startled them both and gave Madeline a chance to escape.

"Yes?" She stepped into the hall to find Maple Thoroughgood there, holding some white cotton garments.

"I've finished, Miss Duncan. Here they are." She raised the bust bodice for Madeline's inspection, her expression a bit nervous. "They seemed a bit plain without any lace, so I added a few pintucks to the front. I hope that was all right. The drawers came out fine though." She held them up and gave them a rub between thumb and forefinger. "Nice, soft goods."

A bit of initiative at last. Madeline could have kissed her.

"You do wonderful work, Maple." She reached for the knickers and inspected the seams and hem, then the overall effect. "They're beautiful!" She looked up at Cole, insisting he admit it too, but he stubbornly refused to concede the point.

"The true test is whether your precious workers will think so." The look in his eyes was challenging . . . and expectant.

How had she let him bully her into calling a meeting to introduce her employees to Ideal's product?

Well, it was too late to back out now.

She stood at the door to the classroom on the first level, taking a mental tally of her employees as they filed in . . . trying to predict which might be counted on to embrace her reform garments and which might actually be thickheaded enough to object to them. Daniel Steadman and his wife, Priscilla; Maple Thoroughgood and Charlotte; Fritz; Tattersall; and Endicott—all definitely for the garments. Ben and Alva Murtry, Will and Molly Huggins, Bernard and Catherine Rush—probably for. Thomas and Bess Clark—possibly against. Matthew, Mark, Luke, and Calvin Ketchum—probably for. Harley Ketchum—probably against. Roscoe Turner and Algy Bates and that other fellow they had talked her into hiring—what was his name? Rutherford . . . Egbert . . . Hubert . . .

Rupert! That was it. She watched Rupert's squinty-eyed examination of the room and his fellow workers and tried to imagine his reaction to producing unconventional ladies' unmentionables. She groaned silently.

The previous evening she had been so confident that her workers would wholeheartedly endorse her garments and her mission. But now, by the cold light of day, watching their dubious faces and recalling their less than enthusiastic response to things like producing free clothing for their own children, some of her confidence was eroding. By the time they had taken all the seats and filled in the spaces between chairs and against the walls, her palms were dampening and her mouth was dry.

"Welcome," she said, walking to the front of the room and reminding herself to keep to the strategy she had outlined in the sleepless hours before dawn. "I have had a chance to greet most of you as you arrived in St. Crispin, and over the last few days I have come to know some of you fairly well. Each of you was chosen for a special task here, and each of you is a valuable part of our factory and community. And since you are such an important part of the Ideal Garment Company, I want you to know that I value your ideas and your opinions and welcome your suggestions. It is my intention that in time you will feel comfortable expressing your concerns and offering suggestions for improving our company and village."

She smiled and paused to take stock of their reaction. *So far, so good. A yawn or two, but no one was asleep and no one was leaving.*

"You know that we intend to produce women's garments. All of you have seen my garments, my tunics and trousers. These are what are known as 'reform' garments. It is my hope that one day we can produce garments like the ones I am wearing. But as it has been said, we must learn to crawl before we learn to walk. Our first product will be much more basic to women's wardrobes, and far more helpful. For too long physicians have warned us of the dangers and health problems resulting from tight lacing. Well, I intend to produce and sell garments that are a healthy alternative to severe, constrictive corsets and stifling layers of petticoats."

A number of heads that had been drooping popped up at the mention of corsets and petticoats. Suddenly all eyes were on her—including Cole Mandeville's. He had just strolled into the room and now leaned against the wall to her left with crossed arms and a faintly amused expression.

"Maple Thoroughgood, our head seamstress, has been working on sample garments of the kind we will produce first." She nodded to Maple, who rose and lifted the sample bust bodice from a flat box on the table at the front.

This was greeted by frowns, shakes of head, and shrugs. They clearly didn't know what to make of it.

"This is called a bust bodice. It is meant to be worn next to the skin as a replacement for a corset, corset cover, and chemise, or the chamois combination worn by ladies of quality."

There were still so many looks of confusion that she took the garment from Maple and held it up to herself, smoothing it over her bosom to show where it would be worn.

The light began to dawn. A loud whisper came from the back.

"Why, it's a titty binder."

Braced though she was for any negative reaction, she was caught a bit off guard by that simple, somewhat incredulous pronouncement. And she blushed. Right in front of Cole Mandeville.

"I-it will provide modesty and support for a woman's body without boning or heavy layering. And it opens down the front to allow a lady to fasten it herself. Only a small percentage of women have the luxury of a lady's maid, yet society continues to insist on fashions that require help putting on and fastening. Our Ideal bodice can change that forever."

She demonstrated the small mother-of-pearl buttons.

"Cal, even *you* could work them," one of the Ketchums taunted another.

"If'n he could get a gal to hold still long enough!" another brother blurted out, drawing a burst of male laughter.

Alarmed by the drift of their comments, she hurried on. "You will notice that some of the fabric we use is unique. It is not woven, it is machine knitted . . . of the finest long staple cotton yarns. That means that some parts of the bodice will be firm and retain their shape and some parts will have a healthful 'give' to permit a range of movement. That should be most helpful for women who engage in outdoor exercise like riding or tennis or bicycling, for women who must work both in the home and in shops, offices, and factories, and for women with chores to do and children to watch."

"Yer sayin' *mothers'll* wear these things?" Bess Clark blurted out. The horror on her face made her opinion of that prospect perfectly plain.

"Well, yes. Women of all ages and stations and stages of life will wear them."

"Girls too?" That came from a Ketchum, Madeline would have staked her life on it. Wicked laughter, mostly male, was followed by indrawn breaths, mostly female. She sought out the nearest Ketchum and pinned his ears back with a look.

"Young *ladies*? Of course." She found the others and gave them glares as she continued. "Will you be able to know that a woman is wearing it? Possibly. Not because her shape will change so much, but because her attitude will. She will be healthier, more comfortable, and have more freedom of movement. The resulting benefits will be visible in her glowing face."

"In her *blushin'* face, ye mean," Harley Ketchum declared, drawing all eyes to his dour countenance. "A proper girl'd be shamed to her toes to wear such a thing."

Madeline's worst fears were being realized. She had asked for opinions and participation—and she was getting it. Now she was being forced to put her own reputation for propriety on the line. In front of Cole Mandeville.

"I consider myself a proper woman, Mr. Ketchum. And I wear such garments without blushing." She prayed that for once her body wouldn't betray her with a flush of embarrassment. It didn't. Harley lowered his eyes in the face of her determination, but from the looks on the others' faces, she wasn't sure it was enough to turn the tide.

"We will also produce a companion garment." She turned to Maple for a second piece of clothing and held up a pair of sturdy knitted cotton knickers. Here was a garment they had no trouble recognizing, and their reaction was predictably mixed. "Some of you know these as 'drawers.' A rather old-fashioned term. These shorter, fuller versions are known generally as 'knickers.' These will be worn with the bust bodice to provide a comfortable, supportive, and entirely proper foundation for ladies' garments."

Tittering began at the back. By the time it worked its way to the front, she had heard the joke being passed along. "Them drawers be so short, a gal's 'nethers' will be hangin' out."

Pretending not to have heard, she held the waist of the knickers up to her own middle, demonstrating the length of them.

"You can plainly see, they are generous enough to provide for modesty, soft enough to provide for comfort, and the cotton makes them easy to launder. They are both less restrictive and of superior quality to other foundation garments being sold." She paused, searching the upturned faces around her—but found mostly puzzlement and uncertainty. She dug down into her repertoire of facts and figures.

"Traditional garments for an average woman have been shown to—wait, there is a much better way to show you." In a stroke of inspiration she beckoned to Emily and Tattersall, sending one off to her house for a box of things at the bottom of her wardrobe and the other down to the shipping room for an old scale recently resurrected. While they were gone, she pulled out a number of sketches she and Endicott had produced together, showing the sorts of garments she hoped Ideal would produce in the future.

By the time Tattersall returned, the workers were buzzing about what they had seen and about the new concept of reform garments. Some were dubious, others skeptical; a few were outright hostile. Then Emily returned carrying a large box, and their attention once again focused on Madeline.

With a determined smile she set the scale and began pulling old garments from the box to place on one side of the scale. "These were my aunt Olivia's—things she had worn and kept as a reminder of how fortunate she was to have been freed from such sartorial tyranny. They are from twenty years ago, but they are all still commonly worn by traditionally attired women. A pair of ladies' shoes . . . stockings . . . chemise, sturdy corset, and cover . . . drawers . . . a small dress improver . . . one petticoat, two, now three . . . a skirt . . . a blouse and jacket."

Even folded lengthwise and drooping over the edges, the garments scarcely fit between the chains that held the pan.

"If we were to put weights on the other side, it would take sixteen or seventeen pounds to balance these clothes. That is precisely how much the average woman must bear and drag around on her person each day. And how much *laundry* must be done. Think of the washing and ironing of all those petticoats, chemises, and corset covers."

There was considerable murmuring among the women, and glowering and head scratching among the men.

"I can see you need something for comparison." She put her proposed Ideal garments on the other side of the scale and added a traditional skirt, blouse, light chemise, stockings, and sensible shoes. Their combined weight failed to even budge the mass of clothing on the other side. "You can clearly see that reform clothing will result in not only greater comfort and freedom and better health, but also in smaller expense and less laundry. The arguments for reform in women's clothing are simply overwhelming."

They were not, however, overwhelmingly *convincing*. Her demonstration had made something of an impact on the women, but she could see many of them eyeing their husbands to gauge their response before responding themselves. Unfortunately male reaction tended to fall into one of two categories: adolescent humor or simmering indignation.

Madeline was genuinely stunned by their resistance to so reasonable and forward-thinking a project. She reminded herself that clothing was an area in which tradition and morality met—and hammered out unwritten laws with the subtlety of an artist's palette, the capriciousness of a summer storm, and the force of all Ten Commandments. True, clothing *was* an expression of who people were: their personal tastes, their values, their economic status, and even the class to which they belonged. But she still couldn't believe that her workers would cling to absurd old notions of fashion propriety, especially when their own financial interests were at stake!

Merciful heavens! What did she have to do to make them see the light?

Then, with the heat of Cole's I-told-you-so gaze boring into her, inspiration struck.

"To produce a good product, you have to know it well. And to truly know a product, you really have to use it yourself. Your opinion and contribution are so important, I want you to have firsthand experience with our garments. That's why I've decided to distribute our entire first run of production to the women of St. Crispin."

There was no time to think it all through, but it felt right . . . the perfect rebuttal to all the doubting Thomases in her workforce.

"Each woman in our employ and the wife of each male employee will be given two sets of our products to wear and evaluate." She relaxed a bit, pleased with her sudden brainstorm. "Call it . . . another of the benefits of working at the Ideal Garment Company."

Everyone began talking at once, such that she could scarcely make out one word in three. Then suddenly Thomas

Clark was on his feet, shoulder to shoulder with a red-faced Harley Ketchum.

"What are ye sayin'?" He jabbed a finger toward the garments on the table. "That our womenfolk got t'wear them things?"

The room went quiet as all waited to hear what she would say. Knowing that how she responded would determine her leadership, she struggled to strike the right tone—neither bullying nor begging.

"What I am saying . . . is that I have such confidence in these designs that I believe the garments themselves will convince you of their worth. Once a woman has tried them, has felt the comfort and freedom they offer, she won't want to wear anything else. That is what I want for our customers, and that is what I want for you as our workers."

But despite her enthusiasm and even the magnanimous offer of free garments to each and every woman, they were still doubtful. Frustration built in her as she saw them huddling back in their chairs, tucking their chins, and wagging their heads. Even Roscoe and Algy and that fellow they talked her into hiring—what was his name?—wore skeptical expressions. And they weren't even working in the factory!

"I told you it wouldn't work," Cole's voice boomed out over the others, drawing every eye in the room to him. He pushed off from the wall and came to stand near the front row of seats with his hands in his trouser pockets and his elbows out, looking for all the world like a great, winged messenger of doom. "The sort of garments you're attempting to produce require a certain . . . *sophistication* . . . to appreciate." He swept the assembly with a look of condescension. "And it appears that sophistication is in rather short supply around here."

Horrified, Madeline planted herself in one of the aisles, among the workers, and turned to face him.

"A woman hardly needs to be worldly-wise to appreciate the advantages of doing less wash each week, in avoiding heat exhaustion in the dregs of summer, or in being able to bend and pick up a child without losing her breath. My workers are perfectly capable of deciding for themselves the merits of Ideal garments."

"Your workers have difficulty deciding which shoe to put on which foot," he declared with a genial smile.

An indignant murmur spread throughout the room.

How dare he! She gave him a look that would have scorched a wet blanket, then turned to her employees with her eyes ablaze.

"I believe we're ready to go to work, are we not?" She looked challengingly from one to another to another. They had not exactly caught fire, but they were sitting straighter, holding their heads higher, and looking resentfully at Cole. It would have to do.

"Good. Endicott and Daniel Steadman will work with the new cutters, showing you how to lay out the patterns and stack the cloth. Maple and Charlotte Thoroughgood will instruct the seamstresses in the order and method of stitching the garments. We all have a great deal of work to do. Let's get started."

As the workers poured out into the factory, talking in hushed tones about what they had just heard and seen, Thomas Clark paused in a group of cutters and hitched up his trousers beneath his belly. "Don't care what they say, my Bessie won't be wearing the likes o' them things. Won't have my woman paradin' about wi' her nether parts hanging out."

Madeline sighed quietly.

When the last worker had returned to the factory and the classroom was empty except for Madeline and Cole, she began to pack away the garments she had used in her demonstration. The longer she worked under his probing, judgmental gaze, the more curt and angry her movements became. She shook a chemise so hard that it made a loud crack, then folded it up into a cramped little square.

"Thank you ever so much for the *help,* your lordship," she said sharply.

But his reply to her sarcasm was not at all what she expected. "You're quite welcome."

Cole turned on his heel and left, the echo of his words lapping like sardonic laughter in his head. She was welcome, he had said, and apparently meant it. On some level he must have known that his condescension would rankle her workers and galvanize them into giving Madeline a chance. He had done it anyway.

Meddling. Unforgivable.

Helping. Even worse.

She was quite welcome. What the hell was happening to him? Getting involved, sticking his nose—his treacherous and damned near indestructible, magnanimous impulses—into places they didn't belong? Her anger at him was the only thing that made it half bearable. As long as she didn't know he was suffering these nauseating little episodes of charity and humanity, she couldn't claim a victory and couldn't use it as an excuse to sink deeper and deeper into a quagmire of altruism.

He headed for the shed behind Netter's tavern, where his horse was stabled, hoping that a ride would help to clear his head. Perhaps seeing the wretched place from a distance would help him regain some perspective on it.

But when he returned some hours later, he found the same quandary waiting for him and made the only decision he could. He would just have to keep telling her and her wretched workers the truth . . . even if it helped.

Roscoe Turner and Algy Bates stood in the garden behind the factory, staring at the devastation they had wrought and seeing in it a job half done. "That Lord Man-de-ville mebbe a testy sort, but 'e knows 'is engineerin'," Roscoe said, then rubbed his grizzled chin. "Know what we need, Alg?"

"What?" Algy stared at him as if awaiting an oracle.

"More horses."

Spotting Rupert Fitzwater crouched at the side of the factory building, bending over something with feverish intensity, they headed over to see what he was doing. When he heard them coming he straightened and hurriedly stuffed what he was working on into his pocket. They could see, as he crammed it out of sight, that it was a writing pad of some sort.

"What ye got there, Rupert?" Roscoe asked, eyeing the edge of the pad sticking out of Fitzwater's pocket.

"Nothing," Rupert responded too quickly. Then he followed Roscoe's gaze to his pocket and hurriedly shoved the rest of the pad out of sight. "Jus' a bit of scribblin'." Their dubious faces prodded him to elaborate. "I keep a diary . . . on my travels an' such."

"We ain't got time fer scribblin'. We got us a rock to move," Roscoe said. "We be headin' over to Stonecrouch to see if they got any horses we can use."

"Fine." Fitzwater removed his hat and ran a hand back through his hair before replacing it. "But there's no need all of us goin', eh? What say I stay here an' get some of this side dug out?"

They eyed the still-covered half of the boulder, looked at each other, and shrugged. "Well, it don't take three men to hire up four horses."

Rupert Fitch removed his coat and picked up a shovel. But the minute the pair were out of sight, he climbed up out of the hole and dusted his hands. Sitting down on the ground by the factory wall, he took out his pad and a stubby pencil and resumed writing.

" 'After spending the long, grueling hours that are required at the factory, the beleaguered workers must turn their dispirited steps toward the hovels that Miss Duncan provides for their housing. The places are in a pathetic state of disrepair, with windows boarded up, roofs with holes, dirt floors, and no water or means of sanitation available. The squalor of the workers' lodgings is a stark and shameful contrast to the comfort and elegance of her own residence in the village, a substantial brick house in which she entertains and beguiles the court's appointed overseer of this outrageous venture.' " He paused and squinted, thinking, then set pencil to paper again.

" 'Burdens of poverty and inhumane working conditions may be borne by oppressed workers with stoicism and heroic forbearance, but the Ideal Garment Company has extended its grim control over its workers to seize even those last scraps of human dignity. Recently, Miss Duncan issued an edict that women workers are no longer permitted to wear conventional clothing, that they must wear the same scanty and indecent garments that she produces in her sweatshop. Indeed, she boasts of wearing such garments herself, and frequently has been seen flaunting her undergarments before the eyes of her male workers.' "

Yes, he told himself with a smile, it was shaping up nicely. There was enough here to create quite a stir in the London papers. Exploitation, indecency, squalor, nonconformity, hints of sexual license—this could be his journalistic coup de grâce, the piece that would gild his name on Fleet Street.

But as he looked over the pages and notes he had written, he thought of the rejections he had suffered over the years from those arrogant bastards at the *Pall Mall Gazette* and *The Times*. They thought of him as a hack, a penny-paper scribbler. If he hoped to get this into anything but one of the scandal rags, he had to have more than just a juicy bit of prose. He needed an angle, something to stir up thinking people, something to give the piece a respectable air.

He thought for a moment, and for some reason the sight of Madeline Duncan and Lord Mandeville, nose to nose in opposition, came to him. She such a do-gooder and he such a skeptic and a scoffer. That image sparked a bit of inspiration.

"Pure genius, old bloke," he mumbled. With his ferret-brown eyes darting over the scene developing in his mind, he flipped to a new page on his pad and began to write furiously. "A second point of view, an opposing opinion. Something staunchly in defense of Miss Do-gooder Duncan and her social experi—"

Suddenly Gilbert Duncan flashed before his eyes—respectable, resentful, and conveniently duplicitous. Grudge-bearing Gilbert had paid him a pretty penny to collect what dirt he could on Cousin Madeline's tidy little enterprise. Perhaps he would pay a bit more to be cast as his dear little cousin's defender. And if Rupert played it right, he might be able to get a third party involved, someone well known but controversial . . . like Sir William Morris.

Beside himself with glee at the possibilities opening before him, he scrambled to his feet, grabbed his coat, and headed for the cottage he shared with those ha'penny dodgers Roscoe and Algy.

Halfway there, in the center of the weedy green, he encountered a small knot of people headed by none other than Madeline Duncan. All of them were staring at the iron water pipe in the main trench. Suddenly there was a faint rumbling and all present held their breath. When nothing happened, Miss Duncan turned to a grizzled workman with a beaming smile.

"I think it's working!" she declared. She rushed into the nearest cottage and a moment later returned with what to Rupert was disheartening news. "Water! The water's flowing just fine!"

Well, he thought minutes later as he sat on his bed in the cottage with a new writing tablet on his lap, whittling a fresh point on his pencil, they might have running water in the cottages now, but the rest of the world didn't have to know that.

10

The day was not without its high points, Madeline thought, using the memory of those modest successes to stave off fatigue. The water was now running in the houses, and they had actually completed a bodice or two. But the day had seemed endless, and the evening seemed to go on forever. It had been dark for some time when Davenport came up the rear stairs of the factory, lantern in hand, and found her perched on Tattersall's stool, rubbing her eyes with ink-stained fingers as she tried to see the letters and bank drafts she was signing.

"We waited supper," Davenport announced, startling her. "For two hours."

"I'm sorry. I should have sent you word. I needed to get a number of things done, and I had so little time today, with production starting. Every time I sat down at my desk, someone came up with another little crisis."

"I thought about bringing you a tray, but decided that would only encourage you to stay longer." She came to lean against the side of the tall clerk's desk. "You'll make yourself sick, Maddy Duncan, if you keep this up. You need rest and food and—when was the last time you took a walk or read a book or ate a proper breakfast at your own table?"

"I can think of more pleasant things than having to face *him* every morning . . . before coffee."

"And I can think of worse," Davenport said tartly. "He's easy on the eyes."

"But hard on the nerves." She glanced down at the paperwork before her and issued a tired sigh. "I suppose this can wait until morning."

She slipped off the stool, collected her shawl, and doused the lamp.

The clock in the hall was chiming half past something when they walked through the front door. Davenport peeled Madeline's shawl from her drooping shoulders and ordered her up the stairs and into bed, promising to bring her a tray. Slipping easily into the pattern of bygone days, she obediently trudged up the stairs, peering over the banister to see the light coming from under the library door.

Every muscle in her body was complaining as she changed her clothes, gave her face a cursory splash of water, and then sank down into the stuffed chair by the cold fireplace. She pulled her bare feet up under her nightdress and wrapped her arms around her knees. While she waited for Davenport, lists of tasks for the following day and details needing attention kept trailing through her mind chanting: *Don't forget . . . Don't forget . . .* And the chant became a numbing drone.

That was where Davenport found her, curled up in the chair, sound asleep, her head resting against the padded wing. The housekeeper set the tray on the table and was about to leave, when she heard movement near the door and whirled.

Lord Mandeville was coming across the room with a finger to his lips. He gestured to the bedcovers, then picked up Madeline and carried her to the bed. Davenport quickly tucked her nightdress around her ankles and pulled the covers over her.

For a moment the pair stood looking at the pale face surrounded by a turbulent cloud of dark hair.

"Headstrong. Stubborn as the day is long," Davenport said. "But you'll never find a truer heart. She was snatched from the jaws of death when she was but a child. Her parents were missionaries, you know. In Africa."

"No. I didn't know," he murmured.

"She comes by her 'giving' streak naturally, I suppose. It's in the Duncan blood. Her grandfather, her father and mother, and her dear aunt Livvy—they all spent their lives doin' good. A pity they didn't *get* as good as they *gave*. Raising children in pious poverty . . . dyin' young and in a heathen land . . . dyin' old and ill without children for comfort. Seems like the Duncans always come to a heartbreaking end. I worry that the same will happen to Maddy if she keeps on the way she's going."

With a final tuck and pat of the covers, Davenport picked up the lamp and led Cole out.

By the time he reached his own room, Cole was roundly annoyed with Davenport and edging toward furious with Madeline. It appeared that St. Madeline of the Endlessly Self-less issued from a whole line of philanthropes who had come to a damned bad end—martyrs to the noblest impulses of humankind. The Duncans suffered from some bizarre inherited compulsion to do good, to give themselves away—substance, body, and soul—to a troubled world. The Duncans of this world were the givers.

And who cared? Who extolled their names or reverenced their sacrifices? Who built monuments to them or wrote songs about them? Certainly not the Mandevilles.

The Mandevilles of this world were the takers.

•   •   •

Hunger was what awakened her this time in the middle of the night. She sat up in bed, feeling her empty middle with her hands, and knew instantly what she wanted. Chocolate. Hot and creamy. It was her favorite treat. She found her soft Turkish trousers and her most comfortable cotton tunic in the wardrobe, put them on, and headed for the kitchen.

The light was out in the library as she passed the door, and she felt a pang of disappointment, which was quickly stanched. The last thing she needed just then was another humiliating encounter with his imperial lordship.

Cocoa, sugar, milk, and a pinch of salt for balance—she soon had the syrup brewing over the coals left in the stove. It smelled heavenly. Her mouth began to water; she could just feel that creamy, chocolaty sweetness sliding down her throat, warming her insides. She turned from the cooler with the milk in her hands—and barely kept from dropping it.

"Ohhh!" Clutching the earthen pitcher tight against her, she flushed with delayed fright. "You just shortened my life by two years!"

"Sorry." Cole was standing behind her in his shirt and riding breeches, leaning a hip against the worktable. His hair was rumpled and his eyes looked as if he had recently been asleep. "Another midnight raid on the kitchen, I see. You know, if you took regular meals like the rest of us, you wouldn't awaken in the middle of the night starving." He smiled with a hint of teasing. "Just a thought."

"I didn't feel like eating earlier," she said. Alerted by the sound of something bubbling, she hurried back to the stove and grabbed her wooden spoon.

He came to peer over her shoulder and sniff the potent aroma of heated chocolate. She looked up just in time to see his eyes close in ecstasy, and jerked her gaze back to the chocolate pot, disturbed by that glimpse of him in the throes of pleasure.

"Chocolate." He leaned over the stove and inhaled deeply. "Ummm. So this is how it's made. Trust you to know how to concoct some decadent culinary delight. Singularly unladylike, you know. Cooking."

"I've never claimed to be a 'lady,' " she said, letting the chocolate drip from the spoon back into the pan. "I was raised to believe a woman should be able to do for herself, whether it's fastening her own garments or managing her own finances or preparing her own food." Judging the chocolate syrup to be ready, she gave him a guarded look and poured in the milk. "I suppose that groan a minute ago meant you would like some."

He grinned. "Clever girl."

"Fortunately for you, I know how to make chocolate only in quantity. Make yourself useful and get two cups out of the cupboard on the right." She stirred and watched the pot, testing it periodically. "There, that should be just right." She poured it into the cups he held, then took one from him and carried it to a stool by the table. He took the same seat he had occupied the other night . . . at the table beside her.

"Where did you learn to make chocolate?"

As he drank, his shoulders eased and his features relaxed. The chocolate was working its spell. She had to make herself look away.

"From Hannah and Davenport," she said, sipping. "They used to allow me to hang about in the kitchen after my studies were finished for the day. I got to help Hannah do all sorts of things. I'll have you know, I can bone fish, pluck and stuff geese, and make jellies and pickled preserves. And my tart pastry will someday be recognized as the Eighth Wonder of the World." She flashed him a smile and he chuckled. "What about you? I imagine you did your share of hanging about the kitchen, angling for a bit of shortbread before supper. Didn't you learn anything from the cook?"

He lowered his cup and his smile faded. "I . . . I learned a lot from the cook."

"Don't tell me, let me guess—how to lick bowls and trade flattery for sweets and sneak raisins out of the pantry."

"That . . . and how to tie my shoes and make my letters and read a book and always tell the truth."

"From the cook?" She puzzled over that. "You didn't have a nurse or a governess?"

"Did you?" He seemed a bit defensive as he turned the question back on her.

"Heavens, no. Well, not in the usual sense. I believe I had a nurse of some sort when I was an infant. But we were in Africa, Sierra Leone, and my mother simply took me with her everywhere."

"They were missionaries . . . your parents."

"Yes. My father used to say he was bringing High Church to low places. And my mother used to laugh and say it was simply his excuse for escaping the clerical kowtowing required here in England. Aunt Livvy often said she thought he went to Africa because he believed that 'low places' were a lot more fun than 'high churches.'" She shook her head with a wistful smile. "He wasn't exactly a jot and tittle sort of reverend."

"So, this altruistic mania of yours tends to run in the family."

She saw the twinkle in his eye. "I suppose it does. That, and blue eyes and a bit of red in the hair—"

"And a stubborn streak a mile wide," he inserted. "Must be a Scotsman in the line somewhere. Or an angel." That slip of the tongue took him by surprise. "A-Anglican—a High-Church Anglican." Fortunately for him, she was only half listening. Angel. It wasn't the first time he'd called her that. When he first arrived in St. Crispin, he had used the term derisively, but, lately he'd caught himself thinking of her that way in earnest—which was appalling.

"What about you?" she asked, interrupting his thoughts. "What sort of family do you come from?"

He was still reeling from letting slip an inadvertent bit of admiration. Perhaps it was that that made him suddenly want to tell her the truth. Or perhaps it was the warmth and darkness of the kitchen, the easy silence between them, and the tantalizing possibility of a unique bit of intimacy . . . and the idea that she might begin to understand.

"I come from a long line of boring, shallow, self-interested clods with a consuming passion for gambling, fox hunting, and boring, shallow, self-adoring women." He said it with a determined insouciance that ironically conveyed just how serious a topic it was to him. She not only recognized that particular defense, she knew precisely how to disarm it.

"Well"—she leaned forward with a mischievous smile—"they do say the apple doesn't fall far from the tree."

He stiffened, searching her expression until he glimpsed the twinkle of humor in it. "Ah, if only I had been a bit more like them. That was always the trouble, you see. I was never quite enough 'Mandeville' to deal properly with my life."

"And what was in the Mandeville line that you coveted so?" she asked.

"The ability to live in simple and uncompromising pursuit of one's own interests. 'Let the rest of the world go to hell in a handcart,' " he blustered in a bombastic voice, " 'just as long as I get my cigar and brandy after dinner.' That's my family motto, you see. To my knowledge, Mandeville blood has never suffered the slightest taint of idealism or altruism, nor been infected with even the commonest strains of decency or generosity."

He studied the perceptiveness in her face and mentally wrestled with something. When he spoke again, his voice was lower and laced with tension.

"It was my misfortune to be the fourth of six male offspring in a noble household. I was not the eldest and Father's treasured heir, nor the baby and Mama's plaything. It was clear from the day I was born that I would never be of interest to either of my parents. The cook in our household had a brother, John Macmillan, who was a tenant on my family's lands. He had a son, Johnny, about my age. When I was old enough, Cook saw to it I spent my time with the Macmillans on their farm . . . being cared for, learning about farming, helping however I could. It wasn't at all unusual for me to be there for a month at a time without anyone from the mansion bothering to check on me."

Bitterness had crept into his voice, and he paused and took a deep breath to clear it. She watched in silence, knowing instinctively that this was a part of him he had shared with few others. Sipping her chocolate and lending him silent support, she waited for him to continue.

"For most of my boyhood I lived as a tenant farmer's son on my family's estate. I wore the clothing they gave me, ate the food they grew, learned my letters and my prayers at their table." He halted and stared into his cup. "They were my family in every way that was important."

"Were?"

Anger, long cooled and hardened, appeared in his eyes. "My noble father, the most Mandeville of all Mandevilles, gambled himself into financial straits and decided to sell off all the family's unentailed lands to cover his debts. Part of the land he sold was the Macmillans' holding. When I learned what had happened, I confronted my father and demanded that he nullify the sale. I was all of thirteen. He gave me a royal thrashing, called me an ungrateful 'get' and a 'whelp gone feral,' and packed me off to Harrow the very next day." His mouth tightened into a grim line as he sorted both his feelings and his words. "I never saw John and Peg Macmillan again."

"What happened to them?" she whispered, feeling his pain migrating into her.

"They went to Newcastle, seeking work. I swore that when I finished school I would set things right, and the day I left Harrow, I went to look for them." His voice thickened. "By then, John and Peg had both died in an influenza outbreak. I finally located Johnny and two of the girls. I gave them what money I could and vowed I would get their land back for them even if I had to go to the courts. Then I went to see my uncle, Sir William, in London, and learned there was nothing I could do."

"Sir William is your uncle?"

"My mother's brother." He smiled sardonically. "A Rayburn, not a Mandeville. Before I knew it, I was at Oxford, preparing to read for the law. I was convinced it was a way— perhaps the only way—to have the power to right injustices and make the world a better place." He rolled his shoulders and slid off the table. "I was wrong."

He padded over to the stove, stirred the pot, and lifted it. "Another?"

"Please."

She offered her cup. He poured. When their eyes met, she glimpsed the old desolation in him. She had to fight the impulse to pull him into her arms.

"It wasn't your fault, you know," she said.

He smiled wryly at her, not bothering to deny the guilt he felt. "No? My blood family reached out to destroy the people I loved, the very people who had cared for and nurtured me in their stead. All the Macmillans got for their love and generosity was ruin and heartache. There is no justice, St. Madeline. It took years in the law to finally convince me, but I learned."

He stood looking down at her, then perched one hip and thigh on the table.

"Don't expect the impossible of people, St. Madeline. They will do what they perceive to be for their comfort, for their pleasure, and for their own best interests . . . in precisely that order. If you expect anything more, you're letting yourself in for a huge disappointment."

"You must not be entirely cold and logical, Cole Mandeville," she said softly, "if you are so concerned about me."

"I don't claim to be perfect." He studied her face, then reached out to brush aside a wisp of her hair. She glanced at his hand, wishing he would touch her hair again. That casual stroke was a tender and telling bit of contact. "Unlike you."

"I have never once claimed to be perfect either, Cole Mandeville."

"Haven't you? Rescuing a whole village full of people, setting yourself up as nurturer of their souls and provider of their needs, their guardian angel."

"Well"—she reddened—"who says guardian angels have to be perfect? They say that many people have 'entertained angels unawares.' If angels were perfect, they would stick out like sore thumbs and we'd recognize them instantly. My own personal theory is that angels are probably the most unlikely people we meet."

He chuckled. "By that theory, the leading candidates in St. Crispin are those two ignoramuses digging infernal blazes out of your garden. Sorry, St. Madeline, but as far as I am concerned, the prime contender for 'resident angel' in this place is you." As his gaze slid into those blue pools of her eyes, he couldn't help adding: "You're probably as close to perfect as a human being gets."

Her heart gave a heavy thud and began to beat faster.

"I'm not even *close* to perfect," she said, drawn to the warmth radiating from him, leaning slightly forward. His features were softening, his eyes darkening. She felt a delicious stirring all through her, heightening her awareness of her body.

"Ahhh, but your blue eyes are. And your soft chestnut hair. And your cream-sweet skin. Not to mention your lips. Although, in truth, they can be gloriously naughty when the occasion calls for it."

"Naughty?" She felt her skin warming and lips thickening under his increasingly hungry regard. "What sort of occasion calls for naughty lips?"

"This one."

He caught her chin in his hand and leaned forward to press a hot, inquisitive kiss on her mouth. Before she knew what was happening, she was on her feet and in his arms and returning that kiss with every bit of warmth and passion she possessed.

Pleasure soared and burst like fireworks inside her, drenching her body in a shower of hot, delicious sparks that could be extinguished only by contact with his. Instinctively, she pressed against him, seeking his warmth and hardness, wanting to explore the feel of him against her, mating his hard planes to her soft curves, covering her, sheltering her. Their kisses deepened, lush and wet, flavored with chocolate. Sweetness, underscored with a hint of ripeness and decadence. Naughty lips. She understood now.

He filled her senses—touch, taste, smell, sight—stretching their boundaries until they began to overlap and she could almost taste with her fingertips the salty heat of his neck, the silky anise of his hair, the wheatlike texture of his broad chest, and the faint musk of his sinewy arms. He was a sensory feast, a passage to wonder, and as she felt herself being turned and her bottom being guided up onto the table, it seemed somehow appropriate to be savoring him in the kitchen.

He poised above her, running his hands up her sides, conditioning her to his touch, reading in each sigh and shiver the pleasure he generated in her. Then with consummate tenderness he traced her features with his lips, absorbing each shape and storing every texture before sinking into her lush, responsive kiss once more.

Soon his caresses grew hotter and more urgent. Her buttons melted under his touch, leaving her tunic to slide helplessly apart, baring her silky bodice, then her sleek skin and tightly budded nipples. His eyes closed as he lavished hot kisses down her chest and across the cool, satiny mounds he had explored so briefly once and nightly in his mind thereafter. This time he explored her with unhurried pleasure, drawing lazy, slowly tightening circles over her breasts, then pouring hot breaths and soft, nipping kisses on their hardened tips.

The feel of his hands, his kisses, his breath on her body, was like long-awaited sun—warm and life-giving. Inside her, new tendrils of feeling were uncurling and reaching toward that sensual sustenance that would fill voids in her being. When his knee nudged hers apart and his weight shifted over her, she welcomed it, responding instinctively, molding herself against him, rubbing her bare breasts against the soft cotton of his shirt, filling her hands with the contours of his back and the thickness of his arms.

The focused pressure of his pelvis against hers wedged a rigid heat tightly against the tender burning in her woman's cleft. A moan of surprise escaped her as his body flexed, raking that ridge along her sensitive hollow and producing a deep, penetrating quiver of response that resonated in every part of her body.

He lifted his head to hers and poured a sweet, lingering kiss over her mouth, sensing the shock in her response, wanting to reassure her. As he braced above her, he pushed up enough to see what he and passion had wrought together.

She was beautiful—fair skin dusted gold in the lamplight, a torrent of dark hair swirling around her smooth shoulders, her eyes dark and luminous with new and compelling desires, breasts voluptuous and nipples proud, her lips swollen like ripe berries. Her tunic lay crumpled about her like an artist's drape, and amid the dark woolen of her trousers, buttons winked, beckoning, promising a quick surrender.

"Cole?" she whispered, running her hand up his arm and along his shoulder. The shy invitation in that touch said she was his now, there.

And when he shifted slightly, relieving his elbow against their hard support, the unyielding nature of that surface caused him to look up and around them. The realization jolted him; they were on the kitchen table.

He was poised on the brink of taking Madeline Duncan—*St. Bloody Perfect Madeline*—on the damned kitchen table!

He sat up and pulled her up with him. Reluctant to face the reproach in her eyes, he had to force himself to meet her gaze. But she was smiling at him with a roused and glowing warmth that sent a trill of guilty relief through him. He should be horsewhipped for putting that smile on her face.

Clutching her gaping tunic together, she swayed toward him and placed a soft kiss on his cheek. He looked down into the centers of her eyes, into the unshuttered feeling in the depths of them. There, in plain sight, were pleasure, surprise, joy, and—*good Lord*—adoration. Not a defense in sight . . . not a single bit of caution, indignation, or common sense.

He recoiled into pure turmoil inside.

"Well, that was a mistake," he said roughly, bounding off the table and retucking his shirt, leaving her to tidy herself.

Madeline watched him withdraw, a terrible sinking sensation in her chest. "Did I do something wrong? I did warn you. I'm not . . . perfect."

He stared at her, emotion rising fast and furious in him. She couldn't have been more wrong. She was perfect in every way, and he would rather be drawn and quartered than tell her so. For if she knew how much pleasure she had given him, he had the dismal feeling that she would go right on being perfectly loving, giving freely of her virtue, her passion, and her affection until he or some miserable hedonistic wretch like him shattered her heart.

"Well, it won't be me," he said aloud, leaving her to interpret it however she would. "I won't have that on my conscience."

In fact, she interpreted that comment and his chaotic emotions, with uncanny accuracy. He didn't want the burden of her virtue on his conscience. With trembling hands she began to rebutton her bodice and then her tunic. Stopping was probably the most sensible thing they could do, but it was disappointing all the same. To be so close to something so breathtaking, and then to have it snatched from your very hands . . .

The real question was *why* he stopped. Did he stop because he was afraid she would be hurt by it, or simply because he didn't want to bother with any sort of entanglement? Did he truly care about her as a person, about her feelings? If so, then there was definitely hope for him.

She didn't know what to think when he took her gruffly by the elbow and steered her out the door into the hallway. In the darkness his grip on her arm gentled, and by the time they reached her door, he released her.

"Let me give you a bit of advice, St. Madeline." His voice was husky with irritation. "If you want to continue in your saintly occupation, you would do well to avoid lovemaking on kitchen tables with jaded noblemen. We're full of unseen hazards and, believe me, the pleasure *won't* be worth the pain."

"Your concern for my welfare seems to know no bounds," she said thickly, swallowing her disappointment.

He took three steps away, then turned back.

"One other bit of advice."

Her eyes glistened in the dim light. "Yes?"

He glanced at the voluptuous outline of her breasts, and his voice sank half an octave. "Get a damned corset. At least they give you a bit of thinking time."

The next morning Sir William arrived in his chambers early, read briefs and petitions, and opened the morning post. He was surprised to find a letter from Cole in it.

"It's not been a week yet, has it?" he demanded of Foglethorpe.

"No, Sir William. Five days by my count," the clerk answered, edging closer to get a discreet glimpse over Sir William's shoulder.

Sir William settled his pince-nez on his nose and held the letter a helpful distance away. As he read, a smile appeared and slowly broadened. "Ahhh. I believe they're making progress. She's a 'stubborn, idealistic little fool who lacks sense enough to come in out of the rain.' She's giving away food, giving away free clothes, and she's hired a passel of *ignoramuses*." He chuckled and removed his spectacles. "Well, at least he hasn't forgotten his Latin."

The sun was well up when Davenport bustled into Madeline's room the next morning and threw back the heavy velvet curtains at the windows. "Rise and shine, Maddy Duncan. You're sleepin' the day away."

"I am?" She groaned as she lifted her head up out of the pillows and squinted at the bright light in disbelief. "Oh, I am!"

She jumped up out of bed, swayed unsteadily, and sat back down on the edge. "I feel as if someone has replaced my bones with rubber."

"Exhaustion, pure and simple." Davenport stood nearby with her hands clasped at her waist and a look of disapproval. "You don't take time to eat and you're not sleeping well. Will you listen to me this once and have a decent breakfast?" She saw Madeline's scowl and guessed its cause. "*He's* been at the table for some time, insisting he'll wait breakfast for you."

"He's waiting for me?" A sudden, intense image flashed before Madeline's eyes: him sitting at the table with his pocket watch in hand, ticking off the minutes that she slept past sunrise. She was up in a flash and pulling from the wardrobe the scarlet tunic and trousers that had become her uniform of late.

As she entered the dining room and took her seat, she could feel his gaze and, without looking, could sense his disapproval.

"You're wearing that again, are you?" he asked, beckoning for a refill of his cup.

"Good morning to you too," she said flatly, refusing to

look at him as she settled her napkin and drank the orange juice by her plate.

"It's just that . . . *I've* seen you in other things, but no one else has."

It was a reference to their midnight rendezvous in the kitchen, she realized, resisting the urge to look up from the boiled egg, toast, and ham on her plate. The heat in her cheeks would only encourage him.

"You know, as I pass through the sewing room, I sometimes catch a bit of the women's talk. Your trousers are something of a topic."

"They are?" She raised her head and saw just what she expected: a sardonic smile.

"They think it odd that you're so dead set on looking like a man, when with a bit of help you could be such a fetching woman."

"I do *not* look like a man."

"That would be my assessment. But then, I've always had an eye for these things. Not everyone is quite so perceptive." He took a bite of toast and washed it down with coffee. "One of the more astute observers did point out the fact that you have a small waist, but the doubters insisted you must secretly wear a corset of some sort." His smile broadened annoyingly. "I thought about providing them a testimonial to your curves, but quickly realized that it might be . . . misinterpreted." He gave a sigh. "Well, what can you expect from the great unwashed?"

"They are *not* 'the unwashed,' " she said, bashing her boiled egg with excessive force.

"Oh, that's right. They have running water now." He was patronizing her. "Personally, I say one would have to be a ninny to think that just because you always wear trousers, you're expecting your women workers to do the same . . . to dress like their men. Why, you've never said the first thing about trousers." He scowled and pursed his lips. "Except perhaps yesterday, at your workers' meeting.

"No, no. Stick to your guns, St. Madeline. No half mea-
sures. I admire that about you. Why should you compromise
your personal integrity and comfort just to cater to their me-
dieval prejudices? Sooner or later, *someone* will put on one of
your bodices and prove to the lot of them that the garments
work just as well under conventional clothing."

That said, he attacked his own boiled egg with gusto.

Madeline, however, had lost her appetite completely.

Was that what her workers thought? That she dressed
like a man? She contemplated that for a moment. She did
love her trousers. But women—whether her workers or her
final customers—would need to know that they could wear
Ideal garments beneath the clothes they already owned. Even
if they thought Ideal undergarments were a splendid notion,
few would be able to afford a whole new wardrobe to wear
on top of them. And fewer still would consider purchasing
and wearing them if they thought their sole use was under
trousers.

She dropped her knife and headed for the stairs.

Cole gave a pained smile and stuffed a piece of slathered
toast into his mouth. *Mandeville,* he told himself, *you are indeed
your father's son.* Sometimes a well-placed bit of arrogance and
condescension were exactly what a situation called for.

When Madeline climbed the stairs to the cutting room floor
later that morning, she was clad in a soft printed cotton dress
with a fitted waist, shirred sleeves, and a gently flared skirt.
Heads turned and a murmur raced along the tables. She held
her chin up and tried to behave as if nothing were different.
But when she paused to talk to Ben Murtry, he snatched his
hat off his head before answering. And when she spoke with
Daniel Steadman about how the pattern templates were holding up, she noticed he stood with his hands behind his back
and seemed especially attentive to what she said. By the time
she spoke with Fritz about the occasional fluctuations in

power levels to the machines, and the engineer—at least fifteen years her senior—called her "ma'am," she was roundly confused. She would never have guessed that the simple act of putting on a dress could make such a difference in their response to her. And she hadn't a clue whether these changes were for good or ill.

By the time she reached the offices, she was beginning to wonder if she was in the right factory. But the instant she set foot in the outer office, she realized she was indeed in her own Ideal Garment Company. The place was positively overrun with small children climbing, crawling, and bawling. It was chaos.

Emily stood in the middle of the outer office with one toddler on each hip and their hands clamped around her neck. When she saw Madeline, she waded across the room and tried to explain.

"Priscilla Steadman's little Michael was so difficult and out of sorts, she couldn't work. I offered to hold him for a while and he seemed to take to me straightaway. Then Alva Murtry's daughter, Polly, started crying, and so I held her too. I've always had a way with babies. It's only when they get a bit older that I have difficulty." She glanced at her two sons, climbing all over her desk, squealing and pulling at each other, and she winced.

"That explains *two* of them," Madeline said as one young creeper pulled himself up, using her skirt for balance, and another fastened himself to her ankle. She peeled them from her and found herself holding one in her arms. "What about the others? There must be a dozen—"

"Nine," Emily demurred. "It only seems like a dozen. Well, the other mothers were having troubles too, and I could scarcely help one and not another. I know how much producing the garments means to you, and I thought if I kept the children busy . . ."

Madeline took a breath and counted to five. Then five more. A glance back through the open door revealed an unprecedented calm in the sewing room. She had to hope it meant unprecedented productivity as well.

"Very well, then care, for them today, if you—" She glanced up and noticed Tattersall's empty desk. "Where is Tattersall?"

Emily looked aggrieved to have to report: "He couldn't work in here. He took his books into your office."

Madeline found poor Tattersall seated at her desk, his mouth drawn tight and his brow knit with irritation. With a wave she ordered him to keep his seat and continue working. But she turned back to Emily with a dark look.

"We cannot keep them here. We won't get anything done ourselves." She jiggled the restless toddler in her arms and tried to think. One of Emily's boys suddenly lunged at the other, upsetting an inkwell all over the stacks of correspondence on the secretary's desk.

"Oh, nooo!" Emily cried, trying to empty her arms of children to rescue what she could of the letters. The tots she abandoned sent up a wail, which started a reaction among the others, and soon the room was filled with caterwauling.

It was the worst possible moment for Cole to arrive. He stepped into the office, looked around in disbelief, and would have ducked right back out the door if he hadn't seen a look of equal horror on Madeline's face. She tried desperately to quiet some of the children while Emily cornered her sons and, between tears, tried to scold them. The moment Emily began searching her pockets for a handkerchief, the pair bolted.

Cole saw two small bodies hurtling toward him and simply reacted, snatching both up in his arms and holding their feet well above the floor until they stopped struggling.

"You two," he growled as he recognized Jonathan and Theodore Farrow. "I'm going to put you down and you're going to stand perfectly still. Is that understood?" His deadly tone made the hair on the backs of their necks prickle, so when he set them on their feet they were as still as mice.

Then he seized each boy by an ear and dragged the pair out the door on tiptoe.

Emily gasped and would have gone after them, but Madeline called her back and insisted that she tend her other charges. After a harrowing few minutes, the fright subsided and they were able to quiet the children. They then discovered Tattersall standing by his desk, hobbled by two young children clamped around his knees and whining. His knuckles were white and his face ashen.

"What do I do?" he choked out, peering down at them as if afraid they were about to gnaw on his kneecaps. Madeline rescued him by peeling them away.

"If you'll permit me to suggest . . ." he said after he was more composed. "There are two rooms on the ground level that aren't being used. If we took a table or two and some chairs . . . Mrs. Farrow could see to the children there today. And perhaps we could find a girl or two from the next village to come and take her place tomorrow."

Madeline heaved a huge sigh of relief. Thank heaven for Tattersall.

In short order she had inspected the rooms, drafted a few workers to help move some furnishings, and begun the process of moving the children. But it became increasingly clear that Emily could never cope with all of them at once. As Madeline stood in the office, her arms full of squirming toddlers, waiting for the workers to ferry the last two downstairs to Emily's makeshift nursery, she was feeling quite disheartened.

This was not how she had pictured running a clothing factory. Wrong shipments . . . slippery contractors . . . lackadaisical and outright reluctant workers . . . unforeseen obstacles . . . brawling boys and squalling babies underfoot—it was just one impossible problem after another. The work she intended to do always seemed to be shoved aside in favor of somebody else's crisis. Now she was finding herself thrust into the role of a reluctant baby-minder. . . .

In strolled Jessup Endicott, fresh from a walk in the nearby woods. He took in the sight of her with her arms full of children and broke into a wistful smile. "My dear Madeline! You were just *made* to cradle babies in your arms." He swooped across the office and held out an artistic hand to the children.

"Do you see that?" he crowed when one cherub reached open arms to him. "Babies adore me, you know. We have something of an affinity, a *simpatico* . . . grounded in a rare mutuality of nature. We share an instinctive recognition of the splendor of simplicity and a deep appreciation of the value of being ourselves. Don't we, my sweet little cherub?" He pulled the little one into his arms and the child nestled contentedly against him. "Babies are so magical," he crooned, patting the toddler's back and glowing with genuine affection. "As far back as I can recall, I've had a magic touch with them."

Madeline stared, openmouthed, as the toddler remaining in her arms leaned and stretched and babbled, trying desperately to get to Endicott too. When the designer extended a lanky arm to accept the child, Madeline willingly handed her over.

"Endicott," she said, breaking into a beaming smile. "Come with me."

In her office sometime later, Madeline sat staring ahead of her blankly, trying to remember just what it was she had intended to do that day. Her reverie was interrupted minutes later by the sound of someone clearing his throat. She looked up to find Cole in the doorway with his hands on the shoulders of two young boys who looked remarkably like Emily's sons . . . except for—

"Their hair!" She hurried over to inspect. "What did you do?"

"I had Cravits cut it," Cole said with aplomb. "He's a

genius with the shears, as these young gentlemen will attest."
He addressed them. "You may wait outside for me." They
nodded with widened eyes, called him "sir," and hurried—
without running—into the outer office.

"Who are those creatures, and what have you done with
Emily's children?" Madeline demanded, peering out the
door, watching them walk upright like real human beings.

"I did what should have been done long ago. I got them
a haircut, gave them a decent breakfast, and threatened to tan
their hides for boot leather if I ever saw such behavior out of
them again." While she was absorbing that, he sauntered into
the office and planted himself in a chair. "What the little
wretches need is a dose of sound discipline and plenty of work
to keep them busy."

"Well, I've engaged a schoolmaster, but it will be at least
three weeks before he arrives," Madeline said, more than a
little perturbed.

"Three weeks?" His eyes glinted. "Well, I'm certain they
can find something to deface, dismantle, or incinerate to keep
them busy for a few weeks. Failing that, they can always find
some*one* to vandalize, terrify, or dismember."

Even knowing he was taunting her, she suffered a hor-
rifying vision of a rampaging herd of Jonathans and Theodores
bursting through the factory and village, trampling everything
in their path. With so many parents at work, the number of
children at loose ends was alarming. All too often "loose
ends" came to "bad ends."

"I suppose . . . we may need an interim schoolmaster,"
she admitted.

"What you need is someone with the eyes of an eagle,
the heart of a lion, and the constitution of a bull elephant,"
he put in helpfully. "In short, a zoological wonder who will
take these little hooligans in hand, glue their bottoms on seats,
and cram sums, letters, and recitations into their heads until
they give in and grow up."

"Well, you certainly make the job sound like every tutor's dream," she declared irritably. "Do you also have a candidate in mind for the post?"

"Actually, one name does spring to mind." He smiled annoyingly. "But I believe Moses has been dead for a few millennia."

"I have a candidate," came a voice from the doorway. They looked up to see Tattersall standing with his hands gripping the edges of his vest. He reddened a bit under their scrutiny. "Myself."

"B-but, Tattersall," Madeline said, staring at him in bewilderment, "you don't know the first thing about children . . . do you?"

"I have impeccable credentials," he said with a sniff. "I used to be one myself."

"Now, here's a possibility." Cole sat back and stroked his chin. "But I must say, Tattersall, I never would have taken you for a man with a death wish."

Madeline heatedly ignored Cole. "But what about your other work, Beaumont?"

"I have the books and ledgers established, and they won't require much time until we're in full production. I can do the books of an afternoon for a few weeks." He fidgeted and lowered his gaze. "I've always fancied having a go at schoolmastering."

"The books and slates arrived some time ago. And I suppose we could use the classroom in the factory while Harley and his sons ready the parish house." She agonized for a moment, then nodded without enthusiasm. "We'll try it, then."

"Excellent," Tattersall said, beaming as he headed out the door.

"They'll send him to rack and ruin," she said, staring wanly after him.

Cole chuckled and headed for the outer office. "Don't be so certain."

Madeline hurried out after him, and they reached the outer office just in time to see the mild-mannered clerk taking

Emily's mischievous boys by the scruff of their necks. A determined fire appeared in his eyes as he looked them over.

"I've been wanting to have a talk with you young gentlemen for some time now." His smile both broadened and tightened. "Come with me."

Madeline watched Tattersall trundling the children out the door and sent Cole a narrow look. "If you've cost me my best employee, I'll never forgive you."

"That's awfully human of you, Archangel Madeline. I might have expected something more in the way of . . . oh, I don't know . . . a host of gratitude, perhaps."

She started. "Gratitude? For what? Annoying and interfering and prodding and meddling and—" She stopped, and her expression evolved into an insightful glare. "And helping."

"Helping?" He jerked back as if slapped, blinked as the sense of it hit, then reddened from the collar up. "There is no cause to be insulting, Miss Duncan!"

As he strode out, she watched the rigidity of his shoulders and the set of his jaw and realized that she had genuinely unsettled him. She had accused him—and justly so—of helping. True, he had done it in a backhanded sort of a way, through nudging and needling with that insufferable wit of his. Just like this morning at breakfast with that business about her trousers . . .

She wobbled over to Emily's desk and sat down hard in the secretary's chair. Twice in one day he had taken it upon himself to bring up changes that he thought needed to be made at Ideal. First he taunted her into setting a more accessible example for her women workers, then he proposed she do something right away about the problem of the older children. Two suggestions in one day.

Helping.

She began to smile, and soon she was positively glowing.

He wasn't half the cynic he professed to be. Recalling the horror in his face as he realized it too, she hugged herself and laughed. It was a hard thing, she supposed, for a proud cynic to realize he bore a shameful streak of hope. Well, she would just have to help him see that such a flaw needn't be fatal. And where better to resurrect defeated dreams than at the Ideal factory?

11

"*Another* report?" Foglethorpe said, eagerly perching on a stool beside Sir William's chair and craning his neck for a glimpse of the letter the old justice held. "He must have a good bit of time on his hands."

Sir William chuckled and resettled his spectacles on his nose. "From the sound of things, that's not all he has on his hands. Listen. 'The place is a bottomless pit, into which St. Madeline nobly unburdens herself of her wealth. Each day there seems to be another crisis requiring a sizable outlay of coin . . . the most recent involving the hiring of baby-minders to see to the women workers' children so that she may have the privilege of paying them to work on clothing for the little wretches to wear. She's an incurable soft touch, and I've grown tired of the incessant naysaying required to keep her solvent. I've given her the strings of her own purse. If you don't approve, replace me. *Quickly.* Your reluctant servant, Mandeville.' "

Sir William lowered the letter and laid his

head back against the chair. "He's coming right along, Fogles. She's gone from 'Mad Madeline' to 'St. Madeline' and he's given up trying to 'cash-starve' the philanthropy out of her." He gave a wistful smile. "I'd give six months off my life to know just how much of her incurable 'soft touch' he's experienced."

Later that same morning, across London in a comfortable house on the edge of Mayfair, Gilbert Duncan was receiving a visitor. He breezed into his parlor, tidying his tie, but stopped instantly at the sight of the scruffy Rupert Fitch parked upon the silk upholstery of his expensive new second empire settee.

"*You.* What are you doing here?"

Rupert smiled with oily self-assurance. "Now, is that any way to talk to a man who's just brought you the keys to a fortune?"

Madeline hurried up the stairs from the storage room three mornings later, a scowl on her face. As she reached the second flight of stairs, the front doors banged open and she was swept up in a tide of children of varying ages rumbling up the steps to their makeshift classroom just off the cutting floor.

She greeted them absently, her mind on what she had discovered in the storage room. Then one little fellow popped up on the step in front of her, demanding her full attention.

"Look wot I can do, Miz Duncan!" he declared, and executed a wobbly handstand right there on the steps.

She gasped.

"Don't do that—not here! You'll hurt yourself!"

"No, I won't! I do it all th' time!" he crowed, standing upside down, red-faced and grinning at her horror.

While the other children clamored past, he proceeded on his hands up the few remaining steps. At the top he righted himself, waved mischievously, and darted off. Belatedly, she recognized little Robbie Steadman—in a spanking new pair of trousers, a middy blouse trimmed with a bit of white piping, and a white cotton tie.

She suddenly realized that many of the children were dressed in the same handsome blue wool jersey. Warmth spread through her. So the children were indeed wearing her design! And Robbie's antic clearly bore out the greater freedom of movement afforded by the garments. She allowed herself a moment of triumph, but then returned to the problem of the nearly empty storeroom shelves.

The time had come to send samples of her Ideal bodices and knickers to the various ladies and mercantile establishments on her list of "influentials." So she had gone downstairs first thing that morning to begin packing—only to discover a mere handful of garments on the shelves, several of which were mysteriously sewn with dark blue thread. Even allowing for plenty of mistakes, there should have been several dozen of each garment by then. Where were the others? And what on earth could they be thinking, stitching white bodices with blue thread?

For the past three days, with only occasional interruptions—like when the Ketchum boys sauntered through and stopped to flirt with Charlotte and a couple of the younger women—her dozen seamstresses had worked steadily on the garments.

Madeline trudged up the rest of the stairs and walked slowly through the sewing room as the women were settling in at their machines and beginning to work.

In her office, she called Maple in and asked her about the shortage of finished garments. Maple seemed a bit uncomfortable as she disclaimed any knowledge of the matter, but promised to give it some attention.

When the head seamstress left, Madeline turned to find Cole standing in the doorway of her office with his hands in his pockets.

"Trouble in paradise, Archangel Madeline?" He strolled in. She busied herself with the letters on Emily's desk. "I couldn't help overhearing."

"I suppose not . . . not with your ear to the door," she said tartly.

"It seems you're having a productivity problem."

"Nothing we can't solve."

"Ummm." He smiled and ambled toward the door. "If you keep an eye out, I suppose."

It was his prickly way of warning her, she knew. She couldn't help wondering what else he knew and wasn't saying. She worked on signing the second round of solicitation letters she and Tattersall had penned the previous afternoon. When she finished, his words were still lingering in her mind. *Keep an eye out . . .*

She headed abruptly into the sewing room, walking with her head up, as if her thoughts were elsewhere. Instantly there was a small flurry at one of the machines along the far side of the room. She couldn't quite locate the source until the sound of someone clearing his throat drew her attention to Cole, who was leaning his arm with determined nonchalance on top of a sewing table. As she changed course and walked toward him, heads lifted and eyes followed her every move. When she neared, Cole turned and sat down on the edge of the table, trapping something beneath him. The woman sitting rigidly at the machine, her face reddening, was none other than Bess Clark.

"Interesting thing, stitchery. I've just been watching Mrs. Clark, here, as she works on"—he rose from his seat on the fabric Bess Clark had been stitching and gave it a puzzled look—"whatever it is she is working on."

What she had been working on was dark blue woolen, part of a pair of trousers. She sullenly snatched it from the table and thrust it into her lunch basket at her feet, then reached for one of a stack of bodice pieces stacked on the other side of her machine. Even without Cole's insinuating smile, Madeline would have been hard pressed not to make the connection.

She backtracked along the machines, looking at the color thread being used, and at the first machine where she found blue, she peered beneath the table at the woman's lunch basket and pulled out a nearly completed girl's dress.

"I believe the mystery of your dismal level of productivity is solved," Cole said as he strolled past her and into the office.

But that was only half true. Finding the problem hadn't been particularly difficult, thanks to Cole. The hard part would be coming up with a solution. The women looked warily at her, wondering what she would do now that they had been working on their children's clothes rather than Ideal undergarments.

She told herself it wasn't surprising that the women were spending most of their time making clothes for the children. Most of them weren't accustomed to thinking beyond the welfare of their immediate families. But they were being paid to work for the Ideal Garment Company, and she needed to control her frustration and irritation before she could speak reasonably about it.

"You've been sewing a great deal but producing very few salable garments." She paused, thinking. "It is of the utmost importance that we have samples to send to merchants and to individuals for endorsements. From now on, Mrs. Thoroughgood will spend her time exclusively in supervision—to be certain you have all the help you require."

She could tell by their faces that they knew Maple would be doing more than just "helping," and they resented it. Eager to make some concession, she added, "But since you obviously feel so strongly about the children's clothes, you may continue to work on the children's garments for the last two hours of each day."

Ignoring the murmuring, possibly even grumbling, she turned and headed back into her office. There, Cole was standing in the doorway in his favorite condescending male posture—arms crossed, chin up.

"That's telling them."

"If you don't have anything to do, I can certainly find something to occupy you," she said, gliding past him to retrieve the letters from Emily's desk.

"Has it occurred to you that thus far you've given away everything you've produced?"

"I consider it . . . a prudent investment."

He followed her and perched on the edge of her desk as she folded letters and stuffed them in envelopes.

"Generosity, as a virtue, is highly overrated. And like most other highly vaunted virtues, it generally flows in only one direction. You give and give, until you can't give anymore, and people will still be there with their hands out." His voice lowered, drawing her gaze to his. "Where will your precious workers be, angel, when *you* need something?"

She studied his worldly eyes, disturbed by the suggestion of painful experience in his words and tone. "Is that what happened to you? You gave and gave . . . until you had no more to give?"

"Me?" In a heartbeat, his defenses were up. But then he took a deep breath and admitted, "I bled for my share of lost causes. In the end, they were all still *lost*."

"In all those years at the bar, you never *won*? Not even once?" she challenged. "I find that difficult to believe."

He considered that a moment, then produced a pained smile. "You do have a way of stripping things down to bare tacks, Madeline Duncan." Then he rose and left the room without any further response.

For a few moments she sat thinking about what he had said. Suppose she reworded his multilayered question. Who hadn't been there when Cole needed something? His family, most certainly. They had carelessly packed him off to live with tenants, then callously ignored his pleas for clemency for his foster family. But those were old hurts. Who in more recent days hadn't bothered to help when he needed it? Someone connected with the law he had loved and then left? Sir William? Someone in his firm?

More important still, what was it he needed now? And what would she have to do to help him find it?

Increased productivity brought problems of its own, Madeline soon learned. The blue-stitched bodices and knickers were set aside to be distributed to the women workers as promised. But what were they to do with bodices that were stitched hastily or crookedly, or that had misaligned buttons? Quality control was one problem she hadn't anticipated. She had somehow assumed that the products would be perfect and desirable simply because she and her workers would want them to be and would work to make it so. It was the first real flaw in her well-thought-out system.

Short of walking the sewing floor herself, peering over the shoulders of her workers and directing every stitch, she had little control over the actual sewing process. She decided to offer a "piece bonus" for correctly stitched garments, and by the end of the third day she was marking down numerous credits in a ledger. Quality had improved drastically, but at some expense and only with her time-consuming inspection of each and every garment.

Mornings began earlier and evenings lasted later than ever now. She ate when Davenport appeared with a tray of food, and nearly always stumbled home well after dark and fell asleep in whatever place or position she landed. There was no time—even if she had been so inclined—for a midnight rendezvous in the kitchen.

Her greatest pleasure each day came when she stood by the front doors as the children entered and saw the new garments they were wearing. The boys liked to demonstrate how they could reach or run or jump in their new clothes, and the girls accepted her compliments and beamed with pride when she commented on the ways their mothers had decorated collars or added cuffs to sleeves to give the dresses more individuality. More than half the children now wore Ideal garments, and when she had a few minutes free or her determination needed a boost, she went to the classroom door and peered in for a glimpse of blue jersey.

Then in the middle of one afternoon Daniel Steadman came rushing up the stairs to the office with a letter from London. When she saw the return address on the envelope, she opened it with trembling hands.

It was from Liberty of London. It seemed that when he was in London, Tattersall had done more than merely buy cloth; he had spoken to his friend at the store about Ideal garments. At the urging of Tattersall's friend, the directors of Liberty had decided to look at her reform clothing with an eye toward offering it to their customers.

"A customer!" she cried, hugging the letter to her, then waved it ecstatically as she danced about the office. "And *Liberty* of all places. The premier mercantile establishment of London's wealthy west side! If we can get them to offer our undergarments, before long a goodly number of the 'upper ten' will be wearing them—I'd bet the factory on it!"

Cole's smile was a bit forced as he refrained from mentioning that she might just be doing that very thing. If Liberty's approval meant success, their disapproval could also mean failure. But she had worked so hard to come this far, and the joy in her face was just too painfully sweet to disturb.

Madeline hurried down to the shipping room to personally locate tissue and pasteboard boxes, then set some of the cutters to packing up the garments stacked in the storage room. In a short while she had composed a letter to accompany the garments. She then oversaw the loading of several boxes into a wagon bound for the nearby village of Stonecrouch, from where they would be put on the next mail coach to London.

When she called her seamstresses and cutters together on

the sewing floor to announce the news, her buoyant mood ignited an explosion of celebration among her workers. They applauded, shouted, laughed, and hugged one another. Some-one produced a mouth organ and a tune, and soon seam-stresses and cutters were dancing up and down the aisles between the worktables. The commotion forced Tattersall to release the children from class to join in the excitement.

Madeline stood in the office doorway, watching, filled with mixed emotions at the disruptive celebration. Cole came to join her.

"Well, you won't get another piece cut or another stitch sewn this day," he said.

"I suppose not," she responded with a tired smile. "But perhaps it will do them good to let off a bit of steam. They've had a great many changes to get used to in the last two weeks. Besides, there are only two hours left in the workday."

He turned his gaze from the merrymaking to her. "If anyone in this place needs a change of pace, angel, it's you."

She looked up at him, his warm autumn eyes, and the handsome mouth, and for the first time in three days gave serious thought to what she must look like. Running a hand over her hair and finding it slightly frizzed, she blushed.

"Perhaps you're right. I haven't been out of the factory in daylight for days. Maybe a walk and some fresh air would do me some good."

She smiled and left him to go down the rear stairs.

After a few moments he decided to go after her and offer his company. He could use a walk too.

The sounds of raised voices and metallic clanking and pound-ing drifted in through the open door at the bottom of the stairs. She slowed, puzzled by them, then quickened her step and was soon standing in the rear yard of the factory.

Her long-anticipated garden was a scene of total devas-tation. All the vegetation and the elevation and planting lines between the factory and the large trees had been trampled or buried under Alp-sized mounds of dirt. In the center of the clearing was that massive rock covered with ropes and ringed with a trench fully four feet wide. On the far side, away from the factory, an earthen ramp sloped up from the bottom of the rock, and logs that resembled small trees were jammed under the side of the rock and up the incline. Roscoe and Algy were at the heads of two teams of massive plow horses straining at the ropes, trying to drag the rock up that slope. But even at the peak of their powerful efforts, the boulder didn't budge.

For a few moments she stood frozen, unable to believe her eyes. When Roscoe and Algy spotted her, they halted the horses. Then they made their way toward her across the trench and mounds of earth.

"Well, miz . . . we almost got 'er done." Roscoe beamed as he looked past her to Cole, who had come up behind her. "Right lucky we heard about them old E-gyptians an' their pyreemids. They moved stones bigger'n this, I hear tell"— he winked at Cole—"usin' these here roller-logs and just a few broad backs."

"Egyptians?" she choked out, staring at the knotty tree trunks they had stuffed down the side of the rock. They were trying to implement some cockeyed notion they had garnered from God knew where about *building pyramids*? Emotion choked off all utterance. She began trembling as the full horror of it descended. They had torn up a perfectly promising garden, wrecked a number of natural flowers and shrubs, and cut down a number of small trees—all to move one cursed rock that would probably never budge!

She turned to Roscoe and Algy, helplessly enraged in the face of their blissfully genuine smiles. They honestly didn't think they'd done anything wrong!

"It's a wreck!" she finally blurted out. "A foul, disgusting mess!"

"It may appear so," Roscoe said, rocking up onto his

toes. "But ye jus' wait until we get Old Cussed outta there. We'll soon have 'er filled and planted an' blooming fine."

"Just leave the wretched thing in there," She spluttered, making frantic scooping motions toward the dirt piles. "Just push the dirt back in . . . put it all back the way it was!"

"Ohhh, no, miz," Roscoe said gravely. "Don't ye be fooled. That rock 'as to go. To make a proper garden, yer plants must put down plenty o' root." He wagged his head ruefully. "Can't do that in rock. And if we wuz t'plant shallow, over the rock, the first dry spell, yer roots'd bake right out. It'd be a right desert out here." He wiped his dripping face with a handkerchief. "We'd 'ave had it out today if that Rupert hadn'ta cut out on us. Dodgy bloke. Always said so." He tapped his temple with a forefinger. "Somethin' not quite right . . ."

A band of anguish was tightening around Madeline's chest, and she suddenly felt light-headed. Her jaw was beginning to ache from being clamped, and a humiliating pricking had begun at the corners of her eyes. The idiots! *This,* on top of everything else of late . . .

She half scrambled, half slid down the pile of dirt where she had been standing, and struck off in the direction of her house. By the time she reached the corner of the factory, she was running.

"Takin' it a might hard, ain't she?" Roscoe said, watching her. "Well, that's women for ye. Never can see the possibilities in a thing . . ."

"Damn and blast it!" Cole lunged and seized him by the shirt, giving him a powerful shake. "I ought to thrash the pair of you within an inch of your lives!"

He released Roscoe with a snarl of disgust. In his mind's eye he was seeing the indelible image of Madeline staring at the devastation, the fatigue evident in her face, the tears collecting in her eyes, the tightly contained anguish that set her trembling from head to toe. He began to go after her, then halted.

He knew what would happen if he caught up with her. He would take her in his arms and comfort her, tell her things she wanted and needed to hear. She would look up at him with tears rolling down her cheeks . . . so sweet and so miserable, so loving and giving and good . . . looking like everything his battered heart had ever wanted in life . . . and he would plunge—headlong and emotions first—into an entanglement with her.

The signs were all there. He was already crazy about her. He wanted to see her, be with her, tease, listen to, or cross words with her. Experience, logic, and wisdom against it, he had already been nudging things into their "ideal" place in her blessed factory. With a word here, a glower there, a calculated presence in the cutting room or the shipping department, he found himself reminding Ideal workers of their obligations. If he went to her now, he'd be walking off his last bridge to safe, impersonal security. He'd be in over his head . . . no going back.

How could he go through all that again? Caring . . . losing . . . hurting . . . He halted, took another step, then halted again.

And if he didn't go? Could he really just turn his head and let her step off the cliff on which she was unknowingly poised?

He thought again of the softness of her heart, the stubborn determination of her optimism, her hope, and her need to give. The world needed a few self-sacrificing souls to keep human life and society bearable. He thought again of the delectable responsiveness of her mouth, the welcoming warmth of her body against his, and how together they seemed to fill some cold, empty region inside him. The hell with the world—he needed something to make *his* life bearable.

"Damn you, old man," he muttered, lurching into motion. "You knew this would happen . . ." Within three steps he was running too.

•   •   •

Algy looked after them with a doleful expression, then sank down on the nearest pile of dirt and wiped his nose. "Roscoe, I think we gone an' made her cry."

Roscoe sat down with a thud beside his cohort, clutching his chest above his heart. But the discomfort in his chest was far more serious than the physical ailment he feared it to be. He was suffering an unprecedented pang of conscience.

"We got to make it right, Alg," he said when that brief sharp pain subsided. "We got to find a way to get rid o' that rock and give Miz Duncan back 'er garden."

"What'll we do, Roscoe?"

Roscoe rubbed his face and thought on it. When it came to him, he brightened. "We'll do jus' what 'is lordship said. *Blast it.*"

With his long stride, Cole caught up with Madeline at the kitchen door. He caught her arm.

"L-let me go—what are you—" She twisted in his grip and tried to resist being pulled down the steps . . . to no avail.

"Come with me, Madeline Duncan." He wrapped an arm around her and all but dragged her around the side of the house.

"Where are you taking me?" she demanded, averting her face so he wouldn't see her eyes as she wiped them.

"Somewhere—anywhere—as long as it's away from this bloody place for a while," he declared hotly, propelling her around the house and toward Netter's Tavern.

"You can't just *abduct* me," she insisted in a choked voice.

"I'm your court-appointed nanny. That *is* what you call me behind my back, is it not? As your nanny, I can do whatever I believe is in your best interest. If I say you need to get away from this place, then—by damn—you'll get away for a while!"

He led her into the shed at the rear of Netter's Tavern and warned her not to move as he saddled his horse. She was in such inner turmoil that it didn't occur to her to run out while he was occupied. By the time she thought of it, he had the reins in one hand and her in the other, leading both her and his horse outside. Seizing her by the waist, he told her to jump and succeeded in hoisting her up onto the pommel of the saddle. Then he managed to climb on behind and pulled her back against him.

They rode straight out of the village and over hills and through valleys, following the road that had brought him to St. Crispin. Exactly how long they rode, neither could be sure, but it was long enough for both Madeline and the horse to begin to tire.

Spotting a stream with banks lined with trees, he headed for it, riding under tall, arching elms and white oaks along the way. There were grassy slopes descending toward the stream, and as they neared the water, they could hear it gurgling over rocks. There they finally dismounted.

"All right, go ahead," he said, looking at her with his hands on his hips.

"Go ahead and what?" she demanded.

"Get it out of your system."

She huddled back with her arms wrapped tightly around her waist. "What?"

"The anger, the disappointment . . . the sadness."

"I'm not angry or disappointed or—"

"The hell you're not," he declared, advancing on her until he was within arm's reach. His eyes were blazing. "Those idiots have torn the hell out of your garden and anyone in their right mind would be bloody, pitching furious about it. Now, unless you truly are *Mad Madeline,* I suggest you get it out of your system. You can't keep it locked up inside forever."

She stared helplessly at him, her emotion too tightly bottled within for her to be able to follow his suggestion. He shook his head.

"Do you even know a single curse word?" he asked in disgust.

"I . . . don't think it necessary to resort to—" Her voice was small and choked.

"Very well, then. *The bloody bastards,*" he declared, shoving his face into hers. "Say it."

"What?"

"Say it," he demanded. *"The bloody bastards!"*

She blinked and turned her face away, but he took her chin in his fingers and forced her to look at him.

"The bastards," she mumbled through tightly clenched jaws.

He winced. "Louder."

"The bloody bastards." It was only a tiny bit louder.

He groaned. "You're supposed to shout it, sneer it, or roar it," he declared. "Blow my ears back. Deafen me." When he saw panic rising in her eyes, he seized her by the shoulders. "Sweetheart, if you haven't got guts enough to blue the air a bit, you haven't got the guts to run a factory or build a village."

She inhaled but couldn't seem to expel her breath. Days—weeks—of draining work and worry and determination had left a pile of promissory notes inside her, one for each withdrawal made on her emotional reserves. Suddenly that emptiness began to fill with hot, churning emotions . . . rising, swelling, billowing frighteningly within her.

He released her and backed a step, looking her over with deliberate disdain. "Then pack it up, angel. Just call it quits and save us both a lot of time and trouble. The place is a shambles anyway, and your workers are nothing but a bunch of lousy, shiftless, stupid clods. You never had a chance anyway." He crossed his arms and snorted. "All those lovely ideals, St. Madeline. And look where they got you."

"Bastard," she said in a raspy voice.

"What?" His eyes glinted as he cocked his head. "I don't believe I quite caught that. Blasted? Blazes? Blamnation?"

"*Bastards*," she said with significantly more heat and volume. *"Bloody bastards!"*

"Why, Miss Duncan"—he stepped back and pressed his hand to his chest—"that sounds almost *peevish*."

"Those idiots!" she shouted, flushing hot and trembling, feeling as if she'd burst if she didn't get it out. "Fools—dolts—oafs—dunces—they haven't got half a brain between them!" She paced back and forth and shook her fists. "They tore the living thunder out of my garden—and had the brass to stand there and lecture me on bloody horticulture! Roots, they say, '*plants gots to 'ave a bit o' root.*' Roots be blamed! Who gives an infernal damn about *roots* when the entire place looks like a battlefield on the day after!" She kicked a stone and sent it skittering. "Stupid clods—don't have the sense God gave an onion—"

While she was busy raving, he cast about for a small branch and now handed it to her, pointing her to a nearby oak. "Give it a few good whacks. Go on, you won't kill it." When she glowered at him, he suggested: "Think of it as a proxy for Roscoe and Algy."

Bark and twigs went flying off the dry branch, and satisfying thwacks resounded along the streambank. She wielded the branch so hard between virulent epithets that Cole began to feel sorry for the tree. She must have felt it too, for, after a time, when her fury was mostly spent, she halted and lowered the bough.

"Numskulls." Her voice was once more choked with emotion, but when she raised her head he could see it wasn't anger. "Why would they do that to my garden?" Tears finally began to roll.

She felt his arms wrapping around her and tried to push away, desperate to regain control, horrified that he would see her cry.

"No, no, no." He overcame her resistance and pulled

her against him, shoving her face into his lapel. "Don't fight it. Let it come. Bawl it out. No mewling or whimpering, now—make those big, obnoxious snuffling noises. The louder the better. Make sure your nose runs and your eyes get good and swollen. Hiccups are always good, if you can manage—"

She smacked him on the chest with her fist, and he stopped. Then his arms tightened around her and she felt his chin settling on her head and his chest move in a quiet sigh.

It was like being enveloped in a living oak. He was warm and hard and smelled faintly of starched linen, wool, and a woody male aura that was oddly reminiscent of the scent of new lumber. In that firm embrace she felt sheltered and valued and wanted in a way that had nothing to do with philanthropic ideals. Pressed against his body, wetting his shirt with her accumulated tensions and fears and disappointments, she was just Madeline. Not factory superintendent Duncan. Not Saint Madeline. Not anyone's guardian angel. Just a woman, being held by a man.

For the first time in days the tightly wound coil of determination in her gave way. Out poured dissatisfactions and setbacks, swallowed insults and small regrets. Tears spilled by the buckets, duly accompanied by jerky gasps and the required runny nose. He slipped a handkerchief between them and she drew back just enough to use it. Eventually, a few deep, shuddering breaths signaled that the worst of the storm was past.

"There . . . that's better." He lifted her chin and smiled at her reddened nose and eyes. "Nothing like a good bawl when you need one. Come, have a seat."

"I . . . I think we ought to get back now."

"Nanny says come and have a damned seat," he said sternly.

She gave her nose another wipe. "You don't talk like a nanny."

"How would you know? You never had one. Until now."

He had her there. And moments later he had her on the ground as well, sitting beside him and leaning against the trunk of a gnarled old oak. After a few blessedly restoring moments of quiet, he reached for her and began dragging her onto his lap.

"What are you—"

"Come sit on Nanny's lap, sweetness, and—"

"Don't be silly—" She tried to fend him off and keep her seat.

"Maddy Duncan," he said quietly, "do you know what Nanny does to stubborn little girls?" He caught her gaze in his and raised his eyebrows in a deliciously complicated threat. For a moment she was tempted to call him on it. But she rolled her eyes instead, and let him pull her onto his lap. Once there, she resisted his efforts to resettle her closer and pull her head down onto his shoulder. After a brief and futile struggle, she heaved a sigh of surrender and relaxed against him.

I had to, Your Honor, he threatened to "nanny" me severely if I didn't.

"That's better," he murmured against her hair.

It was better. So much better that she wanted to never move again.

"Is that what you do when you need to let off steam?" she asked. "Curse and bash things?"

She felt more than heard his chuckle.

"Not quite. My method usually involves about a half dozen bottles of Scotch and a three-day stay in a—" He stopped. "Believe me, this way is better. You won't have a three-day headache afterward."

They sat for a while without speaking, her in his arms, listening to the gurgling stream, the shushing of the leaves moving overhead, and the sounds of calling birds.

"Now, are you ready for your lessons?" he said, shifting beneath her and sitting her up on his lap.

"Lessons?"

"Nanny has a few things to teach you." He held up a pedagogical finger. "Listen carefully. The first is a science lesson." She nodded, watching the glint in his wickedly warm golden eyes. "A body at rest tends to stay at rest unless acted upon by some outside force. Basically, that means that a box or a barrel will just sit there, in one place, unless something comes along to move it. That's a law of physics. That's also a law of human nature. A lot of people are just like barrels, some outside force has to come along and kick them in the bum-bags before they decide to move."

"How . . . *illuminating*." She frowned.

"My point is, it takes a good bit of energy to pick up a barrel or kick a bum-bag. And you've been hefting and kicking quite a bit of late. You can't go on indefinitely supplying the energy needed to move two or three dozen shiftless, uninspired dolts and run an entire factory—no matter how much you want to do so. The laws of science won't permit it." He reached up to stroke her hair and the side of her cheek. "As strong as you are, angel, you still can't bend laws of science."

She looked away, knowing he was right. The explosion of emotion she had just experienced probably came from being so overextended . . . going without sleep and eating poorly . . . worrying about and checking every little detail . . . and finding problems where she hadn't expected them. "But they're learning. I have to give them some time to begin to feel some pride and ownership in the place."

He opened his mouth to say something, then paused, thinking better of whatever it was. "All right. Your second lesson of the day. Mathematics. If you have a dozen eggs in a basket, and you put in a second dozen, what do you have?"

"How big is the basket?" she asked.

He expelled a patient breath. "Big."

"Then you have two dozen eggs in a basket."

"What if you put in another dozen, then another, then several others . . ."

"Then you'd probably have a few broken eggs . . . at the bottom of a basket you might not even be able to lift. Are you sure this isn't science again?"

He made strangling motions toward her neck, and she laughed.

"You'd have too many eggs in one basket," he redirected her answer. "And the more you pile them together, the more danger there is of some of them breaking."

"Oh, then this must be *domestic* science."

"Madeline!" He grabbed her by the shoulders and pulled her close, pressing her nose with his and staring her in the eyes. "You'd have all your eggs in the proverbial 'one basket.' The same holds true of hopes and dreams. Whenever you put all your heart into one project or one ideal, you risk being devastated when something goes wrong."

"*If* something goes wrong. You're saying I need a few additional baskets." She looked down at her hands splayed across his chest as she braced against him. "I have other interests." She was suddenly aware of the heat and hardness of his body under her hands. "A number of them."

"Such as?"

"I read whenever I have time. I sketch and do watercolors. I keep up with my investments. Someday when I have time I'm going to take a trip around the world to check on my properties and other business concerns. Did you know I'm a tea planter? Well, the owner of a tea plantation in Ceylon."

"Any other interests?" He ran his hand up her arm and across her collarbone.

She shivered. "I'm not very good at riding, but I've done it and I'd like to do it more. I own a rather nice stable at Chellingham, I'm told."

"Anything else?" He trailed a finger up the side of her neck and she bit her lip.

"I do love music. I play piano, mostly for my own pleasure, and I adore opera. I don't dance, but I intend to learn. I write poetry and collect wildflowers and grow roses. And when Ideal is on a secure footing, I'm going to establish a charitable trust for the families of missionaries. Then I may buy a steamship and start a trading company, and build a hotel by the sea, and someday, after suffrage, stand for public office."

"Anything else?"

"That isn't enough?" she said, struck belatedly by something deep and resonant in his voice. She looked at him. His eyes were darkening, intensifying, and she knew instinctively what was causing it. It was the same tantalizing awareness that was curling through her body.

"Well, I do have one other interest," she said, feeling a surge of tingling warmth washing through her. "A rather private interest."

"Sounds interesting," he murmured, sliding his fingers into her hair and pulling her lips close to his. "What is it?"

"You."

"Brazen creature." He wrapped his arms around her and pulled her fully against him. "I can see it's time for lesson number three."

"Personal communications?" she asked, her eyes twinkling.

"Very personal." He gave her a soft introductory kiss. Then a firmer, deeper one. An instant later her arms were gliding around his neck and she was returning that kiss with all the passion and pleasure he generated in her. By the time he ended that kiss, her head was swimming and her physical and emotional boundaries felt mushy and indistinct, as if she were half melted. It took a while for her to regain her senses and realize that he had slid her from his lap and was on his knees, removing his coat. He spread it on the ground beside her, then lowered her shoulders onto it and braced above her on one elbow.

"You are a very curious man, Cole Mandeville," she said, tracing his features with her fingers.

"What do you mean, *curious*? You mean: How curious that he's got hairy ears and can play 'God Save the Queen' on his nose? That sort of curious?"

She laughed. "Not exactly. Curious in that you seem to love discomfort."

"I do?" He frowned. "I assure you, angel, I have no peculiar affinity for pain. In fact, I avoid it whenever possible."

"Then why do you continue to wear those torturous collars, miserable starched shirts, and vests that ride up whenever you raise your arm?"

"Well . . . it's . . . it's . . ." Lord, how he hated to use the word "fashionable." And "proper male garb" sounded even worse. He glanced down at his middle and, true enough, his vest *was* creeping up over his shirt.

"It's dashed uncomfortable is what it is," she concluded. "And illogical. And more than a little pretentious. In short, Lord Mandeville, you appear to be in dire need of a good reforming," she said, yanking the knot from his tie. When he drew his chin back to look down at what she was doing, she smiled and ripped the narrow band of silk from his neck. Next she attacked the button of his collar and removed the starched band, flinging it aside.

"Hey!" He followed it anxiously with his gaze, but when her fingers started on the buttons of his vest, he began to reconsider his opposition. "What do you think you're doing?"

"Making you more comfortable. Liberating you. That's what we 'reformers' do, you know."

"Madeline . . . angel . . . sweetheart . . ." His voice lowered. "You do know that you're undressing me . . . ?"

"There." She finished unbuttoning and pushed his vest up and over his shoulders, then down his back. He sat up, and she pulled it from him altogether and tossed it aside. "Isn't that more comfortable? freer? better?"

"*Ummm* . . . better," he concurred, sinking over her and bracing on his elbows. "I think I could come to like this 'reform' business."

"These starched shirts will have to go." She trailed her fingers down his shirtfront. "And we'll have to get you some decent breeches."

"Good Lord. Next thing you'll be smothering me in tatty velvets and telling me cutting hair is a sin against nature." He shuddered. "I'll end up looking like Endicott."

"Don't be silly. Endicott is . . . *Endicott.* What I have in mind for you will be comfortable and graceful. Classical dress, really."

"This won't involve wrapping up in a bedsheet like Marc Antony, will it?"

"Do I look like Cleopatra?"

He gave a relieved grin and ran a hand over her waist. "You look like heaven." He gave her nose a squishy kiss, then lowered his lips to hers and drank deeply of her. "And you taste like the sweetest thing on earth." He kissed her again, then raked her lower lip with his teeth.

His hands began to move over her bodice, exploring her, sending excitement cascading through her. He murmured approval of her soft curves and appreciated them thoroughly through her soft clothing before nudging aside a button, then another. His face was hot and his mouth sultry against her cool breasts. She responded restlessly to his touch, seeking a broader caress . . . wanting to feel him with her whole body . . . urging him, drawing him over her as he had been that night in the kitchen. And when he settled warm and hard against her aching loins, she reveled in the delicious weight of his body against hers.

She felt her skirt rising, felt his hand on her bare knee and gliding up her naked thigh. Then he shifted slightly to the side, and his hand replaced his body against her, stroking, caressing, tantalizing her silk-clad skin. His fingers drifted across her pelvis, drawn to the sultry heat at her core, and she gasped as he touched her.

The movements of his fingers over her sensitive skin drew her body taut and focused her yearning. She shifted slightly, admitting his hand, holding her breath as his fingers stole past that last silken barrier. At his touch her senses began to spiral out of control, calling forth responses embedded deeper than consciousness or even dreams . . . in her very flesh and marrow. She arched and pressed against him, clasping handfuls of his shirt and his hair as she sought a deeper closeness and a more intimate kiss.

Then, when her senses went white and her breath and pulse were so hard and quick that one beat melted into another, she felt herself propelled upward on a sudden hot draft of sensation. Something shattered within her, hurling her into a drenching flood of release.

He ringed her face and throat with soft kisses, calling her back to him, reassuring her. When she opened her eyes, he was smiling down at her with eyes that were warm and golden and features that bore a patina of bronzed heat.

"That, my angel, is as close to heaven as you'll get without wings."

The contentment in her body wrapped sweet tendrils around her heart, and she smiled. "I've never felt anything like this before."

"I would imagine not." He brushed her hair back from her temples.

"Not just in my body," she said, searching him, trying to understand what had just happened between them and what it meant. Her questions must have shown in her face.

"I know. I'm crazy about you too." His smile was a bit pained. "Or maybe I'm just plain crazy. I'd probably have to be to set hands to you like this."

She laughed and placed a kiss on his cheek. "Mad Madeline Duncan and Crazy Cole Mandeville. It sounds like a perfect match to me."

12

They lay for some time in each other's arms, reveling in and exploring the feelings growing between them. Madeline asked about Cole's childhood and he told her about his life on the farm with the Macmillans, and about his tutors and schooling. He asked about her unconventional upbringing, and she described what she recalled of Africa and something of her life with Aunt Olivia. He laughed at her wry observations on the difficulties of being an heiress . . . new to society and money and lawyers, all. And she laughed at his wicked imitations of various people in society, his family, and the legal system.

It was only with great reluctance that they acknowledged the lowering sun and began to straighten their clothing and tidy their appearance. He started to don his vest, but, heeding her scowl, left it off and put his coat on over his shirt. When he looked for his missing collar, he finally found it in Madeline's hand. She refused to give it to him, and he chased her up and down the bank, trapping her at last on a rock at the edge of the stream. With a wicked smile she held it out and dropped it into the water.

"Madeline!" He was now collarless, for good or for ill, for the rest of the afternoon. He watched it float away and wondered how much more was going to change as a result of this encounter with her.

The crimson in the evening sky was sliding toward purple as they reached familiar landmarks that told them they were nearing the village. She was reluctant to let her time with him end and, from her seat behind him on the horse, she tightened her arms around him and laid her cheek against his back.

"Cole, if you were given a million pounds, what would you do with it?"

He contemplated the question. It sounded oddly familiar. After a moment he remembered that it was the question she had asked Sir William in court that first day.

"I'm not certain. I would have to give it some thought."

"Would you use it to find the Macmillans and buy them some land of their own?" He tensed, and she wondered if she had made a mistake in broaching the subject. But after a moment's silence he seemed to relax.

"While I was at Oxford I learned they had used the money I gave them to buy passage to America. Their neighbors said they had talked of a land company that settled people in a place called Kentucky." She couldn't see his face, but she could detect no bitterness in his voice, not even when he said: "They must have not thought too highly of my promises."

"Have you ever thought of searching for them?"

"It's too late for that. It's all water under the bridge now. They've made their life by now, one way or another. And I've made mine."

His words sounded final enough, she thought. Despite lingering traces of guilt and anger at his family's arrogance, he seemed to have made some peace with what occurred. But that didn't explain his disillusionment with the law and his withdrawal from his legal firm and the law society. There was more here than met the eye, and she vowed that sooner or later she'd find it out and help him face it. A heart as strong and caring as his was too precious not to save.

By midmorning the next day it was evident that things were changing at the Ideal Garment Company. The first visible difference was the fact that Madeline didn't appear until well after sunrise. The second was that Maple Thoroughgood and Priscilla Steadman were already at their stations when she did arrive. As she strolled through the sewing room on her way to the offices, the two approached her with an idea for modifying the girls' dresses she had designed. The change, they said, might allow the girls more room for movement and growth. Madeline encouraged them to try their ideas by stitching a sample garment.

Watching them discuss it as they headed back to their machines, she felt a surge of satisfaction that they had invested so much thought and creativity in their work . . . even if it was just for the children's clothing. But by late morning, when the last of the workers came stumbling through the door bleary-eyed and moving slowly after a night of celebration, her anger returned. She remembered what Cole had said about expressing her feelings. Well, there was at least one place that could use a healthy dose of outrage and indignation.

Screwing up her determination, she headed for the garden, bent on dismissing Roscoe and Algy. She had given it considerable thought and decided Cole was probably right; there were some people who would never change no matter how many chances they were given. Much as she hated to admit she was mistaken in hiring the pair, she was more than ready to see the back of them.

But for all her dread and determination, she was unable to sack them; she couldn't *find* them anywhere. No one had seen them since the previous afternoon. Roscoe and Algy had apparently read the handwriting on the wall and absconded before she had a chance to get rid of them.

She walked through the garden, assessing the damage, and was relieved to conclude that it probably looked worse than it was. With a bit of effort most of it could be put right again. But to keep from spreading herself too thin, she decided to leave it for later. She had plenty to do inside the factory.

Cole met her just as she was returning to the factory, and he seemed a bit perturbed. She understood why when he raised his chin and she saw that he was wearing his tie and collar.

"I felt just too naked," he declared, scowling. "Besides, I've just spent the better part of the morning coaxing Cravits out of a heap on my bedroom floor. He took the news of my impending reformation rather hard. I had to promise I would restrict my 'liberation' to private and informal occasions for the present . . . at least until I have something suitable to replace my 'restrictive' and 'oppressive' wardrobe."

She released the breath she had been holding, relieved that the intervening night hadn't completely undone the effects of their time by the stream. There was still hope.

"You truly will give reform garments a try?" She gave him a smile warm enough to make him rather regret giving in to Cravits on the vest and collar business. His mouth quirked up on one side.

"In for a penny, in for a pound. But, I warn you, I won't have you reforming my drawers. An Englishman's drawers are his castle."

She laughed and put her arm through his to turn him and lead him back inside. "I swear to you, I have no designs whatsoever on your drawers." Her voice lowered to a scarcely audible murmur. "But I won't make the same promise about what's in them."

●   ●   ●

Later that afternoon Cole came up the main stairs bearing a letter that had just arrived. He was staring at the return address and wondering what other Duncan might be writing to Madeline. He was drawn out of his preoccupation by the sound of women's laughter in the sewing room. Three of the Ketchums were clustered around what he knew to be Charlotte Thoroughgood's worktable. As he looked in, someone started singing a common ditty, clapping rhythmically.

A surge of fresh feminine laughter greeted the performance and the rest of the women hurried from their work stations to gather around. Judging by the thumping sounds and the bobbing of shaggy blond heads, there was now a dance to go with the singing and clapping. Apparently the celebratory mood of the previous day had carried over.

Unnoticed, he walked closer until with a stretch of his neck he could see Matthew and Luke Ketchum engaged in a parody of a couple dancing. The women laughed and called advice while marking time with their feet and hands. Not to be outdone, Cal Ketchum picked up a pair of Ideal knickers from Charlotte's worktable and flapped and flourished them raucously as he pranced around the circle of women.

Good-naturedly butting the others aside, he tucked the band of the knickers into the waist of his trousers and continued dancing. The hilarity his behavior produced emboldened him to add another pair to his breeches, covering his rear. When someone handed him a bodice, he tried to don it as well, but it didn't fit. He hit upon the idea of tying it to a second one and managed to wrap the two around him. Then on impulse he snatched up yet another pair of knickers and plopped them on his head. Fluttering his eyes and preening, he pounced about and declared in a falsetto voice that he was a new, "reformed" woman.

"I mebee freer in these here new bags"—he said, sidling up to the red-faced Charlotte—"but I still ain't cheap!"

The women howled.

Cole watched the heavy-handed satire with mixed emotions, recognizing both the buffoonish humor and the small-minded sneer underlying the mimicry.

After a few moments he caught sight of Madeline standing unnoticed across the way, her face scarlet, her eyes dark and growing darker.

Before he could react, she turned and retreated to the offices without saying a word.

Fury gripped him, distorting the sounds of their merriment into an insufferable cawing and prating. Pushing his way through the crowd, he came nose to nose with the mincing Calvin, who had just raised his arms for a twirl. Calvin froze and his brothers lost their grins and their adolescent bravado.

The singing and clapping came to an abrupt end.

"Well, well." Cole gave the threesome a scorching stare and almost enjoyed watching Calvin redden and jerk his arms down. "We've a new girl on the floor, I see." His smile would have frosted lemonade sitting in the hot sun. "A fetching little thing too. Except that someone should take the poor thing aside and explain to her a few of the facts of life."

He gave the knickers drooping over Cal's head a flip. "These, for instance—ladies' knickers—are to be worn discreetly. On the *inside*." He snatched them off Cal's head and with a deadly smile deliberately pulled out the waist of Cal's breeches and stuffed the knickers in. Cal lurched back, but Cole's grip wouldn't allow him a retreat . . . dignified or otherwise. With outrageous leisure Cole stripped the knickers from the fellow's waist and one by one stuffed them down the front of his breeches. The resulting bulge was as satisfying to Cole as it was humiliating to Calvin. He turned his head, addressing a wicked aside to the women nearby.

"Really, where *does* Miss Duncan find people who don't even know how simple knickers are to be worn?"

The snickers and titters his comment elicited were too much for Cal. He ripped off the bust bodices and charged toward the stairs, crimson-faced and frantically tossing women's knickers out of his pants as he went.

Matt and Luke slunk off in the opposite direction and were running by the time they reached the rear steps. Cole swept the circle of women with a warning look that sent them hurrying—duly chastened—back to their machines.

Moments later Cole found Madeline in the sample room, staring out the windows. Her eyes were dry but her spirits were clearly dampened. He stopped behind her and put his hands on her shoulders.

"They're thick as clots," he declared. "Don't let it bother you."

"They don't understand at all," she said quietly, as if just discovering it.

"As you said, it may take awhile, but they'll come around."

"The women aren't wearing the garments either. Not even Maple or Charlotte."

"All it takes is one person to start. The others will soon follow." He ran a finger down her neck. "Just be patient, angel."

For a moment they stood quietly together, then she stirred and reached for a tablet, saying she would like to do some sketching for a while. He dropped a kiss on the top of her head and left her.

By the time he reached the factory entrance, he was in turmoil. There he had stood, watching her disappointment and saying that her wretched workers would come around to her way of thinking and everything would be all right. She was finally getting a taste of the reality he had tried so hard to prepare her for—and he couldn't bear it! To escape, he had thrown himself headlong into mindless, mush-headed optimism, spouting witless encouragements, telling her the truth she was finally facing didn't matter. What next, dribbling bad poetry about every cloud having a damned "silver lining"?

He was in serious trouble here, he thought. And he deserved every damned bit of it!

• • •

Sir William hobbled back into his chambers, his shoulders hunched with pain and his countenance positively cumulo-nimbus. Foglethorpe helped him off with his robes, then rushed to the cabinet for the little brown bottle of laudanum. After settling and dosing the old justice, the clerk stood un-easily by with a worried frown and something behind his back.

"Foglethorpe—what in blazes is the matter with you?" Sir William fished his pince-nez from his pocket and peered through it at the anxious clerk. "Something's got you jitter-ing." He gave the clerk's reticence his own interpretation. "Bad news, I gather. Out with it, Fogles—I'm not getting any younger."

The clerk pulled a newspaper from behind his back and stared at it as if he had no idea how it got there . . . or wished he hadn't. "An article in the *Gazette,* Sir William. A rather dubious piece, but touching a case in your venue. I believe Lord Mandeville is mentioned prominently—and in connec-tions one wouldn't wish to be . . . aired publicly."

"Well, give it here, man!" Sir William roared as he low-ered his foot onto the ottoman. He tore it open and with Foglethorpe's direction located the piece on the second page. As he read, his eyes widened. And widened. His face red-dened. And reddened. By all rights the paper should have combusted, but it merely crumpled as his fleshy hand tight-ened on it.

"Damnation!" Sir William thundered, giving the paper a vicious shake. "A scurrilous lot of pig swill!" It agitated him so that he could scarcely focus enough to finish the article. "According to this, Madeline Duncan's a greedy, licentious little tart with all the morality and social conscience of Attila the Hun. She's either running a sweatshop like one of those newfangled socialist communes, or she's running a commune like a foul, suppurating sweatshop. And damn if—from this idiot's yellow prose—I can tell which."

He skimmed the rest and at the bottom caught an item of interest. "Says here that there will be a rebuttal from her cousin, Gilbert Duncan, Esq., printed on the morrow."

He flung the paper across his desk in disgust.

"Horse manure. Plain and simple. I've been thirty years on this bench and I've seen all sorts come and go. Unless I've gone full dotty, she's the genuine article." He scowled. "At least my nephew seems to think so. I don't suppose there's a letter in the post from him. . . ."

Foglethorpe shook his head. Sir William sighed and propped his jowly chin on his hand.

"Dammit, if I didn't have this dickey leg, I'd be on the next coach to that backwater burg this very night."

Across town, in Mayfair, Gilbert Duncan was rolling back on his new silk settee, kicking his heels with glee at the slanderous accusations the *Pall Mall Gazette* had leveled against his wealthy little cousin.

"Oh, yesss! This is too, too good. For all intents and purposes, she is now a hot-tailed little tyrant who thumbs her nose at society and coerces her poor, downtrodden workers to comply with her twisted notions of morality." He sat up and looked at Rupert Fitch, seated on a nearby ottoman, wearing a spanking new suit of clothes but the same old yellow smile. "You do good work, my man. Why, you almost have *me* believing some of this stuff. I only hope my valiant rebuttal will be half so eloquent when it appears in the paper tomorrow."

"It will be," Fitch assured him.

"Good." Gilbert unfolded from the couch and went to pour himself a brandy. "Then perhaps you'd better tell me just what I said in 'my' article . . . so that when I see her in a day or two, I'll know just how grateful to expect her to be."

•   •   •

Over the next two days productivity rose only slightly, but there was a marked increase in the energy Ideal's workers brought to the task of making garments. Here and there workers stopped Madeline to make a suggestion, to relate something they had experienced, or to ask for something they needed to do their jobs better.

Madeline was delighted to see a number of the women taking it upon themselves to devise simple decorations for the knickers and bust bodices. She asked Endicott to speak to the women about his ideas and about ways they could embellish the garments and make them even more aesthetically pleasing. Soon there were a number of experimental variations under way. It was surprising what a creative bit of stitching or a simple flounce could do for both the appearance of a garment and the attitude of the woman making it.

Each evening, after everyone had gone home, she walked around the sewing room, looking at the garments in progress and trying to make peace with what was happening to her dream. She picked up the knickers and an occasional bodice, trying to absorb the changing reality of what she had developed and trying to chart a mental course for what was yet to come. It was so difficult. The future had no safety nets—not for her factory, nor for her heart.

Cole waited downstairs to walk her to her house for dinner. When she reached the front doors, she paused and looked around at the hall and up the stairs.

"It isn't at all what I had planned."

For a moment he was silent. Then he nodded. "It never is. That's one of the interesting things about life. You live it twice, once in your dreams and again in your days." He took the key from her as they stepped outside and locked the doors. "The two versions are never the same. And who is ever to say which is better?"

She smiled and slid her fingers over his, watching with

wonder as he opened his hand and intertwined his fingers with hers.

"Whichever version allows me to do this"—she covered their joined hands tenderly with her other hand—"has to be the best."

The next morning, when she arrived at the factory, two disheveled figures were sprawled on the doorstep, waiting for the doors to open. In a heartbeat they were on their feet and scrambling down the steps to meet her.

"There ye are, miz!" Roscoe said, rubbing his palms nervously on his dirty woolen trousers. "Bet ye wondered what become o' us. Well, I'll tell ye—we been figuring how to fix yer garden. Reckon we owe ye that. I said that to Alg here . . . I said, 'Alg, we got to do somethin' to fix things for Miz Duncan.' " Algy nodded vigorous corroboration. "So we come back. An' this time we'll get 'er done. That garden will be a pure wonder by th' time we're through!"

Roscoe and his dim wick of a partner were dirty and unshaven and looked like they'd slept in a haystack. Bits of straw and the occasional thistle burr were stuck to their rumpled clothes. Only their hats had escaped degradation.

But what got to her was the look in their eyes, the sobering recognition of their wrongs and the irresistibly earnest hope of forgiveness. They wanted to set things right, to prepare and plant the garden as a way of making amends. They believed it was possible to get a second chance.

She stared at them for several moments.

"I should probably have my head examined," she said quietly. "But, all right. You have one more chance to patch up the garden and put it all right." She shook a finger at them. "And I'll be watching every move you make."

•   •   •

No one was more surprised than Madeline when Daniel Steadman came hurrying to the door of the sample room the next morning, red-faced and out of breath.

"Miss Duncan, you've got visitors!" he said excitedly. "A carriage just drove up, right to the door. Fancy rig too. You'd best come and see."

Visitors? Madeline put down the box of pins she held for Endicott, glanced at Cole, who was standing uncomfortably on an overturned box in his shirt-sleeves with fabric pieces draped over his shoulders, and exited for the front doors. Cole seized the opportunity to escape. Over Endicott's protests he cleared his shoulders of fabric, reached for his coat, and headed after her.

Daniel was partly right. There was indeed a carriage stopped in front of the factory. But now three more carriages and a handful of riders on horseback were visible, picking their way along the rutted and difficult lane, presumably on their way to the factory as well. As Madeline stepped out the front doors into the misty morning, a tall, slender man unfolded from the carriage, dusting himself off and resettling his gray top hat with particular precision.

"May I help you?" Madeline asked as she descended the steps toward him.

The fellow gave her an insultingly thorough visual examination, focusing on the scarlet tunic and trousers she had decided to wear again, on an occasional basis.

"You must be the proprietor of this establishment," he said crisply, making it sound an unenviable position. Madeline couldn't help thinking that he looked as if he had made a lifelong habit of sucking lemons.

"I am Madeline Duncan, owner and proprietor," she said. "And you are . . ."

"Sir Reginald Horbaugh, Member of Parliament. I have come, madam, to inspect your premises."

"Inspect?" When she didn't either quail or acquiesce immediately, he grudgingly modified his demand.

"With your permission, of course."

"Not in an official capacity, then?" she asked, annoyed by his condescension.

"Not strictly speaking. However, since I am a member of the white-paper commission on the employment of women and children, I believe it would be in your best interest to open your doors for inspection . . . certainly in light of the reports that have been made in the papers."

"Reports?" Madeline looked over at Cole, who had now joined them. "In newspapers?"

"I've made no reports to newspapers," Cole assured her, "and I cannot imagine Sir William releasing the observations I have sent him in confidence."

Sir Reginald took in Cole's dress and noble demeanor with a skeptical sniff. "You must be Lord Mandeville, overseer of this controversial enterprise."

"I am Lord Mandeville," Cole said icily, "and I have been named the court's appointed observer and agent with regard to Miss Duncan's garment company. May I ask what articles you saw and in which newspapers?"

At that point the riders dismounted. Then the other carriages pulled up before the factory and emptied a motley assortment of people onto the rutted yard. They shook out their clothes, dusted their hats and bonnets and sleeves, and looked around at the Ideal factory and Madeline with bald curiosity.

Shortly thereafter she was inundated by a dozen people, all of whom seemed to know one another by sight and most of whom seemed to find the sight of one another somewhat disagreeable. They began talking all at once, over each other's heads and behind each other's backs.

Overwhelmed by the confusion, Madeline's gaze fell on the person nearest at hand—a robust, bearded fellow with rather coarse features and a ruddy complexion who had planted himself before Sir Reginald.

"Horbaugh, what are you doing here?" he demanded.

"I've come to see if what I've read is true, and if so, to

see that this festering carbuncle of socialism is lanced before it can spread to infect more of our pure English countryside," Sir Reginald declared haughtily. "I might have known *you* would be here, strutting and crowing . . ."

"I'm not at all convinced there is anything here to crow about," the fellow said, then turned to Madeline with fire in his eyes. "William Morris, madam." He presented himself to Madeline and used his nod of respect as an excuse to study her person. His eyes widened when they reached her trousers. "I am something of a craftsman, businessman, and friend of the laboring classes—"

"Oh, I know who you are, Sir William," Madeline said, her eyes alight, brightening her entire countenance. "In fact, I've long been an admirer of your work—from your poetry to your essays on craftsmanship and the principles of design, to your views on the nature of mass production. I dare say . . . they have strongly influenced what I am trying to do here."

"And just what are you trying to do here, young woman?" The imperious question came from a bespectacled older woman dressed in dark, severe garments. With her were two other similarly dressed women. "Flout society's rules and the Almighty's laws . . . coerce people into heathen, free-loving communes?"

An answer came unexpectedly from the rear of the crowd. "She is trying to build a business and rebuild a village society. She is trying to give the poor a chance to better their lot and trying to point the way to a new era of humane and efficient production." Out stepped none other than Gilbert Duncan, dusting off his riding breeches and boots with his gloves. He removed his hat and held out his hand as he approached.

"Gilbert!" She held out her hand, surprised to find a familiar and friendly face among the group. "What are you doing here?"

"Dearest Cousin Madeline," he said, pulling her close

enough to drop a kiss on her cheek. "I came as soon as I could, my dear. It's an outrage—that's what it is. A vile fiction someone has dreamt up to stir controversy and sell newspapers. And I have told them so, assailed them roundly for their despicable treatment of you."

She looked up into her handsome cousin's silver-gray eyes and dazzling smile. "What treatment of me? Will you please tell me what this is all about?"

"The article," William Morris explained crossly. "In the *Pall Mall Gazette*—published in two parts this last week. Stead himself sent me copies in the post and asked me for a response. How can I respond, I said, when I haven't the slightest idea what it's about?"

"Article, *humph*. A call to arms is more like it," the severe old woman corrected Sir William. "I mean to see this squalor and degradation for myself!" She pushed past Gilbert and led her troops straight for the steps.

"Squalor?" Madeline moved to block the way, but Gilbert distracted her.

"I've brought you a copy of the article and my own response—which they deigned to print in its entirety." He produced an envelope out of his inner breast pocket and handed it to her. "Pay no attention to them, Cousin. I'm certain that when these people see what is going on, they will find nothing that will not reflect glowingly upon your splendid ideas and generous heart."

"But who are these people, Gilbert?" she asked in a frantic whisper.

Cole, who had been watching these proceedings with a shuttered look on his face, now spoke up.

"I believe the woman determined to root out 'free love' is Mrs. Sylvia Bethnal-Green, leader of the South London Temperance and Morality Union," he told Madeline. "It looks like she has brought a few of her cohorts . . . including Brigadier Abel Dawes, pamphleteer and apologist for London's moralistic old Whigs. On the other hand, the petite woman in the fashionable hat is, I believe, the labor unionist, Mrs. Annie Besant. Unless my eyes deceive me, the gentleman in the plain woolens is Joseph Lane, founder of the Labor Emancipation League . . . and an infamous 'free lover.' And the others are—"

"Edward Carpenter." A modest, middle-aged man with a bookish look about him paused to introduce himself. "Scholar, political observer, and writer. I wish to make a study of your efforts here . . . with an eye toward their effects on the democratizing of factory work and management."

"Henry Broadhurst, madam." A well-dressed fellow tipped his hat. "Morris insisted I come along. I must say"— he glanced back at the village green and the neat stone cottages—"this is not at all the prison it was made out to be. We shall want to see some of the workers' accommodations as well." He turned abruptly and joined Carpenter on the steps, saying with obvious relief: "Well, I for one cannot smell any raw sewage."

Madeline tore into the envelope and read the scandalous article while Cole looked over her shoulder. As she read, she gasped, clutched her throat, and reddened.

"Misrepresentations, half-truths, and outright lies!" She looked up at Gilbert, then at Cole. "How could they possibly . . . who could have . . ." She looked again at the by-line and the name *Rupert Fitch* fairly smacked her in the eye. "Fitz-water—Fitch—it was that miserable little worm that Roscoe and Algy talked me into hiring!" She stared at Cole. "He came here just to get material for this bit of rubbish!"

Cole put a steadying hand on Madeline's arm.

"Madeline . . ." He nodded toward the lane. There coming toward them were two more coaches and another rider on horseback.

"Oh, no!"

13

By even the most conservative of estimates, there was soon a score of visitors roaming the factory, grounds, and village, each looking for evidence to support a preconceived notion of what Madeline Duncan had wrought in creating the Ideal Garment Company. Madeline tried to gather them together to explain the principles behind her company, but most immediately took issue with her ideas.

"It is not possible to mechanize the work of craftsmen," William Morris insisted. "Mechanization destroys the human spirit. The result will be inferior goods, pure rubbish!"

Mrs. Bethnal-Green held up one of the completed bodices between two fingers. "Replacing women's corsets . . . with these hideous things? Why, that's ludicrous—"

"You have children in the factory—I can hear them," Sir Reginald declared, stalking off to hunt them down. "Child labor—I might have guessed as much!"

"You require your female workers to wear

such garments whether they wish to or not," Henry Broadhurst charged. "That represents a systematic policy of domination. Workers are not chattel! All men possess certain inalienable rights . . ."

"Come with me, Sir William, Mr. Broadhurst," Madeline insisted, taking them by the arms. "When you understand the way we work, you'll see that our workers participate in every aspect of our business. We begin with a mechanized cutting process. . . ."

She led them up the stairs to the cutting floor and had Fritz explain his system. They watched and questioned Daniel Steadman and a number of the other cutters about their work.

"This is all very well," Morris declared brusquely, "but who does the designing? The design should be the natural alchemy of the material, the tools, and the craftsman's hands and spirit."

Madeline suddenly thought of Endicott—"Oh, but of course! I have a marvelous surprise for you, Sir William."

She led the way to the stairs and trundled her visitors through the sewing room and into the offices. "This is where we do most of the design work—our sample room. I believe you already know my chief designer." She beamed as she introduced Jessup Endicott.

Endicott rose from his desk and turned.

The men stared at each other in disbelief.

"You!" Morris roared.

"Morris!" Endicott reddened.

Morris turned on Madeline. "You've just cast your entire enterprise into disrepute. Nothing this mealy little worm produces could possibly have the slightest merit!"

Endicott stalked over, his eyes blazing with more fire than Madeline had ever witnessed in him. "How dare you! Don't listen to him, Madeline. He's a crude and petty tyrant, a ruffian who can no more control his mouth than he can his designs, a glory-grabbing misanthrope who belongs in the Dark Ages, barking at serfs."

"And this"—Morris indicated Endicott's flamboyant dress with a dismissive hand—"is a laughable parody of a craftsman, an elitist who refuses to dirty his hands with the real, honest work of creation. High-flown ideas is all he's ever produced, and not one of those of any value!"

"B-but I thought you were . . ." She looked at Endicott, then at Morris. "I thought he was . . ."

Before she could put words to her confusion, she had to dart between them and call for Mr. Broadhurst's assistance to keep them from coming to fisticuffs.

She urged Sir William back out the door and down the hallway, only to run into Sir Reginald in the outer office, demanding to know why the children in St. Crispin were being kept in the factory, day after day, imprisoned in a locked room.

"Imprisoned! They're not imprisoned, they're in school! Where on earth did you hear that they are kept in a locked—" Then she saw he had Jonathan Farrow by the arm and knew where that misinformation came from.

"Jonathan Farrow, why aren't you in school?" she demanded crossly.

"Mr. Tattersall . . . a bunch of nobs come and started askin' questions an' Mr. Tattersall, he let us out early for dinner."

Madeline had a vision of a horde of children on the loose, running higgledy-piggledy about the work floors. She groaned.

From that moment on, things seemed to spiral further and further out of Madeline's control. The visitors poked their noses into every conceivable aspect of the factory's operation: tools, equipment, lighting, designs, storage, shipping, sales strategy, worker satisfaction. Everywhere she went in the factory, she saw workers stopped and talking to a visitor, explaining how things worked or what they thought of the way the factory was operated. And in every case her workers' words were twisted to suit the preconceived notions of the visitors.

"O'course the women get paid extra . . . by the piece," Thomas Clark said.

"You aren't all paid the same equitable wage?"

"Miss Duncan put our little 'uns downstairs so we'd sew more," Bess said.

"She holds your babies for ransom—to make you work harder?"

"She wants all the women to wear Ideal garments," Priscilla said.

"You're required to wear her questionable garments or you'll be sacked?"

Shortly, Madeline herself was cornered just outside the offices by Morris and Broadhurst, Horbaugh and Carpenter, soon to be joined by others. They demanded to know what she intended to do about the deficiencies in her facility, her manufacturing process, and her treatment of her workers.

"Wages are far from uniform. This Steadman fellow makes half again as much as the other cutters," Carpenter said, waving one of her own documents in her face.

"You have not made adequate provisions for workers to interact with their product," Morris declared. "Where is the pride of creation to be had in cutting hunks of cloth all day?"

"What this factory needs is a workers' association," Broadhurst insisted. "Someone to speak up for the unenfranchised and to organize the workers so that they have some defense against the arbitrary decisions of management."

"I see through this sham of a school, Miss Duncan." Horbaugh shook his finger at her. "Violation of child labor laws is a very serious matter indeed."

She backed against the office window, unable to make sense of their accusations.

All she could see were moving mouths, reddened faces, glaring eyes. Then Cole was pushing his way to her side, his face crimson with rage, his eyes blazing.

"Quiet, dammit!" he roared. "What the devil is the matter with you people?"

All present fell into a stunned silence.

Then Sir Reginald Horbaugh rallied and demanded, "What have you to say for yourself, young woman?"

Madeline straightened and looked from one to the other of these people who had descended on her company in order to pass judgment on her and everything she had tried to accomplish. No doubt they were powerful, influential. No doubt they could ruin her if she refused to comply with their demands.

"What I have to say is . . . What I have to say is *good day to you all*."

When they just gawked at her, she felt fury gathering within her. "Are you hard of hearing as well as pompous, self-absorbed, and insensitive? I'm telling you to leave!"

She took Sir Reginald and Sir William by the sleeves, turned them, and propelled them toward the stairs. "Out— the lot of you!"

"You cannot—"

"Well, I never—"

"How dare she?"

"Out! Leave!" Shooing and shoving, she herded the dozen or so critics gathered around her toward the stairs. Cole joined her in ushering them to the steps, trundling them down and out the front doors.

The ruffled Sir Reginald turned on the steps to wag another finger. "I warn you, young woman, you shall regret this rudeness and unthinkable treatment of us."

"We are not without influence!" Mrs. Bethnal-Green proclaimed.

"How dare you!" Madeline demanded. "What gives you the right to invade my factory, poking and prodding, slighting and sneering . . . Filth, exploitation, oppression, inequity, immorality . . . if you see them here, it's because that's what *your own minds* are full of!" She paused to take a deep breath. "You're no better than that conniving little wretch who wrote those lies in the newspaper!"

With that she turned and headed back into the factory.

Just before the door slammed, she heard one final comment.

"Well . . . I never!"

Cole was there at the foot of the steps, but she couldn't bear to face him just then. She started up the steps. But Gilbert headed her off. He grabbed her hands, drew her close, and lifted her hands to press a kiss on them.

"Madeline dearest, what have you done? They're naught but a bunch of hypocritical old nobs, but they do have influence. People listen to them. They'll slice you up and toast you for breakfast!" When she looked up into his sympathetic face, tears pricked the backs of her eyes.

"Then they shall just have to toast me. I'll not take back a word I said."

"Then I shall be your champion," he said grandly. "I shall go after them and defend you to the limits of my being." He pressed another ardent kiss on her knuckles. "Perhaps a few words with influential friends, another article . . . I shall do what I can."

He strode down the steps, donned his hat, and blew her a kiss over his shoulder as he exited the front doors.

Madeline hurried to her office and slammed the door behind her. How could one wretched article, one mean-spirited and unsubstantiated bit of fiction, wield such influence with intelligent, educated people. With a slight progression of thought, she could imagine that Fitch's one article might now yield five or ten, all written by leading citizens, all reporting on the "deficiencies" and "abuses" occurring at her Ideal Garment Company.

She sank weakly into her chair.

And she couldn't help feeling betrayed by her own workers. How easily they had let the visitors' criticism distort their thinking. How could they misrepresent things so, in light of everything she had done to help them?

But as her anger began to settle, she recalled the way her

workers were questioned. These were proud and simple people, unused to having their opinions solicited. And, of course, they would be embarrassed at any hint that they had accepted charity or been "helped."

In fact, it had undoubtedly been just as humiliating an experience for them as it was for her.

She began to relax, thinking of Gilbert and his gallant behavior. She wouldn't have thought of him as a paladin type; he had always been too busy to bother with family matters. Perhaps Aunt Olivia's death had made him realize the importance of the love and support of family.

And then there was Cole.

He had stood by her and helped her to defend herself and Ideal. Still, how could she face him after such a disastrous confrontation with the "do-gooders" of the world? Somehow, she had gone from being in the forefront of the reform movement to being cast on the other side of the question entirely, among the "owners" and "oppressors" of the world. And all because she had simply tried to put her ideals into action.

She thought of what Cole had said about the way reformers stir up trouble and raise expectations and then walk away, leaving others to sort out the mess they've made. At the time she believed he was simply being pessimistic and close-minded. Now she wondered how he had come by such disturbing insight.

Cole had taken himself straight down to the storerooms, hoping that two floors between him and Madeline would be enough to gain some perspective on what was happening to her. And to him.

He had come so close to committing mayhem that afternoon, it was frightening. Her experience with those "interested citizens"—a self-appointed delegation of hypocritical old cods—was a fair representation of just what her dream was up against in society and in the world at large. In the past few days he had allowed the relative peace in the factory and the seductive intimacy that was developing between him and Madeline to obscure the cold, unpleasant facts of the situation. She was in over her head, adrift on a doomed ship of ideals. And instead of steering her into a safe, sensible dock, he had jumped on board with her, even knowing that the weight of his approval might be all she needed to send her foundering.

The grim thought that he might have done more harm than good set him hurrying through the receiving room to the rear stairs and out the rear door. With his hands in his pockets, he paced back and forth, too preoccupied to respond to Roscoe's and Algy's greetings. Sinking deeper into inner conflict, he struck off for a brisk walk to clear his head.

Behind him, Roscoe and Algy climbed back down into the trench beside the massive rock that had become their raison d'être in recent days.

" 'E's right furious wi' us, I reckon," Roscoe said, arching his aching back over his hands. "Well, never ye mind. Him an' Miz Duncan, they'll be pleased as punch when this old rock is in bits and hauled clean away."

"We'll do it up right this time, eh, Roscoe?"

"Right enough, Alg." Roscoe drew a deep, confident breath. "Hand me a few more sticks of that powder. An' reel off a bit more o' that fuse." He paused to look at the half dozen red paper tubes they had wedged against the side of the rock. "It pays to be careful wi' this stuff, ye know. 'Cause, like the feller said, th' Almighty gives ye only one set o' thumbs."

It was late in the day before Madeline emerged from her office. No one was in the outer office and a peek in the sample room showed it to be empty as well. Collecting herself, she stepped out onto the sewing floor and found it mostly deserted as well. Only Maple and Charlotte were at their machines.

"Where is everyone?" she asked.

Maple looked up, seeming uncomfortable, and finally said: "They quit for the day and went downstairs . . . with the cutters." Something in the way she couldn't meet Madeline's eyes as she said it sent a chill of premonition through Madeline.

Images of Thomas and Bess Clark and Ben Murtry and Will Huggins responding to the loaded questions of their visitors suddenly flashed before her mind. She was on her way to the stairs before she had time to think what she might find or what she might do about it. Maple and Charlotte looked at each other with concern, then abandoned their machines to follow her down.

Sprawled on idle cutting tables and perched on boxes and chairs dragged from the classroom were nearly all of Ideal's employees. Someone was speaking, but the instant she appeared, all fell into dead silence. They looked at her with puzzled, wary, or outright hostile expressions that carried an almost physical impact.

"What is going on here?"

They gave one another knowing and stealthy looks that silently elected a spokesman. Thomas Clark slid from his seat on the cutting table and hitched up his breeches beneath his belly.

"We been thinkin' . . . about what's been going on around here. Them people who come today, they opened our eyes a bit. . . ."

It was some time before Cole returned to the factory. He had walked the ridges and rills in the surrounding countryside, thinking hard and finding very little to be proud of in his behavior of late. Given the insinuations in the article of illicit conduct between him and Madeline—and just how close those insinuations were to being accurate—he realized the wisest thing he could do was withdraw to the nearest inn and confine his overseeing to daily visits for now. It was bad enough that her work had become an object of controversy; she didn't need allegations of personal immorality muddying the waters further.

The seal of finality was put on the decision when he realized that he was sitting on a rock overlooking the village, holding his chest at the thought of being separated from her. He closed his eyes and willed that pain back into the most isolated region of his heart.

By the time he reached the factory, he was trying to think of a way to put it to Madeline without making it appear he was abandoning her. He entered through the rear door, oblivious of Roscoe's and Algy's broad grins and waving arms. As he mounted the steps, approaching the first floor, he heard a muddled mix of voices, only one of which sounded clear and familiar and full of tension. "You believe you deserve a bonus?"

Madeline. He walked faster.

"You think you're underpaid and grossly overworked?" Madeline was saying: "You're bored with your mundane, ordinary tasks? You think Ideal garments are silly and worthless? You believe I've kidnapped your infants daily and held them as ransom to get you to do my evil bidding? You think I've starved and oppressed and exploited and demeaned you?" Her face was crimson, and by then she was shouting at the top of her lungs. "You believe I'm getting rich off the sweat of your brows, and now you demand your *rightful* share of the profits?"

Trembling with the fury of a hundred slights and cuts sustained from them and for them, she looked from one to another of her workers, seeing them through new eyes, seeing them as they really were, stripped of the glow of the virtue she had idealistically—*foolishly*—attributed to them.

Out of the corner of her eye she saw Cole's turbulent face and clenched fists, and was afraid to look at him. He had been right. He had known all along and tried to warn her.

What an idiot she was.

The weight on her chest made it hard to get her breath. Tears stung her eyes.

"All of you—out! I don't want to *exploit* or *imprison* or *oppress* you one minute longer!" She all but chased them out of the room, down the stairs, and out of the building. "You're free!" she choked out, standing on the stoop. "You won't have to suffer my abuse ever again. I'm closing the factory. Go on, go find work with those other employers—the ones who will be perfectly fair and equitable, who will give you lodging and train you for new jobs and put up with your children, who will give you all huge bonuses and make sure your jobs are creative and entertaining and fulfilling every minute of the day! And if you find such a sap, and he hires the likes of you, give him my sympathies!"

There was a heartbeat's pause. Her words hovered on the air.

Suddenly there was a deafening roar and the earth trembled all around them. The building shook so that mortar and dust flew from every window and joint. Thunderous rumbling and quaking seemed to go on and on, pierced here and there by the crack of wood and the shattering of every single one of Madeline's precious windows—the ones she had so painstakingly ordered and installed. Madeline staggered back and Cole rushed to drag her against him and shelter her from the dust and smoke.

Then, as abruptly as it came, the rumble was gone. In its unearthly wake they heard the sound of rubble falling, sawdust and acrid smoke billowing inside the factory, and gasped at the blackened cloud that rolled out the front doors and whooshed out the broken windows.

The shock of it took a moment to register. Madeline pushed back in Cole's arms and looked up at the building in mounting horror and disbelief.

Her factory had exploded before her eyes. And with it all her dreams had gone up in smoke as well.

14

It was well past midnight. The London streets were dark and a light drizzle was falling as Madeline turned her tired mount onto Maypole Street in Bloomsbury.

After the devastation wreaked by the explosion, Madeline's one thought had been to go home—home to the house she had shared with Aunt Olivia. She had gone straight for Netter's stable and Cole's horse, and she hadn't looked back . . . not even as she crested the last rise, leaving St. Crispin. For a score of miserable miles she had driven herself on, her only solace the thought of reaching the familiar old brick house with its stately Gothic windows and fanciful front turret that stood at the end of the lane. But now, as her girlhood home materialized from the gloom, it seemed strangely dark and forlorn. High grass and weeds dominated the front garden, and the windows absorbed the meager light like dark, scorched holes in the walls.

She dismounted on the step, then led the horse around to the carriage house. Numbly, she dried the animal down and found it a blanket and some oats.

"Home," she said, giving the animal's neck a stroke. "I'm home, boy."

When she unlocked the front door and stepped inside, she smelled the familiar must of the old house, the accumulated dust of idle months, and the faint remnant of her aunt's cherished and ever-present lavender. She fumbled at the hall table to light a lamp, then carried it into the parlor.

Everything was draped with dust covers, and in the dim light the room appeared a foreign and forbidding landscape. She ripped off several of the cloths, but felt an odd chill and backed to the cold fireplace, trying to rub some warmth into her aching arms. In the dim light and shifting shadows she seemed to see Aunt Olivia on the settee with a blanket over her lap, looking at her with such love, such hope . . . such disappointment.

Madeline felt tears burn her cheeks and sank to her knees, giving in to wrenching sobs.

This was her childhood, this place. Full of optimism and girlish dreams. Filled with memories of possibilities now forfeit and expectations she had disappointed.

She was suddenly frantic to get away.

But where? Where could she go?

At the break of dawn Gilbert Duncan's houseman answered a persistent banging at his front door and found a young woman on the doorstep, looking damp, chilled, and despondent. Her teeth were chattering so that she could scarcely give him her name. He was on the brink of turning her back onto the street, when the master himself appeared at the head of the stairs in his dressing gown to see what the racket was about.

"Cousin Gilbert!" she called in a raspy voice. He started, glowered at her over the railing, then came racing downstairs.

"Madeline—is that you? Dear God, what's happened?

Are you all right?" When she nodded, then shook her head in confusion, he flung an arm around her and looked about for some clue to her being there. "Are you alone, Cousin? And no luggage? Don't tell me you've come all the way from that horrid place by yourself!"

She raised her head and nodded. "I'm sorry to impose, Cousin, but I couldn't think of anyplace else to go."

"Good Lord!" He felt her hands. "You're half frozen!" He ushered her straight toward the stairs, tossing orders over his shoulder as he went. "Jeffries! A warm bath, some food, and a strong toddy for Cousin Madeline. And be quick about it!"

"There, there, my dear." He steered her into a guest room, guided her onto a footbench at the end of a four-poster, and knelt before her on the rug. "Tell me about it."

"After you left . . . the workers had a meeting and"—she wiped away a stray tear—"and then there was an explosion and the factory windows blew out and everything was ruined . . . because of . . . of—" She shook her head, unable to continue for the emotion clogging her throat.

He handed her a handkerchief out of his pocket and she wiped a few tears before drawing an exhausted breath and sinking back into numbed grief.

"My dear, dear Madeline. You've been through a terrible time—that is all I have to know. What you need now is someone to look after you, someone to see to your interests, someone to guard you against your own selfless and giving impulses."

She looked up at him, and somehow saw Cole's face interposed over his features. She had had someone to care for her. Someone who tried to warn her about her magnanimous impulses. Someone who had tried to help and protect her. She looked away and closed her eyes, holding that bittersweet image a moment longer before it faded. Her shoulders rounded and she sagged against him.

"Oh, Gilbert, what am I going to do?"

"Right now you're exhausted and confused . . . and you've come to the right place, sweetness. Just put yourself in my hands." He pulled her to her feet as housemaids entered with arms full of linen and scurried into the adjoining bath. "There will be plenty of time to discuss your future later."

As soon as Gilbert closed the door to her room, he did a little dance in the hallway, crowing silently. When he looked up, his houseman was standing not far away with an ornate silver tray in his hands, watching with a jaded eye. Gilbert straightened, then swaggered toward the dignified Jeffries.

"Tell the staff they'll be paid all of their back wages by the end of the week," he said quietly, leaning closer. "And there will be a tidy little bonus if my dear cousin Madeline is made suitably comfortable."

Jeffries's eyes lit with understanding. "I shall inform the staff straightaway, sir." He raised one eyebrow. "And how long might we expect the young lady to stay?"

Gilbert gave a wicked laugh. "With any luck, Jeffries, 'until death do us part.'"

In the dark, symbolic world of dreams, Madeline kept seeing that monstrous rock over and over, almost human in its sullen and spiteful refusal to move, then in one sudden, cataclysmic eruption it would shatter into a thousand pieces. Then suddenly Cole would be there, staring at her with pity in his eyes, and the pity would slowly turn to disgust and he would walk away. She called to him over and over, but he would never turn back. And when she ran after him, she never seemed to get any closer despite the fact that she was always running and he was merely walking.

Troubled by her dreams and yet afraid to awaken, she slept through the afternoon, the night, and well into the next morning. When she finally rose, she felt stiff, thick-tongued, and groggy, as if she had drunk too much wine. She stumbled into the bathing room, and when she emerged she discovered a tray had been quietly delivered—tea, toast, and marmalade. Food held no appeal, but she hoped that the warmth of the tea might dispel the chill that lingered inside her. Gathering her voluminous nightgown around her, she perched on a chair and poured her milk and tea. Some of her tension melted as she buried her nose in the fragrant cup.

With a bit of tea in her veins and something in her stomach, she answered a knock on the door some minutes later, and discovered Gilbert, holding a silk dressing gown. He shoved it through the narrow opening in the door and waited for her to don it before entering.

"You look much more rested. How do you feel?" he asked solicitously, leading her by the hand to the fainting couch by the window.

"Better, thank you." She drew her hand from his and lowered her gaze. It occurred to her, now that she was staying in his house, sleeping in his guest room, and drinking his tea; she knew precious little about her only living cousin.

"First thing . . . we must do something about clothes for you." He sat back and produced a winning smile. "There is nothing like new clothes to brighten the spirits."

"Oh, well . . ." She glanced down at her robe. "I suppose I should send for—"

"No, no, Cousin." He laughed. "If you're to make a new life, you must have new clothes to go with it. And I know just the people to provide them for you in a hurry." He leaned close and squeezed her hands. "I've taken the liberty of summoning one of London's finest dressmakers. I told you, I have excellent connections."

He was on his feet before she could mount a serious objection, and it wasn't until an hour later, when he ushered in an officious little man accompanied by a gaggle of harried assistants—a French couturier—that she collected her wits enough to realize that the clothes he meant were the very sort of clothes she had always held to be the very next thing to human bondage.

She stood in the midst of her borrowed bedchamber in a borrowed nightdress, considering the couturier's direction to step up onto the box before the mirrors and thinking of all the times she had railed against the stupidity and oppressive nature of such garments. A powerful ache developed in her chest at the realization that she had been so wrong about so much, she wasn't certain she could trust her judgment on anything. Her entire world seemed to have turned upside down—or perhaps sideways—and just then she was too numb and disoriented to try to right it and chart a true and distinct course.

What if the garments weren't as bad as she had been taught? What if all the horrors of the haut monde had been exaggerated . . . or intentionally misrepresented? If some of her precious ideals had betrayed her, then how did she know others hadn't too?

There was only one way to find out.

Raising her chin, she stepped defiantly onto that wooden box and tried not to shrink or cower when they pulled her nightdress from her.

Several hours later she stood before the carefully arranged pier glasses in her bedchamber, wearing proper knee-length drawers, a frilly chemise, and the first corset she had ever laced up in her life.

Her cheeks seemed to be permanently stained from an afternoon of continual blushing. The couturier and his minions were aghast at the dimensions of her waist and considered her erect posture and substantial rib cage as lamentable natural defects. She would need walking lessons, the little dressmaker advised, speaking in French when Gilbert came to see how things were progressing. And sitting, standing, and probably breathing lessons as well, he added, assuming from her gracelessness that the intricacies of his native language were beyond her. Unfortunately, they weren't.

Now, with her cheeks red, her nose burning from dust, dye, and lint, and her breathing constricted by a merciless set of whalebone stays, she faced herself in the mirror. And her one thought was a bittersweet musing on what Cole would say if he could see her now . . . in the corset he had once admonished her to acquire.

She escaped into the bathing room, locked the door behind her, and ran water to mask the sound of her breathless sobs.

Cole tried the knocker, then the handle of the front doors of the house on Maypole Street. The silence and stillness went on uninterrupted. He peered in a window and saw dust drapes over the dining room table and chairs, and finally admitted to himself she could not be there. He turned reluctantly back down the walk, his hands in his pockets, more despondent than he could ever remember feeling.

Climbing back in his carriage, he sat for a moment, trying to think what to do next. To Davenport's knowledge, she had no close friends in London. Perhaps if he checked the hotels . . .

Pulteney's, the Clarendon, the Midland Grand—none of the respectable establishments had heard of her. In fact, most seemed offended at the mere suggestion that they might have let a room to a young, unaccompanied female, much less one wearing trousers and appearing at the doorstep on horseback and without luggage. When he ran out of reputable establishments, he checked a few less than reputable ones, all to no avail.

Discouraged, he sent his carriage home without him, intending to walk for a while. The thought that she was probably somewhere in London at that very moment, hurting, miserable, perhaps even in trouble, haunted him.

He kept seeing her face as she stared at the destruction after the blast—the horror, brokenness, and despair that seemed unnatural on her lovely features. Over and over he recalled things he had said to her as she struggled against the odds to build something decent and good—jaded observations on humankind, criticisms of her competence and judgment, sneering assessments of her workers, her facilities, and her prospects for success.

Without someone to back her, to bolster her flagging energies, to underwrite her dream, what chance did she have? Even the toughest fighters, strongest leaders, and most powerful revolutionaries—people who built fortunes and governments and empires—had to have *someone* to turn to, someone to share their ideas and victories with, someone to commiserate with on their losses. At the end he had offered her a grudging bit of help . . . a nudge here, a word there . . . only when he couldn't help it, only when he couldn't resist her hope and caring any longer.

By then the damage had been done. His conscience-salving sop was too little too late.

He looked up and found himself on Piccadilly, just a block or so from his club, and headed for it—for the bar in it, to be exact. The dinner crowd had moved into the bar, and there was sufficient noise and smoke to mask his determination to drown his recriminations in a bottle of Scotch whisky. He sat at a table in the corner, shunning company and staring into his first glass of whisky as if expecting an oracle—or perhaps absolution. He found neither, and the merriment around him grew increasingly unbearable.

He headed for the door in high dudgeon, appalled that a man couldn't even get roaring drunk at his club anymore without having to listen to someone else's high spirits. Then, as he was leaving the bar, he overheard the word "cousin" and for some reason stopped stock-still.

When he turned, he found himself staring at the back of a tall, neatly built young man with excessively blond hair. Gilbert Duncan. He wasn't aware he had said the name aloud until the fellow turned to answer to his name.

"Yes?" The icy gray eyes seemed to lose some of their warmth at the sight of him, despite the smile that appeared with them. "Ah . . . another familiar face. Lord Mandeville, I believe."

"Indeed." Cole glanced at the men about Gilbert, most of whom he knew to belong to the "young rakehell" contingent of Brooks's membership. He knew because until the last year or so, he had been a member of that group himself. "Surprised to see you here, Duncan."

"He's just been added to the subscription list, old boy," came an explanation from Lyle Barclay, one of their fellow members.

"Then congratulations are in order," Cole said absently, trying to think of how to broach the subject of Madeline's whereabouts.

"On more than one account," Barclay continued, raising his glass. "Duncan here may be getting 'shackled' soon."

"Wedded?" Cole felt the blood draining from his face.

"My dear cousin Madeline," Gilbert declared, his eyes glittering as they took in Cole's ill-concealed reaction. "She's finally given up that reform madness—some sort of accident at that wretched factory of hers. She's come to stay with me, you know . . . and we've reached something of . . . an understanding."

"You have?" Cole felt like some other being had taken over his body. He was twisting his mouth into a smile and extending his hand toward Gilbert Duncan. "Well, then, best wishes."

Cole fled the bar as quickly as civility allowed, feeling as though something were sitting on his chest, hindering his breathing. Not even the clearer, cooler air of the street could dispel the smothering sensation he felt at the thought of Madeline marrying cloying, boy-faced Cousin Gilbert. It couldn't be true.

But as he walked through rain-slicked streets, feeling the cold drizzle dampening his shoulders and nullifying the effects of the lone whisky he had consumed, he recalled Gilbert blowing a kiss to her as they parted on the steps of the factory and saying something about being a champion and if she needed anything . . . The tumultuous events that followed had eclipsed that irksome incident in his mind. But apparently not in Madeline's. Gilbert had offered her support and solace when she needed it most, and she had gone straight from the ashes of her dreams to the shelter of his arms.

The thought of Madeline in Gilbert's cool, handsome embrace sent Cole into a downward spiral that ended a day later at the bottom of a bottle of Scotch. He awakened in the same clothes, lying facedown on his own bed, with a cotton-lined mouth and a pounding head. Between his discomfort and his distemper, it took poor Cravits the better part of the morning to make him presentable again.

He paced his study and then his parlor and then his hall, and when he could bear it no longer, he stormed out of his house to pace the streets themselves.

He could see now that her heart, her very spirit, had been under siege . . . beset by hopelessness and despair . . . in the person of Lord Cole Mandeville, former barrister and self-appointed king of cynics. With each new criticism, each contemptuous look, and each cutting observation, he had helped to wear her down, to exhaust her loving and creative spirit. In some ways that inner spiritual struggle was the fiercest and cruelest one of all. In the end it was the one that had broken her heart and sent her flying from St. Crispin to London, and into Gilbert's ready and willing arms.

It was his fault.

Again.

Once more he had become the agent of destruction. Once more he found himself in the role he loathed and despised: scrupulously executing the letter of the law while destroying every vestige of true justice. Once more he confronted the workings of the "Mandeville" in him. And this time, three days, three months, or even three years of

Scotch and unbridled sex would not be enough to make him forget the pain.

For the rest of the day he walked the streets, hoping to blot out or at least dull his misery with exhaustion. As evening fell, he found himself walking down the Strand and realized that his feet had carried him to the very person he had turned to for help a dozen years before—Sir William.

The doorman led him down the hallway, where he found his uncle ensconced behind a desk full of briefs . . . in an irascible mood, as usual.

"You!" The old justice staggered up and groped for his cane the moment he saw Cole, and it wasn't at all clear whether he meant to walk with it or use it on his nephew. "What the hell are you doing here?" He waved the cane, then tottered around the desk on it. "You're supposed to be out in St. Clarence—or wherever the blazes it is. And what the devil's all this about you and Madeline Duncan cohabiting and oppressing workers and having orgies in women's knickers? God A'mighty, I sent you out there to keep an *eye* on the girl, not *hands!*"

He had to pause for breath, which was the only way Cole could ever get a word in with him.

"I've come to give you my final report in person," Cole said, sitting down wearily and dragging his hands down his face.

"Final report?" Sir William loomed over him for a moment, then waved to Foglethorpe to bring him a chair and with a grunt of pain settled beside Cole, searching him with that uncannily perceptive gaze. "What's happened?"

"She's given it up. Packed it in. It seems there was a bit of an accident, and, on the heels of several other incidents, it was just too much. As a result of those articles in the *Gazette,* she had a visit from a few notables: William Morris, Joseph Lane, Annie Besant, Henry Broadhurst, Sylvia Bethnal-Green . . ."

"Ye gods. Sylvia Green is still at it?" Sir William muttered. "Then I'm not the oldest living fossil after all." He fixed Cole with a look. "I take it this little delegation didn't entirely approve of her efforts."

"The sods. They marched around poking their noses up everybody's—they were intrusive, arrogant, and belittling. You'd have thought they were a bloody royal commission! They came to see only what they wanted to see, more to accuse and make an example of her than to understand what she was doing. It was intolerable."

"Ummm. And what did your 'Mad Madeline' do?"

"She was as gracious and helpful as she could be—right up to the time when she tossed them out on their blind cheeks."

Sir William hooted a laugh. "And?"

"And . . . Morris and his comrades got the workers so het up that they confronted Madeline about their 'paltry wages' and 'oppressive working conditions.' They were incensed about the supposed callousness and 'inequity' of their treatment."

"And what did she do, St. Madeline?"

"Tossed them out on their hindquarters as well. Said she was closing down the factory." He grew quiet for a moment, staring at his hands as he matched his fingertips, then curled those trembling fingers into fists. "Then the place blew up."

"Beg pardon?" Sir William pulled his gaze from Cole's hands. "*Blew up?* As in 'black powder explosion'? "

Cole nodded and explained about the workmen Madeline had hired, the rock in her proposed garden, and how she had had little enough sense to take the shiftless pair back after they had dug up and destroyed what they were supposed to be creating.

"They repaid her by blowing the place to kingdom come. I suppose that was the last straw. She abandoned St. Crispin for London within the hour."

Sir William sat back, watching Cole's edginess and reading in his despondency that there was another, intensely personal side to the story as well. "So," he said, "it would appear your job is done."

Cole looked up. "If my job was to bully and hound and harass her into giving up her lifelong dream, then I suppose you could say I accomplished it."

"Oh?"

Cole shoved to his feet and began to pace. "I mean, there she was, working so hard and believing in it so much—and all I could do was skulk around like some underfed vulture, telling her how impossible it was and how foolish she was for trying."

"And was she foolish for trying?" Sir William asked as he leaned forward to engage Cole's gaze. Cole knew the old man could read more in him than he wanted to reveal. As usual, honesty was his only recourse.

"I don't know," he said. "She might have made a go of it. Or she might have rocked along for a time, until some catastrophe occurred. Or she might have fallen flat on her face. I don't suppose we'll ever know . . . thanks to me."

"Well, if she was willing to give up something as precious as a lifelong dream on the word of just one man, then she was probably bound to fail, and you've done her a service by ending it sooner rather than later."

"But it wasn't just *a man,*" he said, "it was *me.* And she . . . we . . . I . . ."

"So, it's like that, is it?" Sir William stroked his chin. "You've broken her heart and feel responsible for wrecking her business venture as well."

"I didn't break her heart—well, not the way you might imagine. I saw she was exhausted and stretched too thin, and I kept at her."

"You didn't take advantage of her?" It was both question and statement.

"Not . . . in the way you mean. Not entirely." He sat

down and propped his elbows on his knees. "But in a way what I did to her was probably worse—planting doubts, finding fault, looking for the worst in everything . . . undermining her hopes."

After thirty years on the bench, even in Chancery, Sir William was a master at recognizing a turning point, a crisis of the soul, when he saw it. He scrutinized Cole's burdened movements and grief-ridden expressions. Every line of the boy's long, angular body seemed to slope downward. Sir William smiled wanly. Opportunities like this came his way too damned seldom to suit him.

"So you have regrets," he said, sitting forward and wincing at the pressure it put on his bad leg. "Well, in my opinion, regrets should be outlawed for people under sixty." He waited for that to register, and it did. Cole looked up with a scowl. "In my experience, there are precious few things in life that can't be helped or fixed if someone puts his mind or his shoulder to it. Half the misery in the world is caused by people sitting and wailing about a problem instead of *doing* something about it. If people got up off their arses and applied themselves to whatever bothers them, there would be a lot less blubbering and a lot more done—and the world would be better off on both counts."

Cole stared at his uncle, surprised and angered by his attitude. Of all men, he might have expected his uncle to understand . . . to lend some insight.

"Madeline Duncan is a remarkable young woman. Would you agree with that assessment, or disagree?" Sir William demanded, sitting back.

Cole took a moment, then answered with a hostile "Agree."

"A bit eccentric, but remarkable nonetheless. She built a factory, hired workers, and produced a product—all on her own. According to you, she tossed William Morris, Henry Broadhurst, and the redoubtable Sylvia Bethnal-Green out on their ears, then turned around and did the same to her precious employees. That, my boy, is not the work of a fragile flower of femininity. She's human, not glass. She's hurt, but she can heal." The old man waited to collect his full attention before continuing. *"If you can, she can."*

"Me?" Cole sat straighter. "Heal?"

"The fact that you're in agony over what's happened to this girl is a most encouraging sign. She's done wonders, actually. More than I expected. Resurrected your conscience. Got you to care again. You have to *care,* my boy, before you can *hurt.* Not bad work for a madwoman with an aversion to corsets, eh?"

"Why, you old—" Cole sprang up from his chair, mute with exploding fury, glaring at his uncle—who was smiling like a fat Cheshire cat. Trembling with the effort required to contain his more violent impulses, Cole grabbed his hat and stalked out the door.

Sir William chuckled, watching him go, but soon found himself staring at his scowling clerk, standing in the doorway.

"Lucky man," Foglethorpe said.

"Yes, he is, really." The old justice sighed, feeling quite pleased with himself.

"I was speaking of *you,*" Foglethorpe said, narrowing his eyes. "Any other man would have put your lights out."

Do something . . . do something . . . do something . . .

Wretched old coot, Cole said to himself again and again as he strode furiously along the Strand, headed for the heart of The City. The words beat like a drum in his brain: *Do something.* Who did the old man think he was, handing down opinions as if they were damned edicts, playing God with people's lives? He showed not the slightest remorse at the way his diabolical plot turned out. In the old justice's eyes Madeline had rescued Cole, made him care again, healed him—the hurting was proof.

Well, if this agony was what was required to be *healed,* then perhaps he preferred to stay sick and broken!

Do something . . . do something . . .

Absorbed in his careening thoughts and emotions, he charged along the street, oblivious of other pedestrians, lorries, and even omnibuses. A "Hey—look out!" did manage to penetrate his awareness, and he halted just in time to keep from bashing into a large sheet of plate glass being unloaded from a glazier's lorry. Jolted by the near-miss, he stood a moment, watching the workmen hoist the plate of glass into a shopwindow and work to secure it.

The memory of broken windows came back to him with a vengeance, and he felt a painful ache beginning in his chest. She had been so proud of those windows. . . .

He took in the name of the glazier stenciled on the side of the lorry, then approached and asked the workmen where the firm was located. In moments he was headed for the nearest cab stand, refusing to think too much about what he was doing or to worry about why. He arrived just as the clerk of the establishment was about to lock up for the night. The proprietor, as it happened, was staying late to work on some correspondence and was surprised to have such a well-dressed customer walk in off the street. His surprise turned to incredulity when he heard what Cole wanted.

". . . to the village of St. Crispin, in East Sussex. There, I want you to rebuild a number of factory windows—frame, glass, and all. And I want it started right away." When the glazier wagged his head and opened his mouth to decline, Cole settled the matter by declaring, "Money is, of course, no object."

By the time he had sketched out the windows, approximated their dimensions, and written out a letter to serve as a draft on his own accounts, he was feeling somewhat better. Doing something, he hated to admit, felt better than doing nothing at all. Unfortunately, the salutary effects of "doing" didn't last long. When he reached his home in Mayfair, he was thinking steadily of Madeline——of her in Gilbert's house, perhaps in Gilbert's arms.

Of all the things that haunted him, that was the worst. *He* was the one who introduced her to kissing and caressing. It was *his* lovemaking she had responded to and explored. It was in *his* arms that she experienced pleasure and intimacy for the first——hell, *he* was the one who fondled her knickers and gave her goose bumps and made her dizzy enough to walk into walls!

He paced his rooms and the upper hall of his house, feeling choked and constricted. He began to shed clothes, trying to shed the feeling. Coat . . . tie and collar . . . vest . . . Breath came easier, but he was unable to rid himself of the sense of loss. He was the one who cared about her, who worried about her——who was crazy about her. He was the one who teased her mercilessly, who looked into her eyes and saw into her soul, and who understood how close to being an angel she truly was.

Mad Madeline. St. Madeline. Archangel Madeline.

Do something.

Not far away, in a fashionable town house in Belgravia, Madeline was being dressed for dinner. For the first time since she was four years old she had to be helped into her clothes—— laced into a straining corset, tied into successive layers of petticoats, hung with pads and frames, hooked and buttoned into a viciously tight bodice, and finally draped with a few dozen yards of the finest French silk moiré. And all this after she had spent two hours under the tedious ministrations of a lady's maid with a hot curling iron and a passion for making sausage curls.

She stood looking in the mirror for a moment and glimpsed a total stranger looking back at her. This poor female looked perfectly miserable in a teal blue gown that flattened her breasts and squeezed her waist to a "forgivable" twenty-two inches.

Poor thing, she thought. *She looks like a sausage ready to shoot from its casing.*

Her hair was pulled up so tightly into a knot on the crown of her head that it gave her a wide-eyed look and something of a headache. There were at least two hundred small curls and ringlets on her head, and every one was held in place with a metal pin. And then at each temple were those awful rolls of hair, which—lacking hairpins—were already beginning to droop.

I've seen smarter-looking basset hounds. She sighed. *Certainly happier ones.*

By the time she was duly powdered and perfumed and pinched to put color back into her cheeks, she had completely lost what little appetite she had. It was with the greatest of reluctance that she exited her room and descended the stairs to join Cousin Gilbert for dinner. Following the dressmaker's instructions, she bent forward at the hips and pulled her shoulders back, bowing the small of her back to produce a semblance of the S-shaped curve currently in vogue.

It was like having a parlor rug and an entire tea table lashed to your waist and being asked to walk without spilling. She withdrew a bit more inside herself, trying to escape the discomfort relayed by her aching senses. *I suppose you get used to it.*

She paused in the doorway to the parlor to locate Gilbert and found him by the fireplace, looking quite dapper and obviously pleased by the sight of her. He hurried to take her hand and lead her into the room, talking all the while. It was hard to appreciate, much less produce witty repartee when she had to concentrate so much on the mechanics of breathing and walking. She looked up to find he was introducing her to someone. Lord Somebody. And Lady Something—who didn't look like a tortured sausage.

"I thought perhaps you wouldn't mind a bit of company and conversation tonight," Gilbert said privately as he led her into the dining room. "One has to start somewhere." Then he gave her one of his aren't-I-just-too-charming-for-words smiles and declared, "You look ravishing. Madeline, my dear, you were made for such clothes."

If I was made for such clothes, then why can't I even sit down in them? she thought as she caught her bustle cage on the corner of the chair a second time and fumbled to free it. It took three tries to get her seated properly. Lord and Lady Something-or-other pretended not to notice. She sighed. *Breeding tells.*

By the time she reached her room four hours later, her back and ribs were aching, she was dizzy from the wine and lack of air, and every nerve in her body was screaming for relief. When the maid finally removed her corset, she melted into a puddle on the bed and refused to rouse herself again, even to let the girl take down her hair. She lay there for a long time, looking up at the ornate ceiling, tracing plaster cherubs, pomegranates, and grapevines with her gaze.

"Maybe I just won't eat dinner . . . ever again."

15

The next morning Cole trapped the membership secretary of Brooks's in the Great Subscription Room and got him to render up Gilbert Duncan's address, on the pretext that he had a wager to pay off and it was not the sort of thing one could reasonably handle across a civilized card table. He approached the house on Chester Square, repeating to himself the excuse for his intrusion: It was his legal duty to oversee her affairs, at least with regard to Ideal, and advise her on same. And if circumstances required it, he would be willing to confess to a concern for her welfare, and then demand to know why the hell she was marrying her oily cousin Gilbert.

Braced and prepared, aching for the sight of her, he was roundly disappointed to be told that neither she nor Mr. Duncan were at home, and that they were not expected for some time. He walked back through Mayfair, stifling the impulse to go searching high and low, and feeling thwarted and irritable. Rousing from his dismal thoughts, he was surprised to find himself on Regent Street, in front of Liberty, staring intently at a display window filled with children's clothes.

Liberty . . . the one store in all London that carried Ideal garments. He truly was a glutton for punishment.

Entering, he made his way to the ladies' department and strolled about for a while, weathering stares of indignation from the female clerks. After a time he approached one of them and identified himself as a representative of the Ideal Garment Company. He had come, he explained, to learn something about their customers' reaction to Ideal's garments.

Mollified somewhat by his explanation, the clerk explained that she was not authorized to make such reports, but, in confidence, related that the ladies generally seemed a bit skeptical. A good idea, many said, and they liked the lines and appearance. They thought the goods were nice and the design supportive. But all but the most adventuresome were reluctant to make such a drastic change in their wardrobes.

As he thanked her and turned away, he was glad Madeline hadn't heard that assessment. Silly women, not to recognize an inspired bit of design and a chance for freedom when they saw it. He headed for the door with Madeline's disconsolate image burning in his mind, but found the way blocked by a crowd in the aisle. A number of perambulators, women, and assorted children were collected around something on display. He craned his neck to look for another route, but the nearest alternative was also clogged with middle-class matrons and the occasional nanny, all with children in tow.

Children again. The world was positively overrun, these days, with the little—

"Ideal. They certainly are aptly named," one of the women was saying.

"So much better than those little gentleman suits or Fauntleroy velvets."

"Smart and yet sensible. You know, the head clerk said

the originals were designed by the old queen herself, when the prince was just a boy."

The display under discussion consisted of a tiered table topped by two wire forms approximating children's shapes and dimensions. One wore a middy blouse, and the trousers were trimmed in white piping. The other wore a dropped-waist dress with a sailor collar and tie, made of dark blue wool jersey. A carefully lettered placard on the display proclaimed them to be Ideal garments produced by the Ideal Garment Company.

He tried to slip past the two women ahead of him to get a closer look at the display, and they promptly jostled him right back to his former place. "How dare you, sir? Take a place in the queue and wait your turn like the rest of us."

"Wait? For what?" He stared at the dress and sailor suit, taking in their details.

"Ideal clothes, of course. They're only taking orders, you know. You can't get the actual garments today," one of them said before they all turned their backs on him.

There was no doubt; those were the very garments Madeline had designed for the children of Ideal's workers. Somehow they had made it to Liberty with the shipment of samples, and were mistakenly being offered for sale too. He glanced around at the number of women waiting to give the harried clerk their orders for the garments, and was caught off guard by a surge of pleasure. If Madeline could only—

But Madeline hadn't seen it and wouldn't see it. And the garments these women were so eager to order probably would never be made.

He turned and barreled through the increasing crowd and was halfway down the block before he could draw his next breath.

Walking, sitting, standing—Madeline was having to relearn virtually every movement living required. Life in a corset wasn't really so difficult once she got the hang of it. She only had to remember to limit her exertions—no hurrying, no reaching or carrying or climbing, and no laughing, not that she had had many opportunities for the last in recent days. Dragging around twelve pounds of fabric, steel framework, and horsehair padding was bearable once she got used to the way it rubbed and bumped her bottom. Sitting, however, required something like a military campaign; a flanking approach, a bit of tactical positioning, engagement of forces, and, finally, occupation.

It was probably a tribute to the hardiness of her sex, she decided, that some women were capable of engaging in riding or punting or badminton while encumbered in such garb. She, however, would probably be relegated to the ranks of those ladies identified as "delicate." Her lungs and brain were accustomed to a full complement of air, and, with their supply greatly reduced, they had a disconcerting tendency to rebel and produce dizziness and dark spots before her eyes. When Gilbert took her shopping for hats and for refreshments in a tearoom, she had to sit down no less than four times.

But being of delicate constitution did have benefits, she discovered. Women prone to swooning were never expected to engage in lively interactions or to say anything clever or witty. And according to her maid, fragile females were never required outside their chambers before three in the afternoon and were always excused from arduous activity and potentially difficult or unpleasant situations.

Well, she reasoned, corsets couldn't be all bad if they allowed her to be excused from life for at least half of every day.

Being excused from life was precisely what she had craved for the first several days after her explosive departure from St. Crispin. She sat for long periods in her room, staring at upholstery patterns and the print in the books of popular romantic poetry that Cousin Gilbert provided, grateful to feel nothing, to be numb all the way to her bones. If she could have arranged it, she would have stayed in that dazed and sensationless state forever. It certainly made her new clothing, her new acquaintances, and her attentive cousin Gilbert more bearable.

But all good things, as the saying goes, come to an end. Her rebounding sensitivity awakened to small things; at first, pricks with hairpins, a dinner partner who was overperfumed, the incessant clatter of dishes at dinner, and the nasal whine that crept into Gilbert's voice. It seemed she was constantly being pestered for her opinions on purchases, and she noticed that whenever she was alone with Gilbert for five minutes, he began driveling bits of that treacly poetry he had given her. "Rapturous hours unending" and "Hearts overarching, to meet in sweet divine"—that sort of nonsense.

She could have told him a thing or two about "hours unending."

The cracks in her protective insulation, once noticed, widened all too quickly. By her seventh night in Gilbert's house, her merciful insensitivity was a thing of the past. She found herself constantly on edge, alert to the slightest discomfort or annoyance and reacting with increasingly volatile thoughts and comments. The maid, scuffing her heels across the carpets, sounded like a column of Prussians. As she dressed for her first evening engagement—a dance given by a wealthy earl—her garters kept feeling like they were sliding down, her corset seemed tighter than usual, and her bodice kept drooping off her shoulders. By the time she descended the stairs to join Gilbert and his friend Lord Glenroven in the parlor, her new shoes were pinching her toes, her skin itched from the perfumed powder, and she was in a ripe mood indeed.

Did Gilbert always sound like a donkey when he laughed? And this Glenroven fellow had hands like limp noodles—he even left spots on her gloves!

When the carriage was brought around, Lord Glenroven declared that riding backward made him ill, and Madeline found herself wedged between the two for the ride to Belgrave Square. By the time they arrived at Lord and Lady Reardon's elegant house, the poufs and silk violets on her bustle had been crushed, and she felt pressed and crowded by Gilbert and his ever-present hands. As they waited in a line in the entry hall, to be announced, he kept bending to her ear and whispering instructions for what she was to do and say to various people he was keen to impress. His constant nattering about details only added to her case of nerves.

Can't he see that his breath is loosening some of my curls? Don't these people have anything better to do than stand around staring at my crushed poufs?

The music was very nice, she admitted grudgingly as they entered the heavily mirrored drawing room for a circuit of the first floor. The doors had been thrown back between rooms and guests were mingling freely amid lavish flowers, lilting chamber music, and liberally poured champagne. Gilbert was beaming, obviously in his element. He seemed to know a good many people, and they were all more than eager to meet her. On occasion there were comments or questions about her being "the one," but Gilbert slyly deflected them and smiled.

Three days earlier such comments would have passed her by altogether. But now she noted them and grew tense and uneasy, interpreting them as proof that a good many of these people had read the wretched articles about her and wondered how much of them was true. If she was to make any sort of life in this society, she had to start then and there. Surpressing her anxiety, she forced herself to greet these new acquaintances with more enthusiasm. Then Lord Reardon, their host, joined them and asked to be put on her dance card. When she demurred, saying that she did not dance, Gilbert seemed mortified and whisked her away for a private word.

"You truly cannot dance?" He made it sound a hanging offense.

"I cannot, Cousin. There was never an occasion for it,"

she answered, trying to contain her surprise at his ill-concealed outrage.

"Had I known, I never would have brought you *here*." He gave his vest a jerk and glanced about to see if they were being noticed. "Then we shall have to keep you well away from the ballroom." He noticed the surprise on her face and checked his reaction, producing an ingratiating smile. "It wouldn't do to subject you to the onslaught of admirers you would undoubtedly attract until you're ready for them. Unfortunately, I have already bid for several dances with other ladies. Perhaps I can get Dunroven to take care of you for a while."

Take care of me? Like the family embarrassment who can't be trusted in polite company? she thought, furious at the insinuation that she had to be "handled." *Or an unruly child?*

Cole's handsome black coach rumbled through the warm spring evening, swerving this way and that to avoid pedestrians and rain-washed ruts. Inside, a harried Cravits was fussing with Cole's tie—"Do hold still, sir. I simply cannot have you seen looking like a scruffian"—up to the very moment the coach stopped in the street outside Lord Reardon's house.

"Good enough, Cravits." He reached for the door handle but was stopped cold by the valet's grip on his collar and had to wait for the final twist that set a perfect pucker. "For God's sake, I'm not a guest. And I doubt they hold gate-crashers to the same exalted standards."

He stepped over the clothes on the floor of the coach and sprang down the coach steps. After instructing his driver, he headed for the massive front doors of the grandest house on Belgrave Square.

This was madness, he knew. He had returned to Gilbert Duncan's residence a short while before, intending to see Madeline and tell her about the success of her inadvertently "ideal" garments. When informed that she was out, he man-

·aged to prize her location out of the houseman, then returned home just long enough to grab his evening clothes and Cravits. Now his morning clothes lay on the floor of the coach and he was about to barge into the Earl of Reardon's home uninvited.

But, in truth, lack of an invitation was the least of his worries. Upon entering, he paused for a moment by the door, located an acquaintance in the entry, and made straight for the couple with an effusive greeting. As soon as the doorman assumed what it was natural to assume and looked the other way, he headed immediately up the grand stairs to the ballroom. A quick circuit of the room told him Madeline wasn't there, and he hurried downstairs, pausing halfway to search the crowd. He had no luck—until it dawned on him that he was looking for a young woman with a plain chignon, a scarlet tunic, and trousers. She would hardly be wearing those here, and he hadn't a clue what she might look like in regular clothing.

A woman drifting through the colonnade at the rear of the long entry hall caught his eye. Something familiar about her movement sent him flying down the rest of the steps. When she paused outside the conservatory doors, he slowed, praying it was Madeline and strangely both eager and reluctant to confront her.

She turned slightly, presenting a familiar profile—a straight nose, and neatly squared chin—and he relaxed. Nothing else would have identified her as the same fiery young woman who single-handedly battled the legal establishment, built a factory, resurrected a dead village, rescued a dozen families from London's slums, and considered flaming scarlet and Turkish trousers ideal mourning apparel. This young woman was clothed in the height of London fashion: a delicate white satin gown with a narrow waist and a delectably low neckline, trimmed with a drape of violet velvet and alternating flounces and poufs of satin and velvet, with silk violets down a substantial train. She wore twenty-button gloves, a cameo on a velvet ribbon around her throat, and an air of misery that was palpable.

When she entered the conservatory, he followed at a distance, unsettled by the sight of her in conventional evening dress. The gown was exquisite even by Paris standards, and she filled it to perfection. Until a month earlier he would have considered her appearance—voluptuously curved, faintly aloof, and swathed in luxury—to be the epitome of genteel womanhood. She would have been his ideal woman.

But just then, when he looked at her, what struck him most was the heartache that drained her features to a ladylike pallor and the tightly reined sorrow that others probably mistook for languorous poise. She looked to him like a woman who was wearing someone else's clothes . . . living someone else's life.

"There you are," he declared, startling her. She whirled, and at the sight of him staggered back, tripping on her train. If he hadn't darted forward and grabbed her, she would have fallen bustle-first into Lord Reardon's prize equatorial ferns.

"Cole." For a moment there was a flare of light in her eyes, then she quelled it and pointedly removed her arm from his grip. "What are you doing here?"

"I might ask you the same," he said, moving closer, looming over her and watching her tense more with each degree he advanced.

Madeline looked up, feeling her senses jolted by him and aching at that impact. He was dressed in elegant evening clothes, with a pristine shirt and embroidered silk vest and perfectly tied neck cloth. His dark hair shone and his autumn-forest eyes glowed with emotion she found both absorbing and painful to see. He looked as if he might have just stepped out of her turbulent dreams. When his image began to swim before her eyes, she realized she wasn't breathing and gasped air just as he spoke.

"Are you going to marry Gilbert?" he demanded.

"What?" She opened and fluttered her fan. "Don't be absurd. He's my cousin."

"A *distant* cousin," he corrected her. "And I understand you are now staying with him in his house. That may have given rise to certain . . . *expectations*."

"Not on my part," she snapped. But even as she said it, an embarrassingly large piece of logic fell into place in her mind, and she suddenly saw her situation as others might— as Cole apparently did . . . as *Gilbert* did! All of his adoring looks, incessant hand-kissing, and babbling about "hearts overarching" suddenly came together in her mind. Her eyes widened and she lowered her fan. Gilbert *was* angling to marry her!

She looked up at Cole's knowing expression, appalled at having him watch her discover the mess she had made in seeking to escape an even bigger mess. Arrogant wretch— why did he always have to be *right* about everything?

"Then if you're not marrying Gilbert, what in blazes are you doing in those clothes?"

"I've had a change of style"—she fumbled furiously with her train, then kicked it out of the way so she could step back—"to go along with my change of heart."

"Oh?" He gave her a slow, thorough look. "About this change of heart—"

"It's none of your business, actually," she preempted his comment.

"I beg to differ."

"You're relieved of duty, absolved of all responsibility." She came straight to the point. "You needn't worry about my magnanimous impulses ever again." Gathering her train over her arm, she straightened with as much dignity as she could muster. "They're dead. Gone. Defunct. I shall be happy to write Sir William a letter to that effect, if you wish."

With each word between them, a bit more of the emotion roiling deep inside her escaped, and she found herself beginning to tremble. Alarmed, she backed another step. His presence was rousing memories and feelings in her that she was not prepared to handle.

"Forgive me, angel, but I've suffered enough of your little homilies on the nobility of giving to be more than a little skeptical. I believe you and I should have a talk."

"We have nothing to say to each other," she said irritably. "I have decided to heed your suggestion that I face the grim realities of humankind and reform my hopelessly gullible life." She couldn't help the trace of bitterness that crept into her tone. "Congratulations, you've succeeded in reforming the reformer."

When she started past him, he didn't prevent her from leaving. In fact, he took her elbow and propelled her along, out of the conservatory and straight down the side hallway, where he opened door after door, looking for an unoccupied room.

"What do you think you're doing?" she hissed as they passed other guests.

Without answering, he pushed her through a doorway into a dimly lighted room. When he turned to close the door, she jerked free and backed away.

"Insist on your pound of flesh, do you?" She folded her arms around her waist and stuck out her chin, trying to combat the feel of those burnished autumn eyes tugging at her. "Very well, you won. You were right. It was just as you said. Now let me go."

"You don't really believe that," he insisted.

"Oh, but I do," she said tightly, desperate as she felt her barely contained emotions slipping bit by bit out of her control. "You were right about everything. Reform garments *are* absurd, impractical, and utterly unsalable. Heavens, why should women wish to breathe when they can be excused from so much unpleasantness if they don't? And you were dead right about my precious workers—they were nothing but a bunch of whiners, shirkers, and opportunists." Every word seemed to carry a bit more heat than the last as she paced away, then back.

"And as for reformers . . . our exalted visitors bore out your predictions entirely. They stirred up nothing but trouble and discontent. They offered no solutions, no attempt to resolve or improve things—just judgments, accusations, and a lot of patronizing moralisms. Rather fitting, was it not? That I, who believed so wholeheartedly in reform, was undone by a pack of rabid and overzealous reformers." The hostility raging in her was her only defense against the tears threatening at the backs of her eyes. "I'm sure the irony of it hasn't escaped you."

The way his eyes slid over her and the troubled look on his face said that very little escaped him. Her hands curled into fists as she contained the urge to throttle him. How dare he stand there looking so cool and in control, so perfectly wise and impartial. The wretch!

"What hasn't escaped me is the amount you were able to accomplish—against great odds."

"Accomplish?" She gave a humorless laugh. "All I *accomplished* was the squandering of nearly a quarter of my aunt's legacy to me. Not on luxury and fast living, true. Instead, I wasted it on feeding four or five dozen greedy, shiftless, malingering ingrates, giving them places to live and clothes to wear, caring and providing for their children. And through it all I managed to keep them quite entertained with the absurdity of my notions about clothing reform. They *took* with both hands. And why shouldn't they if I was gullible enough to offer?"

"You *are* hurting, aren't you, angel?"

"I am not an angel. Nor am I a saint or a madwoman or a willful, troublesome child. I am just a person who tried to make a difference . . . in a world that doesn't like differences." She had to swallow the tears collecting in her throat to continue. "I don't intend to let that ruin what is left of my life."

He stared at her for a moment, invading her gaze, laying

bare the hurt and disillusionment she tried to hide. She could feel him examining the conflict of her ideals and experiences. Then his piercing gaze softened, his eyes darkened.

"I don't intend to let it ruin your life either."

He grabbed her by the wrist and headed for the door.

"How dare—Cole Mandeville, I will not be manhandled!" She took a swing at him with her free hand, only to have him catch it and use it to drag her along as well. Without making any more of a spectacle than necessary, she tried balking, twisting, and finally kicking, all to no avail. He pulled her through the drawing room, along the colonnade that ringed the main hall, then straight out the front doors—under the stunned scrutiny of their lordly host, Reardon, and at least a score of London's elite.

When they reached the street, a huge black coach came hurtling up and Cole hoisted her up the steps and shoved her inside, where her feet tangled in her skirts and she fell back against the seat. Between the lurching of the carriage and the binding of her rigid corset and cumbersome bustle frame, she had difficulty righting herself. Scorning his offer of assistance, she finally struggled up on her own and fled to the other side of the carriage. There she braced against the rocking rear-facing seat, and tried to recover both her breath and her dignity.

"Take me straight back to Cousin Gilbert's—this minute!"

"Changed your mind about marrying him?" he said with a taunting smile. She came within a hairbreadth of launching herself at him with nails bared.

"I mean it. I consider this an abduction—I'll have you brought up on charges and given the fullest measure the law allows!"

"You know, I'm really rather surprised at you." He sprawled back against the tufted velvet seat, looking every bit as calm and in control as she was furious and frantic. "I wouldn't have expected you to just give up and walk away."

"I did not just give up. If you'll remember—I was *blown* up!"

"When things got a little rough"—he shrugged—"you cut and ran without putting up a fight. It amounts to the same thing."

"Without a fight?" She looked around for something to throw at him, seized a pillow from the seat beside her, and heaved it at him. It surprised him, but he managed to catch it. "And what was I supposed to fight? Indifference? stupidity? laziness? Wasn't that what I was doing all along? I worked my fingers to the bone for Ideal. I gave those stupid workers everything I had—my money, time, energy, faith. They took what they could and then destroyed the rest!" Desperate for another missile, she resorted to jerking off one of her shoes and flinging it at him. He dodged, then seized the shoe, opened the window, and tossed it out.

"Ohhh!" She yanked off the other one and hurled it at him. He was prepared this time, caught it, and sent it to join its mate on the London streets.

"Pray do continue. But I should warn you, if you continue to throw clothes at me, you may start to feel a bit chilly before we reach St. Crispin."

"St. Crispin?" Panic invaded her anger, chilling some of its heat. "I am not going back to St. Crispin."

"Oh, but you are," he said.

"The factory is a pile of rubble, no one wants the stupid clothing, and the village is a pathetic mud hole populated by bum-bags who have to be kicked again and again to get them moving!" She was trembling, having to force every word past a constriction in her throat. "There is nothing in St. Crispin worth fighting for."

"Nothing . . . but your heart."

The pained understanding in his eyes unleashed a smothering wave of grief in her. She didn't need reminding that she had left her heart behind her in pieces on the steps of the factory. That was why for the last week she hadn't been able to feel, to think, even to mourn. Suddenly the enormity of that loss came crashing down on her.

"Stop—" she choked out. "Stop this carriage and let me out—here—now!"

"You can't run from it, Madeline." His voice came low and earnest, like the whispering of conscience. "The failure, the pain, the disillusionment . . . you'll carry them with you wherever you go. They will always be just a turn of thought away. And no matter how you try to drown your sorrows or fill your days, they will always find a way to remind you. You have to go back and face it down . . . deal with it."

"Like you dealt with it? Like you faced it down?"

Her angry words lay burning on the air.

"Like I'm facing it this very minute," he said tightly. "I've made mistakes, Madeline. Disastrous ones, monstrous ones. But none worse than the one I made with you."

The words were like a punch in the gut. Mistakes. Instantly, the memories of his kisses, his caresses, his tenderness, rose inside her. Those were all mistakes too? Now she had not even *that* to hold on to?

She gasped and suddenly found it impossible to exhale. Reduced to shallow, panicky breaths, she knew she had to get away and dove headlong for the door.

Cole lunged after her, caught her by the waist, and pulled her back against him. As she thrashed, he managed to maneuver her between his legs, bracing his feet against the opposite seat. He was panting by the time she was secured.

"Are you mad, trying to jump from a moving carriage? What in heaven's name's gotten into—" His eyes widened as he felt the severe boning beneath her gown and connected it to her troubled breathing. "What the hell is this?" Wrapping his legs around her to hold her, he began to work the buttons and hooks at her back.

"Stop—" She struggled on two fronts, trying both to breathe and to escape him. Tears were welling in her eyes and she put her hands to her face to keep him from seeing them. She didn't want to be near him, didn't want him to see her out of control.

"It's this damnable corset. Lord, no wonder you're acting like a lunatic—you can scarcely breathe!"

Threads popped and buttons and hooks flew as he seized the fabric with both hands and pulled open the back of her dress. Muttering, he fought his way through the buttons, tapes, and ties of petticoats, past the fastenings of her bustle frame, then through a corset cover.

Her vision was blurring, her head reeling. Why was he doing this? Why did he have to invade her life again, drag her back to St. Crispin, make her relive all the pain and humiliation of the last month? What did he want from her? Her struggles weakened. Again and again she felt him grabbing the laces and pulling. As each round of lacing slid, she felt her resistance to him sliding as well.

The pressure on her ribs suddenly eased and she drew a starved breath, expelled it, then breathed deeply again. But more air meant better thinking and a clearer understanding of her situation. Anguish settled over her once more, weighing on her heart, and she went perfectly still.

"I can't go back," she said in a whisper raw with pain "There's nothing to go back *to*."

He felt her trembling and her attempts to control it, heard the desperation in her voice, and saw the strain on her face and the fluttering of her pulse in her throat. Yet he sensed that this was just the tip of the iceberg. She truly was terrified. For a moment he stopped to think what it would be like for her to be back in St. Crispin. A harrowing image of her in a deserted factory, sifting aimlessly through rubble, mired in defeat and anguish, flashed into his mind. He recoiled. It would be nothing short of cruel to take her back to all that, to force her so soon to confront something so devastating.

"Please . . . let me go. Just stop the coach and let me out."

"I can't let you go," he said gently, tightening his arrns

around her waist and pulling her up onto the seat beside him. "But I won't take you back to St. Crispin."

What she needed was a neutral place, somewhere without memories and worries attached. Someplace safe and comfortable. Someplace he could have some time with her, talk to her, stuff some heart back into her. When it came to him, he rapped on the carriage, then opened the sliding panel to give his driver a change of destination.

"Home, Caldwell."

Minutes after Cole and Madeline disappeared in the coach, a storm broke among the guests in Lord Reardon's entry hall.

"An outrage!"

"Simply criminal!"

"Stolen right out of the earl's home!"

Gilbert was summoned instantly and he negotiated the tempest with a blend of styled outrage and genuine fury. The scene Mandeville had caused—it could have been only Mandeville, though it had happened so quickly, no one present could positively identify the wretch—was potentially disastrous to his hopes for a marriage with Madeline. But in a masterstroke Gilbert quickly assumed the dual role of anguished family member and aggrieved suitor, putting his own interpretation on events and redirecting reaction into usable channels of opportunity.

When Lord Reardon declared in a flurry, "We must call the police. Scotland Yard will track the fiend down soon enough!" Gilbert quickly drew him aside.

"No, no, your lordship, please. This is my *beloved* cousin, a lady of some standing, to whom I am devoted. She must not be subjected to any more notoriety than necessary. It must be some sort of misunderstanding, and I feel beholden to sort it out in as private a manner as possible. You see, her trustees have asked me to interest myself in her affairs and see to her welfare. I fear I may have disappointed their confidence in me. I will not know a moment's peace until I have found her and returned her to the bosom of her family."

Flush with good wishes and godspeed, Gilbert accepted the use of his host's carriage and hurried out to rescue his beloved lady cousin.

But once away from Belgrave Square, he told the driver to head for St. James's and settled back in the plush carriage to plot his strategy. Two names came to mind. He decided he had two stops to make.

If anyone could find the little witch for him, it was that useful piece of slime, Rupert Fitch. It was said there wasn't a fart let in London that the scribbler didn't know about. But his second stop of the evening was even more important. He had spoken the truth when declaring he had been in contact with Madeline's trustees in recent days. He had quite an illuminating visit with Sir Edward Dunwoody three days before . . . in which he revealed the collapse of Madeline's enterprise and her status as a guest in his home.

A master in the use of selective candor, he had confided in Dunwoody concerning his "deep affection" for Madeline. Then, playing on the fact that she had flown from St. Crispin to his arms, he insinuated that she was coming to feel the same. The priggish solicitor was so relieved to have his rebellious client show inclinations toward female conformity that he virtually opened the estate's coffers to Gilbert. The extravagant new clothes had come from Madeline's own money, and the staff who had assiduously attended her every whim had also been paid for with her coin.

He smiled, freeing his mind to spin its cleverest webs. If she welcomed his "rescue," there would be a quick wedding to silence any untoward comment. If she refused his magnanimous "remedy" for her disgrace, the scandal of her abduction could be used to help prove her erratic and unstable behavior in the courts.

Either way, he would be seen as a devoted kinsman acting

in her best interest. And her lovely fortune would tumble straight into his appreciative hands.

It was only minutes before the coach pulled up before Cole's house on Berkeley Square. He removed his coat and put it around Madeline, but when he climbed down and reached up to help her down, she refused to move.

"Where are we?" she demanded, looking up at the imposing brick facade, elegant doors, and well-tended greenery boxes on either side of the entrance.

"My house." When she started to protest, he reached for her waist and hauled her from the coach bodily.

The doors seemed to open magically and he trundled her quickly inside. The marble entry hall was bathed in the light of two gas lamps that were turned low, but she had little chance to see the place. He tossed a string of orders to the houseman who met them, while propelling her to the steps and up.

"What are you doing?" she demanded, trying unsuccessfully to wrench away but succeeding in finally dragging him to a dead stop in the middle of the stairs. "Why have you brought me here?"

"We need to talk, and this is the safest, most private place I know."

"Safest for whom?" She glanced up the stairs and glared at him.

He studied her resentment, belatedly seeing his choice of venue through the broken trust visible in her eyes. Reversing direction, he dragged her back down the steps and pulled her down a long hall and into a paneled room lined with bookshelves, furnished with a massive mahogany desk and heavy leather upholstery, and smelling faintly of fresh tobacco and aged whisky.

"Will this do?" he asked, his tone carefully neutral.

She pulled his coat tighter around her and surveyed the

room with rising discomfort. It seemed very much the way she might have expected his private study to be. Elegant but substantial . . . venerable . . . comfortable . . . a refuge from the responsibilities of the powerful male world. Just now *she* needed a refuge. And the very last thing she needed was to be closeted someplace "comfortable" with Cole Mandeville.

"It depends on what you have in mind," she said, struggling to protect herself by feeding the embers of her anger. It was the only defense she could seem to muster against him and her need for him. "I don't see any whips or chains—or thumbscrews."

"Is that what you think? That I brought you here to torture you?"

"I haven't the foggiest why you'd take me anywhere. I would have thought you'd be more than glad to see the last of me. " She told herself not to look at him, not to listen to the undercurrents of warmth in his tone, and fastened her gaze on the desk. "Or perhaps you've brought me here to take me up on my offer of a letter to Sir William."

"Or perhaps because I care about you and I know you've had a rough time of it these last few days."

That jolted her. Him caring? How dare he do this to her!

"Or perhaps because you have a guilty conscience about something," she snapped. "A stolen kiss here and there perhaps? Well, who could blame a wealthy nobleman for indulging himself to pass the time when he's sentenced to rusticating?"

His gaze grew intent, but his voice stayed treacherously soft. "All right. I'll admit it. I do have a guilty conscience. It's something of a novelty, and I've decided to prolong and even enlarge the experience by doing something about it. *Apologizing.*"

Surprised by his declaration, she felt her determination ravel and tensed. "You expect me to believe you brought me here to apologize?"

"I made a terrible mistake with you, Madeline."

"So you said. I don't really need or want to hear any more of this."

"I never meant to hurt you or to add to your problems."

"You wouldn't happen to have any pins in your desk?" she said purposefully, heading for the top drawer to look.

"In fact, I thought I was helping."

"I need only two or three, and I can be on my way," she declared with increased volume and vehemence, to blot out his words.

"I could see the disappointments, the problems coming a mile away, and I wanted to warn you, to prepare you."

"If you would please just find me a parlor maid and a bloody box of silk pins!"

"What I couldn't see was that I was as much a part of the problem as anyone."

"You won't help, fine, I'll just wear your damned coat over my gown!" she shouted, feeling both her tears and her panic rising.

He reached the door slightly ahead of her and stood blocking the way. She couldn't look up, not with her eyes burning with tears and her broken heart so visible in them. As she stood struggling for control, he brought his hands from behind his back. In one of them was a fringed pillow. He offered it to her.

"I don't seem to have a tree on hand at the moment, but you can use the desk or the couch." His voice softened dangerously. "Or me."

She looked up, her eyes brimming, her whole body trembling . . . wanting . . . needing him . . . and so very afraid. She snatched the pillow, but before she finished swinging it once, the dam holding back that flood of anguish broke.

Suddenly his arms were around her, and his body was hard and warm and real against hers. And though she knew she could be walking off another cliff, she wrapped her arms desperately around him and let the tears come.

"That's it," he said softly onto the top of her head. "Get it out. Good, big sobs, remember. The louder the better."

She pounded him on the shoulder, then proceeded to do exactly as he said, giving in to wrenching sobs. But, strangely, they didn't last for long. The feel of his strong embrace and of his warm, supportive shoulder beneath her cheek somehow softened her grief. He led her to a seat on the couch and produced a handkerchief. She wiped her face and blew her nose, and when he drew her into his arms again, settled back against him. The silence was so sweet that she was reluctant to break it for some time.

"How do you know?" she finally asked.

"You start talking furiously and you get a certain tight, you–can't–hurt–me look." He lifted her chin so he could see her eyes. "I just know, that's all. Are you ready to hear my apology now?"

She nodded and he gave her a bittersweet smile.

"I didn't mean to add to your problems, Madeline. I truly was trying to help. I saw you headed for disaster and wanted to save you from it. Do you have any idea how long it's been since I felt the urge to save someone?" When she shook her head, he shook his. "I don't know either—it's been too damned long to remember. I'm totally out of practice. I couldn't see that warnings and advice weren't what you needed. You needed someone to believe in you, someone to support you and take care of you. And every time you turned around, there I was, croaking gloom and doom and telling you how impossible it was."

"It *was* impossible." She wiped her wet cheek, then let him pull her head down onto his shoulder again. "I see it all so clearly now, and I feel so foolish. It was probably obvious to everyone on earth but me. Whatever made me think I could plan and build and run a factory, much less a whole community?"

What was it about her that made him suddenly want to rearrange, reform, and reconcile the whole blessed world just to see her smile again? Perhaps it was that old saying about nothing being sadder than an angel's tears. . . .

"There was nothing wrong with your plans, sweetheart. Your grasp of what it takes to run a business would put most bankers to shame. And as for strength and fortitude, I don't know another single person—male or female—who could single-handedly plan and carry out what you managed to do." He gave her reddened cheek a stroke. "The fault wasn't in your knowledge, your ability, or your courage. It was in your lack of experience with people. You were just too trusting, too generous, too willing to believe the best about everyone."

"So you're saying the factory failed because I was too *virtuous*?" She sat up straight, sniffed, and shrugged out of his coat. "You don't think having the bad judgment to hire helpless widows, drunken engineers, randy young hulks, and village idiots might have had something to do with it?"

"Very well, I admit your employees presented some problems. But Fritz seemed to do some of his best work with a few belts in him. And much as I hate to say it, Emily Farrow did have a flair for organization and correspondence. As for the Ketchums—if you could have imported a few more eligible seamstresses, they might have settled down nicely. They did a fine bit of carpentry when they could get their heads out of their—"

"Children—there were all those children I hadn't counted on," she said, scowling.

"Which you took care of rather nicely, I recall. With a schoolroom and nursery."

"And there were problems with production itself."

"Which were mostly solved. You had straightened out your supply problem and were working on smoothing the various stages of production, giving the workers a bit more say in what they did, encouraging their initiative and independent efforts."

She felt a small bloom of hope and realized he was responsible for it. But a moment later she made herself come back down to earth, telling herself he said such things only to make her feel better. He didn't truly believe them.

"Well, it's all moot now, isn't it?" She avoided his gaze. "Everyone hated our products, even my employees."

"A lot of products take a while to catch on. I was in Liberty yesterday. That's one of the reasons I came to see you tonight, to tell you—" She looked up from her hands, tensing, feeling a bubble of expectation rising in her middle. "It seems there was something of a mix-up when they packed the samples for Liberty. Some of the children's clothes you designed were packed in with the sample bodices and knickers. And at Liberty customers were queuing up to place orders for them."

"The children's clothes?"

"Those dark blue things that make them look like little sailors. The clerks had set up a special display and put up a sign touting them as 'Ideal' garments." He took her face between his hands. "Madeline, I know they aren't what you planned, but they are reform garments and a viable product. Your knickers and bodices might not change the way women dress overnight, but, who knows, when word gets around, they may sell better than you think. The clerks said most women seemed to like the idea. . . ."

"They liked my children's clothes?" She grabbed his tear-soaked shirt. "They really like them? Wanted to buy them?"

"They did."

"You wouldn't just say that, would you?"

"False hope is crueler than no hope at all. I'd never do that to you, Madeline." He was utterly serious as he took her by the shoulders. "Do you hear what I'm saying? Your Ideal Garment Company can succeed, can still work. You can still have your dream. And to prove it to you, I'll take you to Liberty first thing tomorrow, so you can see the display for yourself."

At that moment he wasn't just putting a gloss on the world to make her happy, he was telling the truth—to himself as well as to her. It *could* work. She *could* make a going concern of it.

The idea hit him square between the eyes, sending ripples of shock radiating through him. Until that moment, as he encouraged her and defended her dream to her, it hadn't occurred to him that he might actually have been wrong about Ideal. So many of his dismal expectations had been borne out, he had simply assumed he was right. Yet he had given her piece after piece of evidence to show that his skeptical conclusions did not tell the entire story. Mired in his own stubborn cynicism, he had ignored the other half of what was happening—the good half.

If he had been right, he had also been equally wrong.

It was as if he had suddenly smacked into a wall and found himself moving in an entirely different direction. It was all so clear that it astounded him. There was real potential in Madeline's work, in her employees, in her ideas. With a bit of support she could have heeded sound advice, withstood the inevitable disappointments, and solved Ideal's problems before they became cataclysmic. And if he was coming to that conclusion rationally and reasonably, that meant he was looking at things very differently from the way he was two months before. It meant he had—he could scarcely make himself think it, much less say it—*hope.*

"But what if I can't make it work?" she said quietly. "I will have to hire all new workers and rebuild the factory. There has probably been damage to the machinery. . . . " She looked up and bared her deepest fears. "What if I can't do it all?"

With his heart strangely full, he smiled and hooked a hand behind her neck, drawing her face close to his. She had just given him something priceless, and he wanted nothing more than to return the favor.

"Who says you have to do it all?" he said. "Hire people you can trust and then make them responsible. And then . . . I intend to be there . . . helping you, supporting you."

"You do?" she whispered, her heart suddenly beating erratically.

"Every step of the way, angel."

Her face lit with pleasure and she looked at his mouth, needing, anticipating. . . .

"Under one condition," he continued, holding her away for one minute longer.

"And that is?" She wet her lips.

He reached for the shoulders of her bodice and pulled them straight down her arms, wrenching a surprised protest from her. Batting her hands away, he seized her corset and began wrestling it from beneath her dress. It took some doing to free it beneath the layers of petticoats and beneath the bustle paraphernalia, but when she realized what he intended, she twisted and shifted to allow him better access.

Holding the offending piece up in the dim light, he studied the thick canvas ducking, inch-wide stays, and heavy-duty grommets, and gave a low whistle. "This thing is built like a Turkish prison."

He thunked one of the stays with his finger and gave her a wondering look—just before he carried it over to the window, opened it, and dropped it out.

"Hey! That is an expensive corset."

"It was a damned torture rack. Spanish inquisitors used lighter machines to force confessions out of heretics." He settled a hot-eyed smile on her and strolled back to join her on the couch. "I'll go with you to St. Crispin and help you and support you, on the condition that you never, ever put on one of those things again."

She blushed, and as she was pulling her gown back up onto her shoulders, he grabbed the neckline of her bodice and held it for the ransom of her agreement.

"Promise me," he demanded, his eyes like glowing coals.

"I promise," she said breathlessly.

He pulled her into his arms and she finally got the kiss she wanted. It was long and liquid and lingering, the kind that made her toes curl and her breasts tingle and her skin come alive with a hunger for sensation. When his kisses began to drift, she abandoned herself to their tantalizing explorations, drinking the pleasure into her bruised but healing heart. And when he made her squirm with his naughty tweaks and delicious nibbles, she laughed and decided to give him a taste of his own medicine.

Wriggling her knees under her and sitting up beside him, she reached for his silky tie and stiff collar. Then, as he protested, she jumped up, carried them to the open window and dropped them out. Settling half on his lap, she attacked his vest and even the studs of his shirt. Soon his neck and chest lay bare beneath her hungry gaze.

"Ohhh, Madeline," he groaned as she nibbled her way across his chest. "Is that any way for an angel to behave?"

16

"Wait—I'm losing something—" As they mounted the stairs, she had to pause to gather her skirts and loosed petticoats together in her arms. Soon she was so bundled and bound, she could scarcely walk, and yet she was in imminent danger of losing her bodice and bustle frame at any minute. She looked up at him with eyes wide in the dimness. "I'm falling apart!"

"Women!" He scooped her up in his arms and carried her the rest of the way.

There was just enough moonlight coming through the windows at the base of the domed ceiling to allow them to navigate. Once upstairs, they could see by the light coming from two open bedroom doors down the hallway.

By the time he reached the guest bedroom, he was panting and laughing at the same time and she was in grave danger of being dropped right on her drooping bustle. He lowered her legs and she turned just enough to slide down his body. Releasing her petticoats to put her arms around him, she realized they hadn't fallen and looked down at the ball of muslin, silk, and velvet trapped between them.

"You do seem to have a problem with your clothing, Miss Duncan," he said, kissing her nose and stepping back enough to let the balled-up skirt fall. To her dismay, he continued back another step. "Let 'Nanny' give you a few lessons in fashion, my dear," he said in a crotchety voice, shaking a finger. "Firstly . . . a woman as lovely as you should never wear light-colored satins." He reached for the skirt of her dress and began to pull it up over her head. "The fabric will always turn pink, don't you know."

"Pink?" She laughed, suffering his ministrations.

"From blushing. Satins are vain, child. They can't bear to be outdone." He grinned and his voice returned briefly to normal. "Especially by a woman's skin."

She shivered with expectation and watched him throw her skirt aside. "Anything else?" Suddenly he was "Nanny" again, crackly voice and all.

"And these low-cut gowns . . . a medical hazard, you know."

"They cause . . . pneumonia?" she said as he dragged her bodice down her arms.

"Eyestrain," he announced. "For all the gentlemen ogling you. Better stay away from them." She laughed, feeling a familiar tension rising between them.

"You're awfully knowledgeable about these things, Nanny. I had no idea."

He stared at her petticoats and shook his head. "Too many layers. They should really warn young women against this." He began to peel them off one at a time. "Traps the heat against their bottoms . . . makes them think unhealthy thoughts."

"I can see how 'hot bottoms' might be a serious problem with young women." She laughed softly, watching him strip her clothes, delighted by his impersonation.

"And this thing . . ." He strolled around, considering her,

and gave her bustle frame a swat. Then he abruptly lifted it up to look under it. "As I thought." He began pulling it from her. "Bustles are for females without enough padding on their bones. You, my dear, have *plenty* of padding."

"Plenty of—" She gave him a shove and walked away with her nose in the air. He gave chase and caught her near the window, in a shaft of moonlight. "Padding?" she said indignantly. "I have plenty of padding?"

He pulled her hard against him and laughed. "That's not necessarily a bad thing, you know." He slid his hands down her back and cupped her buttocks. "I happen to like your padding. In fact, I like it very much." He gave her a brief, heated kiss, then released her and stepped back to scrutinize her.

"Hmmm." *Nanny* was back, shaking her head with a "tsk." "These old-fashioned unmentionables, they're apt to cause chafing." His eyes widened. "And chafing leads to redness and redness leads to sores . . . and sores lead to infections and infections lead to gangrene . . . and gangrene is nearly always fatal." He began tugging frantically at her long, ruffled drawers. "Get out of those bags at once, child—before you die of gangrene!"

She laughed so hard, he had to do all the work. And when he reached for her chemise, she let him slide it down her arms without the slightest demur.

"Ahhh, much better," he said in his regular voice.

There she stood in the moonlight, naked, bathed in gold and silver, precious . . . but, oh, so warm to the touch. Self-conscious, she wrapped her arms over her breasts, and he smiled, catching her gaze in his and then catching her warmth in his heart.

"That's the way I'll always see you," he said, his voice suddenly low and full. "Dressed only in the beauty your Maker gave you. My lovely, loving Madeline. My own personal angel. Rescuer of my heart."

Suddenly the playfulness was gone, and deeper, fuller passion took its place. He picked her up and carried her to the bed. When he hesitated at the edge, she grabbed his sleeve and pulled him down beside her. He braced on one elbow, searching her face and stroking the hair from her temples.

"Stay," she said softly.

He closed his eyes. "There won't be any turning back, angel."

"There's already no turning back, Cole. I can't just decide suddenly to stop loving you." She saw the impact of her words when he opened his eyes. They were full of powerful new emotions that lent fresh heat to their autumn fires.

"I do love you, Cole."

His mouth poured over hers softly, exploring every nuance of every contour and every movement she made. The sensations strengthened with all the urgency of a feather falling . . . unhurried, inevitable . . . deepening the pleasure of his mouth on hers by slow, maddening degrees. He opened her lips with his and plundered her with tender, expert strokes that made her bones go soft and her blood catch fire. When he raised his head, she had difficulty focusing her eyes.

"You're an extraordinary woman, Madeline Duncan," he said, bracing above her on his elbows. "You're bright and loving and beautiful and strong and generous. In a more perfect world you'd be matched with a man who was just as strong and bright and generous and loving as you are. But we both know now that the world is far from perfect. And, for once, that works in my favor." He smiled smugly. "Instead of Mr. Perfect, you've somehow been matched up with me.

"You may be asking yourself, what do I get out of this wretched bargain? A very good question indeed." His voice lowered and thickened. "You get a man who may be a bit opinionated, stubborn, and arrogant but who is also bright enough to actually have ideas on things, has enough character to stick by the things he feels strongly about, and is confident enough to speak his mind honestly—no having to guess what he's thinking." His mouth canted into a soft, compelling half-smile. "I have money and some property and I'm not at all tightfisted. And best of all: I can make you see stars or rainbows or Chinese fireworks or lightning bolts—whatever it is you see when the earth quakes and falls away beneath you—every night for the rest of your life."

She stared at him, tracing his features, delving into the depths of his opening heart, feeling a oneness with him that awed her.

"Not a bad bargain," she said, her eyes glistening, her chest aching softly. Then she grinned, returning to the pleasure of his body against hers. "Especially that last part . . . about the Chinese fireworks." She grabbed the open collar of his shirt in determined fists and parted it forcefully. "Now, get out of those awful clothes, Nanny, and come and teach me more. There are a few things I've just been dying to learn."

He stripped his clothes eagerly, flinging the shirt thither and the trousers yon. When he rejoined her on the bed, she laughed and pulled his head down to join their mouths. The tingling eddied from her mouth down through her throat and chest, and soon her entire body was alive with hunger and anticipation. As their kisses deepened, he slid his chest over hers and traced her sides with feathery strokes that made her squirm and giggle.

They took turns touching, exploring, and caressing each other. He learned about the bends of her elbows and the backs of her knees. She found the spot on his back that made him shiver and shudder with pleasure. He discovered the pressure and rhythm required to bring the tips of her breasts to taut, burning points, then how to control the flames with the wet heat of his mouth. She traced the lines of his back and the curve of his buttocks, then explored the male parts of him and discovered the power in a simple touch.

They dallied and stroked and teased until he found himself atop her, his legs entwined with hers, his body molding, reshaping hers with its heat. He nudged her knees apart and slid between her legs, fitting himself tightly against her most sensitive flesh. She welcomed him, knowing that this was both what she had craved and what she had promised. He joined their bodies by slow, tantalizing increments, giving her time to adjust, reassuring her, enjoying her sense of wonder and discovery. And when, at last, he lay embedded deep inside her, feeling her untried body holding him in a tight caress, he clasped her to him and poured the depths of his soul into her eyes.

"I love you, Maddy Duncan. I don't know if I always have. I know only that I always will."

She looked up at his beautiful angular face and knew it was true. Nothing else could make a man like him do the things he had done.

"I do love you, Cole Mandeville." She cradled his face in her hands and urged it down to give him a lingering kiss. And when it ended she demanded to know: "Now what about those rainbows and Chinese rockets you promised me?"

He laughed and kissed her, and soon her passions were simmering, rising, and expanding. Then, when her senses could hold no more, they burst in a shattering climax and suddenly there *were* colors everywhere—fiery golds and reds and yellows that slowly cooled to rich, textured purples and blues and greens. The colors stirred to a second surge of brilliance as he took his pleasure in a long, arching movement that stopped her heart, then filled it with tenderness and pride.

As they drifted to sleep, still joined and reveling in the delicious intimacy, she heard what she thought must be humming. It took her a minute to put words to that familiar tune.

Old King Cole was a merry old soul . . .

And she smiled.

The next morning Madeline awakened to a sun-warmed chamber and the sight of Cole, clad in shirt, trousers, and coat, propped on one elbow beside her. She stretched extravagantly, feeling a new confidence inhabiting every inch of her body.

"Good morning, sleepyhead."

"Yes, it is a good morning." She lifted her chin to collect a kiss, then glanced at his clothes. "A wonderful morning. What are you doing dressed?"

He laughed. "Only one night and already you're a flaming hedonist. I shall have to see that 'Nanny' has another talk with you, young lady."

"Oh, good." She gave a sensuous wriggle. "Every time we talk, I seem to learn quite a bit. She really is a very wise old girl." He chuckled and rolled from the bed.

"So wise, in fact, that she rousted me at the crack of dawn and sent me down to Regent Street." On the table were several packages wrapped in brown paper. "She was afraid you'd cause a stir wearing only her favorite clothes, so she sent me out to find some that won't . . . give you gangrene."

"Cole, how thoughtful!" Her eyes lighted and she scrambled from the bed, bringing the sheet with her. Tearing into the packages, she found a delicately embroidered white blouse, a softly gored blue skirt, a simple cotton petticoat, stockings, and a pair of French-heeled pumps. "They're wonderful!" She looked up at him. "How did you know what to get?"

"I made a thorough study of your wardrobe once, remember," he said. "I just looked for garments that approximated what you already had."

"Looked where? Where did you find such clothes readymade?" She looked through all the things once more, as if looking for something and frowned.

"At Liberty of course. And here . . ." He handed her one final package from behind his back. "You may need *these* before you can put on *those*."

She opened it and inside was a bust bodice and a pair of soft knitted-cotton knickers. Her knickers. Her product. She clasped them to her heart and looked up at him with love and tears shining in her eyes. He had bought her and brought her her very own set of Ideal underclothes.

"Cole Mandeville, you are without a doubt the most . . . wonderful man in the world." She threw her arms around him and he chuckled, wrapping her up tightly in his.

"That's a relief," he said, teasing. "I wasn't sure you'd like them."

He waited for her to dress, stealing kisses and sharing with her his cup of coffee. Then he took her downstairs, where his butler, Saggett, and staff had laid out a sumptuous brunch. She began racing through her food, and he demanded to know why she was in such a hurry. She looked up, licking marmalade from her lip, her eyes alight.

"You promised to take me to Liberty, remember?"

He nodded, but admonished teasingly, "Clean your plate first, Madeline. Nanny says."

Fortified by a hearty meal, they sent for the carriage, and while they waited, Cole showed her the rest of his house.

When they came to his study, she had a chance to inspect the books and artifacts that stuffed the shelves. Many of the books dealt with law and legal matters, and she turned with a book of case precedents in her hand to study him.

"You know, of course, you'll have to tell me someday," she said.

"About what?"

"About whatever it is about the law that made you quit doing what you so obviously loved to do."

She watched his guard rising and was considering whether this was the time and place to press the issue, when Saggett appeared at the door looking quite unsettled. "Excuse me, my lord, but there are . . . is . . . a delegation of some sort demanding to see you." He glanced at Madeline. "Concerning Miss Duncan."

In the entry hall a delegation of three men stood just inside the still-open door, wearing their top hats and gloves. At first glance it was clear this was not a social call, but Cole and Madeline were still astonished to have one of the men wheel, point at Madeline, and declare: "There she is—I said she would be here!"

She stopped dead in the center of the entry hall, watching in horror as Cousin Gilbert and two of her aunt's solicitors swooped down on her. They rushed to surround her, shunting Cole aside, and bombarded her with questions.

"Are you all right?" "Has he harmed you in any way?" "Dearest heaven—has he kept you here all night?" That last question lay burning on the air as she tried to make sense of their presence and heated demands.

"I am perfectly fine, thank you, Cousin Gilbert." She tried to pull her elbow from his clammy grip, but he wouldn't release her. Cole shouldered one of them aside and took his place, drawing her protectively against him. "Cole, these gentlemen were my aunt's solicitors and are the trustees of her estate."

"We've met," he said tautly.

"Sir Edward, Mr. Townshend . . . whatever are you doing here?" she asked.

The trio stared at her rosy face and at Cole's proprietary hand on her wrist, and sent each other looks of alarm.

"Since your abduction last night—I have had half of the city of London out looking for you," Gilbert said in his most aggrieved manner. "I have been *frantic* with worry! Not knowing where to turn, I went to see your trustees to solicit their help. And when word came a while ago that Lord Mandeville was seen wrestling a woman from his carriage, Sir Edward and Mr. Townshend insisted upon accompanying me."

"How dare you, sir?" Dunwoody addressed Cole. "Enter a gentleman's home and abduct one of his innocent lady guests—"

"But he didn't truly abduct me," she began, glancing up at Cole.

"Mr. Duncan has witnesses to the incident," Dunwoody insisted.

"Infringing upon a young woman of impeccable reputation—a young woman for whom you bear not just moral but legal responsibility—this is unforgivable!" Townshend blustered.

"I have done nothing to Miss Duncan except rescue her from a life that she wanted no part of," Cole declared. "It's true I did escort her from Lord Reardon's—"

"He freely admits it," Townshend exclaimed, aghast.

"You are beneath contempt, Lord Mandeville," Gilbert said, his face filled with genuine loathing. "Come, dearest Madeline, we shall take you out of this place." He pulled on her arm, trying to pry her free of Cole's grip. "Unhand her, sir."

"I will not go!" Madeline jerked her arm from Gilbert's grip and glared at him. "I am the supposed injured party, and I say that no injury occurred. It is true that Lord Mandeville and I crossed words and that he escorted me from the party. It was so that we could sort out our differences . . . which we have done." She glanced up at Cole's angry face. "And since it was rather late, Lord Mandeville generously offered me the use of his guest room. He was just about to take me . . . home . . . to my house in Bloomsbury. I've decided to move there, Cousin Gilbert. You have been most gracious, but I have imposed upon you quite long enough."

"You see? I was afraid of this," Gilbert said to the others, shaking his head. "Madeline, you must let us help you. You don't know what you're doing, saying."

"I'm afraid we must insist that you accompany us out of this house, Miss Duncan," Dunwoody said, straightening to his fullest height. "This very minute."

"She will do no such thing," Cole declared with fiercely. "I have suffered your absurd charges and abuse for Miss Duncan's sake. But if you are not out of my house in fifteen seconds, I shall toss your vultures' carcasses out into the street myself!"

They were suddenly face-to-face in searing quiet, three men to one, each side waiting for the other to blink.

"Please go, Gilbert," she said, frantic to defuse the potentially violent situation. "You're not needed here."

Gilbert transferred his gaze to her, examining her and finding something about her changed. With a seasoned voluptuary's perception, he sensed instinctively what that something was.

"So." He gave Madeline a look of pitying contempt. "That is how it is." He glanced meaningfully at Dunwoody and Townshend. "I believe we are too late, gentlemen. I believe *the damage* has already been done."

The others caught his inference and turned looks of outrage and disgust on Madeline. She reddened and lifted her chin.

"Lord Mandeville," Dunwoody said with a regal disdain polished by years of practice, "you have violated not only this young woman, but also your sacred duty before the bar. It appears that you have used your legal office and function for tawdry personal gain, and that, sir, we will not tolerate! Good day."

The three strode out and onto the street, where they were joined by a fourth figure who had been lurking in the doorway, largely unnoticed. Rupert Fitch scurried along after the threesome, tucking his pad and pencil away and falling in behind them with his ears cocked. He heard nothing of additional value until they paused on the green of the square and Gilbert Duncan faced the others.

"Clearly, she is not responsible for her actions, gentlemen. It pains me. I am only glad that Aunt Olivia has been spared seeing sweet little Madeline sinking into the depths of depravity and derangement."

"There is but one recourse," Townshend declared. "We must seek a remedy in the courts."

"A fat lot of good that will do, with Mandeville's uncle sitting on the bench," Dunwoody said with a snarl. "The man's a vile, eccentric old wreck who feathers his nephew's nest out of his judicial privilege and our—Miss Duncan's pockets."

"Of course, I don't know much about the law," Gilbert said, watching their reactions. "But I think it a crime that there is not some way to have a justice removed from a case in which he or his family has become too personally involved."

Dunwoody and Townshend looked at each other, the same idea blooming in both their minds. "That's it," Dunwoody said. "We shall petition to get Rayburn removed from the case. Penobscott-Holmes, head of Chancery, is an old school chum of mine. . . ."

Gilbert watched the partners hurrying off, checked his watch, and struck off across the square for the cab stand. Fitch tagged along.

"Smooth as silk, Mr. Duncan," Fitch said with genuine admiration.

"I thought so." Gilbert reached into his pocket and handed the news writer a small purse. "Good work finding the little trollop. Check with me from time to time, Fitch. Who knows when I may have another little job for you?"

As he settled back in a hansom cab, headed for Brooks's, Gilbert sighed with satisfaction. Who would have guessed that Madeline's avid, idealistic exterior concealed a hot-tailed nature? He couldn't have planned it any better; her illicit passion for Mandeville had played straight into his hands. Soon they would have their day in court and "crazy Cousin Madeline" would be placed in his charge—fortune and all.

Madeline was still reeling as she watched Cole's face harden and saw him turn away. She followed him into his study, feeling as if she were watching a stranger.

"Cole?"

"I won't be very good company just now," he said, keeping his back to her and looking out the window into the rear service yard. Beneath his tight control and deliberate movements was an icy fury that she sensed was partly directed at himself.

"Cole, it doesn't make any difference."

"Doesn't it?" He didn't turn around. "You heard them. I've damaged you irreparably, taken advantage of my office and responsibility toward you."

"Don't be absurd. You haven't damaged me or taken advantage—"

"Haven't I?" He turned, and the darkness in his eyes took her breath. "You heard them. They blame me for your conduct, and in large part they're right. I allowed you to run your course at St. Crispin, even when I saw how things were going, I didn't interfere or help. I did nothing. And now that I've finally done *something,* it appears to be all the wrong things. It seems that I'm destined to destroy the things I love the most. The Macmillans, the law . . . now you."

"Don't be absurd, Cole, you haven't destroyed me and it wasn't *your* actions or your love for the Macmillans that caused their problems. And it's not—"

The law. Again. That nameless beast that claimed and overshadowed half of his heart, his life.

"All right, tell me. I want to know just what it is that still has its claws in your heart. Greedy creature that I am, I don't want to share your heart with anybody or anything." She closed the door and leaned back on it. "We're not leaving this room until I hear what it was that broke your heart and sent you fleeing from the law." When he looked up, he saw that she was serious and utterly determined.

"It's old news. It doesn't do any good to bring it all up again," he said.

"Tell me," she demanded, stalking him with her eyes crackling. She could see the conflict her demands generated in him. If there were any other way . . .

"You told me I had to deal with my problems, face them

down. And then you helped me do just that. Cole, I love you, and if you know what that truly means, you'll tell me what happened and let me help you deal with it, face it down."

She saw him wavering, saw the need and pain mingled with the anger and knew she had to help him. She pulled him to the couch and pushed him down on it. Then, hiking her skirt, she abruptly straddled his lap, serving notice that she intended to keep him there until he capitulated and talked to her.

Then she kissed him with everything in her. Long, and fierce. Gentling slowly against his hardened mouth, coaxing, loving him, drawing whatever poison was there to the surface.

When finally his lips began to soften under hers, then to respond, she lifted her head and looked at him. His eyes were full of dark, troubled emotions.

"All right." He looked away for a few minutes while he conjured long-suppressed memories of painful events.

"I told you about my childhood, about why I went into the law. I honestly tried to do some good. I helped people, won a number of cases, and believed I was doing what was right. Then gradually, somehow, without my knowing it, my clients' wishes began to replace my personal values and judgment. I stopped making decisions about what was right or wrong. Winning the case, coming out on top, became my justification for everything, my whole reason for being." He glanced at her eyes and his voice grew hoarse as his throat constricted.

"I don't know if that makes sense to you at all. I didn't need money. I didn't need connections or position or power. What I needed was purpose. And I found it doing battle daily in a courtroom full of other men who were just as hungry as I was."

"It does make sense," she whispered, touching his face to bring him back to her. She, too, had known what it was to need a reason to get up each morning. "It makes all the sense in the world."

His eyes shimmered as he struggled with old memories and fermented pain. "I slowly lost myself in it . . . working constantly, forsaking friends, and abandoning other parts of my life. I was a man driven. It didn't matter anymore what was right—as long as I won."

"And something happened."

He nodded and drew a deep breath, preparing himself.

"I took on a case. A nobleman with a large fortune and a hunger for more. He owned a parcel of land in London's East End, near the river, and was determined to clear the tenements on it and make a fat profit selling it to a company that wanted to build new docks. A few social reformers heard what was afoot and protested, saying that the tenants would be turned out on the streets and have no place to go. A suit was brought and the justices ordered a stay. The deal was turning bad—the buyers were ready to seek property elsewhere." He rubbed his eyes as if wiping away a disturbing vision.

"My greedy landowner was angry and he threatened, in my hearing, to burn the place to the ground." His eyes filled with tears. "I laughed. Said it might be the best solution. God help me . . . I saw the look in his eyes. I knew what kind of man he was. And I let him walk out of my office. *I did nothing.*" His voice cracked. "Two children died in that fire."

"Oh, Cole . . ." She shifted, gathered his shoulders in her arms, and pulled his head against her breast. She held him that way for a time, then looked down at him. "It wasn't your fault. You didn't set that blaze."

"But I did and still do bear some of the blame. I suspected he might do it and I did nothing to stop it." He set her back and sat up. "Don't you see? It was history repeating itself. It was the Macmillans all over again. The same damned situation . . . a landlord dispossessing tenants. Only this time I was on the wrong side. I had gone into the law to fight bloated, unfeeling wretches, and I ended up becoming one of them.

"That's why I left the law, Madeline. I lost my morals, my ethics, damn near lost my soul." He set her from him; he had to get up, to move. He paced back and forth, his voice and face were bleak.

"I probably should have told you before last night." He glanced away. "I won't hold it against you if you decide to . . . now that you know what sort of man I am."

Her heart ached for him. She slid from the couch and invaded his vision, causing him to step back, then back again. She followed him, her eyes rimmed with tears.

"Oh, I know exactly what sort of man you are. You're a silver-tongued devil, a backslidden cynic, and a meddlesome but adorable nanny. You're also the rescuer of my heart, the rock in my shoe that annoys me enough to make me do what's right—you're my mate and my friend. You tell me the truth even when it isn't an easy or pleasant thing to do. You care about me. You are willing to admit when you're wrong. . . .

"Cole, there isn't a person alive who doesn't have things to regret or be ashamed of. Aunt Olivia used to say that pain is nature's way of making us pay attention to something that needs attention. Perhaps regrets do something similar. Perhaps they're supposed to spur us on, to drive us to be better, to do better. You won't let me give in to my regrets, you're making me put them to work. Well, perhaps it's time you started listening to your own advice."

She backed him into the desk and wrapped both arms around him. He was trembling, scarcely breathing for the conflict crowding his lungs. He was terrified to look into those warm, engulfing pools of blue, afraid that they might contain pity or obligation or just the altruistic urge to save.

"Look at me," she said authoritatively, punctuating her demand with a shake of his shirt. He did look at her. And he looked into her. "Tell me how you feel about me."

"You know how I feel about you."

"Say it anyway."

"I love you. With all my heart." He wrapped his arms around her, feeling some of his grief lifting, as if it were being shifted onto her shoulders. It wasn't his solitary burden anymore; he had her to share it. And that did indeed make a difference.

"But you heard what they said," he began, returning to their present predicament. "They believe I've used my position as your overseer to have my nefarious way with you. They could go to the law society . . . to the courts themselves. And, of course, there's still the little matter of your Ideal Garment Company. After the explosion and the delays, they'll have more ammunition to use against you."

He had good points, she realized. As of now she had no factory, no workforce, no profit to show. And what if they decided to bring charges against Cole for misusing his influence?

"All right, there are problems. But we'll find solutions. We have a product that people seem to want. We can show them the demand for our children's clothes at Liberty. We still have nearly two months. By then we can have the factory up and running again. . . ."

He looked at the hope in her face and prayed that he hadn't helped to restore it to her only to have it wrenched away again. Life in the law had taught him that more often than not, one should prepare for the worst in a situation—not the best.

17

The day after Madeline's trustees discovered her in Cole's house, Sir William stormed into his chambers like a typhoon run aground; blowing papers off Foglethorpe's desk as he passed, waving his cane and piercing the air with verbal lightning bolts.

"Bugger Gerald Penobscott-Holmes—bugger the Judiciary Review Commission—bugger the whole damned Court of Appeals!" he roared. Swinging his cane wildly, he knocked a stack of books off a nearby table. "Not once in thirty-five years on the queen's bench have I ever been accused of 'harboring personal interest.' " He wheeled on Foglethorpe and reiterated: "Not once!"

Foglethorpe, a man of imminent good sense, said nothing and waited for details.

"Holmes required me to recuse myself from Madeline Duncan's case. Said I was personally involved, can you imagine? Why, I was hearing cases before he cut his first tooth! I should certainly know whether the hell my judgment is impaired by personal feelings or connections. And it damned well isn't in Madeline Duncan's case. That was a piece of judiciary brilliance, that was. Solomon-like. Inspired. I'd like to see jelly-livered Gerald come up with something that rescues a dream, two hearts, a number of London's poor, and an entire village in——''

He halted and turned to stare at Foglethorpe. Straightening slowly, he squared his portly shoulders. The gleam that entered his eye made Foglethorpe groan silently, pluck the pencil from behind his ear, and grope for his pad on Sir William's desk.

"Clear my calendar for the next two weeks, Fogles! Shunt all new cases off to the juniors. Send word to the parties in my current cases that they have just been granted magnanimous extensions to revise and resubmit their briefs." Sir William thudded back and forth over the worn rug, his eyes darting over some tableaux in his mind. "With a new justice they'll be hearing all the evidence . . . and Holmes dropped word of a countersuit. She'll need someone a damn sight better than old Dickie Pendergast this time. Send a messenger to Benjamin Calvert telling him I need his services desperately— a family emergency. Then send for my carriage and find out where the hell my nephew is. We've got a case to prepare and only three or four days to do it!"

The halls and lobby of Chancery, in the Strand, were clogged with people when Madeline arrived on the first day of her case's hearing. A number of people were milling around the doors of the courtroom when she and Davenport approached, and one spotted her distinctive clothing. "There she is! That's her—with the trousers!" Instantly, she was besieged by news writers asking questions.

"Is it true that you're bankrupt, Miss Duncan?"

"Did you really make your workers wear nothing but women's undergarments?"

"How about givin' us a peek at them knickers too!"

Madeline and Davenport fought their way through the jostling group and the bailiff shoved them safely through the glass-paneled doors and the darkened vestibule. By the time she emerged into the court, she could barely breathe. She stood at the side of the chamber, staring up at the filled pews of the gallery, stunned by the contrast it presented to its emptiness on her first day in court. There were news writers, Chancery case followers, law students—not to mention potential witnesses, legal scholars, and the odd friend or associate of the barristers on the floor below. Word was spreading of a rarity in progress, an interesting case in Chancery.

Suddenly news writers were prowling the halls of Chancery, searching for tidbits of information to sensationalize. Unfortunately, tidbits were plentiful. The facts of the case alone made for juicy reading: an unmarried heiress, recipient of a large fortune, flouting society's expectations for women by wearing trousers, advocating the abandonment of corsets, and attempting to set up a business and a bit of a social experiment in the same enterprise.

A murmur swept the court as people caught sight of her, and Davenport gave her hand a squeeze before heading for the steps to the gallery. Davenport had arrived in London the day of Lord Reardon's party, having stayed in St. Crispin just long enough to pack Madeline's things and close up the house. Her report of having seen loaded carts leaving the village had sent Madeline's spirits tumbling. But her presence in Aunt Olivia's house also had made living there bearable again.

Madeline located Cole, who had saved a seat in the front row of the gallery for Davenport. Exchanging a smile with him, Madeline made her way past the packed opposition tables to the plaintiff side. There sat her two overage barristers, one already nodding sleepily and the other trying to adjust his spectacles.

Sir William had done his best to secure top representation for her, but his first and second choices were already hotly engaged in trials, and by the time he got to his third choice, a chill wind had blown through the Inns of Court. Sir William had to turn again to old Dickie Pendergast and to a retired barrister who was his personal friend, Mr. James Crofton. But even more worrisome than her counsel was the selection of Sir Henry Samuels as presiding justice.

"It that bad?" she asked Cole when Sir William brought the news of his appointment.

"It's worse than bad," Cole said. "Henry Samuels and I have crossed words and locked horns so many times, I've lost count. To put it bluntly: He hates my very liver. And my testimony, as the court's appointed agent, is the bulk of our case."

When the bailiff called the court to order and the honorable Sir Henry entered, Madeline's heart sank. He was a gaunt, pallorous man, a contemporary of Cole's who appeared well beyond his years. He didn't look the sort to indulge impassioned arguments about creativity and idealism and doing good in the world. And he would probably have even less sympathy for ladies' reformed undergarments. His first words to the court confirmed her fears.

"A caution to you all," Sir Henry began, glowering first at one side, then at the other. "This is the second hearing of this case, required by circumstances that are most regrettable. Fortunately, since a final disposition ruling had not been given, the shameful deficiencies in the previous proceeding may be remedied without recourse to lengthy and absorbing appeals." He turned then to the plaintiff's table and fixed Madeline with a steely gaze.

"You will find my courtroom an orderly place, where the issues of law are given grave and respectful consideration. Unlike my predecessor in the hearing of this case, I shall not tolerate caprices, eccentricities, or demonstrations of any sort." He looked up at the rear of the court, and Madeline wondered if the dark look on his face was for Cole. "The gallery be warned as well. We shall have dignity and decorum in this proceeding, and anyone breaching either will find himself—or herself—quickly expelled.''

"*Humph*," came a muffled response from the gallery, loud enough to carry to the floor but not quite loud enough for Sir Henry to differentiate from a cough. Madeline turned just enough to see Sir William thumping and swaying down the steps. When she turned back, Sir Henry's pallor had changed to an unflattering pink. It was considered a discourtesy for one justice to invade another's courtroom without first asking permission, but to have a removed justice invade his successor's proceeding . . . Watching Sir Henry's reaction, Madeline wished Sir William had used more discretion.

"Proceed, Mr. Crofton, with your opening statement!" Sir Henry snapped.

It was easy to see, a half hour later, that the venerable Crofton had been saving up words during his retirement and intended to spend them all that morning. He read, elaborated on, and interpreted his opening statement for what seemed an eternity, but without so much as a hint of impatience from Sir Henry. Indeed, the justice might have been a statue borrowed from the court lobby, for all the reaction he displayed. Then barrister Farnsworth was called upon for an opening statement, and every drowsing head in the gallery popped up. Not only was his bombastic style of delivery quite a change, but the content of his orations was compelling.

"Miss Duncan is a well-meaning but utterly misguided soul whose eccentric and sadly impractical ideas have placed her in a most vulnerable position, a vulnerability that has been exploited by a number of unscrupulous persons. We intend to show, Your Honor, that Miss Duncan's affairs have deteriorated to the point where her judgment, morality, and even competence are in question."

Judgment, perhaps. Morality—how dare they! But mental *competence*? She grabbed Mr. Crofton's arm. Cole and Sir William had tried to prepare her for the sort of allegations that might be leveled against her, but, seated in her own comfortable parlor, she had thought they were overstating the case a bit. It was a jolt, hearing her actions misconstrued and listening to callous assaults upon her character, ideals, and efforts.

By the time dinner recess was called, she was genuinely shaken by the accusations and by the realization that those comments were just the beginning. Cole tried to allay her worries by reminding her that he soon would be taking the stand to give a positive account of her efforts. "And Sir Henry, of all people, will know that I may be counted on not to put too high a gloss on things," Cole ruefully assured her.

When court resumed, Mr. Crofton called Lord Cole Mandeville to give testimony, and Cole made his way down from the gallery to the witness box.

"I was pressed into the court's service as 'overseer' of Miss Duncan's financial dealings," he said by way of explaining his role with regard to Madeline's enterprise. "I was to approve or disallow large purchases and generally 'protect her from her magnanimous impulses,' which I took to mean that I was to prevent her from spending too much or unwisely."

"And were you to keep the court informed of the progress on her venture?"

"I was to send weekly reports to the court . . . and did."

"Please tell the court your impression of Miss Duncan's Ideal Garment Company when you first arrived in the village of St. Crispin."

"The building was old and in need of significant work. She had spent considerable money on new windows for light and ventilation, and had engaged—at some expense—an engineering firm to pipe running water into each of the cottages in the village. She had also hired an engineer to develop and install machinery for cutting cloth and for powering numbers of sewing machines. Carpenters were at work repairing the factory and building worktables needed for production. Much work had been done, but there was a great deal yet to do."

"And what about Miss Duncan's workers? Did she have employees?"

"A number of them. New workers and families were arriving daily. Miss Duncan met each one with a supply of food to tide them over as they settled in."

"Did you have occasion to speak with Miss Duncan regarding her expenditures?"

"I did. I questioned the wisdom of providing so much for her employees. She insisted that it was only humane to offer them assistance for the first week or so. I believed it ill advised at first. I later came to see that it saved her workers considerable time procuring food and supplies in those first days."

"Upon seeing how her policy contributed to the functioning of the factory, you changed your mind," Crofton rephrased it. "And were there other things you changed your mind about as time went on?"

Cole related a number of issues, from the need for a water system to the establishment of a temporary schoolroom for the workers' children, which illustrated that he had come over time to respect Madeline's views and to see Ideal's progress as a direct result of her thorough planning and tireless efforts.

"I learned that she had a clearly defined schedule and a timed plan for producing, marketing, and advertising her garments. I saw her hold meetings with her employees and solicit their ideas and cooperation. I watched her make decisions and grapple with problems as they arose—and found her to be bright, thorough, surprisingly competent, and uncommonly dedicated to her work." He glanced at her with as much dispassion as he could manage.

"She frequently worked past sunset, well after her workers had gone home. She missed meals and sleep, and generously offered to design and supply goods for all the women to sew garments for their children. And when—because a number of the seamstresses she had hired were married to the cutters she had hired—she was inundated with squalling babies, she opened a little-used storage room, furnished it, and arranged to have girls from the neighboring village come and take care of the youngest children during the day."

"So you came to see Miss Duncan's enterprise as a viable business concern."

"I did. I still do," Cole said.

"Please tell the court how much profit Miss Duncan's business has generated for her," Crofton instructed, hanging his hands on his robe.

"I believe there has been no profit as yet." Cole glanced at Sir Henry, then at Madeline, and hastened to add, "But few enterprises of this magnitude would show a profit at this stage of development. There is considerable interest in Ideal's products. Liberty, in Regent Street, for example, has shown considerable interest in placing an order for Ideal clothing. If this proceeding had been held as originally scheduled—after a three-month interval—she would have shown significant sales, possibly a profit."

"And if you were asked to advise the court in the matter . . . to suggest whether or not Miss Duncan should be given leave to continue development of her company and to control her own fortune . . . what would you say?"

"I would say, without reservation, that she should be permitted to continue. Her understanding of what it takes to develop and run a business concern has grown considerably in the last six weeks. I believe that Ideal will someday be a sound business, known for its humane working conditions as well as its high-quality products."

Madeline listened to Cole's words with love and pride swelling in her heart. He had told the truth, and yet managed to make it sound as though she had progressed considerably in a very short time. And indeed, she had. How could anyone find fault with his balanced and objective account?

Crofton thanked Cole and Sir Henry, then retired. Sir Henry offered Farnsworth the opportunity to examine the witness and he leapt at the chance. Swaggering toward the witness box, he grasped his robe and gave Cole a thorough look before taking aim.

"Tell the court, Lord Mandeville, what was your opinion of Miss Duncan's competence when you first arrived in St. Crispin?"

"I believed her to be naive and in some instances misguided in her efforts."

"You were skeptical?" Farnsworth questioned, striking a pose.

"I was."

"Would it be fair to say that you were *more* than skeptical?"

"I don't think so," Cole said, knowing his former associate's badgering technique in court and working to control his rising annoyance.

"Would it not be fair to say that you characterized Miss Duncan as a *madwoman*? That you frequently referred to her as 'Mad Madeline'?" Farnsworth hurried back to the table and picked up a document.

Cole straightened and his jaw clenched. "If I used that term, it was in jest."

"And were you jesting when you wrote in your first weekly report to the court"—Farnsworth looked at the paper in his hand—"and I quote: *'She is a madwoman . . . get me out of here!'*?"

A murmur ran through the gallery, but the spectators were no more surprised than Cole. He had written that facetious assessment in the heat of anger and the grip of insufferable pomposity. How the hell did Farnsworth—

"Is this or is this not the letter you wrote to your uncle, Sir William Rayburn, the justice who presided over the first hearing of this suit?" He thrust the paper into Cole's face, and when Cole stared at it, unblinking, he prodded, "Yes or no, sir. Is this your writing? Are these your words?"

"They are," Cole was forced to admit. "But they were

written at the spur of the moment . . . and in a . . . facetious mood.''

"*Facetiousness* in a report to a duly constituted court of law is not acceptable, your lordship." He turned to Sir Henry. "The defense offers into evidence this letter."

"Where did you get that letter, Farnsworth?" Cole demanded, gripping the rail.

"I'll tell you where he got it—he stole it out of my chambers!" Sir William thundered from the front row of the gallery. When they looked up, he was on his feet, his face scarlet and his fist shaking.

"Order!" Sir Henry banged his gavel furiously and pointed it at Sir William. "I shall not tolerate such outbursts in my court!"

"Don't be a dolt, Henry, the man's a thief—or at very least in league with one!"

"Sit down, Rayburn!" Sir Henry thundered back. "One more outburst and I shall have you *removed*!" He turned to his clerk and held out his hand for the letter.

Madeline recovered enough to tug on Crofton's sleeve, and he objected.

Sir Henry had both counsels approach the bench, and after some consultation had them step back. "The letter is entered into evidence. Any other letters will be considered one at a time, as they are authenticated."

"Other letters?" Cole said, turning to Sir Henry. "I object, Your Honor."

"You cannot object, Mandeville, you're a witness," Sir Henry responded in a choleric mood. "The rules of the courtroom have not changed. Proceed, Farnsworth."

"You have testified in this court that at first you believed Miss Duncan to be 'naive' and somewhat 'misguided.' " Farnsworth smiled. "But, in fact, your feelings on the subject were quite a bit stronger. Is it not true that in your second report to Sir William you stated that she was 'a stubborn, idealistic little fool who lacks sense enough to come in out of the rain'? You further informed your uncle that she was 'giving away food, giving away free clothes' and that she had 'hired a passel of *ignoramuses* . . . two of whom are digging a hole all the way to China in her rear yard.' " He dangled the paper he had been reading before Cole's eyes. "Is this or is this not the very letter you sent to your uncle?"

"It is," Cole said. A muscle flexed visibly in his jaw.

"Another little jest?" Farnsworth said nastily, then hurried on. "And you have further testified that as time went on, your opinion of Miss Duncan and her abilities as a manager of workers rose. Well, it hardly could have *fallen,*" he said, flashing a smile at the gallery and drawing a round of laughter and a banging gavel. "How closely did you scrutinize Miss Duncan's finances? Did you examine her books?"

"No." Cole reddened slightly. "My function was to oversee, not to perform a clerk's work."

"Then did you at least review and authorize each expenditure?"

"Only the larger ones . . . of which there were not many," Cole said.

"Truly? If that was the case, then why were you prompted to write to your uncle: 'The place is a bottomless pit, into which St. Madeline nobly unburdens herself of her wealth. Each day there seems to be another crisis requiring a sizable outlay of coin . . . the most recent involving the hiring of baby-minders to see to the women workers' children so that she may have the privilege of paying them to work on clothing for the little wretches to wear. She's an incurable soft touch and I've grown tired of the incessant naysaying required to keep her solvent'?"

There was another murmur in the courtroom. Out of practice and cast in the unfamiliar role of a witness, Cole had been caught off his game. Now he jolted back into form and answered a question that hadn't been asked. "I decided to eliminate the burden of requiring her to get approval for capital expenditures because I wanted to let her make those decisions herself."

"You wanted the woman you called an idealistic fool to make her own decisions?" Farnsworth focused intently on him. "In spite of her frequent and growing expenditures on a factory that was fated never to produce a single product, you gave Miss Duncan the strings of her purse. You abandoned your duty to oversee Miss Duncan's expenditures, Lord Mandeville. What I want to know is why?"

"I believe I have said. I thought her to be capable of spending her own money. And I believe it has yet to be established that the Ideal Garment Company is incapable of producing—"

"Are you certain there was not another motive involved?" Farnsworth looked to Sir Henry, to the counsel tables, then to the gallery. "Why would a man wish to aid a woman in emptying her coffers?" He turned on Cole with a daggerlike gaze. "Unless it was perhaps to curry favor. Were you 'grooming' Miss Duncan?"

"Absolutely not."

"Then why did you give her the strings of her purse?" Farnsworth demanded fiercely, his neck veins bulging. "Was it not because you hoped to benefit materially from her misguided and indiscriminate generosity?"

"No," Cole said emphatically.

"Was it not because you wanted to get your hands on the rest of her money?"

"No!"

"Was it not to take advantage of the young woman yourself?"

"No," Cole roared back, "it was because I fell in love with her!"

A murmur of excitement raced through the court as Farnsworth recoiled. Clearly, that answer, vehemently delivered, was not what he had anticipated. But a heartbeat later, he smiled.

"How admirably romantic of you, Lord Mandeville. You were willing to allow the woman to ruin herself financially *because you fell in love wih her*. No more questions, Your Honor."

"It was a damnable fiasco," Cole growled in the carriage on the way back to Madeline's house in Bloomsbury. "A performance that would have embarrassed the greenest junior on the last bench in the lowest court." He glanced at Madeline, who was facing the window.

"You couldn't have known they would have those letters," she said without looking at him.

He could feel Davenport's eyes on him as well and ran a hand over his face. Madeline had every right to be upset at hearing herself described in such unflattering terms. He waited until they reached her house and they were alone to continue.

"Madeline, I apologize. I wrote to Sir William whenever I was annoyed, which was a frequent state of affairs those first days in St. Crispin. For what it's worth, I do believe that you are competent and capable of managing your own affairs."

"Then that makes you a minority of one in the entire city of London."

"Don't you mean two?" he said, catching her gaze, then her waist.

She gave in as he wrapped his arms around her, and she leaned her head against his shoulder.

"I don't think so. I'm not certain I would trust me with my own affairs just now, much less the fate and livelihood of two dozen families."

"Well, then let me believe in you for both of us," he said, a pained look that she didn't see on his face. "Borrow my faith in you, angel. You've more than earned it."

•   •   •

Some distance away, near the corner where the Strand becomes Fleet Street, very nearly in the shadow of the new Law Courts themselves, two scruffy, ill-dressed men sauntered along, gawking at the buildings and people they passed. One had a partial loaf of bread jutting from his coat pocket and the other had a sausage visible in his. They had just come from the Victoria Embankment, where the new gardens had been recently inaugurated.

"We could go see th' super'ntendent of that Victoria Park. See if'n he needs a hand or two," Roscoe said, watching his partner.

Algy scuffed his worn heel against the pavement and shrugged. Roscoe gave a heavy sigh. Algy hadn't been the same since they left St. Crispin three days before.

"C'mon, Alg—ye got to snap out of it. We done what we could. Hauled away what we could . . . buried the rest o' Old Cussed. We leveled 'er out good an' proper."

"We coulda stayed, Roscoe. Planted somethin'," Algy said, shoving his hands into his trouser pockets and looking away. Whatever Roscoe said next was lost on him, for he spotted someone familiar across the street. He grabbed his partner by the arm and pulled him into the nearest doorway.

"What the—what is it?" Roscoe said, coming alert and squinting to follow Algy's stare. "Somebody we owe money?"

"Naw," Algy said, his long face set with vengeful determination. "Somebody what owes us." He pointed across the street to where a short, wiry figure in a fancy bowler hat was pausing just outside a food counter, lighting up a cigarette.

"Old Rupert Fitzwater . . . Fitch . . . whatever he calls hisself now," Roscoe said with his eyes narrowing and his fists clenching. "Y'know Alg, we ought to have a sociable word wi' our old pal Rupert."

They waited until the reporter sauntered off down Fleet Street and followed him, walking quietly, saying nothing. The streets were increasingly empty as people hurried home for dinner. When they reached Bouverie Street and Rupert turned down it, Roscoe elbowed Algy and they headed after him. Down Temple Avenue they followed him, until they reached a small alley leading through to the fields of the Inns of Court. There they rushed him from behind and each grabbed one of his arms in a viselike grip. Hoisting him up onto his toes, they trundled him down the nearest alley and tossed him up against a wall.

"Hey, Rupert, remember us? Yer old pals Roscoe an' Algy?"

"The plaintiff, Miss Madeline Duncan, to the stand," came the call as the first order of business on the second day of the proceedings. Madeline took her oath, took her place, and prayed the knocking of her knees wasn't audible.

"Miss Duncan," her counsel, Mr. Crofton, began, "please tell us in your own words how you came to hit upon the idea of a garment company . . . and why you were willing to spend a sizable portion of your inheritance to create it."

She proceeded to speak of her years with Aunt Olivia and to tell of the "million-pound game" and her surprise at learning she was a very wealthy woman. By the time she got to the notion of reform garments and her meeting with Emily Farrow in the lawyers' offices, the gallery was utterly silent, totally absorbed in her story.

"And now, as to the venture in question," Crofton directed. "Describe for the court the intent and progress of your business."

"It was my intent, at the beginning of this venture, to produce reform garments to replace the torturesome and unhealthy cinchers worn by women and to provide for employment and a better life for people who needed it."

"You wished to help those less fortunate than yourself," he reiterated. "A laudable goal. And what progress have you made?"

She related the developments at Ideal, the two kinds of products that had been produced, and the great interest in children's clothing that was shown by customers at Liberty. When questioned about profits, she admitted that there had been none as yet, but that production had not yet begun on a meaningful scale. As soon as possible, she intended to hire additional workers and fill orders for garments. Final questions centered upon her organization and what sort of records were being kept of expenditures and income. She was pleased to report that she had most capable help, in the person of Beaumont Tattersall, who until a few months before had worked for the defendants.

It was with genuine dread that she watched Farnsworth approach the witness box to question her. When she looked out into the gallery, her eyes fell first on Gilbert, seated in the first row with his arms crossed and wearing a particularly ugly smile.

"If all is as straightforward as you indicate, why is it, Miss Duncan, that you have denied my clients' request that you produce your books and ledgers? Can it be because there are none?" Farnsworth's voice rose. "Or is it because they were destroyed in the blast that demolished a good part of your factory nearly two weeks ago?"

Madeline paled, but insisted: "I have not denied their request. I simply have not yet received them from my clerk, Tattersall. There was a small accident in which we lost a few windows, but the factory was far from destroyed."

Farnsworth gave her a smile that said he knew far more about the situation than she wished. With a glance at Gilbert's sneer, she could guess where he had learned it.

"And how would you know what is still there, Miss Duncan?" he challenged in a booming voice while facing the gallery. "You fled St. Crispin shortly after the explosion and have not returned since. Is that not true?"

"I have not been back since the blast," she said, feeling the starch draining out of her spine. Was it wisdom or cowardice that had kept her from returning? she asked herself. "I have been occupied here in London—with hiring new workers, contacting potential customers . . . "

"And 'consorting with' Lord Mandeville, is that not true?"

She gasped, stunned by such a blunt accusation. Crofton lodged an objection, which was sustained, and Farnsworth, his point already made, announced he had no more questions. Crofton rested the plaintiff's case while reserving the right to present another witness when Tattersall arrived from St. Crispin.

Dinner recess was called and, during the break, Cole said he had errands to run and left Madeline in the company of Davenport and Sir William. She couldn't eat, could scarcely keep tears from forming. "It all seems so unfair," she said. "All I did was try to build something, to share my good fortune with others in a loving way."

"Don't you worry, Madeline," Sir William said, laying his fleshy hand over hers on the tabletop. "It will be all right. Sir Henry is a bit of a prig, but he has a fine mind. I believe we can count on him to see through Fartsworth's damnable obfuscations."

But Sir William's kind words were little comfort that afternoon when the defendants began to present their case. They announced they intended to call several witnesses who had seen firsthand the conditions and practices employed at Ideal. And when Sir Reginald Horbaugh's name was called, Madeline couldn't help the groan that escaped her.

The member of the Royal Commission on the Employment of Women and Children approached the witness box with a bearing that betrayed his years in the India Corps. When Farnsworth asked him to describe his observations at Ideal, he fixed Madeline with a vengeful stare.

"The place was substandard in virtually every respect. I saw children in the factory and soon discovered that Miss Duncan kept the children of her workers locked up for the bulk of each workday. She claimed to be operating a school, but I saw no books, slates, or other instructional materials. I caught several of the wild creatures and posed them a number of questions to test their knowledge. They showed not even the most rudimentary knowledge of geography or Latin, and when questioned in private claimed they were kept in the factory against their wills and made to help with factory work for long periods without rest or recompense."

When asked about the situation of the women workers, he dismissed the question with: "She employs a low and common sort . . . ill educated and lacking in the self-discipline and the skill to control their children." Then he added with a sniff of indignation: "I saw no shackles at the worktables. But then, I was not permitted a full and comprehensive investigation."

"And why was that, Sir Reginald," Farnsworth asked solicitously.

"She went quite hysterical, began raving, and threw us out—all of us who had gone to investigate her operations. Ordered us out . . . and using most vulgar language."

There was an outbreak of comment in the court, on the floor and in the gallery. And when Mr. Crofton examined the witness, asking if he had bothered to ask about the location of the school, or to speak with the children's teacher, or to speak civilly with Miss Duncan concerning these matters, Horbaugh insisted it was impossible to deal with her in her overwrought state.

The second witness of the day was the redoubtable Joseph Lane, labor organizer and self-proclaimed expert on wages and working conditions. When asked to describe working conditions in the Ideal Garment Company factory, he was more than prepared.

"The factory, of course, is old and has been refitted. I paid particular attention to lighting, ventilation, and sanitation, all of which could stand improvement. And as to safety, there are open ditches and huge holes all over the area, and inside the factory are exposed shafts and belts that nearly took the life of one child already."

"One child nearly died?" Farnsworth looked up at the justice in horror.

"So I was told. The child was sent up into a perilous region above the machinery to retrieve something. If a quick-thinking worker had not risked his own life and limb, the child would most certainly have been caught in gears and belts and crushed."

"That's not true!" Madeline cried, lurching to her feet. "Theodore was playing up in the rafters and slipped. And it was Lord Mandeville who saved him!"

"Order, order!" Sir Henry banged his gavel furiously and admonished Mr. Crofton to control his client or she would have to be removed.

When things settled in the court, Joseph Lane testified that there was no union and that Miss Duncan had made it clear she would never permit organizing activities. He said that workers reported they were told not to ask questions, just to work. And in a final stroke he offered the opinion that wages at the factory were low for the kind of skilled labor required. Mr. Crofton managed to get him to admit, upon cross-examination, that most of Madeline's workers were still being trained for their jobs and that they were compensated with lodgings and food as well as money.

Madeline sat with her face aflame, aching with outrage and tension, telling herself that things couldn't possibly get any worse. Then they did. The next witness was Mrs. Sylvia Bethnal-Green. Farnsworth wanted to know her opinion of the "nursery" Madeline had established.

"I was not permitted to see it," she responded. "But the women workers told me about it. Dark and damp . . . many of the children have contracted ailments from their exposure to it. But what concerned me most was the general moral atmosphere of the factory." She reddened and grew agitated. "A most unhealthy environment. There are women's un-

mentionables everywhere . . . constantly in view . . . constantly under discussion. What sort of effect would such sights
have on impressionable children? I'll tell you what sort." She
shook a pudgy finger. "Overstimulation, that's what. And the
dangers of *overstimulating* children are well known to the medical community."

"Unhealthy? By thunder, I'll tell you unhealthy. Unhealthy is walking around with that much filth in your mind!"

Madeline didn't have to turn around to know who had
spoken . . . or to know what the subsequent thumps and
growls and occasional yelps and laughter meant. Sir William
was no longer in the gallery. And some poor bailiff probably
had a bruised shin.

By the time four o'clock came, Madeline could scarcely
put one foot before the other. "I feel as if I've been mangled,"
she said, staring numbly ahead in the carriage on the way
home. "Pounded, bleached, blued, and put through a
wringer." When Cole put an arm around her and drew her
against his side, she looked up with eyes dark and filled with
pain. "I don't know if I can take much more."

Cole spent that evening in the guest bedroom where he and
Madeline had spent the night together. He paced and fumed
and hurt and raged, feeling more impotent than he ever had
in his life. It was the Macmillans all over again. Someone he
loved was being hurt, and he was just sitting by in the gallery,
doing nothing.

He thought of the weariness, the strain, the hurt in Madeline's beautiful eyes and wanted to take on the whole world
for her with his bare knuckles. She needed a champion.

Champion, hell. She needed a damned guardian angel!

He thought of the love she had poured into his heart and
of the healing it had produced, and he realized that there was
no one else. She was his mate . . . his match . . . his love . . .
his life. It was up to him. But to help her, he would have to

do as he had advised her—stand and face the things that haunted his soul, reclaim his place in the law. *Do something.* He looked over his wingless shoulder and gave a wistful sigh.

He was going to make one very unlikely angel.

The next morning the courtroom was shocked to see Lord Mandeville, in black robe and periwig, sitting at the plaintiff's counsel table. But the spectators' surprise was only a pale shadow of that experienced by Madeline when she walked into the court and found him there. "What . . . how . . . why . . . ?" She couldn't think what to ask except, "Are you sure?"

He looked her in the eye and said quietly, "I've never been more sure of anything in my life. Except that I love you." He squeezed her hand. "I'm going to fight for you, angel. With everything I've got."

Cole explained that he had gone to see Sir Henry in chambers, to request permission to join Madeline's counsel. After some prickly questioning, Sir Henry had finally permitted it. And indeed, he opened the session with a directive to his clerk recorder to add Lord Mandeville to the list of the plaintiff's counsel. Farnsworth stood with his face reddening and his mouth working soundlessly.

Two additional witnesses were called by the defendants that morning. But even under Cole's clever questioning they maintained a hostile attitude toward Ideal and Madeline. The evidence against her continued to pile up . . .

. . . until the doors at the rear of the courtroom banged open and a crowd of people came pouring down the center aisle. Everyone at both counsel tables turned; Sir Henry frantically pounded for attention and ordered his bailiffs to remove them. The interlopers put up a hue and cry, demanding to be heard, and put up something of a scuffle as well.

Madeline sat stunned and speechless as Roscoe and Algy wrestled two burly bailiffs to a standstill while begging Sir Henry for "a hearin'."

Suddenly Cole was on his feet and before the bench, identifying the motley group as workers from the Ideal Garment Company and asking Sir Henry for a moment to confer with them. Rubbing his face, looking to be at wit's end, Sir Henry permitted it.

"Since their treatment and welfare has been made a central issue of this suit, I submit that they should be heard," Cole said moments later. "They have traveled a long way to see justice done."

Madeline stared at them, her eyes stinging as they smiled and waved and whispered eager greetings to her. It was clear they had not come to complain. She had never seen anything quite so beautiful as the determination shining in their faces.

There were Tattersall and Emily, Daniel and Priscilla Steadman, Ben and Alva Murtry, Maple and Charlotte Thoroughgood . . . and, of course, all four Ketchum offspring. Endicott was languishing near the back, and Fritz was bringing up the rear. But in front, asking permission to speak, were Roscoe and Algy. And while Roscoe spoke for the group, Algy waved at Madeline and gave her a gap-toothed grin that tugged at her heart and caused it to overflow.

"Yer Worship . . . " Roscoe bowed from the waist and Algy awkwardly followed suit. "We're Miz Duncan's workers. We come because we heard they been sayin' things what ain't true in here. We been there at th' factr'y from the first. We know the truth and we want t' set things right."

Sir Henry closed his eyes, struggling for self-control or wisdom, or both. He dragged his hands down his face and sighed. "Very well. Proceed, counsel."

"I object," Farnsworth declared. "Your Honor, we have not finished our case."

Sir Henry glowered at him. "Unless I've lost all touch with reality, Sir Harvey, these people *are* your case. And I for one intend to hear what they have to say."

After some pushing and coaxing at the back of the court—a sort of democracy in the rough—Roscoe Turner was elected to take the stand first and explain how they came to be there. He stood, hat in hands, looking a bit dwarfed by the machinery of the law, but little daunted by it.

"Don't be nervous, Mr Turner," Cole said. "Just tell the court in your own words, how you came to be here."

"Me an' Alg—that's Alger-non Bates, Yer Worship"—he addressed the justice and pointed to the grinning Algy at the back—"we seen old Rupert Fitch on th' street a day or two ago, not far from here. We had us a right cozy little chat—on account of he worked wi' us out in St. Crispin. He told us about Miz Duncan's troubles and we decided somethin' had to be done. It weren't fair that somebody as goodhearted as Miz Duncan has so much trouble. So . . . we shanked it straight out to old St. Crispie to tell th' others. But . . . honest Miz Duncan . . . we never meant t'blow out yer windows like that.

"We helped clean up th' glass. Them Ketchums and their pa, they carried out all the wreckage and boarded up the holes. And then we hauled off some parts o' that old rock and buried the rest." He grinned and looked at Madeline. "Old Cussed won't bake yer roots, now, miz. Everythin's nice an' level now. Ready for plantin' yer garden."

Tattersall took the stand next, carrying his precious ledgers under his arm. He detailed the sort of accounting that he had employed in setting up Ideal's books, and related the incident involving the mix-up over the cloth.

"It turned out to be a wonderful mischance," he said. "We had a great deal of dark blue jersey on our hands and a lot of children who were calling each other names . . . partly because they were dressed so differently. Miss Duncan designed them some 'reformed' clothes and our designer, Jessup Endicott, made up some patterns. The women loved working on the children's clothes . . . showed quite a bit of initiative in making them up.

"Then some were included by mistake when samples were sent to Liberty. The store clerks put them on display and they've created a good bit of excitement. Mothers seem to love them." He looked at Madeline, grinning, and raised an envelope. "Apparently two wrongs *can* make a right. We have our first official order . . . for dozens and dozens of children's garments."

"Let me see that," Sir Henry said, holding out his hand. The letter was duly passed to the clerk, then to the justice, who read it with some interest. When Farnsworth cross-examined, there was little to do but demand the books. Tattersall turned them over, beaming a smile at his former employers.

Daniel Steadman testified next, relating the story of Madeline's meeting to introduce Ideal's workers to their product. " . . . all a bit skeptical at first. She could see that, but she wanted us to understand. So she did a lesson for us. Brought in a balance scale and put old style women's clothes on one side . . . and reform clothes on the other. When we saw how much less buying and washing and ironing and wearing— well, it seemed to make sense. To most of us, anyway."

"There were those who didn't like the clothes?" Cole asked.

Daniel shifted uncomfortably. "There was some that didn't like the idea . . . like that Thomas Clark and his wife, Bess. All they did was complain . . . about everything. The cottage Miss Duncan gave 'em was too drafty, they said. The stove was too small, the bed was too hard, and the ham she gave them was too salty. Hardly ever struck a tap of work. They were the first to pack up and go, after Miss Duncan left." He reddened a bit as he looked at Madeline. "Odd thing, about that . . . after them and a couple of others left, the rest of us—we started feeling better. We got together and talked and realized what his lordship said was right. We never had it so good. Miss Duncan was nothing but good to us. We all wanted to stay and make a go of it. So we got busy and cleaned it up and started to fix things." He turned to Madeline. "You'd be right proud if you could see it, miss."

Madeline was "right proud" right here, right now. As she watched her workers coming forward, braving the imposing majesty of the royal courts and speaking before a packed courtroom, both her heart and her eyes began to fill. They did care. They did understand what she had tried to do for them. And now that she needed help, they wanted to do something for her in return. They had made her dream theirs . . . and were willing to defend it. She looked up to find Cole looking at her with emotion working in his face. It was all she could do to hold the tears back.

Emily Farrow was next. She had brought with her a stack of letters . . . responses to the sample garments Madeline had sent to a number of leading women. Several had pledged her their support and written to endorse and encourage her efforts.

"And I just want to say that . . . I don't know what I would have done if Miss Duncan hadn't offered me a post with her. I was a widow with two small boys and no income. She didn't give me charity, she gave me a chance to learn and work and do for myself. She's done that for each of her employees . . . training us, teaching us, tolerating our mistakes, even when they're big ones." She looked at Madeline. "Thank you Miss Duncan."

She slipped down from the witness box and Priscilla Steadman testified next.

"I was skeptical, like the rest, about the women's . . . unmentionables. When Miss Duncan gave them to us to try, none of us did, at first. Then, just before she left . . . I broke a bone in my stays and I didn't have another. So I put on the Ideal garments. And you know . . . " she brightened with artless surprise, "they worked!"

Laughter broke out in the courtroom and she flushed crimson.

"Well . . . I wear them all the time now . . . and they're really comfortable and easy to care for . . . " She caught Alva Murtry's eye and nodded. Alva hurried forward with a large box in her arms. When she got to the front, she climbed the steps to the dais to thrust a bust bodice and a pair of flounced knickers into Sir Henry's hands.

"Here ye are, Yer Worship. 'At's what we make. Part of it anyway," she said.

Sir Henry stammered and flushed and behaved as if he didn't know whether to examine them or drop them as if they were a contagion. The courtroom sat in shocked silence for a moment, then erupted in noise when Alva invaded the ranks of the opposition counsel and the gallery itself . . . handing out bodices and knickers to everyone in sight!

"Your Honor!"—Farnsworth was on his feet in a flash—"This is an outrage!"

"Stop it! Stop it at once! Order—order!" Sir Henry pounded his gavel ferociously, and ordered the bailiffs to intervene. But he had to threaten to clear the court before the gallery settled down. He rubbed his now-blotchy face, wondering where he lost control of the proceedings, and what grudge Sir Gerald Penobscott-Holmes bore him, in assigning him this case. He called Cole and Farnsworth before the bench and demanded that they maintain order and decorum amongst their witnesses, or face contempt charges.

Then Maple Thoroughgood took the stand to speak to issues of worker satisfaction and the quality of the garments. But when she produced a pair of knickers to demonstrate a point, Sir Henry looked as if he were choking and dismissed her before she finished.

"I shall have no more ladies' undergarments flung, fondled, or flashed about in my courtroom!" he snapped, punctuating his order with a blistering smack of his gavel. And from the back of the gallery came a low, sympathetic rumble of a laugh. Everyone turned to find Sir William standing in the gallery door holding his sides.

Priscilla whispered to Cole and he frowned and whispered back. Looking a bit uneasy, he requested to approach the bench. "A demonstration?" Sir Henry said. *"Not another one."*

"Not that sort of demonstration," Cole assured him. "There are some other products the court really must see to understand. . . . '' Taking Sir Henry's indecision for permission, he turned and nodded to Priscilla Steadman, who opened the rear doors and led in a row of children.

"What on earth—Mandeville!" Sir Henry glowered and raised his gavel, but was somehow unable to lower it. His gaze and indeed the attention of the entire room were focused on the nine children holding hands and being led before the bench. They ranged in age from four to twelve . . . all with shining, freshly washed faces and neatly combed hair . . . and all wearing garments made of fine dark blue wool jersey.

Some of the children looked a bit uncertain, some were smiling broadly . . . all the picture of health and well-being.

"These are our children, yer lordship," Priscilla said. "We brought them so you could see what we make . . . so you could see how good Ideal clothes work for children."

"Can I now, Ma?" a boy of about seven pulled at her skirt. She gave him an affectionate nod. "Watch this—look what I can do in my clothes!" He proceeded to upend himself and walk on his hands for several steps. Cole plucked him off the floor and turned him right-side up again, fearing that if it continued, they would soon have a full scale outbreak of gymnastics on their hands. Then, holding the boy in his arms, Cole stepped into the midst of the children and drew the eyes of the entire courtroom.

"This is Madeline Duncan's dream, Your Honor. Children free to play and move and grow . . . families whole and working and building something together." Spectators and participants alike quieted and strained forward to catch his every word.

"Madeline Duncan is one of those unique people the world produces on its rarest and finest days. She is a dreamer . . . a woman with vision . . . a person who looks at things beyond and around and above them . . . one who sees possibilities not deficits. She embodies the creative spirit inherent in all humankind. For her the drive to create and build is as necessary as eating and breathing are to the rest of us."

He turned to look at Madeline, whose face was wet and whose fullness of heart was visible in her eyes. He had never wanted anything in his life more than he did Madeline Duncan.

"Dreamers, even grand and visionary thinkers, are not especially rare. What makes Madeline so exceptional is that she is both a dreamer and a *doer*. She harnesses her creativity and yokes it to her boundless energy. She does what many dreamers never even attempt . . . she works to make her dreams come true. And in the process, she livens and brightens and betters the world for everyone around her.

"The vaunted reformers of this world descended on Madeline Duncan in the midst of the hardest work of her life . . . trying to create a factory, trying to revive a dead village. They came with their prejudices and their grand ideas . . . but without the slightest inkling of what a dream in action looks like. They found older facilities, and a few malcontents and a lot of work yet to be done, and—shortsighted—they quit looking. They didn't bother to look for the dream taking shape inside the grit and dirt and sweat." He smiled. "How many of the so-called experts who have testified these last two days would have seen Michelangelo at work and sniffed that he was just a dirty little Italian stonemason?"

He sat the boy down on the counsel table and went to stand by Madeline.

"The world needs to find and treasure and cultivate minds and hearts like hers . . . whether they come in the shape of men or women, young or old, rich or poor. Your Honor, we ask for a direct and favorable ruling against the defendants . . . to enable Miss Duncan and the workers of Ideal to get on with their dream."

Sir Henry considered that, then said, "I believe I have heard quite enough. I am ready to make my ruling."

"D-do something, Farnsworth!" Gilbert was fuming in the gallery.

"B-but, Your Honor!" Farnsworth blustered, fearing a repeat of the last ruling.

It wasn't a repeat. It was worse.

"I hereby direct that the entirety of Miss Duncan's fortune be turned over to her own keeping . . . with the stipulation that she continue to consult with and seek the advice of Lord Cole Mandeville for the foreseeable future." He banged his gavel sealing it, and in the stunned silence, began collecting his papers. Then he looked up to see Madeline rising, sliding into Cole's arms. "And Lord Mandeville . . ."

"Yes, Your Honor?" Cole straightened and the rising noise in the gallery damped to see what he wanted.

"You do intend to marry the woman, do you not?"

Cole glanced at Madeline's surprised face and laughed. "I do indeed, Your Honor . . . if she will have me." He looked down at her. "Will you? Will you have a reformed cynic and renewed believer for your husband and partner?"

"Marriage? Goodness. Well . . . " she stammered, looking up into his warm gaze. "What would I do? I mean . . . I don't know anything about being a wife. I've never really expected to get married and do all the regular things."

"Angel, with you nothing will ever be 'regular' or 'usual.' " He chuckled, pulling her against him. "I think I rather like that idea."

"Would you want children . . . and summer picnics . . . and family Christmas trees . . . and punting on the river . . . that sort of thing?"

He couldn't tell if that was hope in her eyes or horror. "I believe all of that is negotiable. Except perhaps the 'children' part. I'm not sure that's entirely in our control. But, I think I might like to see a little Mandeville or two running about in Ideal clothes."

"Say yes, consarn it!" came a roar from the gallery. "My leg is killing me!"

She laughed and slid her arms inside his proper legal silks.

"I think I might like that too. Oh, yes, Cole Mandeville. I'll marry you."

Epilogue

The mantle was being hung with garlands of fresh pine and balsam, festooned with holly and red velvet ribbon, and extra candles had been placed for lighting, all over the Duncan-Mandeville house in St. Crispin. The tantalizing aromas of pudding and gingersnaps and all manner of cakes and candies filled the house as Davenport and Hannah worked to finish treats for the Christmas party Madeline was giving for the village children, the next day.

Madeline heard Mercy answer the front doors and shortly Beaumont Tattersall appeared with a sheaf of papers in his hands. When he saw her up on a chair putting the finishing touches on the ribbons over the mantel, he gasped.

"Lady Madeline! You must come down from there." He hurried to take her hand and help her. "His lordship would have a conniption if he were to see that."

It was true. She looked down at her mounded belly beneath her cleverly draped jersey gown and sighed. Cole had become a "nanny" in earnest, these last few weeks . . . curtailing her physical activity and endlessly fussing over her. Of course, he also rubbed her back and massaged her feet at night . . . and made her midnight cocoa . . .

"Don't tell on me and there'll be a little something extra in your Christmas stocking," she said.

"There already is," he said with a mischievous twinkle. "Emily has . . . well, she has agreed to marry me."

"Why Beaumont, how wonderful! Congratulations!"

There had been a veritable epidemic of matrimony in the last six months. Three of the four Ketchums had married newly hired seamstresses and settled down this autumn. Fritz Gonnering and Maple Thoroughgood married on Sweetest Day. And recently, Jessup Endicott and Charlotte Thoroughgood had stunned the entire village by announcing plans to wed . . . sending Calvin Ketchum off to join the Foreign Legion. Cole shook his head at that last pairing and declared that there was no accounting for taste. Madeline laughed and agreed, saying: "Just look at us."

"Now, about these production figures, Lady Madeline—"

The parlor doors flew back with a bang, and in from the hall waggled one very large balsam fir tree . . . with two human creatures embedded in it. Roscoe peered at her through the branches. "Here she is, yer ladyship. Th' finest tree in all England."

"In the tub in the corner," she said, pointing and watching as they struggled to erect and stabilize the Christmas tree. It fell twice, beaning Algy once, before they finally set it properly. It was a beautiful tree indeed . . . perfect for candles and garlands and ornaments made by the village children. When Roscoe and Algy finally got somethng right . . . it was really, truly right.

"The figures?" Beaumont called her attention back to the papers in her hand.

"Oh, yes." She looked them over and frowned. "Not much improvement in the bodices and knickers, I see."

"But in the children's clothes—every time our output doubles and the orders quadruple. We can scarcely keep up. And those new styles you introduced, with the new collars and trims . . . everyone agrees they're going to sell like lemonade in July."

She carried the figures into the library, where Cole was working on a brief for a case he was bringing in London, after the turn of the year. He had gone back to practicing law, but in a newly created firm that specialized in serving philanthropic organizations and charitable trusts.

His eyes lit up at the sight of her and he put down his papers and slid back from his desk to welcome her onto his lap. "Why so serious, angel?" He scowled and peered over the edge of the papers she held.

"It's the monthly sales figures. The children's clothes are absolutely booming. But my knickers and bodices are sitting still by comparison." She looked at him with an exaggerated pout to her lip. "Why doesn't anybody like my knickers?"

"Ohhh, angel," he said with a chuckle, giving her bottom a suggestive pat. "I like your knickers. In fact, I'm crazy about them. . . ."

In Devonshire, at Mrs. Southerby's School for Young Ladies, the senior girls were getting ready to depart for Christmas with their families. And in the dormitory, three friends were opening gifts they had gotten each other.

"Oh! Just what I wanted!" one declared holding up a pair of Ideal knickers.

"I got one too!" said the second girl, inspecting hers, admiring their simple ruffles and soft fabric. "Look at the embroidery . . . that blue stitchery looks like cutwork."

"I hope, I hope—yes! Ideal knickers!" The third girl

giggled, holding them up to her waist. "Won't Mistress be scandalized!"

On the palatial estate of the wealthy Earl of Cortland, the beautiful young countess was selecting jewels to wear for the dinner party she was giving in half an hour. "Mimi, I have a little something for you," she said, holding out a box with a lush red bow to her French lady's maid. "*Joyeux Noël.*"

"*Pour moi, madam?*" Mimi said, her large, liquid brown eyes lighting with pleasure. She tore open the ribbon, plunged through the tissue, and came up with a ruffled, flirtatious pair of Ideal knickers and a satin-trimmed bust bodice with pearl buttons. "*Ohhhh, madam. C'est délicieux!*"

"Aren't they, though," her ladyship said, casting an eye over her shapely little maid. "But Mimi, bear in mind . . . if *his lordship* ever sees them, you're fired."

In the ladies' retiring room of the East India Building, a number of typewriters had met for a bridal party for one of their members, who was marrying a young law office clerk. "We all chipped in on the silver candlesticks and there was money left over. So we got a little something just for you," one said, handing the glowing bride-to-be a box from Liberty of Regent Street.

The bride opened the box, held up the Ideal bodice and knickers, and blushed thirteen shades of red. The others howled.

Across London, Temperance and Morality Union President, Mrs. Sylvia Bethnal-Green was preparing for bed. Behind her dressing screen and beneath her heavy brushed flannel night-dress, she peeled off her stays and gave a great sigh of relief.

On the bed, watching avidly, was round and ruddy-faced Colonel Nesbitt Bethnal-Green.

"I have a little something for you," he said in a voice one would use to coax a wary kitten to one's hand. He produced a box from behind his back. "Christmas early."

"Don't be silly, Nesbitt. I couldn't," she declared, scowling. But as she stared at that glossy red ribbon, curiosity got the best of her. She settled gingerly on the side of the bed . . . a safe distance away and tore into the box.

"I have it on good authority that this is the coming thing," the colonel said with a hopeful bit of lust in his voice. "I hope you like it . . . *buttercup*."

Sylvia Bethnal-Green pulled back the tissue and stared, aghast, at a ruffled pair of Ideal knickers.

Author's Note

Rarely have two characters wormed their way so deeply into my heart as Cole and Madeline have. I wanted their midnight chats over cocoa to go on forever.

I owe debts of love and gratitude to my sister, Sharon Stone, and to editor Wendy McCurdy, for their contributions and support during the writing of this book.

The Victorian clothing reform movement began as far back as the 1850's, both in England and the US, largely in reaction to those extremes of fashion, the corset and the crinoline. Medical practitioners and midwives had railed against the evils of tight lacing for decades, but it was the later Victorians with their zeal for reform and their yen for the romantic and classical styles, who produced the first serious effort toward eliminating corsets. The intrepid Amelia Bloomer, of New York, and her friend Dr. Mary Walker experimented with female trousers, wore them for nearly twenty years, then later abandoned them. By 1881 and the birth of the Reform Dress Society in London, other factors were making clothing changes possible. Women were taking more active roles physically, encouraged by the resurgence of interest in physical fitness and culture. Believe it or not, the general acceptance and popularity of the bicycle played a major role in clothing reform. A woman could have an eighteen-inch waist or a bicycle . . . not both. Increasingly, women chose the bicycle.

As to the specifics of the story . . . reform garments were indeed offered for sale at Liberty on Regent Street in London. As in Cole and Madeline's story, the general desire for fashions requiring corsets proved to be stronger than logic, reason, hygiene, and comfort combined. Women did not abandon corsets *en masse* until after World War I, and then, most often, because they were relieved to give up the extra pounds of linen in the weekly wash.

As in the story, the one true success of the clothing reform movement in late Victorian times was in the rethinking and redesign of children's clothing. Until then, children were dressed as adorable toys (Lord Fauntleroy), as miniature men and women (corsets, stiff collars, and all), or in cast-off adult clothing . . . seldom altered to accommodate their smaller frames. As a result of clothing reform and new Victorian ideas of childhood, children were liberated from the horrors of lacing and backboards before their mothers.

And on a final note . . . there are a number of ideas in Cole and Madeline's story that I find intriguing. I strongly believe that we generally see what we look for, that we often get just what we expect in life. Thus, it behooves us to cultivate hope and goodness and caring in ourselves and others. If we look for it, it's there. This does not negate the pain and sorrow and difficulty in life, but it does give us something to live by and to hope for.

Lastly, I do believe that many of us may have indeed been influenced, perhaps even rescued by unlikely angels. And if we are open to the possibilities for good in the world, we may find ourselves called upon to be "unlikely angels" too.

Thank you, Irwyn Applebaum.

ABOUT THE AUTHOR

Betina Krahn lives in Minnesota with her two sons and a feisty salt-and-pepper schnauzer. With a degree in biology and a graduate degree in counseling, she has worked in teaching, personnel management, and mental health. She had a mercifully brief stint as a boys' soccer coach, makes terrific lasagna, routinely kills houseplants, and is incurably optimistic about the human race. She believes the world needs a bit more truth, a lot more justice, and a whole lot more love and laughter. And she attributes her outlook to having married an unflinching optimist and to two great-grandmothers actually named Pollyanna.

DON'T MISS THESE FABULOUS
BANTAM WOMEN'S FICTION TITLES

DON'T MISS THESE FABULOUS
BANTAM WOMEN'S FICTION TITLES